The Big Leagues

By Chris Petersen

FOR STEVE

(It's not your fault.)

CONTENTS

ACKNOWLEDGMENTS

This book would not have become a reality without the support of some very important people to whom I owe endless thanks. First, to my wife, Vicki, for her unwavering belief in my ability to do this and her patience through season after season of often-irritating baseball. To my parents, Wulf and Georgia, who always indulged me when I would rather stay inside and write stories than do anything else. To my friends, Staci, Brian, and Jennie, who volunteered their time to make sure all of this made sense. To Jason, designed this book's amazing cover. And, finally, to Steve Ontiveros, who hit a go-ahead home run on June 26, 1977, and ensured my team started my life with a win.

1. A LONG TIME AGO...

Ten-year-old Sparky Katakura rolled the ball around and around in his right hand, his fingers turning it over until the seams were lined up perfectly. Sixty feet and six inches away stood his brother Ken, waving his bat around behind his head in tight little circles. More than thirty miles away was the closest big-league ballpark, Zevon Field in San Carlos, home of the Stars. Sparky was one pitch away from striking out his older brother. They both were ten years, three months and fourteen days away from the most devastating moment of their lives.

"So what are you going to throw me?" Ken called out to his little brother on the mound.

"Do you think Duke Hobbs tells every batter he faces what he's going to pitch them?" Sparky answered, trying to squint imposingly.

"You know," Ken said, "if you were as good as Duke Hobbs you'd be able to just announce what you were going to throw me and I wouldn't be able to hit it." Ken turned his lip up into a sneer and dug his feet into the dirt. "Don't you think you could be as good as him someday?"

Sparky gripped the ball behind his back. It felt like a perfect four-seam fastball. He could already see the look on Ken's face when it blew by him. In the fading afternoon sunlight, Sparky swore he could see a little trickle of sweat forming on the back of Ken's neck. They had been practicing all day, and Sparky could feel it coming. He was going to strike his brother out. He knew it.

"Okay, brother, check this out." Sparky stood straight and hid the ball inside his mitt. "Here comes the heater, straight down the middle!"

Sparky raised his arms over his head, lifted his left foot and with one complete motion of his lanky body sent the ball whizzing across the plate. With his eyes following the ball the entire way,

Ken tensed himself and took a full swing at the pitch. Bat met ball with a loud "crack," but Ken had gotten under the pitch, and the ball shot straight up like a rocket. It burst through the leaves of the big gnarly oak tree the boys were using for a backstop, causing several leaves to rain down on Ken's head. The ball landed with a "plop" behind Ken, where it rolled against his heels.

"That's an out!" Sparky declared, pointing with his mitt at the spot where the ball had landed.

"Nope, nuh-uh," Ken said, tossing the ball back to him underhand. "That would have been back into the stands, foul ball. Count's still two-and-two."

"Based on what?"

"Based on the fact that if the tree hadn't been there, that ball would have carried out of play."

"No way, the catcher would have gotten under it, no problem." Sparky slammed the ball into his glove to demonstrate what it would have sounded like.

"Who's your catcher?"

"Terry Schulman, of course." The question confused Sparky. Why wouldn't he be pitching to the Stars' veteran catcher?

"Schulman wouldn't chase a ball like that anymore anyway, not with his knees," Ken said. "Besides, he wouldn't have had a play on it because it would have carried into the seats at Zevon Field."

"Stop pretending to be so flipping smart."

"Stop pretending to pitch," Ken laughed. "Now are you going to try striking me out or are you going to stand there whining at me until dinnertime?"

Sparky spat at the dirt of his backyard's makeshift pitching mound. The spittle landed directly in the path of an ant, who quickly and quietly changed direction to avoid it, no time spent thinking. Sparky leaned in to stare down his brother, who was smirking confidently and twirling the bat behind his head again. Taking a deep breath, Sparky rolled the ball around in his hand until, like a safecracker trying to find the combination, his fingers found their perfect spots. The last pitch had almost fooled him, it just needed to be a little bit faster, just a little less time for Ken to react. The sun was almost set, and the smell of pan-fried salmon stretched from the kitchen across the yard. Either way, this was going to be Sparky's last pitch of the day.

Sparky got into position. He drew another deep breath. His arms reached up to the sky. He pulled his right arm back as far as it could go. He planted his left foot on the front of the mound. His shoulder began to burn with effort. His pitching arm snapped forward. Sparky let the ball go.

The ball turned in the air, causing the air around it to whistle over the spinning seams. There was a wisp of smoke dancing around the ball as it hurtled through the air toward the plate. Suddenly, the ball seemed to catch fire, and it trailed flames behind it like the tail of a shooting star. Sparky's eyes grew wide as the flaming pitch nearly completed its journey. Ken gritted his teeth and whipped the bat out in front of him.

The sound was unlike anything Sparky had ever heard before. The sizzling of the flames was followed by the intense wind of Ken's swing, which was followed by the sickening "pop" of a direct hit. Without even watching the ball jump off the sweet spot of the bat, Sparky knew exactly what had happened as the scream of a long home run carried over his head and into the deepest part of the backyard. The sound was soon replaced by the sound of Ken's laughter.

"Man, I thought you almost had it there, dude!" Ken said as he trotted around the makeshift bases. "Anybody else might have swung right through that!"

"Yeah, but you didn't," Sparky said mournfully as he watched his brother's cleats kick up little clouds of dust from the mound. The ant was still poking around at the edge of the hill.

"Little bro, what do I keep telling you?" Ken said as he arrived at home plate. He slowed down, taking exaggerated strides before finally hopping up and landing with both feet on home, throwing his hands up in the air triumphantly. "You are never ever ever ever going to get me out!"

"Says you." Sparky continued kicking at the mound. Ken put his bat on his shoulder and put his arm around his brother to lead him inside for dinner. Sparky knew Ken wouldn't let him forget about that last pitch for the rest of the evening.

"Hey, you know what, kid? It's not going to matter, anyway. Because you and me? We're going to both be playing for the Stars someday, and we're going to win the championship with your arm and my bat. And my speed, my glove, my charisma, my clubhouse leadership, et cetera, et cetera."

"Aw, shut up!" Sparky said, giving his brother a little elbow in the ribs. "Your defense sucks."

"What the heck are you talking about? I'm flashing all kinds of leather out there!"

"Yeah, right! Remember last Saturday during our Pee Wee game?"

"Hey, that's no fair, the sun changed position on me all of a sudden!" Ken pushed Sparky away as he began laughing at him.

"This is you," Sparky said, flailing his arms around like an inexperienced juggler. "WHOA-WHOA-WHOA-WHOA! Katakura drops the ball! One run will score! Two runs will score! Here comes the runner from first and now HE will score!" Ken ripped his cap off his head and whipped it at his cackling brother.

"Knock it off, or I won't let you pitch to me after school anymore."

"Okay, okay!" Sparky dusted off Ken's cap and tossed it back to him. "Hey Ken?"

"Yeah?"

"That was a pretty good pitch, wasn't it?"

"Best one I've ever seen you throw, little bro. Seriously." Ken slapped Sparky on the back as they walked back to the house for dinner. "One of these days, Spark. You and me are going to win a championship, and I'm going to do whatever it takes to make that happen. And you're going to owe me...big time."

Later that night, after his parents had kissed him goodnight and shut his bedroom door, Sparky reached under his bed and pulled out a small radio. Waiting until the light from the hallway went out, Sparky put in his earbuds and within a few seconds he could hear the mellow sound of Vince Hatcher, as familiar as his own mother's voice.

"Hello, San Carlos! Vince Hatcher with you once again for another thrilling game of Big League Baseball on the voice of the Stars, KMVP!" Sparky settled back into his pillow and felt himself sink into the soothing white noise of the buzzing crowd. Late-night ballgames were strictly prohibited for Sparky and his brother, except for Friday and Saturday nights. On this Tuesday night, Sparky risked the threat of a full grounding for the opportunity to hear this game.

"Tonight, the Stars of San Carlos open up a three-game series with the Osaka Tsunamis, currently in first place in the Oceanic League's Green Division, and both teams are bringing the heat to get this battle off to a blistering start!" Vince was in rare form that night, Sparky thought, although he wasn't sure if it was the intensity of the pitching matchup or the illicit thrill of listening to a game so many time zones away that made him so excited.

"Taking the hill tonight for your Stars is the ace of aces, the Stars' No. 1 man, the ever-loving idol of millions, Duke Hobbs!" Sparky smiled broadly, confident that Hobbs would be setting them up and knocking them down all night, and he was going to hear every pitch. "Duke brings a record of 11 wins and 3 losses to the ballpark, with an ERA of 2.34. Not to be outdone, the Tsunamis will counter with their top starter, Turk McGillicuddy, himself a leading candidate for the Big Leagues' top pitching honor. Bearing a record of 12 and 4, McGillicuddy boasts an ERA of 1.78. Of course, he has a doozy of a defensive lineup behind him to keep that total down.

From left to right, the Tsunamis' outfield setup tonight includes..."

Two and a half innings later, the score was knotted at 1-1. Hobbs was on the mound in the bottom of the third in his first real trouble of the evening. Vince's voice had become hushed and more serious, as if he knew exactly how important this game was to Sparky. "Runners on the corners, one out," Vince said solemnly. "Hobbs was ahead of the batter Gollenbock 0-2, but now six pitches later Gollenbock has battled back to a full count, three balls and two strikes."

Sparky dug under his bed to find the shoebox where he kept his baseball card collection. He quickly flipped through them to find his Tsunamis team set and zeroed in on Gollenbeck, the awkward-looking shortstop. Sparky gripped Gollenbeck's card tightly between his fingers and stared him down, looking for some flaw Hobbs might be able to exploit. Gollenbeck's image stared back, his bushy eyebrows like caterpillars performing some kind of ballet on his forehead.

"Hobbs is set and here comes the 3-2 pitch to Gollenbeck," Vince said. There came a quick crack and a gasp from the Osaka crowd. Sparky's stomach jumped. "That ball is hit high in the air on the left-field side...but it bends foul into the stands and we'll do it again." Sparky relaxed his shoulders and went back to staring at Gollenbeck, that ugly little troll. The fans in Osaka were chanting and banging their inflatable thunder sticks together: "TSU-NAM-I! TSU-NAM-I! TSU-NAM-I!" They continued to chant right up until Hobbs went into the windup.

"Here's the 3-2 pitch," Vince said, punctuated by the sound of contact. "That ball is on the ground between third and short, Snyder ranges over to his right – makes a diving stop! Over to second, there's one! The throw to first is...in time!" Sparky tossed Gollenbeck's card back in the box and silently pumped his fist in the air.

"A double play gets Hobbs out of the inning!" Vince gushed. "The Stars showing that Osaka doesn't have a monopoly on defense – oh have mercy! We're going to the top of the fourth, and the score remains tied at 1 apiece!" Settling back into his pillow, Sparky sighed deeply, thoroughly enjoying the commercial for Wally's Wingnut World that followed. It was the best commercial he had ever heard.

When Sparky woke up the next morning, it was to the sound of the morning newsman droning on about changes to zoning laws. He stashed the radio and rushed through his morning routine – dressing, brushing and combing in a blur to make it down to the breakfast table. If he was lucky, the sports section of the paper would have the late scores from Osaka. That is, if he could pry it away from his father in time. Sparky imagined the shame of having to ask one of his friends at school the final score, the laughs he would get if it came out he couldn't make it through an entire night game without nodding off. He could see Duke Hobbs pointing and laughing at him among his classmates, too.

At the breakfast table, Sparky's father had set up shop behind the sports section, bringing a slice of toast behind it and returning it to the plate a moment later much smaller than before. Ken, likewise, was hiding behind an economy-sized box of Curveball Crunchies. His arm and spoon were in constant motion, a regular "plink, plink, plink" marking each trip of the spoon from bowl to mouth. He kicked his feet under the table in time with the sound. Sparky took a slice of toast from the middle of the table for appearances.

"Morning, Dad," he said.

"Well, good morning, Sparky," his father said without coming out from behind his newspaper.

"Are you almost done with the sports section?"

"If you're looking for the score of the Stars game, it ended late. You know how it is with those Pacific Rim games."

"Oh. Okay."

"I'm sure one of your little friends at school knows how old Duke did, you can ask them when you get on the bus."

"Sure, Dad. Thanks." Sparky stuffed as much toast into his mouth as possible and started chewing – anything to keep from screaming. Ken noticed his brother and leaned across the table toward him.

"Psst, hey," Ken said, motioning for Sparky to lean in closer. Sparky guarded himself against a punch on the arm. "Hobbs went the whole nine innings, struck out eight, one walk. Stars won 6-3." Ken snapped back to his upright position behind his cereal box, and didn't say a word to Sparky the rest of the morning. Sparky could only look back at his brother and feel sort of mad at him – there was something else he was going to owe him for.

2. THE ROOKIE SEASON

"Welcome back, baseball fans! Vince Hatcher coming to you live from a sold-out Zevon Stadium for Game 7 of the Worlds Series between the San Carlos Stars and the London Champions!" The air inside the ballpark was cool – a combination of the night chill and the breeze coming off the ocean – but the stands were filled with 51,050 people sweating bullets. None of those fans, however, were as nervous as the young man standing in the center of the diamond, on top of the pitcher's mound: 20-year-old Sparky Katakura.

"It's almost hard to believe the story of this season," Vince continued from his perch in the press box. "The Stars and their young captain Ken Katakura rocketed all the way from the bottom of the Intercontinental League's Orange Division in the early going of the season to take the pennant, storm their way through the playoffs and take a very strong London team all the way to the brink of elimination in an 0-3 hole." Sparky kicked his cleats into the dry brown dirt and stared down at home plate. The Champions' hitter was standing just outside the batter's box, taking a few casual practice swings. Sparky rolled the ball around in his hand with the tips of his fingers.

"However, a series of miscues, gaffes and outright strange occurrences have allowed the Champions to come right back and tie the series up at three games apiece, forcing the definitive Game 7," Vince said. "And there on the hill right now is young Sparky Katakura, who was called up from the minors mid-season and has contributed so much to this incredible run the Stars have had. But now he's in a situation no pitcher wants to be in, regardless of their age. One has to wonder what is going through the mind of this young man right now."

Sparky rolled his shoulders in an attempt to loosen up and looked over his shoulder at first base – one London baserunner. He looked behind him at second base – another London baserunner.

Over at third was another London baserunner. All around him, Sparky could feel the crowd watching him. In the months leading up to the Worlds Series, the San Carlos crowds would rock and spill over onto each other like sloshing water, always in motion. That night, they stood almost still, like a garden of statues.

He could see a little girl standing in the front rows behind home plate – she had her hands folded in front of her face, as if she might be praying. There was a look of panic in her eyes, and Sparky could tell she was pleading with him silently. It had to have been the same look Sparky had given his Duke Hobbs baseball cards over the years. He knew what she was thinking, too, because it was the same thing he asked Hobbs for so many times: "Please, Sparky, just this once. I'll never ask you for anything else ever again if you just get this last out."

"Katakura faces a bases-loaded situation here in the top of the ninth inning," Vince continued. "The Stars cling to a precarious two-run lead, and with two outs the Champions send their cleanup hitter Lewis to the plate. Lewis started the series slowly, but has been on a tear in the last four games, as have most of the London nine. Lewis is 3-for-4 already tonight with a double and three RBI."

At the plate, Lewis spit a sunflower seed into the dirt and prepared to step into the box. Behind Sparky, at second base, Ken must have noticed the sweat dripping from underneath his brother's cap, because he motioned to the dugout and out came the Stars' manager, Eddie Garson. "Time!" barked Eddie as he came trotting out of the dugout.

Ken and Eddie joined Sparky on the mound. "You don't look so good, Sparky," Eddie said. "How you feeling?"

"I'm all right, I'm all right," Sparky said. "I can get Lewis."

"You think so? He tagged you pretty good the last time up, and this is what you call one of your classic big-time situations, here." Eddie's crinkled face was locked right on Sparky, and all Sparky wanted to do was run away.

"He's going to be fine, Eddie, come on," Ken said. "He's just a little nervous, isn't that right, Spark?"

"Y-Yeah, I guess that's all it is."

"See? Just let him get Lewis and it'll all be over!"

"Ken, I'm not saying I don't want Sparky to close it out, but let's be realistic here," Eddie said. He looked back at Sparky and clapped a hand on his shoulder. "You did a hell of a job tonight, kid, but why don't you let someone with a little more juice in the tank finish it out for you, hah? I'm going to bring Olvera in from the bullpen."

"No!" Ken said, grabbing Eddie's arm. "Eddie, come on, you have to let Sparky finish this game!"

"Dang it, Kenny, this isn't a sandlot game we're playing here, this is Game 7 of the ding-dong Worlds Series! Your brother's given it everything he's got, and I want to make sure we win this ballgame!"

"We will win this ballgame, but only if you leave Sparky in!" Ken protested. He suddenly dropped his voice lower. "You know why he has to stay in, Eddie."

Eddie didn't have a response at first. He lifted his cap off, scratched the top of his head and then calmly smoothed the cap back over his hair. He looked Ken right in the eyes. Sparky wiped the sweat off his forehead with the back of his glove. The home plate umpire came plodding up to the mound.

"Hey, fellas, let's go," the ump said impatiently. "Either make a change or let's play ball, okay?"

Eddie heaved a deep sigh and patted Sparky on the shoulder. "Okay, kid, get this guy out and let's enjoy the champagne, how 'bout it?"

"Yeah, sure thing, Eddie, you got it," Sparky said, nodding frantically. Eddie turned back to the dugout, leaving Sparky and Ken alone on the mound.

"Okay, all right," Ken said as he backpedaled his way to second base. "You can do this, Sparky. You're going to do this. And you're going to owe me big time, I promise."

Sparky nodded again and turned to face Lewis.

As the Champions' team leader in batting average, on-base percentage and home runs for the last five seasons, Lewis already was an imposing figure at the plate. The way Sparky was feeling at that moment, he may as well have been 10 feet tall. Sparky looked in at the catcher, who signaled for a slider and then slid a half-step closer to Lewis. He held his mitt low, expecting Sparky to have the pitch break low and inside. Sparky reminded himself that Lewis was known to bite on a bad pitch on the inside corner. Exhaling, Sparky nodded and set himself.

The pitch was near-perfect, starting out at knee-level right down the center of the plate and then broke inside, just a few inches from Lewis' bright purple stirrup socks. Lewis took the bait, swinging the bat right over the top of the ball. The umpire called "STRIKE ONE!" and the crowd punctuated it with a tremendous roar. Lewis cursed himself and tapped the end of the bat on the plate.

The crowd was still buzzing as Sparky looked in for the next sign – a fastball down and outside. He nodded and snapped his arm forward. The pitch whistled through the air, straight as an arrow. The speed of its rotation caused the ball to catch fire halfway between the mound and the plate, and by the time it reached Lewis it was a streak of flame and smoke, not even recognizable as a baseball. Once again, the ball struck the mitt without Lewis even coming close to it.

"STRIKE TWO!" called the umpire, and again the crowd let out a joyous cheer. Sparky glanced back over his shoulder and saw his brother smiling back at him. He could see Ken mouth the words "You got him," then pointed confidently at him. Even though his arm felt sore and weak, and he was well over his usual pitch count, Sparky knew he had one more left in him. All season long, Ken had been telling him that he had what it takes, so he had been right every time. "Why should now be any different?" Sparky thought.

Sparky saw the signal – fastball down and in. If he could get the same velocity on this one that he did on the last pitch, there was no way Lewis would be able to hit it way down there in his blind spot. He reared back and put every last bit on energy he had into his arm, felt the extreme force of the pitch tearing at his shoulder and elbow. The ball left his fingers like a bullet from the barrel of a gun. It closed the gap between Sparky and Lewis with terrifying speed, another flaming comet scorching the air around it.

Lewis planted his back foot in the batter's box, dug his heel into the dirt and began his swing. His teeth were clamped together so tightly it looked like he might grind them into powder. His eyes were shut. The bat came speeding across the plate in a perfect arc. Sparky could see he had started his swing late – he was going to swing right through the tail end of the pitch. At least, that's what it looked like what was going to happen.

At the last second, just as the ball was about to cross the plate, the flames suddenly blew out, leaving the ball as visible as the sun in the sky. Much to Sparky's surprise and horror, the ball even appeared to hang in the air, perfectly motionless. But Lewis' bat continued to slice through the air, closing in on the ball. Where there was raucous cheering before, there was dead silence. But that silence was soon punctured by the sound of the bat connecting squarely with the ball.

The ball came rocketing to Sparky's left, but well out of his reach. He wheeled around to see Ken in position to make a play on the ball. It took a hard bounce off the infield grass and skipped up directly in front of Ken. His glove was in perfect position to cradle the ball, his feet were set to make the easy throw to first. Lewis was only halfway down the first base line. The ball dropped perfectly into the palm of Ken's mitt. Ken reached into the glove and threw in the direction of first, but the ball was nowhere to be seen.

Instead, the ball sailed through the air in a high arc directly behind Ken. It had slipped out of his fingers just before he made the phantom throw, and now the entire assembled crowd of Zevon Stadium held its collective breath as the London baserunners dashed around the bases. By the time the ball landed on the infield and was claimed by the third baseman, three runners had crossed home plate. The Champions dugout was jubilant, high-fives exchanged so enthusiastically they were the only sound heard throughout the ballpark.

On the mound, Sparky felt his stomach sink like a 12-6 curveball. He looked up at the scoreboard: "E4," it read, error charged to the second baseman. Champions 6, Stars 5. All 100,000 eyes in the stands were on Sparky, but he could only think of two. And there she was, the little girl was had pleaded with him silently just a few minutes before. Only Sparky couldn't see her eyes – she was weeping into her hands. Her father, a broad-shouldered man with a beaten-up Stars cap on his head, rubbed her shoulders and whispered comforting things in her ear. There were tears in his eyes, as well.

The next batter came up, a pinch hitter, and on the second pitch he popped up to the shortstop. Sparky never even saw who it was – he just jogged back to the dugout and tried not to look in his teammates' eyes. Ken didn't say a word to him.

Although Eddie walked the length of the dugout clapping his hands together and sounding upbeat, none of the words landed with Sparky. The first Stars batter of the ninth trudged up to the plate, and was caught looking on a curveball that nipped the corner for strike three. The second batter made contact but only managed a weak dribbler up the third baseline that made him easy pickings for out number two. Ken stepped out of the on-deck circle and adjusted his helmet. He waved his arms in circles, bent his knees and shook his head – his own particular little ritual at the plate. Sparky had seen him do it a million times before, but never like this, never like he knew he was going to strike out.

Sparky decided to watch the crowd instead of the plate. Maybe if he didn't add to the pressure on Ken, it would give him just enough breathing room to get a hit, he thought. The first pitch crossed the plate with blazing speed for strike one. The crowd grimaced in pain. The next pitch fooled Ken badly, and he almost tripped over his own feet after twisting himself up on the fruitless swing. An old man in the stands dropped his head and shook it sadly.

"Ain't over yet," Eddie said softly. "It ain't over yet."

The third pitch came whizzing off the mound, and Ken stepped into his swing. The bat came around with magnificent force, and with a deafening sound it collided with the ball, sending it skyward at an intense speed. The crowd jumped to their feet, some even began cheering, but Sparky only watched Ken track the ball through the air. He tossed the bat aside and began running down the baseline as fast as he could, keeping his eyes on the ball the entire time. Ken kept his eyes fixed on the ball, and Sparky kept his eyes fixed on Ken. The crowd was roaring, almost bursting out of their seats like popcorn kernels. Ken churned up a cloud of dirt as he tore around first base.

And then, Ken stopped.

With his eyes still glued to the sky, Ken stopped halfway between first and second. The crowd fell back into their seats, suddenly silenced. Sparky looked out to center field and saw Lewis, the Champions' MVP of the evening, clinging to the top of the outfield wall. His arm was extended into the now-cold night air, and at the end of his arm was his glove, and in his glove was the ball.

The Stars filed silently into the clubhouse, but Sparky stayed behind. He watched the Champions celebrate on top of the mound, watched Lewis hoist the championship trophy above his head, watched them don the freshly-stitched "World Champions" caps. Some of the crowd stayed behind – either they were Champions fans who had made the long trip across the Atlantic or they were Stars fans still too stunned to understand what had just happened.

When Sparky finally entered the clubhouse, he found something he didn't expect to see. The entire team was still there, still in their uniforms, still sitting at their lockers. Their faces were ashen, their expressions vacant. To Sparky they looked like they could have been dead. Ken stood up from his locker and hugged Sparky tightly.

"Spark...it wasn't supposed to happen like this," Ken said, his voice choked with tears. "I'm so sorry, bro, I'm so sorry..."

"It's my fault, Ken," Sparky said, hugging his brother back. "I shouldn't have thrown that pitch. I didn't think there was any way he could have hit it!"

"That's the funny thing about this game, isn't it?" Suddenly a sharp, cackling voice rang out from the back of the clubhouse. Sitting on one of the trainer's tables was a short man, dressed in a shabby, ill-fitting suit. He had black, slicked-back hair that looked as oily as fried chicken, and eyebrows that were sharpened into little points that met just above his pug nose. He hopped off the table and marched confidently into the center of the clubhouse.

"Yes sir, that is the funniest thing about this game...you spend all your time setting lineups and comparing statistics and plotting strategy," the little man said as he twirled his stubby fingers in the air. "But when it all comes down to it, one bad hop can ruin your whole season. Evening, gents."

Ken ran up and grabbed the little man by the lapels, lifting him an inch off the floor. "What the heck is going on here? This wasn't supposed to happen!"

"Really? And just where was that stipulated?"

"Ken? What's with this guy?" Sparky asked. The rest of the team just hung their heads. The little man slapped at Ken's hands and Ken dropped him back on his feet. The stubby man made a show of dusting himself off and strode forward to shake Sparky's hand.

"I don't believe we've been properly introduced yet," he said. "The name's Mr. Stitches, and I represent your new employer."

"What are you talking about? Did they sell the team?"

"Mmm...in a manner of speaking." Stitches chuckled to himself and looked back at Ken, who was sitting at his locker again, defeated. "Your brother never mentioned me? Never mentioned our little agreement?"

"Ken, what is this stumpy weirdo talking about?" Ken rubbed his eyes and tried to fight the tears.

"Sparky, I came to your brother and his teammates at the beginning of this season with a little proposition," Stitches said. "I could guarantee them a championship so long as they pledged to sign their contracts over to my employer – in perpetuity, of course."

Stitches reached behind his back and produced a leather-bound binder. He held it in front of himself and theatrically opened it to show Sparky its pages. It was a baseball card binder, like the many Sparky had once kept on his bookshelf after he decided a shoebox was for little kids.

Unlike the cards he had kept meticulously arranged and cataloged, the cards in Mr. Stitches' binder were mostly blank. They had the positions listed, but the spaces for names and photos were empty. If he looked into the blank spaces for too long, Sparky started to feel sick to his stomach.

"Let's not waste any more of our time, shall we?" Mr. Stitches said, and suddenly there was a sound like a burst of wind, and a flash of light so bright Sparky had to shut his eyes.

When he opened them, Sparky was standing alone with Mr. Stitches in the clubhouse. The cards in Stitches' album were no longer blank, each one bearing the name and image of one of the Stars. They looked no different from any other baseball card, with the players either smiling or wearing expressions of intense concentration. In the center of the page was Ken's card, and Sparky saw a look of deep regret on his brother's face as he looked out from his cardboard prison.

Stitches looked up from his album and jumped back a step when he saw Sparky still standing in front of him. He flipped through the album furiously and then gave Sparky an angry look.

"That's never happened before," Stitches said. "Why aren't you in here with the rest of your teammates?"

"Why are you asking me?" Sparky said, shoving Stitches backward. "I don't even know what just happened!"

"Your brother and your teammates are in here for safe keeping," Stitches said as he patted the cover of the album. "They'll be fine, don't worry. But I'm not finding a card for you in here, and that is...troublesome." Stitches hid the album behind his back once again and it disappeared. From inside his suit jacket, he produced an envelope, and from that envelope he removed a folded piece of paper. He began reading it intently, then folded it back up and returned it the envelope. He scowled at Sparky.

"When did you join the team?" he asked in an accusatory tone.

"I was called up from the minors a few months ago," Sparky said. "Ken convinced Eddie to give me a shot in the bullpen, and a few weeks later I was bumped up into the rotation."

"So you never signed this contract? Your brother never told you about the agreement?"

"He never said anything to me, just kept telling me we were going to win a championship."

"This is unfortunate," Stitches said as he adjusted his tie. "My employer prefers that these contracts come through without any hitches, but sometimes they are unavoidable. Goodbye, young Mr. Katakura. I have a feeling we will be meeting again." With a little wave and a devious smile, Mr. Stitches vanished from sight.

"Wait!" Sparky reached out to grab the little man, but his hands passed through nothing. He was alone in the clubhouse, and the only sound he could hear was the muffled roar of the Champions celebrating down the hall. Sparky stood in front of Ken's locker, where his brother was sitting just seconds earlier. Ken's batting gloves were crumpled on a shelf, and Sparky quickly stuffed them into his back pocket. He was surprised by a knock on the clubhouse door.

"Sparky Katakura?" a young man, one of the stadium's grounds crew, stood at the clubhouse door.

"Yeah, that's me," Sparky said quietly. "What do you want?"

"I'm sorry, but I was asked to give this to you right away." The young man handed Sparky a crisp white envelope bearing his name in clean, printed letters. "They told me it was from the league office."

"Who told you it was from the league office? Who gave you

this?"

"He…he didn't say," the young man said nervously. "Just told me to give you this and left. It sounded pretty important."

"Okay, thanks." Sparky took the letter and opened it.

"Dear Sparky," the letter began. "The Commissioner of Big League Baseball requests your presence at a special hearing to be held tomorrow at 1:20 p.m. at the league offices in New York City. Please note: Attendance is mandatory. Signed, The Office of the Commissioner of Big League Baseball."

Sparky let the letter fall from his hands as he looked at the nameplate over his brother's now-empty locker. "Commissioner? New York? Mandatory? Ken, what in the world did you do?"

Sparky hadn't slept at all the night before, crammed into a seat on a cross-country train, and he hadn't been on the road without Ken since before their parents' funeral. He was wearing a suit he normally wore only for about 15 minutes at a time on road trips as he went from the team bus to the hotel – the necktie clutched his throat, the shoes pinched his feet and the cuffs of his shirt cut off his circulation. Even so, with his eyes dry and tired and his head aching and throbbing, Sparky found himself in awe of the gleaming white marble façade of Big League Baseball headquarters.

The building sat in the middle of a plaza filled with bronze statues of legendary players of the past. Even without getting too close, Sparky could recognize the unmistakable batting stance of Hector Macias, the unstoppable side-arm delivery of Louie Fuller and the three heads of Vortax the Merciless, frozen in polished metal, enduring for all time.

The rush of enormous fountains drowned out the usual New York City noise of car horns and police whistles, and somehow the scent of freshly-cut grass and hot dogs overwhelmed the city's normally gritty scent. It was no wonder the plaza was filled with people, some taking pictures of the statues, but most simply enjoying the oasis of baseball in the middle of one of the world's busiest cities.

In the center of the plaza stood the Big League Baseball headquarters itself, looking like a 10-story block of solid marble carved by the gods to resemble home plate. Legend had it that the building was actually donated from Mount Olympus, but most knowledgeable fans knew that Zeus would never part with any piece of his beloved personal baseball diamond, no matter the reason.

Sparky passed through the turnstiles at the massive front gate and was immediately stunned. He wasn't sure if it was the lack of sleep, or if he was dazed from the chaotic cab ride, but the lobby was the most beautiful thing he had ever seen. He wished he and Ken could have made the trip there before, together and under better circumstances. Rather than cold marble floors, the building was carpeted in grass as green and as alive as the best-kept outfields in the game. On the shimmering white wall directly in front of him, a massive marquee flashed messages like, "Welcome to Big League Baseball HQ!" and "It's a beautiful day for a ballgame!"

A dirt basepath marked with a perfect chalk line led to a large box office in the center of the room. Sparky approached one of the open windows, where a smiling old woman sat perched on a stool counting ticket stubs. She wore glasses that dwarfed her wrinkled face, and a blue Big League Baseball cap rested on top of her curly white hair.

"Welcome to the Big Leagues, sonny!" she chirped. "How can I help you? Are you here for a tour? Buying tickets? Getting a jersey customized?"

"No, I'm Sparky Katakura of the San Carlos Stars...I was given this letter after the last game of the Worlds Series and just spent all night getting out here." Sparky pulled the now-crumpled letter out of his pocket and flattened it out in front of the old lady. She leaned in so close her forehead almost touched the window.

"Oh, you're here for the special meeting of the league presidents!" the old lady said with surprise. "Yes, of course, it's all anyone's been talking about here today!"

"Really? Can you tell me what it's about, exactly?"

The old lady waved her hands in front of her face dramatically. "Oh, no, no, I'm afraid the details are top secret! Top secret! But you're kind of early, aren't you?"

Sparky checked his watch and realized he was more than an hour early for the meeting. "Yeah, I guess I am," he said as he took another look around the lobby. "Uh, how long does a tour normally take?"

"Oh, you have plenty of time!" the old lady said, her smile showing off teeth as white and polished as the lobby's marble. "Tell you what – why don't you jump in the next tour and I'll make sure you're in the Commissioner's office in time for your meeting?"

"Really? That would be great, thanks."

"No problem! Just tell the tour guide that Hortence sent you!" The old lady flashed a loony smile at Sparky and returned to counting ticket stubs.

Sparky stuffed the letter back into his pocket and followed the baseline to the left. The entire building appeared to be carpeted with grass, which accounted for the smell outside in the plaza. Sunlight streamed down through the many enormous skylights built into the ceiling. Within a few moments, a young lady in an immaculately clean and bright baseball uniform appeared with a gaggle of gawking visitors in tow. Sparky was swept up by the group's momentum and he was on the tour, whether he liked it or not.

"In this direction, we will take you through the offices where many of the most important decisions governing Big League Baseball are made," said the tour guide in a perky Southern drawl.

His eyes drawn upward to the skylights, Sparky collided with an older man in a bow tie who was power-walking in the opposite direction. He had the face of a turtle and a haircut like a first-grader.

"Excuse me," Sparky said. "I'm really sorry about that, but it's my first trip to Big League Baseball Headquarters and I'm just a little excited about seeing the central meeting hall."

"The central meeting hall is one of Big League Baseball Headquarters' most sacred and sacrosanct locations," the turtle-like man said, not looking at Sparky. His eyes drifted up toward the ceiling and the blue skies beyond the skylight. "For generations, the minds behind the grand old game have gathered in this holiest of holies to celebrate the game's glorious past and plot its ascendant future."

"O-kaaaay," Sparky said cautiously. "Do you know where it is?"

"The obvious answer to the question is to merely give a location, but the most correct answer is to say that the soul of the game resides in all of us, deep within our hearts..." At this point, the tour guide separated herself from the head of the group and stepped between Sparky and the little man.

"I'm sorry, George, you just run along to wherever it is you were going," she said, sounding like a mother comforting her child. "I'll help this young man find what he's looking for." George went back on his way down the hall, muttering softly to himself about flannel uniforms.

"What's the deal with that guy?" Sparky asked.

"He's from the Nostalgia Department, I'm afraid he isn't much good for anything else," the woman said. "Now if you don't mind, we're almost at the next stop on our tour, okay?"

The group came to a stop in the center of a large office staffed by dozens of artists working at dozens of easels. On each easel was a drawing of a different baseball uniform. The rest of the room was wallpapered with similar drawings, each one of a different uniform and a different activity – some of the drawings were pitching, some were hitting, others were fielding or just standing around looking vaguely happy about something.

Suddenly, Sparky was grabbed by an older woman clutching a clipboard to her chest the way a drowning person would hold a life preserver. She guided Sparky to an easel and the harried-looking artist laboring in front of it.

"Does this look right to you?" The young woman gestured to the easel.

"What do you mean?" Sparky asked.

"The uniform! The uniform! Does it look right to you?" Sparky scanned the drawing for anything that looked out of place, but didn't see anything.

"Uh, it looks okay to me..."

"You see, Paul? It looks fine. This guy said so."

"It's ridiculous," Paul spat back, sneering at the drawing he had just completed. "They're the Greensleeves, they should have green sleeves!" Sparky took a closer look at the drawing and noticed that it was indeed a new uniform concept for the Mumbai Greensleeves, only the jersey's signature green had been replaced by a day-glo purple. Even the name "Greensleeves" across the front of the jersey had been re-colored purple.

"Actually, now that I get a better look at it..." Sparky protested.

"You see, Mary? It does look wrong!" Paul slumped over his drawing table again and shook his head.

"But this is what people are buying right now!" Mary said, pointing emphatically at the drawing as if Paul just wasn't seeing the right one. "Purple is in right now, people love purple! This kid is the exact demographic we're looking for!"

"Purple has no place in baseball!" Paul shouted. "Especially when the team has 'green' right there in its frigging name! The team's going to hate it!"

"Purple is the new aquamarine! It's hip!"

"Purple is the color of evil!"

"Purple rules!"

"Purple sucks!"

"Hey!" Sparky yelled, grabbing both Paul and Mary's attention for the first time. "I'm just here for the tour, okay? Oh, and purple does look really stupid on the Greensleeves' uniform, by the way."

"That's not what my market research says," Mary sniffed. "So anyway, Paul, back to the uniform – what are your thoughts on the socks?"

"Stirrups!" Paul shouted as Sparky raced down the hallway to catch up with his tour group. They had scuttled ahead to a large room dominated by a gleaming golden statue. The tour guide waited for Sparky to reach the edge of the crowd before she began her presentation.

"Now that everyone's caught up again...we have reached one of my favorite parts of the tour by far. This, of course, is the statue of the man without whom we would not have the Big Leagues, the minor leagues or even the game of baseball at all." The tour guide lifted her hands high above her head in adulation. "This...is Major General Abner Doubleday!"

Sparky craned his neck to see the enormous statue, which depicted the mustachioed general holding a baseball in one outstretched hand and a bat resting on the opposite shoulder. He was wearing an ancient Egyptian headdress, the kind normally reserved for the pharaohs. The look on his face was one of absolute seriousness, and engraved at the base of the statue in foot-high letters was the question: "Who Says I Didn't Invent Baseball?" Sparky gazed at the statue in amazement as the tour guide's sugary voice faded in and out of his awareness.

"...and of course it was that mysterious time-travel accident that sent the general's ghost back to the dawn of civilization, and from there he laid the foundation for the game of baseball and modern society as we know it," the tour guide continued.

Later, Sparky followed the tour down a hallway that opened into a cavernous room lined with large banners in every color of the rainbow. Hanging underneath each banner was a photograph, nearly blown up to life-size, of a team of triumphant players celebrating on the mound. The banners stretched on for what looked like miles. The tour guide stopped in the middle of the room and simply spread her arms open wide.

"Welcome to the Hall of Champions," she said in a hushed voice. "Please feel free to take a look at some of the greatest moments from the history of Big League Baseball."

The crowd spread itself throughout the hall, pointing and smiling at cherished memories and laughing over the shared experiences of seeing their favorite teams hoist the Commissioner's Cup above their heads. He stopped in front of a banner in the purple and gold of the Machu Picchu Pinnacles, with the photo depicting the exact moment Vince Block made contact with the ball that would break a scoreless tie in the 17th inning of Game 7 in the '72 Worlds Series. Sparky's parents hadn't even met when that ball skipped over the shoe of Guillermo Peralta, but he had seen that play happen so many times on TV that he could recall it as clearly as his first day of high school.

Further down the row and deeper into history, Sparky found the solid black banner of the '21 Ninjapolis Shadows, the only team in history to exit the stadium before the presentation of the Commissioner's Cup. In fact, the photo underneath the banner showed only the bewildered members of the Ivy Town Professors, who found themselves alone on the field within seconds of the final out being recorded.

Further still, Sparky took a moment to marvel at the team photo of the '02 Casablanca Suspects, their steely gaze and defiant expressions telling the entire story of their difficult but ultimately triumphant championship season. To be kidnapped by a jealous sultan and forced to play in a different uniform was one thing, but to escape and make up the entirety of their original schedule without a single off day and winning the title was nothing short of a herculean effort.

Even though each photo depicted a different team, a different moment, a different hero, they all shared one thing in common: they all captured the ultimate moment for the nine players on the field at that time. They all showed champions, and Sparky felt his heart sink as he wondered how history would remember him and Ken.

Finally, the tour ended, and Sparky was shooed by the guide down another long hallway. At the end of hall was a door that read "Central Meeting Hall." He opened the door, and found a room no bigger than a closet. On the floor was what looked like the rubber from the top of a pitcher's mound. Sparky cautiously stepped onto the rubber, and suddenly he was rushed straight upward as if he was being sucked through a gigantic straw.

As soon as his feet hit solid ground again, Sparky looked around. He was standing in total darkness, and the sound of his feet echoed as if the room went on for miles. Suddenly, a bright spotlight snapped on directly over his head, illuminating a thin column around him. A deep, resonant voice came thundering into the room.

"Sparky Katakura…" the voice droned. In the air, high above Sparky's head, a giant glowing head came out of the darkness. The head of an older man, completely bald, with a pair of tiny glasses perched on the tip of his nose. His face had creases in it that made his frown stretch all the way down past his chin. He glared at Sparky with a look of intense disapproval.

"Y-Yes?"

The head raised one eyebrow. "I am the great and all-powerful Commissioner of Big League Baseball. Do you know why we have summoned you here?"

"Does it have anything to do with what happened last night? Because I have no idea what's going on or why I'm here!"

"I can explain," came a sickeningly familiar voice from the other side of the room. Another beam of light dropped from the ceiling, illuminating the figure of Mr. Stitches. He looked as unctuous and smug as the previous night back in San Carlos, but he obviously had been through an easier night than Sparky had.

"Silence!" The Commissioner bellowed. He took a moment to let his voice carry to the far ends of the room. "It has come to our attention that your brother and your teammates had made a deal with…the Baseball Devil." With those last three words, the Commissioner's voice grew even deeper and darker. He said the words as if it caused him great physical pain to do so.

"My employer finds that term uncomfortable," Stitches said.

"The Baseball Devil?" Sparky said. With that, the Commissioner's glowing visage was instantly surrounded by 10 more glowing heads, all older men, and flanking him five on each side. These, Sparky realized, had to have been the fabled presidents of the 10 major leagues. They too glowered at Sparky disapprovingly.

"The Baseball Devil is the representation of all that is evil in the game," the Commissioner said.

"He is every lazy outfielder who won't track down a foul ball," one of the presidents said.

"He is every team owner who charges too much for tickets," said another.

"He is every player who cares more about his own stats than helping his team win," said another.

"He is every hot dog vendor who won't walk all the way up to the last row of the upper deck," said another.

"These are all unfair characterizations," Stitches said.

"The Baseball Devil is, simply put, an insidious influence on the game," the Commissioner said. "And we have been trying to expel that influence from the game for some time now. Unfortunately, he continues to gain greater hold over the game, such as through his contract with your brother, for example."

"I'm sure that if the Big League Baseball offices would thoroughly examine the contracts signed by Mr. Katakura and the rest of the Stars, they would determine that everything about them is perfectly fine," Stitches said. "My employer simply wants to determine the status of young Sparky, over there."

"Sparky Katakura was not a member of the San Carlos Stars' roster when they signed their contract with your employer," the Commissioner stated. "He cannot be claimed."

"But he is free to negotiate with our organization on his own, is he not?"

"Of course," the Commissioner said, confused.

"Sparky, how badly do you want your brother back?" Stitches said.

"I'll do anything," Sparky said.

"Then I have a proposition for you." Stitches adjusted his tie and ran his hand over his shiny black hair. "If you can win a Worlds Series championship next year, I will release your brother and his teammates from their contract, no strings attached."

"And what if I don't?"

"If you don't, then the Commissioner's Office agrees to keep its nose out of my employer's affairs forever." Stitches smiled and looked around the room at the worried faces hovering in the light above him. "Does that sound agreeable?"

"I'll do it," Sparky said.

The presidents looked at each other, then nodded at the Commissioner. "The Commissioner's Office agrees to the terms," he said.

"The one stipulation..." Stitches said, "...is that Sparky must win the Worlds Series with the team that finished with the worst record in all of Big League Baseball last season."

"All right, I'll do it," Sparky said. "Just tell me where to go."

"Sparky Katakura," the Commissioner said solemnly, "you are hereby declared a free agent, and by the power of the Commissioner's Office I assign you to the Go-Town Goats."

"Where's Go-Town?" Sparky said. "Who are the Goats?"

"You have one full season to win the Worlds Series and save your brother's soul," the Commissioner answered. The enormous glowing heads of the Commissioner and the league presidents began to fade out of sight.

"Play ball," the Commissioner said, just as they disappeared completely.

3. SPRING TRAINING

The bus ride home was long and quiet, as was the winter that followed. Sparky kept up his usual offseason training regimen, spending long hours at the gym and repeatedly tossing a ball against the big tree in the backyard. Ordinarily, he could count on Ken either offering him encouragement or laughing at his mistakes, but instead there was only the sound of the ball whizzing through the air, the thump of the horsehide against the tree bark. He would walk to the tree himself, gather the balls up in a big white bucket and carry them back to his makeshift pitching mound to begin throwing all over again.

At night, Sparky would pour over his books, scan the Internet and flip through the few baseball cards he held onto, looking for any clue at all about Go-Town and its Goats, but there was precious little to be found. A card might provide a stat line for a player traded to another team years earlier, but invariably all Sparky could glean from it was that there was indeed a team called "Goats," and no Goats hitter he could find had ever hit higher than .240. The Internet revealed that Go-Town was located in the middle of the country, was famous for building most of the world's hover-cars, and had some very nice restaurants that were perfect for enjoying a meal after visiting a museum. None of this was very helpful to Sparky.

One day, Sparky received a letter in the mail, with a return address in Go-Town. The envelope had a tiny, smudged picture of what looked like a cartoon goat wearing a baseball cap and swinging a bat. The goat was either smiling or gritting his teeth angrily, it was difficult to tell.

The letter read: "Dear Sparky, My name is Arthur J. Mint IV, and I am the owner, president, chief operating officer and general manager of the Go-Town Goats. I was informed by the league office today that you had been assigned to my team by special order of the Commissioner's Office. I must admit to being slightly perplexed by this situation, especially because I can find no record of you ever playing baseball before in my scouting reports. However, I'm sure we can get to the bottom of this unusual circumstance through friendly conversation. I would like to invite you to visit me at my office here in Go-Town before the start of Spring Training. Further information and a bus ticket are attached. I look forward to meeting you. Sincerely, Arthur J. Mint IV."

Sparky watched San Carlos gradually get smaller through the back window of a bus. The ticket Mr. Mint had provided turned out to be several years old, and Sparky had to spend some money out of his own pocket to cover the fare increases. He watched the gleaming spires of the city's skyline recede into the horizon, almost like they were being retracted into the ground by some unknown mechanism. Sparky began to feel like the city might not be there anymore, if he ever returned to that spot, and he wondered if he would ever want to.

There were five million people who loved baseball once upon a time in San Carlos, but in the months since Sparky's cursed Worlds Series the city learned to stop talking about it. They stopped gathering in bars and restaurants to watch out-of-town games, children stopped wearing their caps outside, and no one had stopped Sparky for his autograph at the bus station. He could tell in their eyes that they knew who he was.

Eventually, the view out the back window flattened to an endless horizon, nothing but ground and sky, separated neatly into two equal portions. Sparky drifted off to sleep several times, only to awaken to the same view, making it impossible to tell how much time had passed. A copy of the book "Great Pitchers of History" sat untouched on the seat next to him.

Go-Town appeared at first as a small blur on the horizon Sparky glimpsed through the windshield. The landscape had changed from the dry desert beige to a snowy white. Farm fields were bordered by groves of trees arranged in tight columns like schoolchildren lined up for recess. Soon the bus was swallowed up by the city, and the streets were filled with hovercars zipping by and making high-pitched burbling noises.

As he stepped off the bus, Sparky was greeted by a fat little man with red cheeks and a crew cut. "Are you Sparky Katakura?" the little fat man asked him. When Sparky nodded his head, the little fat man handed him a white envelope and walked away as fast as his stubby legs could carry him.

Inside the envelope was a one-page letter, written in what appeared to be a girl's handwriting. Sparky had gotten lots of fan letters in his short time with the San Carlos Stars, and he had become very familiar with different types of female handwriting.

The letter read, simply: "Dear Sparky, Welcome to Go-Town! All of us who love the Goats are very excited to have you here, and we wish you great success in a Goats uniform. There is at least a 25 percent chance that the Goats can win 50 games this season, so the entire city is pulling for you! Best, The Go-Goats Girl."

Sparky folded the letter and put it in his pocket. He took a quick look around the bus station. There were dozens of people all going about their business, but none of them even noticed Sparky. Was that little fat guy and the letter supposed to be his welcoming committee? If the entire city was excited to have him there, why was everyone ignoring him? Why didn't this "Go-Goats Girl" come out to meet him in person?

All the confusion, combined with the exhaustion from his long bus ride, caused Sparky to slump down onto a nearby bench. An older man wearing a crisply pressed business suit sat next to him, reading a newspaper and whistling a jaunty tune. The noise burrowed into Sparky's head like a woodpecker, digging deeper with each note.

"I'm sorry, but would you knock off the whistling?" Sparky sighed. "I've got kind of a headache and you're sort of driving me nuts."

The man in the suit folded up his newspaper into a neat little rectangle and looked Sparky up and down. "Well, I'm sorry about that, friend," he said without a hint of sarcasm or annoyance. "I guess I was so wrapped up in enjoying my paper that I didn't even think about it."

"It's cool, man, don't worry about it," Sparky said.

"Say, you look like you're having a rough day, if you don't mind my saying," said the man in the suit. "Anything I can do to help?"

"Actually, yeah. You wouldn't know how I could get to the ballpark, do you?"

The man in the suit twitched a little at the word "ballpark," and he began fidgeting in his seat. "Heh, ballpark? I, uh, that is to say, I'm not really sure what you, uh, what you're talking about there, sport."

"The ballpark, where the Goats play? Do you know where it is?"

"Whoa, hey now, kid…let's calm down here," the man chuckled nervously. "What's all this about a goat? Heh-heh."

Sparky became annoyed. "This is Go-Town, right?"

"Oh, absolutely! Go-Town it is, you betcha! But say, why don't you take a tour of one of the hovercar factories here in town? Maybe go to the opera and take in a show? Why, there's any number of walking tours of the city where you could learn everything you need to know about Go-Town!"

"No, no, no," Sparky interrupted. "I just need to find the ballpark. What's the matter with you?" He began looking around the station and noticed that most of the people milling about were looking in his direction. "Does anybody know how I can get to the ballpark?" Sparky asked out loud to no one in particular. No one in particular answered. Many of them dropped their heads and hurried away.

Sparky felt a tap on his shoulder, and he turned to see the little fat man from before standing behind him. The man in the suit hurried to gather his briefcase and newspaper before rushing off to wherever it was he needed to be. The little fat man handed Sparky another envelope.

"Here," he said before hustling away again. The new note read: "Dear Sparky...By now you probably need directions to the ballpark. Go north on Louis Street and into the woods. You can't miss it. Good luck, The Go-Goats Girl."

The directions led Sparky into the center of the city, but he was surprised to find an immense forest of tall trees that covered several square blocks. The street continued straight into the heart of the forest, and after a few minutes of walking Sparky found it hard to believe he was even in the city anymore. The sounds of the traffic were replaced by the rush of the winter wind through the bare branches, and the sight of snow-covered trunks took the place of the streetlights and street signs.

At the end of the road, Sparky found a massive brick building, built around the forest so that the trees stood like columns in a Greek temple. Above the main gate was a large red triangular sign that read, in big white letters framed with neon, "WELCOME TO ZIGLEAF FIELD." Then, in much smaller letters, it read, "Home of the Go-Town Goats."

The gate was open, which Sparky thought was unusual for a Big League ballpark in the middle of winter. He stepped inside the dark concourse and listened to his steps echo off the brick and concrete walls.

"Hello?" he called out. Almost immediately he heard the sound of someone behind him clearing their throat. Behind Sparky was a very short, very elderly little Japanese man, an oversized red-and-orange baseball cap teetering on top of his head.

"The office is at the top of the ramp, third door on the left," the little man said.

"Oh, thanks," Sparky said. "Mr. Mint's office, right?"

"Yep."

"How did you know I needed to see Mr. Mint?"

"I'm the clubhouse manager," the little man said. "Yoshi

Kawaii. I know everything that goes on around here. I have to, it's my job."

"Yeah, I guess you would, right?" Sparky said.

Yoshi straightened his cap and puttered slowly down the concourse. "Be seeing you around, Sparky. Welcome to the Goats. Hope you survive the experience."

Sparky watched Yoshi hobble out of sight and shook his head. "Everybody in this town is absolutely out of their freaking minds," he said to himself.

When he finally entered Mr. Mint's office, Sparky almost believed he had stepped into a large cave. It was very dark, and there seemed to be an opening to the outside at the other end. Once his eyes adjusted, he saw Mr. Mint's broad desk at the other end of the room, with a picture window behind it. The window looked out directly onto the muted green grass of Zigleaf Field. Seated at the desk, naturally, was Mr. Mint. He was a man shaped almost exactly like a pencil – tall and thin, practically without shoulders. He stood up as Sparky entered the room and invited him in. Sparky's feet practically sank up to his ankles in the ultra-plush carpeting.

"Welcome, my boy," Mr. Mint said in a voice that sounded just like a clarinet. He shook Sparky's hand, but his grip was so weak Sparky wouldn't have known unless he had watched it. "I hope you're enjoying your time here in Go-Town so far?"

"Yeah, I mean, it's been okay so far."

"Splendid. Well, I wanted to bring you here because I always like to introduce myself to our new players before they put on the uniform. I like to get a feel for the type of person they are. Chemistry is so important to a ballclub, wouldn't you agree?"

"Oh, sure. Of course." Sparky felt like he was being swallowed by the high-backed chair he was sitting in.

"I can't tell you how many times I've had to let a player go simply because he wasn't a good fit for the team. So few team players out there these days. It's a real shame." Mr. Mint cocked one eyebrow at Sparky and waited.

"Oh, uh, yeah, I guess so, sir."

"Take, for example, that dreadful business that just took place in the last Worlds Series, with the Stars." Sparky reflexively dug his fingernails into the soft velvet of the chair's arms. "Too many players thinking only of themselves and not what was best for the team. I'm sure you saw the game, you know what I'm talking about."

"Did YOU see the game?" Sparky asked incredulously.

"I had my assistants read the wire reports to me the next day," Mr. Mint said, shuffling some papers around his desk for effect. "But I get the sense just by talking to you that you're not one of those types of players, am I right?"

Sparky slumped back into the chair. "No, sir," he said wearily.

"Of course not. I consider myself an excellent judge of character, you know." Mr. Mint stood up and turned to look out the window onto the silent field below. "My grandfather was an excellent judge of character, too. He chose my father to run this team when he retired, and my father then passed it to me. The Mint family has owned the Goats for more than 100 years, and in that time we've had a lot of success, thanks to hiring the right people."

"But I've never even heard of this team until a few months ago," Sparky said. "No one in town will even admit that it exists. What kind of success are you talking about?"

"Naturally, the Goats haven't had the kind of success that makes the front page of the sporting press," Mr. Mint sputtered. "But our accomplishments are historic all the same. Did you know, for example, that the Goats hold the Big League record for the most triple plays in one season?"

"Your infield was that good?"

"No, as a matter of fact the triple plays were all against us, but that's still quite an accomplishment, wouldn't you say? I mean, one team wins the championship every year, but running into 32 triple plays in one season...that only happens once in all of history!" Sparky was beginning to feel like this would be the longest season of his life.

Spring training opened a few weeks later, out in the middle of the desert of Calisota. When Sparky arrived at the Goats' training camp, he was surprised to be met by Yoshi, who led him down a long, dusty trail to a dock at the edge of a narrow river. A tiny rowboat decorated with the Goats' logo bobbed in the water next to the dock.

"Before you start asking a lot of questions," Yoshi said with a weary sigh, "the camp is at the end of this river."

Sparky just shrugged and dumped his duffel bag into the boat. Out of all the things he knew about this team now, having to use a rowboat in the desert was far from the strangest. Yoshi methodically paddled the boat down the river, and in time a large lake came into view, a shimmering blue mirror in the middle of the sand. In the center of that lake was a large island, dotted with buildings. Sparky could see the yellow foul poles of the practice fields poking into the blue sky.

"Is this-?"

"Yes, welcome to the spring training home of the Go-Town

Goats," Yoshi said without enthusiasm. "Mr. Mint's father built this island 50 years ago, and more than 500 million gallons of sea water are pumped into the artificial lake every year. Mr. Mint's father believed the combination of the hot desert air and the salt from the sea water would help invigorate the players."

"Huh, that's weird," Sparky said.

"You think so?" Yoshi said sarcastically. "Hm, maybe you're right."

The clubhouse was deathly silent when Sparky arrived, and he made it to his locker without seeing another person. He unpacked his bag, set up his locker and took a look around. The clubhouse was nothing special, except for the weight room – at least, Sparky thought it was the weight room. Instead of the usual arrangement of benches and weights, the room was lined with what looked like big metal coffins. Opening one up, Sparky saw the insides of the chamber were lined with big horseshoe-shaped magnets, exactly like the kinds used in old cartoons to catch roadrunners or mice who had been tricked into eating ball bearings.

The mess hall looked normal enough, except for the fact that none of the tables had ketchup, mustard or hot sauce. The only condiment present on each table was a bottle of some thick green substance labeled "Dr. Horton's Restorative Root Marm." The labels had a picture of a muscular man with a handlebar mustache holding a horse over his head with one hand. Sparky unscrewed the cap and took a whiff – it smelled like the inside of a lawnmower bag.

When he got back to his locker, Sparky found another player sitting in the clubhouse. The young man literally jumped out of his seat when Sparky entered the room. Sparky half-expected him to salute. He was a dark-skinned young man with very short hair, skinny and short. He couldn't have been older than 18, so he was only a couple of years younger than Sparky. Sparky imagined he probably looked just like this kid to some of his older teammates in San Carlos.

"Hi!" the kid said. "Are y-you on the team, too?"

"Uh, yeah."

"Of course you are, that was a stupid question. I'm sorry, I'm just kind of nervous."

"Don't worry about it," Sparky said, shaking the kid's hand. "Sparky Katakura, how you doing?"

"Katakura, oh yeah! I heard you were going to be here this year. Carlos Caballeros, nice to meet you, man. So what are you doing here this year?"

"Ah, it's kind of a long story, maybe I'll tell you later,"

Sparky said as he rubbed the back of his neck. "Hey, what's the deal with those magnet things in the weight room?"

"Huh? Oh, wow, I don't know," Carlos said, his eyes wide. "This is kind of my first season here. Well, it's kind of my first season anywhere, to be honest."

Just then, the clubhouse door was thrown open with a bang. It was then that Sparky saw the first truly familiar face he had seen since arriving in Go-Town a few weeks before. It was the mustachioed face of Fuzzy Fernandez, former shortstop for the Brooklyn Batsmen. Seven summers ago, it seemed that Sparky couldn't open up a pack of baseball cards without finding Fuzzy's smirk lurking within. Sparky wound up using a stack of them to prop up one of the legs of his desk. It had been three summers since Sparky had even heard his name – he vaguely recalled hearing something about a suspension.

True to the smirk on his ubiquitous baseball card, Fuzzy came striding into the locker room as if his arrival was what everyone had been waiting for. His long, lanky arms and legs still looked capable of making a diving play to his right to keep a ball from shooting into left field. His Goats cap sat on top of his head, surrounded by a magnificent halo of frizzy hair. It was a miracle the hat didn't pop right off his head, given how thick and plentiful the hair on his head was.

"Aw man, look at this," Fuzzy said with a cackle. "Fuzzy's not the first one at Spring Training this year! I'm gonna lose my reputation as a gamer, oh boy!" Fuzzy continued giggling to himself as he unpacked his duffel bag and then stretched out on a bench.

"Hey kiddo," Fuzzy called out to Carlos, "do Fuzzy a favor and wake me up before Skip gets here. I want to make sure he sees me in the weight room."

Astonishingly, a sudden gust of wind tore through the locker room, lifting Fuzzy off the bench and dropping him on the floor with a thud.

"Get thine hindquarters off yon floor!" The voice came booming from behind Sparky, and he turned to find the doorway filled with a mountain of a man, at least seven and a half feet tall, with wild red hair and a beard that swirled around him with the wind. He carried a massive bat on his shoulder and in his other hand he held a frightening mallet made of stone.

Fuzzy dusted himself off and stood up. "Aw come on, man, I was just making a little joke," he said. "Why you gotta start busting my hump on the first day of camp, huh?"

"Know this, mortal...the God of Thunder doth not tolerate teammates who slacketh off!"

"God of Thunder?" Sparky said.

"Aye!" The giant took Sparky's hand and shook it heartily –
so heartily that he almost lifted Sparky off the ground. "I am Thor
Odinson, the mighty Norse God of Thunder who doth defend left
field from opponents' line drives and pop flies!"

"Yeah, except he couldn't catch a fly ball if he was wearing
a mitt the size of a minivan!" Fuzzy said.

Thor stood so close to Fuzzy that the bill of Fuzzy's cap was
touching one of the buttons on Thor's jersey. Thor's voice was a
low rumble, like a distant storm. "I am the God of Thunder," he
said, "and the power of the storms is mine to command. When thy
bat can strike the ball with force enough to send it as far as mine
doth, then perhaps the son of Odin will take heed to thy prattling."

There was a moment of silence. Neither Thor nor Fuzzy
moved, each keeping their eyes fixed on the other. Thor's nostrils
flared with rage.

"Dude, nobody here knows what the flip you're saying,"
Fuzzy said finally. "Like, ever. Do you even understand what you're
saying?" Thor grumbled to himself and stomped to his locker.
Sparky heard him use the words "pitiful mortals" as he unpacked
his bags. As he watched the rest of his teammates unpack in
silence, Sparky felt a hard slap on his back. He turned around and
saw a chubby guy in a t-shirt and shorts standing next to him,
grinning broadly.

"How you doing there, buddy?" he said grabbing Sparky's
hand and shaking it. "You on the team, or are you somebody's kid
brother? Ah, I'm just kidding, take it easy, sport. Bobby Munson,
third base."

"Sparky, starting pitcher. Nice to meet you, Bobby." Bobby
took the locker next to Sparky and unzipped his bag. On top of the
rumpled clothing was a box of pink-frosted donuts. Bobby
immediately stuffed one in his mouth, crumbs and sprinkles falling
from the corners of his mouth and collecting on top of his sizable
gut. Bobby noticed Sparky staring at him in disbelief.

"Oh, sorry, bro," Bobby said. "You want one?"

"No, but thanks," Sparky said. "I don't want to sound like a
jerk or anything, but are you sure you're going to get back in
playing condition eating those things like you are?" Bobby already
had another donut in his mouth, but he let out a muffled guffaw
anyway.

"What the heck are you talking about?"

"You're completely out of shape," Sparky said, still trying
not to sound like a jerk. "How did you ever get on a Big League
Baseball team like that?"

"Oh," Bobby said, brushing the crumbs off his t-shirt but
picking the sprinkles off to eat. "Mr. Mint saw me playing for the

Go-Town city softball champs, and he said he really liked the way the crowds cheered for me, so he signed me right there on the spot. I've been with the Goats for four seasons now. Isn't that awesome?"

"Yeah, pretty awesome," Sparky said. "Hey, so tell me something, Bobby. Is the clubhouse always this messed up? I mean, with Thor and Fuzzy getting in each other's faces all the time?"

"Them? Oh yeah, totally," Bobby said through another mouthful of donut. "That's nothing, though. Just wait until Mr. Wonderful gets here."

"Who's that?"

"Oh-ho-ho-ho! Man, I could tell you, but I'm pretty sure you'll know him when you see him, dude."

The clubhouse filled up steadily, but Sparky didn't see anyone who might have fit Bobby's mystery man. In fact, none of the players seemed to have any interaction with each other, aside from Fuzzy and Thor's altercation from before. The majority of them sat around in front of their lockers, looking beaten down and depressed. Many of them were texting on their phones or reading magazines. Carlos was twirling his glove in the air and catching it between his hands. Bobby was reading a worn-out copy of "Fishing and Stuff That's Related to Fishing." Fuzzy was stretched out on the bench again. Thor took lazy practice swings, first with his bat, then with his hammer.

"Aren't we going to go...you know...practice?" Sparky said.

"Fuzzy don't do anything unless he has to," Fuzzy said without opening his eyes or moving at all. "You wanna go practice so bad, you go find Skip. The rest of us are cool just sitting here."

"He's got a point, little guy," Bobby said. "Skip's workouts are bru-hoo-hoo-tal."

"Well maybe you guys need someone to be brutal on you," Sparky said. "How do you expect to win the Worlds Series if you're..." Sparky didn't get to finish his thought, because the entire clubhouse minus Carlos burst into laughter.

"Young friend, the God of Thunder has known victory on every field of battle on either side of the Rainbow Bridge," Thor said, shaking his head. "But here, on Midgard, with these as his compatriots on the field of baseball...well, there are certain things that not even the gods are capable of."

"Redbeard sounds like a dork, but even Fuzzy's got to agree with him," Fuzzy said, still not moving. "This place is the end of the line, man."

Sparky could only stand there for a moment as the rest of his new teammates went back to their slacking. There was a lot more he wanted to say to them, but he could feel the words sinking like a base hit dropping onto the outfield grass.

Instead, Sparky went trudging through the halls of the clubhouse, until he found an office marked "MANAGER." There was a light on inside, and he knocked on the door. There was no response. He tried again, but still there was nothing.

"Hello?" Sparky pushed the door open slowly and leaned into the room. The office was cramped, filled with file cabinets and a dented old steel desk. At that desk, studying a wrinkled depth chart, was the equally wrinkled Skip LeRoche. He squinted at Sparky through his thick glasses.

"Hey, can't you read the sign on the door?" said the one-time Big League Baseball record-holder for most times hit by a pitch. "I'm busy in here."

"There's no sign on the door," Sparky said. Skip jumped to his feet and shuffled to the door, brushing Sparky out of his way.

"Ahhh, look at this! Some joker pulled down my sign! I tell ya, these young punks today got no respect for the position of manager, that's what I'm saying!" Sparky noticed a hand-lettered sign reading "KEEP YER MOUTHS SHUT! MANAGER WORKING IN HERE!" stuck with a piece of tape to the back of Skip's pants. "Whaddya staring at, kid? What's yer problem?"

"Nothing, the guys in the clubhouse just wanted to know when practice started."

Skip's eyes grew wide. "Practice? Whaddya talking about? What day is this?"

"It's the first day of Spring Training, don't you know that?"

Skip stood silently for a moment, and then the confusion dropped from his face and he began pushing Sparky out of the office. "Sure, sure, of course!" he said. "I'm the manager, fer crying out loud! Get back in that locker room and tell the rest of those bums Skip's coming to whup the lazy outta them, toot sweet! Hey, by the way, what's yer name, kid?"

"I'm Sparky Katakura."

"Oh yeah! Hey, I've got to talk to you, son. I'm thinking I'm going to have to move you from the bullpen into the starting rotation."

"But I'm already a starter," Sparky said.

"Oh, you are, are you?" Skip said with mock surprise. "I'm gonna clue you in on something right here because you're new: I don't like guys who come into the ballpark with delusions of grandeur, you got that? You want a spot in the rotation, you got to earn it! Now get out there!" The office door slammed shut behind Sparky.

Out on the practice field, Sparky watched as Yoshi emerged from the equipment shed with a pile of jump ropes, all tangled together like a plate of spaghetti. The other Goats trudged over and began trying to separate them. Skip came hobbling out of the dugout, adjusting his belt to no avail as his pants were simply too baggy.

"Awright you bums," Skip said, punctuating his greeting by spitting a wad of bubble gum at his feet. "Get those jump ropes undone and get to work. Then we're gonna get the medicine balls out and really work the sissy outta ya!"

"What is this, gym class?" Sparky asked Fuzzy, who only shook his head. "Hey, Skip! When do we start working on pitching drills?"

"Whuzzat? Pitching drills?" Skip marched over to Sparky and jabbed a bony finger into his chest. "Listen here, kid, do you know the average pitcher makes nearly 3,000 pitches a season?"

"Yeah, so?"

"So? You can't just jump right into pitching on the first day! There's all kinds of conditioning and restorative treatments you've gotta do before you can even think about pitching again! You don't do that now, and all of a sudden you're out of gas before the playoffs even start!" Skip's statement drew a few sarcastic snorts from the other Goats.

"That's crazy," Sparky caught himself saying without thinking. The wrinkles on Skip's face began to arrange themselves in a frown that reached from his eyebrows down to his neck.

"Where the heck do you get off calling me crazy, kid?" Skip stepped directly onto the tops of Sparky's feet – a technique he often employed when arguing with umpires – and got so close Sparky could tell what the manager had for breakfast. It was scrambled eggs, with bacon and seemingly two full pots of coffee.

"Why don't you go take 30 laps around the field and then come back and tell me I'm crazy?" Skip spat. Sparky pulled his cap down over his eyes and started jogging. From the middle of the field, Carlos watched Sparky take his laps before focusing his attention on the knotted ball of jump ropes in front of him.

The next few days progressed similarly to the first one. Each day, Sparky was introduced to a new team exercise of dubious benefit to a ball club, and each day he found himself running laps around the field for questioning it. All the while, Skip would angrily insist on the necessity of his training regimen:

"Listen, kid, electrical stimulus is scientifically proven to build muscle growth, so grab that Tesla coil or it's another 30 laps for ya!"

"Listen, kid, a ground ball can take a lot of bad hops, so if you can catch a jackrabbit with a lit match up its butt, you can make a routine play, don't ya think?"

"Listen, kid, a Big League ballplayer's gotta be able to perform under extreme pressure. So get back in that batting cage and if I see you looking down at those rattlesnakes again, it's another 30 laps!"

One night, as Sparky laid awake in his bottom bunk, he thought back to where he was just one year before – in Spring Training camp with Ken and the Stars. It wasn't long before Sparky was sent to the minor-league camp, but for the first few days he was practicing with the Big League club and, more importantly, his brother. He remembered Ken laughing at his swing, encouraging him to keep his arm angle up and calling out from second when he was tipping his pitches. Now, he was stuck listening to Bobby snore as his stomach did somersaults from another meal slathered in Dr. Horton's Restorative Root Marm. His eyes were itchy and his nose was dripping – apparently he was allergic to jackrabbits. He felt like crying.

Before he did, though, he heard a soft thumping noise against the far wall of the clubhouse. Tip-toeing around his sleeping teammates, Sparky crept outside and found Carlos wearing his uniform pants and a glove, bouncing a ball against the wall.

"Hey Carlos."

"Oh, what's up, Sparky?"

"What are you doing out here?"

Carlos looked at the ball in his glove as if he had been caught robbing a bank. "I'm sorry, I just wanted to come outside and get in some practice. I used to do this all the time back home, to learn how to field short hops, you know? My hometown is kind of small, so there wasn't always someone to play with."

"That's cool. It's not like we're getting any real training done here, anyway." Sparky held up his hand and Carlos lobbed him the ball.

"Is Spring Training always like this? In the Big Leagues?"

"I've never seen anything like this," Sparky said as he tossed Carlos the ball. "Even my Pee-Wee League practices were better than this, and we were always stopping because some kid would pee his pants."

"At least you didn't have to chase any jackrabbits," Carlos said. "I don't like how they scream."

"Me neither. You're the only other guy here who gives a crap about winning, Carlos."

"I just want to win a championship, make my mother proud of me," Carlos said. "But it doesn't look like that's going to happen with this team."

"It's going to have to, Carlos," Sparky said, tossing the ball back a little harder than before. "Or else I don't know what I'm going to do."

The next morning, Sparky and the Goats sat bleary-eyed around their lockers. Sparky and Carlos were tired from their secret training sessions, but the rest of the team had gotten even less sleep thanks to Bobby's snoring. Sparky was tying the laces on his cleats when there came a loud hollering from down the hall.

"Ya-HOO!"

Sparky and Carlos nearly jumped out of their chairs, but Fuzzy only sighed and shook his head. "Great, here comes Mr. Wonderful."

Through the clubhouse door stepped a big, beaming wall of a man, all shoulders and arms with a tiny duffel bag slung over his shiny sportcoat. His thick blonde hair was sealed around his head like a helmet. In one hand he carried a big black boom box, which he set on a chair in front of an empty locker.

"Howdy, fellas! Have no fear, your Lance is here!" It was then that Sparky overcame his initial shock and recognized the big slab of human being who had just invaded the clubhouse – Lance Bright, one-time home run leader of the Solar League with the Las Vegas Magicians, only his familiar smiling face had become creased and droopy with age. The way the rest of the Goats clubhouse ignored him immediately answered Sparky's unspoken question as to where Bright had been since the last time he heard Bright's name called. He had been in Go-Town, and apparently he had made himself very comfortable.

Unfazed by the silence he was greeted with, Lance switched on his boom box and filled the room with the twangy sound of a country guitar and a woozy warbling kind of singing. "Girl, I'm hustlin' for your heart," the voice crooned. "I'm standing here on third, waiting for the the word, so I can make a break and steal home!"

Lance tapped his foot with the song and nodded his head. He slapped Thor on the shoulder and pointed at the boom box proudly. "What do you think, Thor old buddy? The album drops on Opening Day! Fifteen brand-new country-western tracks, all of them written personally by yours truly. So, you think there's at least one multi-platinum hit in there, old buddy?"

"I say thee nay," Thor grumbled. "Thine music doth remind the Odinson of the cries the Frost Giants would make as they fell in battle."

"All right, so we know the big guy likes it," Lance pointed at Sparky. "How about you, little man? Record of the year, right?"

Sparky could only stammer a little. He was admittedly a little star-struck by Lance, who was still imposing despite the fact that he was clearly out of his prime.

"All right, that's great," Lance said, not waiting for Sparky to collect his thoughts. "Lance Bright, right field. Nice to meet you, rookie."

"Oh, uh, hey," Sparky said, snapping out of his daze. "I'm not actually a rookie. I'm Sparky Katakura, starting pitcher."

"Oh, okay," Lance said flatly. "Where did you play before coming here, then?"

"San Carlos," Sparky said.

"Weren't you guys in the Worlds Series last year?" Lance said. "I was in the Marshall Islands shooting a little cameo scene for a movie that'll be hitting basic cable in a few weeks, so I didn't get much chance to watch the postseason this year. The Bright-man is an in-demand cat, in case you didn't know."

Lance turned away from Sparky and addressed the locker room. "So, what's new around here, Goats? Skip made you all toss the medicine ball around yet?"

"Yeah and it sucks just like it always does," Bobby said.

"Hey man, why do you think Mr. Bright always comes to camp late?" Fuzzy laughed. "He's the smartest guy on this stupid team."

"If he was really smart he wouldn't even be here," someone else said in the back of the room.

"All right, you bums, suck it up and get it together," said Skip as he came charging into the locker room. "We're doing jackrabbit drills again today, so let's be out on the practice field in five, come on!"

The team groaned in unison. As the Goats filed out of the locker room, Sparky hung back and got Skip's attention.

"Skip, you're killing us with these stupid drills," he said. "Is there any chance we could get some actual baseball in today?"

"Look, kid, I know you think I'm some kinda kook, but I've got my training regimen and I'm sticking to it," Skip said. "That is, unless you want to go to Mr. Mint yourself and convince him to do things differently."

"All this stuff is Mint's idea?"

Skip looked offended. "Whadda ya think I am, some kinda spineless jellyfish? The jackrabbits were a hundred percent my idea. Mr. Mint said we should use ferrets."

The next day, Skip called Sparky over to the bullpen. He gladly dropped the jackrabbit he had just caught, letting it scamper away to a nearby bush.

"Our new catcher just arrived today, a trade with the Outlaws," Skip said. "I want you to make a few tosses to him, get him loosened up."

"You mean pitching? I can start pitching now?"

"Yeah, yeah, yeah, don't wet your pants or anything, just get over there and make sure he gets nice and loose," Skip grumbled. "And just so we're clear, I expect double rabbit drills from you tomorrow!"

Sparky chose to ignore the last thing Skip said as he trotted into the bullpen and picked up a baseball. The catcher made his way slowly into the bullpen. He was a tall, tired-looking man no younger than 45, with a mustache that spread from his upper lip like the wings of a hawk soaring on the breeze.

"How you doing, kid?" he said in a deep raspy voice as he slowly crouched into position. "Gimme a second here. You're that hot-shot from the Stars, ain't you?"

"That's me."

"Lou Houston, pleased to make your acquaintance." Lou grunted in pain as he rocked back and forth on his heels.

"You were with the Outlaws?"

"That's right," Lou said. "Also the Scouts, the Clockwatchers, the Freezers, the Streaks, the Majestics, the Blue Shoes...ah, but I could go on forever and you don't want to spend all day listening to me read my resume."

"That's okay, it beats listening to Lance talk about his awful country-western album," Sparky said.

"Hey, what's wrong with country-western music?" Lou said.

"You'd know if you heard this album."

Lou spat at the ground and laughed. He punched the center of his mitt and held it in front of him. "All right, kid, show me what you got, don't go easy on me."

Sparky looked in at the fragile old man squatting at the other end of the pen and decided to start off a little slow. He reared back and whipped a medium-speed fastball at Lou. The pitch caught his mitt dead-center, but the force of it sent Lou staggering back half a step.

"You all right?" Sparky called out as Lou tossed the ball back to him.

"Oh yeah, just caught me a little by surprise, that's all." Lou shook it off and got back into position. "Go ahead on, give me the real heat."

Sparky shook his head. The old guy was asking for it, so why not give it to him? He decided to cut loose and try out the pitch he had been developing, the Blazing Fastball. Sparky took a deep breath and focused on tapping into the energy he needed for the pitch. He cocked his arm, planted his front foot and sent the ball hurtling out of his hand. The ball picked up speed as it tumbled across the bullpen, the seams buzzsawing through the air at speeds so fast the friction began to burn the cowhide. Wisps of smoke trailed off the ball, followed by flickering tongues of flame. By the time the ball collided with Lou's mitt, it was a solid ball of fire, extinguished only when he closed the leather around it in a puff of smoke. Despite his earlier trouble, Lou didn't budge an inch on impact.

"Holy smokes, kid," Lou said in appreciation. "You've got more than a little zip on that fastball of yours, you know that?"

"I've been told that," Sparky said.

"This is the end of the line for me, so I know what I'm doing here, but how'd a young buck with real talent like yourself end up with the goldurn Go-Town Goats?"

"It's a long story," Sparky said. "Let me ask you a question, Lou, since you've obviously been around the Big Leagues for a while."

"Shoot."

"What are the odds of this team winning the Worlds Series this season?"

Lou took a look out at the practice field, where he watched Bobby and Lance collide as the jackrabbits they were chasing crossed in front of each other. He looked back at Sparky with a solemn look on his face. "Kid, I'd be surprised if this bunch even knew how to spell 'Worlds Series.' What makes you ask?"

"It's, ah, a contractual thing."

"What, you mean like an incentive?"

"Something like that."

Lou stared into Sparky's eyes for a moment, then spat at the ground again. "I think I know what you mean, kid," he said, shaking his head. "And for what it's worth...I'm sorry."

The next morning, Sparky tossed a few pitches in the bullpen with the rest of the Goats' pitching staff. Lou shook out his hand after every other fastball, making Sparky wonder if the old man was even going to make it through a full season. Maybe he should really crank it up and break the poor guy's hand, he thought. It would practically be an act of mercy. He looked over his shoulder to see one of the other pitchers bounce a pitch off the dirt and way over the head of the bullpen catcher. The catcher fell backwards trying to stab at the ball mid-flight, but the pitcher didn't look bothered by his wildness at all. Instead, he twirled his thick, curly mustache and smirked with a satisfied look on his face.

"Dude, that was a nasty pitch," Sparky said.

"Oh, you think so?" The other pitcher pointed his nose up in the air and sniffed loudly. "Hmph, I would be angry at you for saying such a thing, but how else would a philistine like yourself react to that pitch?"

"What? Are you saying you pitched like that on purpose?"

"No no no, you silly person. Antonio De La Goya does not pitch on purpose." Antonio took a deep bow, sweeping his hands in front of him as if presenting a fine seven-course meal on an invisible table. "No, my friend, Antonio De La Goya pitches with purpose. Observe."

Antonio took a new ball and twirled around on the mound before throwing a wide, hooking slider that broke across the plate and well out of the catcher's reach, sending him sprawling to the dirt. Antonio turned and smiled smugly at Sparky.

"What the in the wide world of sports was that?" Lou called out from the other end of the bullpen. All other activity in the pen had stopped to watch Antonio's impromptu clinic.

"That, sir, was only one piece in a much larger work," Antonio said.

"Say again?"

"Pitching is an art form, and I am, therefore, an artist. Each pitch is a brush stroke toward the greater masterpiece. You look at this pitch and see only 'high and tight' or 'low and away,' but the true artist sees the curve, the speed, the arc of the ball adding texture and color to the pitch that came before, and the pitch that came before that pitch, and so on. Layered all together, these 'nasty' pitches, as you say, come together to form a living, breathing work of art!" Antonio ended his speech by throwing his arms into the air.

"That's great, Mister Art-teest," Lou said, "but what was your ERA last season, if you don't mind me asking?"

"If you are concerned with such petty things, fine, I cannot change your mind. The number, good sir, was 8.47, but I hardly see how that has any bearing on the quality and sincerity of my art."

"I didn't think you would," Lou said as he pulled his mask back down over his face.

The only other pitcher in the bullpen was a young woman with a shock of multi-colored hair sticking out in random streaks from under her cap. She had a tiny metal loop in her left nostril and a shifty look on her face. As Sparky continued to warm up, she slunk up next to him like a snake. She raised her eyebrows when Sparky finally made eye contact.

"Hey," she said quietly. "What do you use?"

"Excuse me?"

"That's a heck of a fastball you got there, buddy," she said, nodding in Lou's direction. "What's your secret? Kerosene?"

"No."

"Lighter fluid?"

"No."

She looked around and lowered her voice even more. "Voodoo?"

"No!"

"You're telling me you can do that all by yourself?"

Sparky raised his eyebrows now. "Yeah."

The girl laughed out loud and punched Sparky in the shoulder. "That's hilarious! You're a funny guy, buddy. I'm Willie Wilbur, starting pitcher."

"Sparky Katakura," he said, shaking her hand with its long, rainbow-colored nails. "Nice to meet you. Those are some nails, Willie. Don't they mess up your delivery?"

"Heck no, I need these babies. Every game I stash a little something extra under each one. You know, petroleum jelly for a little more slickness, some rubber cement to give the ball some extra weight." Willie held up her pinky finger, which was topped with a hot-pink nail that bore a serrated edge, like a steak knife. "With this one I can even scuff it up a little, maybe tear out a few seams."

"Isn't that cheating?"

"It's not cheating if you lose anyway," Willie replied.

4. Opening Day

Three days and a dozen rabbit bites later, it was time to pack up for Go-Town. Sparky and Carlos stood side-by-side at their lockers, stuffing socks and jocks and hats and bats into their duffels. The last thing Sparky pulled out of his locker was a single baseball card – Ken's rookie card from his first season with the Stars three years before.

"You ever seen Zigleaf Field, Sparky?" Carlos' smile could barely be contained by his face. "I hear it's pretty wild, man."

"Yeah," Sparky said as he snapped out of his fog. "I was there over the winter."

"What's that park that has the waterslides that go around the outfield bleachers? That's in San Diego, right?"

"Uh, yeah, I think so."

"Is that in the Central League? That would be awesome to play in a park with waterslides, right?"

"No…San Diego, that's the Oceanic League, I don't think they're on our schedule this year."

"Aw, man. But the Canaries are in our league, right? Man, that's going to be awesome, right? I think I could get a hit off Marshall Harris, don't you think so?"

"Sure, Carlos, yeah. I'll bet you will."

"This is going to be amazing, it was worth getting bitten by all those rabbits to play in the Big Leagues! This is all I've ever wanted, Sparky."

"Yeah, I know." Sparky closed his locker. "It was all I ever wanted once, too."

In the week before Opening Day, a conversation very much like the one below was a common thing to hear in the barber shops, playgrounds and bars throughout all of Go-Town:

"So, how do you think the Goats are going to do this year?"

"UGH."

It was the same conversation 21-year-old Katie Spalding had

been having for the last three weeks. She would ask one of her friends how they thought the Goats would do in the upcoming season, and whoever she was talking to would invariably say "UGH." Despite this, Katie Spalding found herself standing outside Zigleaf Field on Opening Day, a ticket in her hand.

Katie gazed up at the marquee: "WELCOME TO OPENING DAY – GOATS VS. FORT CLARK CANARIES." A steady stream of people shuffled their way through the gates into the ballpark, many wearing the Goats' orange and red, but a good number of them decked from head to toe in Canary yellow. Katie tucked her red hair under her orange hat and sighed deeply.

"Okay, here we go again," she said to herself as she stepped through the turnstiles.

Inside the park, the pale spring sunlight covered the field like a warm blanket. The zigleaf trees had only started to bud, leaving the branches entirely bare. In the absence of leaves, the reams of red-white-and-blue bunting gave the ballpark its color. The familiar chatter of the roving vendors rang out throughout the stands, announcing fresh, fluffy popcorn, ice cold soda pop, warm salty peanuts and red-hot hot dogs. Katie carried her hot dog and soda to her seat, a seat she could have found blindfolded – good old aisle 424, row 3, seat 101. Katie dropped her knapsack into seat 102. No one would be there to claim it.

A couple rows down, Katie spotted a pair of Canaries fans making their way to their seats. There had always been a lot of yellow in the stands when the Canaries came to Go-Town. Fort Clark was only 40 miles or so down the river from Go-Town, and the Canaries had, in general, been a bit more successful than the Goats, ensuring that practically anyone who didn't live within the city limits of Go-Town claimed being a Canaries fan, at least publicly.

The taller of the two Canaries fans eased into his seat with the care of someone afraid he would be bitten by a snake. He took a hesitant bite of his hot dog and chewed it thoughtfully. He held it at arm's length and nudged his friend. "Does this look like an all-beef hot dog to you?"

The shorter one leaned in and sniffed the frankfurter, wrinkling his nose. "Mm, I'd have to say no," he said.

The taller fan smiled. "I'd have to say you're right," he said. "An inferior beef/pork blend, not even grilled properly for the consistency. Another epic fail for this franchise."

"Well, what else would you expect?" the shorter one waved his hands to include all of Zigleaf Field in his criticism. "This team has been a blight on Central League baseball for generations."

"Mm-hm, too true," his taller friend agreed. "How anyone

can show their face wearing the Goats' particularly putrid shade of orange, I'll never understand."

Katie rolled her eyes and started filling out her scorecard with the starting lineups. It already was difficult for Goats fans to watch their team stumble around the field, but it was even worse when the Canaries were in town. Katie didn't know whether she should feel pride or shame in being one of the few who did both regularly.

Most of the Goats' lineup would have been easy for Katie to fill out even if she hadn't read a single Spring Training report from the Gazette, but there were enough new faces to make things a little bit interesting. She couldn't deny feeling a little flutter of excitement as she penciled in "SP: Katakura," but she quickly tamped it down.

Meanwhile, in the clubhouse, "SP: Katakura" was looking at his name on the lineup card and frowning. He pulled Fuzzy over and tapped a few names. "Who are these guys?" Sparky asked. "I never saw them in Spring Training."

"Second base is some new guy," Fuzzy said. "They just signed him a couple days ago. Supposed to be pretty good."

"Yeah, but what kind of name is 'Blerk Hurzberk?'"

"Hey man, if he can cut off a throw from center without tripping over his own feet, Fuzzy don't care how his name's spelled."

"Okay, and what about center? 'VORP?' Is that short for something?"

"Hey, Skip!" Fuzzy called out. "You forgot our star center fielder, man!"

Skip looked up from tying his shoes and took a quick look around the clubhouse. "Aw, heck! Yoshi! Go get the kid outta storage, huh?"

"'The kid!'" Fuzzy snorted as he nudged Sparky. "That thing's so old its warranty probably ran out long before Skip's!"

Yoshi returned from storage with a large wooden crate on a handtruck. With effortless speed, Yoshi pried the front of the crate off with a screwdriver. Inside, standing upright, was one of the oddest things Sparky had seen, up to that point. He recognized the dented, rusty frame of a vintage robot player immediately. Its eyes were like two Christmas tree lights, and its joints were stained with old grease. The baseball cap built onto its head was spray-painted Goats orange, but bits were flaking off of it. The thing looked more like a water heater than a baseball player, but when Yoshi flipped the switch on its back it jumped to life and came jogging out of the crate clapping its steel hands together.

"All right, all right!" the robot shouted enthusiastically, its metal jaw clanging as it spoke. "Awesome day for baseball! Awesome! Let's play another one!"

"We ain't even played one yet, you crazy pinball machine!" Fuzzy shook his head as the robot continued creaking and squeaking around the room. "Ugh, Fuzzy's gonna have to retire early, man, I swear to God."

The robot grabbed Sparky and Carlos simultaneously and squeezed them close to him. "New teammates, all right! I'm so excited to meet you both! I'm your Value Outfield Robot Player, but you can go ahead and call me VORP!"

"Nice to meet you, VORP," Sparky croaked. "Would you let us go now?"

Moments later, the teams had lined up along the foul lines for the introductions and the national anthem. During the anthem, with his cap over his heart, Sparky noticed that most of the Canaries fans were watching not the flag but a man dressed in a bright yellow suit and tie. He appeared to be conducting them like a choirmaster.

The Goats took the field, with Carlos practically sprinting to his spot, VORP doing cartwheels on his rusty limbs and the rest of the team dutifully trudging into position. Lou eased into his crouch behind the plate and nodded to Sparky on the mound. As he took his warm-up tosses, he thought to himself, "Just get out to a good start. Make your pitches, hit your spots and the rest will work itself out. Just win the first game."

It was something his coach in high school had always said: "The only game you can win is the one you're playing right now." Sparky just had to concentrate on winning the first game, worry about winning the rest of them as the schedule allowed. "Sure," he thought, "this team is pretty lousy, but I almost won the last game of the Worlds Series a few months ago. I'm good enough to win, and that has to be worth something."

He took a glance behind him and finally got his first good look at the second baseman, Blerk Hurzberk. No more than four feet tall, Blerk didn't look like any player Sparky had seen in the Big Leagues, or even on the planet, for that matter. His shiny blue skin made him look like a balloon animal in a baseball uniform, and his eyes were large, lidless and black. Blerk stood just behind second base, and gave Sparky a little wave when he saw him looking back. Sparky gave him a tiny wave back but then motioned for him to move a few steps over, away from the base and more in a second baseman's natural position. Blerk looked down at his feet and shuffled a few steps to his left. He gave Sparky a thumbs-up and Sparky was free to concentrate on pitching again.

Sparky took a deep breath as the Canaries' lead-off hitter

stepped into the box. Lou flashed the signal for a fastball – the index finger, pointed straight down. Sparky reared back and sent one whistling across the plate and into Lou's mitt with a resounding "THWAP!"

"Steeeeeerike one!" the umpire bellowed, and the Goats fans in the stands made their voices heard. The signal for the next pitch was the same, and Sparky followed with another blistering pitch that the batter didn't even have a chance to flinch at.

"Steeeeeeeeerike two!" Sparky couldn't help but smile a little to himself. If nothing else, he knew he could rely on his fastball. Lou silently requested another. Sparky put a little extra into the third pitch, but this time the hitter tracked it from his hand and was able to put the bat on it, sending a chopper bouncing across the infield grass to second. Blerk shuffled to his left, scooped it up, but instead of making the throw to first he plucked the ball out of his glove and examined it closely. The Canaries' batter, who had slowed down upon seeing Blerk field the ball, quickly hustled to the bag and made it to first safely. The stands rocked with the pained groaning of the Goats fans and the boisterous laughter of the Canaries fans. Sparky could only throw up his hands in frustration. Carlos looked bewildered, Lou hung his head and Fuzzy appeared to be giggling to himself. Blerk trotted to the mound and cheerfully deposited the ball in Sparky's glove.

"Hey man, what the heck was that all about?" Sparky demanded.

Blerk smiled broadly. "I collected the ball, isn't that the objective of the game?" he said in a voice that sounded like a video game.

"You're supposed to throw it to first base after you collect it," Sparky said. "Haven't you ever played second base before?"

"I'm sorry to say that I haven't," Blerk said. "In fact, the rules of this game are quite new to me."

"You've never played baseball before?" Sparky asked urgently.

"To my people, baseball is a foreign concept," Blerk replied. "I was sent here to learn the game and bring it back to my home world. We hope to form our own team, join the Big Leagues and finally bring honor to our people by defeating the Rigel 7 Conquerors in a game! Your Mr. Mint was gracious enough to give me a place on this team to observe and learn."

"Mr. Mint is pretty gracious about a lot of things," Sparky said. "Look, just stand over there where I showed you, and if you end up collecting the ball again, just throw it over to Carlos as soon as you do, okay?" Blerk grinned and gave Sparky another thumbs-up before scampering back to the infield.

"Ya bum!" Skip shouted from the top of the dugout steps. "I ever catch you doing that again and it's fifty push-ups, you got that?" Blerk gave Skip the same weird smile and a thumbs-up.

Sparky looked in at the next hitter, and Lou just shrugged in a way that said, "Ain't the worst I've ever seen, kid." Lou called for another fastball, and Sparky whizzed it past the late-swinging hitter for a strike. The next pitch was fouled off behind home plate to make it an 0-2 count. Lou signaled fastball again, and Sparky hurled a heater that was smoking when the hitter swung over the top of it.

"Steeeeerike three!" The batter flipped his bat in the air, tugged his cap down over his eyes and sulked back to the dugout. There was some noise coming from the stands, nothing like what Sparky had heard in San Carlos, but enough to let him know someone was paying attention. The next hitter stepped to the plate, his eyes fixed on Sparky. He tapped his bat on home plate and spit at the ground. Lou signaled fastball again, and Sparky delivered. The batter made contact, sending the ball on a high arc over the infield into left field. Thor pounded his glove with his fist and camped out underneath it.

Or, Thor camped out under where he thought the ball would be. Instead, it dropped safely to the ground about a foot and a half in front of him. By the time he realized what had happened, the runners had made it all the way to second and third. There were still no outs.

The next man in the order was the Canaries' clean-up hitter, Bert Backlin. Backlin was a big man, even by baseball player standards. His shoulders were as wide as a pickup truck, and his square head sat in the middle of them like a cereal box on a store shelf. He was known for his thick handlebar mustache almost as much as he was for his ability to drive a ball over the bleachers of most Central League ballparks. Indeed, many of the Canaries fans in the stands wore thick, curled mustaches of their own, either real or simulated.

"Afternoon, friend," Backlin said to Sparky as he took his practice swings. "Nice to see a new face in old Zigleaf Field, even if he is wearing a Goats uniform. I assume you've heard of me."

"Don't let him get in your head, kid," Lou shouted. "Just keep your eyes on the strike zone."

"Just to let you know, my diminutive friend, what I'm about to do is in no way intended as a personal affront," Backlin continued, ignoring Lou. "You see, it's simply what I do. Birds have to fly, fish have to swim, and Bert Backlin destroys baseballs."

"Just step in and we'll see about that, dude," Lou said. "Come on, kid! Let's remind him that chickens ain't never flown before."

Sparky pounded the ball into his mitt and looked in for the sign – slider down and away. Lou set up with his mitt just outside the zone. Sparky pulled back and unleashed a slider that edged just outside the zone, but Backlin didn't swing. Lou called for an offspeed pitch high and outside, which Sparky lobbed in, but again Backlin didn't swing.

"He wants me to pitch around this jerk," Sparky thought. "After all that stuff about finding the strike zone and chickens and all that, he wants me to settle for a walk!"

Lou signaled for the 2-0 pitch, another slider down and away. Sparky shook it off. The next signal called for a high curveball, and again Sparky shook it off. Appearing frustrated, Lou finally gave the signal for fastball, and Sparky nodded.

The ball hurtled toward home plate with scorching speed, but Backlin's bat cut a mighty slice through the air and caught it right on the money. The ball rocketed through the sky, becoming smaller and smaller before it finally disappeared into the frothing crowd in the right field bleachers. Lance didn't even so much as look up at it as it soared over his head. The stands were boiling over with yellow, while the few orange patches remained as still as frozen puddles.

Backlin rounded second base and shouted over the din of the crowd: "Once again, friend, please don't take this as anything personal. Bert Backlin is only doing what Bert Backlin was born to do. Perhaps you are only doing what you were born to do, as well, eh?" Backlin stepped on home plate and accepted the high-fives of his teammates before sauntering to the dugout.

In the stands, Katie could only sigh and mark Backlin's homer on her scorecard. One-third of an inning into the new season and the Goats were losing already. The Canaries fans in front of her were beaming.

"No better way to start the season, hm?" the taller one said.

"Oh, most assuredly," said the shorter one. "It seems the game always rewards those who appreciate it properly, wouldn't you say?"

"Without a doubt. I would venture to say that the poor souls here to support the home team have only themselves to blame for the poor showing their team has put up here thus far." Katie hated being by herself for this game. In the margins of the scorecard, she drew a makeshift chart detailing the flight path of Backlin's home run. She would have to check it against the actual chart when it hit the Internet later this evening, but Backlin's power still showed no signs of deterioration over the past few seasons. All the empirical data suggested that she would be listening to

Canaries fans crow about their team for a long time to come.

Lou, grimacing in pain, came running out to the mound as fast as he could. "Kid, I don't know what to tell you here, but don't let this get to you, all right?"

"Oh yeah, no problem," Sparky said. "Are you even watching the same game I am?"

"Listen to me, kid. When I was in Kansas City, we had a chimpanzee playing shortstop. I ain't lying to you – he was a real-live goldurn chimpanzee. They had to make special little batting helmets to sit on his noggin."

"And? What does that have to do with anything?"

"Just thought you might find that interesting," Lou said as he walked back to home plate. "I sure as heck did."

Sparky was baffled. What did a chimpanzee have to do with the situation he was in? Was the chimp a better fielder than any of his teammates? Was there something the chimp did that Lou wanted him to do? Sparky began to think he had had just about enough of people saying things to him that didn't make any sense.

"Steeeeeerike three!"

Sparky looked up and realized that while he had been contemplating Lou's chimpanzee, he had struck out the next two batters in the order. He hurried to catch up with the outfielders jogging to the dugout.

"Hey," Sparky said to Lou as the old man stretched his legs at the end of the bench, "Why did you tell me about the chimp?"

"I figured you could have used something else to think about while you were out there, take your mind off Backlin and the rest of those dudes. I guess it worked, huh?"

"Yeah, I guess. Uh, thanks."

Lou waved him off. "Forget about it, partner. Just try to keep your head straight out there. I only got so many stories, you know."

Lance led off the bottom of the first for the Goats. He watched the first two pitches miss the zone, then fouled off the third for a 2-1 count. Sparky watched Lance narrow his eyes and set his feet before the next pitch. Lance's breathing appeared to slow down and his eyes remained fixed on the pitcher's hand. The fourth pitch came tumbling off the pitcher's fingertips as Lance stood as still as a statue.

Suddenly, like a coiled snake, Lance sprung into his swing and met the ball right in front of the plate with a solid "CRACK!" Lance smiled to himself and flipped the bat casually in the direction of the dugout. By the time he finally stepped out of the batter's box, the ball landed in the furthest row of the right-field bleachers, further than Backlin's homer had landed.

Lance trotted across home plate just under a minute later and back to his spot on the bench.

"Atta way, baby! Atta way!" Skip clapped Lance on the shoulder, but that was the only thing anyone else said to him before he sat down next to Sparky.

"Nice work, Lance," Sparky said.

"Hm? Oh, yeah, thanks. It always feels good to get it out of the way early in the game."

"What do you mean?"

"You know…if I can pad my stats in the first couple of innings, then I don't have to work so hard late in the game, right?"

"Huh?"

"Take it from the Bright-man, kiddo – April and September are the best times of the season for me. April because guys are still a little rusty and there's a lot of rookies pitching – no offense – and September because guys are tired and you get a lot of call-ups who shouldn't be in the Big Leagues in the first place. Again, no offense."

"Right." Sparky sat silently on the bench as he watched Carlos step in. Carlos was clearly nervous, his fingertips twitched as he squeezed the handle of the bat. Beads of sweat rolled off his forehead. He kept repositioning his feet in the batter's box, trying to get comfortable. He watched the first pitch breeze by for a strike. Carlos continued fidgeting as the next pitch missed high and away for a ball. The 1-1 pitch came in lightning-quick and Carlos swung through it for strike two. He quickly mopped the sweat off his forehead as the catcher tossed the ball back to the mound. Finally, the 1-2 pitch was a slow 12-6 curve that started out high and ended up low, but crossed the plate right in the zone, with Carlos watching it all the way.

Carlos hung his head all the way back to the dugout and slumped onto the bench. As Lou took his bat to the on deck circle, he tapped the bill of Carlos' cap. "Ain't nothing to be ashamed of, kiddo," Lou said. "I remember Apollo Church's first Big League at-bat. He swung at three straight that missed the plate by a mile. He turned out okay." Carlos didn't say anything, didn't even look up at Lou.

The next batter of the Goats' half of the first, with two outs, was Fuzzy. On a 2-2 count, Fuzzy reached out and slapped one between the shortstop and second baseman for a clean base hit. He held his batting helmet onto his head with one hand as he ran to first, afraid it might pop off. With a man on first and the Goats trailing 3-1, Lou stepped to the plate.

After carefully watching two pitches just miss the outside

edge of the plate for a count of two balls and no strikes, Lou hit a chopper that bounced past the first baseman and into right field. Fuzzy was able to hustle into second base without a problem, but Lou wasn't more than halfway to first when the right fielder caught up to the ball. Lou clenched his teeth and tried to run through the pain in his knees, but he was thrown out easily, more than three steps away from the bag.

In the dugout, Skip waved a hand at the field in disgust. Sparky gathered his glove and started for the mound, but stopped to take a look at the lineup card again. "Why does Skip have Lou batting in the clean-up spot when he's obviously so slow?" Sparky wondered. The lineup card, etched in Skip's shaky penmanship, spelled it out: "1. Bright 2. Cabarellos 3. Fernandez 4. Houston 5. Hurzberk 6. Munson 7. Odinson 8. VORP 9. Pitcher's spot."

"Oh my God," Sparky said out loud, "It's in alphabetical order. The batting order is…alphabetical order."

"I know," Lance said as he stretched and slowly stood up from his nap, "Works out great for me!"

Sparky settled into a groove as he worked through the rest of the Canaries' order, getting two groundouts and an easy fly ball to VORP in center field in the second. The Goats' half of the inning was just as productive, but far more eventful.

First, Blerk struck out looking, holding the wrong end of the bat and swinging it downward at the pitches like he was trying to chop wood. He smiled and handed the bat to the umpire as he was called out. Then, Bobby came up and actually hit a little bloop single that dropped in front of the right fielder. It was Thor's turn at bat next, and he came to the plate with his hammer tucked into his belt. Thor let the first two pitches by for a pair of gimme strikes, but before the third pitch he closed his fingers tightly around the bat handle. His eyes began to glow, and tiny lightning bolts danced over his fingers. When he swung at the next pitch, there was a terrible sound of rushing wind and the skies over Zigleaf Field darkened suddenly. A flash of lightning blinded the crowd, followed by a thunderclap that shook the mighty branches over the field. But when the rumble faded and the skies became clear blue once again, Thor stood with his bat smoking, the smell of ozone in the air. The ball was resting comfortably in the catcher's mitt, and he was called out on strikes.

VORP practically skipped to the plate, his built-in cleats kicking up dust and pebbles that ricocheted off his body with little "PING"s.

"Boy oh boy, do I feel good today!" VORP gushed while waiting for the first pitch. "Nothing better than the first at-bat of a new season, unless you're talking about the second at-bat of a new season! Heck, even when you're in September and it's an OLD season, nothing beats the first at-bat of the ballgame!"

WHAP!

"Steeeeerike one!"

"Wow! That was a real scorcher there, buddy! You've got a heck of an arm, I'll say that! Nothing I like more than facing a pitcher who really knows what he's doing, you know what I mean? A guy who's firing on all cylinders! Me, I had most of my cylinders stripped and replaced a couple of seasons ago – never felt better in my life!"

WHUP!

"Steeeeeerike two!"

"Holy smokes, is it 0 and 2 already? Looks like you've got me in a pretty deep hole here, pal! A true pitcher's count, that's what they call it. I'm completely at your mercy now! You could throw me another fastball, try to blow it by me. You could try and offspeed pitch and fool me looking, that's always a good choice. Or, you could confuse me with the breaking ball, make me swing at a ball in the dirt! Oh man, the strategy is one of the things I love most about this game!"

CRACK!

VORP stopped talking just long enough to knock the next pitch over the second baseman's head and into the gap in right-center field. Sparky could hear him talking even as he ran down the first base line. "Woo hoo! There's a way to start a season, lemme tell you! How awesome is it to get a hit for all these amazing Go-Town fans..."

Bobby, who was picking his teeth at first base, looked up at the crack of the bat and almost tripped trying to run to second. VORP rounded first and almost immediately he was right behind Bobby, babbling away as Bobby huffed and puffed his way from first to second.

"Come on, Bobby! Let's get some hustle in that muscle, whaddaya say? Pick 'em up and put 'em down, Bobby-boy! Atta way!"

"Hey man, would you shut up for a sec-" Bobby stumbled over his own foot and took a hard tumble face-first on the infield. VORP couldn't stop himself in time and ended up tripping over Bobby, crashing to the ground with the sound of a car crash. The center fielder was scooping the ball off the warning track when the second base umpire signaled VORP was out for overrunning the lead baserunner. The inning was over, and the Goats had only one run to show for their three hits. The Canaries still led 3-1.

In the stands, Katie heard her cell phone buzz. The text message read: "How bad is it?"

"Same as always," she typed back.

"That bad, huh?"

"Might get better. New guy pitching okay."

"Okay. Just let me know when you're ready to stop wasting your time."

"Bye, Mom." Katie turned off her phone and dropped it back in her purse. Now she was really upset that she was by herself. She tried to clear her mind by penciling the weak grounder to third the Canaries had just hit into her scorecard. The numbers, cruel as they were, at least never took any joy in being that way, unlike the opposing players or their fans.

Sparky notched another strikeout and a fly ball to center for the next two outs. The third inning went by uneventfully, except for a bloop single by Lance that was erased when he was picked off first base easily. Lance, he later admitted, was trying to give a girl in the front row his phone number.

In the Canaries' half of the fourth, Sparky had mowed down the first two batters, but now faced Backlin again. The beefy slugger stepped casually to the plate and twisted the ends of his mustache to give them a little extra curl.

"Good to see you again, friend. I hope our last encounter gave you an opportunity to learn a little something that might make this at-bat a little more challenging, eh? I prefer to match skills with players who are at the top of their game. It helps keep me at the top of mine, you know?"

"Keep talking, and I'm going to knock you onto the bottom of your butt," Sparky grumbled.

"Oh-ho! A spirited back-and-forth!" Backlin responded. "Adding some spice to the rivalry – I love it!"

Sparky whizzed the first pitch straight down the middle – the radar gun on the scoreboard read 102 mph. Backlin nodded his head in appreciation, but Sparky couldn't have cared less about earning Backlin's respect – he wanted the strikeout. He gritted his teeth and whipped in his next pitch, another fastball that reached 105 mph. Backlin swung the bat underneath it, looking like he was thinking about something else.

"I say, hurler, those were some very fast fastballs! I should like to see what you can offer me next, if you would!"

"You bet I would," Sparky said. There was no other pitch for him to throw, despite Lou's frantic signals to the contrary. Sparky was going to get him out with the Blazing Fastball. He had to get him with that pitch and that pitch alone. No way was he going to let this preening gasbag show him up twice in the same game.

Pouring all his concentration into his shoulder, Sparky let

the ball fly. More than mere smoke this time, the ball tore through the air so fast it actually caught fire. For an instant, Sparky watched this leather fireball, a shooting star made of horsehide, carve a burning trail straight to the plate. He watched the air shimmer and dance around the ball, distorted by the sheer heat coming off of it. He watched Lou's eyes grow wide in amazement as he steeled himself to stop the screaming missile. He watched the Goats fans start to gasp at the sight.

And, finally, he watched as Backlin effortlessly swatted the ball high into the air and over the fence for his second homer of the day. What he didn't watch was Backlin's confident trot around the bases. It was now 4-1 Canaries in the top of the fourth, but already Sparky could see streams of orange-clad fans making their way to the exits, heads down. The next hitter grounded weakly to second, and even though Blerk needed Fuzzy's help determining where to throw the ball, he had plenty of time to record the out.

The rest of the game went by normally. That is to say, the Goats continued to make mistakes and the Canaries continued to take advantage. A line drive to left field skipped all the way to the wall when Thor misjudged it and fell over backwards trying to make a back-handed stab at it. A stolen base attempt went awry when Blerk jumped in the baserunner's path. Later, Blerk was picked off when he tried to steal during a pitching change.

Sensing Sparky's frustration, Fuzzy came up to him in the dugout and slapped him on the shoulder. "Don't get so down, kid," Fuzzy said. "It's not always like this."

"Really?"

"Yeah, sometimes it's a lot worse."

Finally, the bottom of the ninth arrived, and the Canaries had staked themselves to a 9-1 lead. Sparky had not been pulled from the game, something that had more to do with Skip not paying attention to the game than it did with Sparky's performance. Bobby had managed a base hit and made it to third on sacrifices from Thor and VORP. Sparky was at the plate with a chance to drive in a run, even though he was 0-for-3 to that point. He tried to clear his previous failures from his mind. The first pitch from the Canaries' relief pitcher slid right over the top of Sparky's bat for strike one. The next pitch caught him off-guard and he watched it drop in for strike two. Sparky prepared himself for the 0-2 pitch, but instead the pitcher threw to third, where the third baseman gently tapped Bobby on the backside. Bobby had lifted his right foot off the base to tie his shoe. He had just untangled the knot when he was called out to end the game.

The Canaries high-fived and congratulated each other in the middle of the infield as their fans whooped and hollered from the

Zigleaf Field stands. Sparky just dropped the bat and made his way silently back to the clubhouse.

In the stands, Katie watched Sparky's sullen march off the field. She saw Carlos still sitting on the dugout bench, biting his lower lip and trying very hard not to cry. She saw Blerk grab his glove and jog out to the field, only for Fuzzy to grab him and explain that the game was over. Lance was on his cell phone, Thor was shaking his head sadly and looking to the sky with sad, pleading eyes. In the bullpen, the Ballpino brothers were having a heated game of rock-paper-scissors – it was quite possible they weren't even aware what had happened. The other pitchers had left.

Katie glanced down at her scorecard and marked the final out of the game – Munson, caught stealing. That was the official way to score what had happened, but Katie found herself wishing there was an official symbol for "being an idiot." She felt like giving herself a spot on the scorecard for that particular symbol, too.

Sparky sat at his locker for a few minutes before showering and getting back into his street clothes. He didn't say a word to anyone, although he could tell Carlos was waiting for him to say something.

"Hey Sparky, how did you think I did today?" Carlos finally asked.

"You did fine, Carlos, fine." Sparky couldn't remember seeing any of his friend's at-bats – he was mainly preoccupied with making a mental list of everything about the Goats that needed to be fixed, and on Opening Day it was already a pretty long list.

"Yeah, you did a heck of a job out there, rookie," Lance said as he dried his hair. "Just one thing, though."

"What is it, Mr. Bright?"

"Far be it from me to tell a teammate how to play the game..." Fuzzy let out a loud "Ha!" from the other side of the room. "As I was saying, I don't want to tell you how to play the game, but in the sixth inning I noticed you stretching your hamstrings trying to dig out a bad throw by Munson over there."

"Is there any other kind of throw by Munson?" Fuzzy shouted.

"Shut up, dude!" Bobby retorted.

"That kind of play will get you an out and a pat on the butt from your manager, but don't forget that if you tweak something down there it can be a real bummer for your power numbers," Lance continued. "And that's the kind of thing that really matters when it's time to sign a new contract. Again, just something you might want to keep in mind, courtesy of the Bright-man."

Suddenly feeling sick to his stomach, Sparky tossed his

glove into the back of his locker angrily, at which point a plain white envelope came fluttering down from the top shelf. Inside the envelope was another note just like the one he had been given at the train station when he first arrived in Go-Town:

"Tough break today, but we have a feeling you can get through it. You just need something besides the fastball. Talk to Yoshi – he'll point you in the right direction. Good luck – The Go-Goats Girl."

While the rest of the team goofed around, Sparky found Yoshi hunched over a work table in the equipment room, sharpening a set of cleats with a comically large file.

"Hey Yoshi, do you know anything about this note I got in my locker?"

Yoshi peered over the top of his glasses to get a better look at the note. He wrinkled his nose and returned to his work.

"So...does that mean no?" Yoshi continued filing away at the cleats. "Okay, so then everything about this team is weird beyond belief, gotcha. Thanks a lot, old man. Guess I'll go check my locker for any other stupid riddles. Maybe somebody left me a treasure map while I wasted my time over here!" Sparky crumpled the note and hurled it into a nearby recycling bin. Yoshi gently cleared his throat.

"You're one of the most impatient young people I've ever met, you know that?" Yoshi said. "And that's something, considering that pretty much everyone is younger than me. Be here tonight around 8 o'clock, and be ready to throw."

"What, you mean like practice?"

"You're going to wish we were just practicing," Yoshi said without looking up.

5. THE HUSTLE

Sparky arrived at the ballpark just after 8 o'clock. The city was noisy with nightlife as hovercars burbled through the streets carting people from one hot spot to another, but Zigleaf Field was a pocket of tranquility surrounded by forest. The lights were on, but there was no one on the field.

"Hello?" Sparky called out, but there was no answer. Suddenly he realized what must be going on – he was being hazed. He was the new guy on the team, so the other guys were going to put him through the paces and make him look like an idiot for their own amusement. He remembered his first day in the minor leagues when his hitting coach sent him around the ballpark looking for the "keys to the batter's box." Hilarious. Now somewhere Fuzzy and Bobby were having a good laugh over a basket of buffalo wings as they imagined Sparky running around an empty stadium in circles. He sat down on the mound and waited for the punchline.

A moment later, a baseball came flying out of the darkened stands and rolled across the infield grass until it came to a stop just before the base of the mound. Sparky squinted into the darkness and made out the shape of a tiny person sitting in one of the front rows.

"So you have a Blazing Fastball," Sparky heard Yoshi call out to the mound. "Let's see it."

Picking the ball of the ground, Sparky wound up and let loose, hurling a flaming pitch that struck the backstop with a splash of flame and smoke. From the stands, Yoshi whistled in appreciation.

"Not too bad, but a thumper like Bert Backlin can still catch up to it, right?" Yoshi stood up and began hobbling his way toward the mound.

"Backlin got lucky a couple of times, I'll figure him out," Sparky said.

"Mm, well, that's one way of looking at it. The other way of looking at it is that you need to be able to show him something different every once in a while. You need to learn something new."

"From who?"

Yoshi stopped in his tracks and glared up at Sparky. "Go get that ball," he said as he pointed at the backstop. Sparky retrieved the scorched baseball and flipped it back to the mound. "Now stay there and get ready to catch this."

Sparky crouched down into a catcher's stance. "Catch what?"

Yoshi frowned and let the ball settle in his hand. He then proceeded to go into a windup that incorporated some strange movements Sparky had never seen before. The old man's wrists seemed to undulate like snakes and he balanced on his toes like a ballet dancer. The windup was almost hypnotic, so fascinating that Sparky didn't even notice that the ball was coming right at him for a second.

The way the ball looked to be coming in off the outside edge of the plate, Sparky figured the pitch for a slider, and adjusted his glove accordingly. Then, about halfway between the mound and the plate, the ball just vanished without a trace. Sparky's eyes darted around for any sign of it, but the only thing he could see was Yoshi, finishing his follow-through on the mound, his reddened cheeks huffing and puffing with the effort.

Sparky was about to stand up and ask Yoshi what had just happened when the ball reappeared on the other side of the plate, only giving him a fraction of a section to react and catch the ball. He looked down into his glove and saw the ball, no different than before he had tossed it to Yoshi.

Yoshi was still wheezing on the mound by the time Sparky's mind caught up to what he had just seen. "How did you do that?" he asked.

"The same way you throw that fastball," Yoshi finally answered once he caught his breath. "The same way all the greats do what they can do. It's a matter of hustle."

"Yeah, hustle, I've heard all about it," Sparky said, rolling his eyes. "Every coach I've ever had kept telling me I showed hustle. 'Way to show some hustle out there, kid! Nice hustle today, Sparky! Everybody look at Katakura, he's got real hustle!' Never really knew what that meant."

"That's because every coach you ever had wasn't me," Yoshi said.

"No offense, Yoshi, but you're not a coach, you're the clubhouse manager." Yoshi hopped up and smacked Sparky so hard on the back of his head that his cap nearly flew off.

"You don't know anything about me, Katakura, and you

sure as heck don't know the first thing about hustle." He retrieved a bucket of balls from the dugout and dumped them out in front of the mound. Picking up the nearest ball, Yoshi nudged Sparky off the pitching rubber and straightened his crooked body into near-perfect posture. With another unusual windup, Yoshi threw a pitch that fluttered off his fingertips so slowly that it seemed to be traveling underwater rather than through the air. And it was still slowing down.

The ball continued its mid-air crawl toward the plate, giving Sparky enough time to practically count the number of times it rotated on its journey. The longest game Sparky had ever seen before in his life was an 18-inning game between the Stars and the Cairo Scribes that lasted more than five hours. It felt like he could have fit two of those games in the length of that pitch.

Suddenly, as if he was waking up in the middle of a long, lucid dream, Sparky saw the ball snap back to regular speed, bolting across the plate and into the backstop. He shook his head, and looked down to see Yoshi chuckling to himself.

"Whoa," Sparky said. "What time is it?"

"Time for you to get to work," Yoshi said. "Now do exactly what I tell you…"

Sparky returned to the ballpark each night for the next two nights. During the day, he sat helplessly in the bullpen and watched the Goats lose the next two games handily to the Canaries. In the second game, Antonio de la Goya gave up a grand slam after loading the bases on three straight walks. As Lou told Sparky after the game, all Antonio could talk about between innings was how the placement of the grand slam pitch provided "texture and color" to the at-bat. "It really was one of my better works," Antonio told the newspapers after the game.

In the third game, the Goats sent Willie Wilbur to the mound. The punky pitcher tested the Canaries with an array of pitches that flitted and darted around the plate under some highly suspicious circumstances. Several times, she chose to throw a ball into the stands rather than let the umpire inspect it. She counted a few strikeouts in her stats for the day, but she also gave up three home runs in her first start of the season. When she returned to the bench, she gave Sparky a wink and stuck her tongue out at him. "They don't suspect a thing!" she laughed.

Sparky continued to work with Yoshi that night after the game. The little old man had him throwing harder and longer than he would ever feel comfortable doing even in an actual game, but instead of pain Sparky could feel something different in his arm. He watched in amazement as one of his breaking pitches started to get fuzzy and pixelate as it swung across the plate, like a glitchy online video. His face alight with excitement, Sparky turned to where Yoshi sat tossing sunflower seeds into his open mouth.

"Did you see that?" Sparky asked. "It almost disappeared!"

"Yup," Yoshi replied flatly. "Almost. Keep at it."

"Are you finally going to tell me what we're doing here?" Sparky asked before throwing another pitch. "All my life I've been a fastball pitcher. I never knew I could have control on offspeed stuff like this."

"I wasn't going to tell you right away because I thought you'd let it go to your head right away," Yoshi sighed. "But I guess if you've been out here this long without complaining you're in it for the long haul. You can go ahead and sit down for a minute."

Yoshi dragged the overturned ball bucket underneath him and sat down on it. His legs swung free over the grass. "There is a thing in this game called hustle, and some guys have it but others don't."

"Do I have it?"

"Shut up for a second, will you? Let an old guy say something so you can learn a thing or two. Hustle is like a power source, something every ballplayer draws from once or twice in his or her career. Usually, it means a player has a little extra strength for a clutch home run, a little extra movement on a breaking ball, or a guy can move a little faster, jump a little higher. But in a few rare cases, a player can tap into the hustle whenever he or she needs it. It lets them do things only a handful of players could ever do."

"Like throw a fastball so fast it catches fire," Sparky said quietly.

"Now see, this was the spot where I was going to say that you were one of those players, but you had to go ahead and just blurt it out." Yoshi just stared at Sparky for a moment with a cockeyed frown.

"I'm sorry."

"Eh, it's okay." Yoshi hopped off the bucket. "I just don't get to give that speech too often, and I'm starting to think I'm getting pretty good at it."

"How many times have you given that speech?"

"I didn't always used to be the clubhouse manager of this dump, you know," Yoshi said as he looked up into the branches towering over their heads. The star-speckled night sky poked through between the leaves. "A long time ago, I wasn't that bad of a pitcher myself. Yeah, I thought I really was going to be something in the Big Leagues, but then one season me and my team, well, we ran up against something way bigger than all of us put together. It was something cold, something evil."

The night already was still chilly with the remains of winter, but as Yoshi started his story Sparky could swear the temperature dropped a few degrees more. There was a look in the little old man's eyes that said what happened to him was a long time ago, but was as close and familiar to him as an old friend.

"I was with the Capital City Generics, long before they joined the Transmetropolitan League," Yoshi began, his voice losing the hard edges it normally had. "We weren't that consistent, but we were a tough bunch of scrubs. Scratched and clawed our way to the top of the standings, fighting all season. Finally, we're a half-game behind the Peacocks and, wouldn't you know it, we're playing those guys on the last day of the season. Well, we won that game, and now this group of losers who spent most of the year before in the cellar is in the divisional round of the playoffs." Yoshi paused to draw a deep breath.

"I should have known we were in for trouble, because we got the Whales in the first round, and they were on a hot streak. Our bus pulled into San Diego at 10 in the morning, and by 2 that afternoon we were getting our butts handed to us. Whenever we swung the bat, the ball stepped out of the way. Whenever we tried to catch the ball, it found a way around us. It was like the ball was the tenth man on the field for those guys. That first game, nothing went right." Sparky sat in silence as Yoshi stopped to wipe his forehead.

"You play 162 games a season, and you think you learn how to bounce back from a bad outing," Yoshi continued. "You think you can put a bad day behind you. There's always tomorrow, after all. There's always next season. But a day like that…" Yoshi turned and looked Sparky right in the eyes. "A day like that and it's like the game itself is telling you to give it up. The Whales didn't end up winning the Worlds Series that year, and the next season they had a whole new roster, but it didn't matter to us. We were beaten. We weren't ever the same again, any of us. I caught on as a pitching coach in the minors, eventually got bad enough at that job that I made it all the way down to equipment manager, and now I'm here." Yoshi swept his hands across all of Zigleaf Field.

"Since then, I've seen a lot of teams like those Whales come up through the Big Leagues, always getting so close, always with everything looking like it's going their way, always ending up on the short end of the box score in the Worlds Series. But that wasn't the only thing those teams had in common. They all had the same guy in the front office. Not really the same guy, mind you, but the same kind of guy. He's a slick guy, a smart guy, a guy who knows everything there is to know about the game except why it exists. I think you know who I mean."

"I think I do," Sparky said.

"Well, ever since then I've been waiting here, waiting for a phenom who has that connection to the hustle, who can maybe break through against that dark haze hanging over the game. I've seen a lot of kids I thought might be that guy, and now you're one of them."

Yoshi bent over to pick a ball off the ground and flipped it to Sparky. "So you can see you've got a lot of work to do. The Phantom Slider – keep working on it."

Sparky arrived to the ballpark early the next morning to get in a little more practice with his new pitch. The rest of the team began showing up for batting practice, with Carlos taking the field about 20 minutes later than the others.

"Hey roomie," Sparky said as he jogged out from the bullpen to meet Carlos. "You all right?" Carlos moved as if he was carrying a bookcase on his back. His eyes were bloodshot and his hair was a mess.

"Sparky, hey. Yeah, I'm good. I just hung out with Lance and a couple of the guys last night, no big deal." Carlos' voice sounded like a rusty door hinge.

"Jeez, Carlos, what time did you get back last night?"

"Oh, uh, kind of like...right now?"

"Dude, why did you do that? You know we've got a day game today!"

"I know, but you've been out the last couple of nights and I guess I got bored or something. Then Lance said he and some of the guys were going out to find something to do and ... oh, man, you really missed something! You know how they have a monkey house at the zoo? Well, normally it's closed at midnight, but Lance knows this guy. Anyway, we went in there with Bobby's radio-controlled cars and we ... hey, where have you been lately?"

"It's kind of a long story," Sparky said, suddenly feeling a lot less enthusiastic about his sessions with Yoshi. "Just make sure you stay awake. We need you to be sharp at first today."

"Why?" Carlos asked as Sparky walked away. "Lance says first base is the easiest position to play!"

Soon it was game time, and Sparky was able to make it through the first inning by relying on his Blazing Fastball. Lance led off the bottom of the first with a booming drive that sent the right fielder racing for the corner of the outfield. Lance stood frozen at the end of his swing watching the ball arc high in the sky, but instead of landing in the bleachers it bounced off the very top row of bricks in the outfield wall. Realizing the ball was still in play, Lance finally began running to first, where he arrived just a half-second before the ball did. Skip tossed his cap to the dugout floor and stomped on it before slapping it back on his head, rumpled and dusty.

Carlos stepped to the plate and teetered awkwardly on his feet as he raised his bat. He swung late at three outside pitches and slumped back onto the bench, where he promptly fell asleep. Sparky glared at Lance, who stood at first base doing little stretching exercises and chatting with the Canaries' first baseman. He pantomimed what Sparky assumed was what a monkey looked like while it was being chased by a radio-controlled car, to the great amusement of the first baseman. Fuzzy grounded into a routine 6-4-3 double play and the inning's promise was snuffed out unceremoniously.

At last, Sparky took the mound in the top of the second to face Backlin once again. The mustachioed muscleman walked to the plate with the demeanor of a man approaching an ice cream stand on a hot day. He reacted to the sight of Sparky on the mound as one would when recognizing an old friend on the street.

"Marvelous day today, isn't it, old boy? Just splendid." It took every bit of self-control Sparky had not to say anything back. Lou called for the fastball, and Sparky let him have it. Backlin's knees bent just slightly, but he did not swing. Strike one. Lou wanted another fastball for the second pitch, and Sparky uncorked a Blazing Fastball that left a scorch mark over the plate. Again, Backlin would not swing.

"I don't want to end this at-bat too quickly, you understand," Backlin said. "I know how important it is for a young pitcher such as yourself to get in some practice."

Lou called for the fastball again, but Sparky shook him off. He also said no to the offspeed, the curve and the splitter. It was only when Lou reluctantly signaled slider that Sparky finally agreed. "Okay, kid," Lou said to himself behind the plate. "If you feel good about it, so do I."

"Practice is important," Backlin continued, "but even the patience of Bert Backlin has its limitations. Therefore, I hope you don't mind too terribly much if I end this little session with this next swing."

Behind his back, Sparky fumbled to grip the ball the way Yoshi had shown him. He checked and double-checked to make sure his fingers were in exactly the right places on the ball. He made sure to relax his wrist and slow his breathing, just like Yoshi instructed. Sparky went into his motion and let the ball fly.

From behind the plate, Lou watched as the pitch started out

straight and slow, a total meatball pitch, batting practice. Then, the corkscrew motion of the ball as it tumbled through the air began to steer it to the outside half of the plate, but it didn't look like nearly enough break to pull itself out of Backlin's wheelhouse. Backlin tensed and began his swing, looking for all the world like he would meet the ball violently with the barrel of the bat. But then, just before the ball crossed the top of the plate, it vanished. Lou panicked – Had Backlin hit it already? Was it already halfway back to Fort Clark? But there had been no sound, no thunderous crack of wood on horsehide. Backlin was still in the middle of his swing.

Lou's eyes were still adjusting to the disappearing ball when he instinctively reached out past the outside half of the plate. He saw nothing, but felt the sting of something striking the inside of his mitt. There was a sudden rush of air as Backlin completed his swing, and then silence. Both Backlin and the umpire looked at each other in confusion, then they looked down at Lou, who was just as surprised as they were to see the ball resting comfortably in the center of his mitt. Strike three, Backlin went back to the dugout without another word.

After the inning was over, Lou waited for Sparky before returning to the dugout. "The heck was that pitch, kid? Looked like the old Phantom Slider to me."

"That's exactly what it was, Lou. Good eye."

"Now, I ain't calling you a liar, Spark, but would you mind explaining to me how it was you learned to throw a pitch that ain't never been thrown by anyone in the Big Leagues other than a handful of dudes?"

"I have connections, okay?" Sparky hustled to make it back to the dugout before Lou. "Now if you'll excuse me, I've got a game to win."

With the help of the Phantom Slider, Sparky cruised through the next four innings without allowing a run. Even after Blerk rolled a soft ground ball to home when there was no one on third, Sparky was able to strike out the next two batters. He was able to hold on through the top of the ninth, striking out Backlin another two times while the normally serene slugger began to gnash his teeth in frustration. He had no kind words for Sparky his last time up, only a string of expressions that the newspaper writers omitted from their game stories out of respect for any children or elderly women.

With the game still scoreless in the bottom of the ninth, Blerk was the first Goat to the plate. His false nose and mustache was sliding off his face, but he managed to adjust them before he was completely exposed. With the first pitch on the way, Blerk reached out and caught the ball with his left hand. He curved his lipless mouth into a smile and proudly showed the ball to the umpire.

"I caught it!" Blerk declared. "What is my reward?"

The umpire called the other umps in from the field and they stood in a tight circle discussing the incident for a long time. Skip and the Canaries' manager eventually came out of their respective dugouts for an explanation, but they were both shut out of the deliberation. Meanwhile, the crowd grew restless and began jeering the umpires from their seats.

After several minutes, the home plate umpire signaled for Blerk to take first base, indicating that Blerk had technically been hit by the pitch. Cyrus O'Malley, the Canaries' manager, went into a rage.

"What are you talking about?" he shouted a few inches from the ump's face. "That's clearly interference! This little weirdo should be out, you moron!"

The ump kept his arms folded over his chest protector and his eyes closed. "Cyrus, all I saw was the ball hit that little guy right in the hand. If you think he did it on purpose, let me ask you if you think a guy would ever stick his bare hand out to try and catch a 95-mile-per-hour fastball?"

"Of course not!" O'Malley sputtered.

"Then it had to be an accident, hit by pitch, batter takes first base. Another word out of you on the subject and it's the showers for you, Cyrus."

O'Malley didn't say another word, just trudged back to the dugout with his face red from shouting. His disposition didn't improve even after Bobby and Thor both struck out with Blerk still standing proudly at first. From the on-deck circle, Sparky could see the red-headed and now red-faced skipper dictating a letter to one of his bench coaches to send to the Central League commissioner's office.

VORP was up next and managed to slap a base hit into right field. The Goats' third base coach had to physically restrain Blerk from running past third base as the shortstop received the ball from the right fielder. There were two outs, but the Goats had a man in scoring position and Sparky was due up.

Sparky tightened his batting gloves and tried to appear cool and collected as he walked to the batter's box. Last season, Sparky had rarely been in this position. He knew he could count on Ken to drive in a couple of runs and give him a comfortable lead to pitch from. Even without the help of the Baseball Devil, Ken seemed to be able to coax a fly ball into dropping in front of an outfielder at will, almost as if he had trained the balls to do what he told them to.

There was no Ken today, not even a single hitter in the lineup that Sparky could count on to come through in the clutch. If he missed this chance, there was nothing. His arm was tired, and he would likely be lifted for one of the Ballpino brothers in extra innings. Any of them would certainly give up at least one run immediately and the game would effectively be over. Sparky believed he had tried too hard to lose this game. If there was no one else to believe in, Sparky would have to win the game by himself.

Sparky spit into the palms of his hands and rubbed them together before gripping his bat. It was something he had seen countless other players do in his life, but he had never noticed it helping him with his grip. Still, now was not the time to just rule out anything that might help him. From Little League on, hitting had never been Sparky's forte, but he could at least make contact and read pitchers' delivery, so he wasn't entirely helpless at the plate. He had been in position for a game-winning hit exactly once before, in high school. He popped out to short, but Ken was up next in the leadoff spot and got the job done with a gapper to right center field.

The Canaries' reliever wore a blank expression that was almost definitely practiced. If the thought of facing Sparky made him nervous, he didn't show it. The first pitch was a direct challenge – a fastball down the middle that Sparky watched fly into the mitt for strike one. The mass of yellow-clad fans in the stands pulsated with excitement, while the pockets of orange began melting into the aisles and draining out the exits.

The next pitch was another heater, straight down the center of the plate. It made a sound like a rocket buzzing Sparky's knees. Again, Sparky only watched it find its target like an arrow from Robin Hood's bow. Robin Hood also had been known to throw a pretty nasty fastball himself, if Sparky remembered his history right. The roar of the Canaries fans at Zigleaf Field threatened to drown out the umpire's call of strike two, but Sparky didn't need help identifying that. The pitcher allowed the corner of his mouth to turn upward into a tiny little smirk, a smidgeon of swagger that tipped Sparky off – the next pitch would be identical to the last two.

Sparky twisted the bat handle in his hands as he waited for the next pitch. Blerk was stationed at third, with the third base coach keeping a very close eye on him. VORP flexed his rusty knees at first with a squeaking that was audible at the plate, even with the crowd screaming for a strikeout. The pitcher got set, Sparky took a deep breath, and then the pitch was away.

It was another fastball, just as Sparky predicted. He planted his front foot and swung as hard as he possibly could. The impact of the bat meeting the ball sent shockwaves up Sparky's arms. His hands stung painfully and went numb for a moment. He dropped the bat and began charging toward first. The ball struck the front of the mound and shot straight up in the air off the dirt. The shortstop pulled up underneath it and waited for it to come down. It hung in the air, spinning like a satellite reaching orbit. The third base coach shoved Blerk off third base toward home. VORP's spindly legs drove him in the direction of second base. Sparky knew he was running as fast as he could, but it felt like forever between each time his foot hit the ground.

Meanwhile, the ball finally began to fall from the sky over the infield. Sparky was within five steps of first base. Blerk was nearly home, with VORP sliding into second. The only play was at first. The Canaries' shortstop plucked the ball out of the air and in one motion rifled it toward first. Sparky's foot was inches above the bag. He tried to will it down faster but gravity wouldn't be bullied. There were two sounds: Sparky's foot hitting the bag and the ball landing in the first baseman's glove, but it wasn't clear in which order they had happened.

The next sound, however, made it clear – the thunderous roar of joy that erupted from the Fort Clark fans. Sparky had reached first base just a fraction of a second too late. He was out and the game was still tied.

The tenth inning moved by as a blur to Sparky. He watched it all happen as if he were remembering a nightmare that had woken him up one night as a child. He watched Skip send him to the clubhouse in favor of Ted Ballpino. He saw Ted give up a towering home run to Bert Backlin that drove in two runs. He caught a glimpse of Fuzzy grounding out to the pitcher to cap a 1-2-3 bottom of the tenth and seal the game and the sweep for the Canaries. Sparky saw all of it, but he wasn't thinking about it. It wasn't until after the game, in the clubhouse, that Sparky finally had something to say about it.

"What is wrong with you guys?" Sparky shouted, slamming his locker door. The rest of the team looked up from what they were doing and just stared at him for a moment.

"Uh...what do you mean?" Bobby asked, his mouth half-full of sandwich.

"Yeah, so we lost to the Canaries," Ted Ballpino said.

"Yeah, we always lose to the Canaries," Todd Ballpino added.

"Yeah, Todd especially," Tad Ballpino said.

"My ERA against the Canaries is lower than yours, Tad!"

"Ooh, good for you! 7.50 versus 7.60, big freaking deal!"

"Those guys always kick our butts, man," Fuzzy said. "You can't get used to it, you better find another league to play in."

"Come on, guys!" VORP chirped. "I know we're going to get them next time!"

"Oh shut up, Rusty!" Fuzzy retorted. He threw a towel at the robot that draped itself over his head.

"I don't know what Sparky's complaining about, he struck out Bert Backlin three times!" Lance said. "Why don't you try just being happy with that, okay, buddy? Take a chill pill, you'll live longer."

With that, the team murmured in agreement and went back to their lockers. Sparky was left standing by himself in the middle of the locker room, physically and emotionally exhausted. Only Lou approached him to offer any kind of support.

"Your method ain't too hot, but I agree with the message, kid."

"I've never been on a team with so little..."

"Esprit de corps?"

"Yeah, I think that's what that is. What am I doing wrong?"

"You're trying to win these games all by yourself, and ain't nobody in the Big Leagues who can do that consistently, not even Big Bad Bert Backlin himself," Lou said. "You need to herd all these steers in the same direction, or else they're going to just keep grazing wherever the heck they feel like."

"And how do I do that?"

"That's the thing, Sparky. With this bunch, I don't know if you can." Lou put an arm around Sparky's shoulder and punched him in the bicep. "I think I have a pretty good idea of what you're doing here, kiddo, and what's at stake for you. Much as it pains me to say it, you might have to start thinking about chalking this one up in the loss column already."

It was hard for Sparky to ignore Lou's advice as the Goats started the season with a 10-game losing streak, with the sweep by the Canaries followed by a pair of three-game series sweeps against the Astro City Skywatchers and the Omaha Actuaries. The days became indistinguishable from each other. A game was lost on a baserunning mistake, or a dropped ball in the outfield, or a swinging strikeout on a pitch in the dirt. Sometimes it was all of those things and more. The bottom line was that the Go-Town Goats were already looking up from last place at the Fort Clark Canaries, and no one but Sparky seemed to care.

6. ROAD TRIP TO TRANSYLVANIA

Given everything else he knew about the team, Sparky fully expected the Goats to travel in a broken-down old bus. In reality, however, there was a stylish and modern private jet awaiting them at the Go-Town Airport. Word around the clubhouse was that Mr. Mint used the jet himself during the offseason and claimed it as a business expense by letting the team use it. Besides, Fuzzy said, Mr. Mint always took his vacation in October, and when would the Goats ever need an airplane then?

Sparky was jolted awake by the plane landing hard on the runway. He rolled up the shade on his window and looked out to see the entire landscape shrouded in dense, rolling fog. The sky was gray, with only the blackened branches of leafless trees providing any contrast. Carlos was peering out the window on the other side of the aisle with a look of terror on his face. He made the sign of the cross and turned to Sparky.

"Sparky, what is this place?" Carlos said. "What kind of an evil place have we come to?"

"Ah, quit your whining, Caballeros," Skip said as he came trudging down the aisle with his duffel bag slung over his bony shoulder. "Cleveland don't let you smoke in a movie theater, that's evil. This is just Transylvania."

Of course Sparky was familiar with the Transylvania Blood Sox from his baseball card collection, but when he was growing up the Stars had never played against them or any of the other teams in the mysterious Midnight League. That's why he felt so uneasy walking into Shreck Field, with its stone parapets that loomed over the field and its dank, candlelit corridors. The visitor's clubhouse was cold with floors made of stone, so no one dared take their socks off. Despite the fact that the Blood Sox had just hosted the Keystone Combines for a four-game series, the visitor's lockers were covered in thick spider webs that needed to be brushed away before opening.

As Bobby opened his locker, the team got a fright as a pale, trembling young ballplayer in full uniform leapt out, screaming. The Goats jumped out of his way as he skittered into a corner of the clubhouse and covered his face.

"D-don't let them take me!" the player croaked. His road gray uniform read "Tampa Bay" in baby-blue script across the front.

"Who?" Sparky asked.

"My team! Don't let them find me here, I just want to go home! My name's Dan Freeny, I play right field for the Tampa Bay Sunbeams."

"Tampa Bay?"

"We're an expansion team, but the Commissioner's Office told us there weren't any open spots in the Solar League or the Oceanic League. So we were put in the Midnight League and I can't take it anymore!" Freeny clutched his knees and rocked himself back and forth on his backside. His eyes were fixed on some unknown point miles away from the Goats and the clubhouse. "It's insanity, playing in this league. You go to Monroeville, and you're playing against zombies! Have you ever tried to hit a curveball that the pitcher's hand was still holding? In Crystal Lake, they steal bases and you can't even see them! You'll be standing at second base and all of a sudden he's right behind you, just breathing real heavy... And Arkham..." Freeny shuddered. "I never want to go back to Arkham ever again!"

At this point, Skip had pushed his way to the front of the group and without a word he slapped Freeny hard across the face, stunning him for a moment. "Listen to this little milksop!" Skip said to the team. "In my day, we played double-headers in graveyards with honest-to-God werewolves! But did we go diving into lockers like little rabbits? Heck no! Now get off your duff and run on home back to Tampa Bay before they miss you, but if this is any indication of what kind of ballplayer you are I'll bet you've got a lotta time before that ever happens!"

Freeny grabbed his powder-blue cap out of the locker he was hiding in and ran off into the darkened corridors and disappeared from sight. Apparently there was only one thing scarier than spending a season in the Midnight League – Skip LaRoche.

The game began, appropriately enough, well after dark. The stands were full of ominous shapes, obscured by shadows but punctuated with glowing sets of red eyes and the occasional popcorn bag or red-and-black pennant waving. Vendors floated through the aisles filling plastic cups with a deep red beverage Sparky told himself was probably just fruit punch.

Thanks to Sparky's new one-two punch of the Flaming Fastball and the Phantom Slider, he managed to hold the Blood Sox scoreless through eight innings. What's more, he was lucky enough to have been on base in the fifth when Lance clubbed another of his self-serving home runs. Things were actually looking up for a change, but in the bottom of the ninth, the game started to take an ugly turn. Back-to-back singles and a walk loaded the bases with no outs. As Sparky kicked at the dirt on the mound, Skip and Lou came out to talk to him.

"All right, Sparky, gimme the ball," Skip said. "You did a heck of a job against them vampires, but I'm going to the pen."

"Come on, Skip!" Sparky pleaded. "You and I both know that if you turn this game over to any one of the Ballpino brothers, it means we're gonna lose!"

"Hey! I'm not gonna tolerate anyone bad-mouthing their teammates on this club!" Skip said, squinting one eye and shooting a harsh look at Sparky with the other.

"You said yourself yesterday that the Ballpinos are the sorriest bunch of dopes you ever seen, Skip," Lou said.

"Are you telling me I don't know how to run a ballclub?" Skip said, tapping Lou in the chest protector with a finger. "You wanna take over filling out the lineup card everyday, cowboy?"

"Nah, that ain't what I'm trying to say...listen, Sparky, why don't you just do what Skip says and hit the showers, okay?" Lou spat at the ground and pulled his mask down over his face. "Maybe we'll get lucky this time."

"No," Sparky said simply. "I can finish this game. Forget luck, I'm going to win this ballgame." He tightened his grip on the ball.

"Aw heck, Skip, the kid's got his mind made up," Lou said. "Whadda you say you give him one more batter and then yank him? It's not like he's going to be any worse than a Ballpino brother would be."

Skip stood there for a moment, squinting at Sparky and Lou. Then he slapped Sparky on the shoulder and left the mound. "That Ballpino kid still looks pretty stiff in the pen," he said. "I'll give you one more batter, but if you can't get an out I'm gonna pull you no matter what. And that's all I've got to say about that."

"Lookee there," Lou told Sparky. "You got what you wanted. Now all you have to do is live up to your end of the bargain."

The next Blood Sox hitter was Dimitri Dragos, an imposing figure even without his pale white skin, pointed ears and visible fangs. He smiled menacingly at Sparky as he took his practice swings. The first pitch was a blistering but normal fastball that Dragos swung right through.

"Bleh!" Dragos exclaimed after the umpire signaled strike one.

From first base, the Blood Sox baserunner cupped his hands to his mouth and started taunting Sparky. "Dragos is going to destroy your next pitch, blood bank! You're going to wish we would just bite your neck and end your misery!"

Carlos, who was cringing as far away from the baserunner as he could without taking his foot off the bag, shouted back with a quiver in his voice. "D-don't listen to him, Sparky! He hasn't hit you yet!"

"Ha-ha!" the vampire laughed. "Dragos hasn't gone hitless in a game in more than 400 years, you mortal loser!"

The next pitch came in high and tight, but Dragos was able to make contact, popping it up straight behind home plate. Lou scrambled to his feet and positioned himself underneath the ball.

"I got it!" Lou called out, but the ball bounced off the heel of his mitt and rolled harmlessly to the backstop. "Aw, shoot!"

"Foul ball, 0 and 2!" the umpire yelled.

On the mound, Sparky had to stop himself from showing any sign of frustration. The look on Lou's face made it clear no one was more upset about it than he was. Shaking his head, Lou slowly got back into position and signaled for the Phantom Slider. Sparky hurled the pitch with deadly accuracy, watching it break over the plate and vanish for the split-second Dragos attempted to drag the bat through its flight path.

"Steeerike three! Yer out!"

"Bleh!"

Sparky heaved a sigh of relief as Dragos buried his fangs deep in the barrel of his bat. He glared at Sparky, his red eyes burning with hatred.

The next batter was Pierre LeStrat, the Blood Sox' dainty left fielder. He strode up to the plate adjusting his white batting gloves and taking a moment to make sure his silk cravat was properly ruffled and tucked into the neck of his jersey.

"That was some lucky pitch, mon ami, but I have your timing all figured out now," LeStrat said as he brushed his long hair over his shoulder. "You can't fool LeStrat so easily!"

"That's funny," Lou said, "because the scoreboard up there says you're 0-for-2 already today."

LeStrat only hissed at Lou – a terrible, animal-like sound – and showed his fangs before swinging at the first pitch and sending it rocketing on the ground in Fuzzy's direction. The Goats' shortstop picked the ball cleanly off the dirt and whipped it to Lou, who had plenty of time to step on home to force out the runner from third. Lou then threw the ball to Carlos at first to try and get LeStrat and a double play.

Carlos reached out for the throw from Lou, but LeStrat just

smiled and transformed into a thick, glowing mist that still carried his fearsome red eyes. With an eerie, echoing laugh, he swept down on Carlos like a sharp wind from the underworld, causing Carlos to jump with fright off of first base before he caught the ball. The mist quickly reformed back into the shape of LeStrat, standing calmly on first.

"Safe!" the first base umpire called out, which sent Skip charging out of the dugout.

"SAFE?" Skip screamed. "What the heck are you looking at, ump? How's he supposed to put the tag on a puff of fairy dust, huh?"

"His foot came off the bag, Skip," the umpire said. Skip began furiously kicking dirt over the umpire's shoes while LeStrat took his time pulling off his batting gloves one finger at a time.

"Oh, too bad!" LeStrat giggled.

"You know, back when I was playing," Skip sputtered, "umpires knew better than to fall for any of that fancy-pants vampire hocus-pocus!"

"Yeah, well, you ain't playing anymore, Skip," the umpire said wearily.

Sparky put an arm around Skip and steered him back to the dugout. "It's okay, Skip, don't worry about it," he said. "I'm gonna get the next two guys out, you'll see."

"Ah, ya lousy, no-good...bums..." Skip said to no one in particular.

As he took the mound again, Sparky saw the next batter was Gunther Shreck, a hulking, purple-skinned galoot of a vampire with a mouth wider than Lou's catcher's mitt. Sparky couldn't imagine a brute like Shreck being able to sneak up behind anyone to bite their neck – he looked like he would trip over his own enormous feet before he got the chance. Despite his size, however, Shreck also was hitless against Sparky that day, and he looked especially stupid by swinging and missing badly at two down-and-outside balls to end each of his two strikeouts.

With the bases still loaded and only one out, Sparky was eager to ring up Shreck for a third strikeout and just focus on getting the last out. However, his eagerness caused him to release the ball just a fraction of a second too late, and the ball broke well outside the strike zone away from Shreck. But instead of taking a hack at it, Shreck vanished in a puff of smoke just before the pitch reached the plate and rematerialized on the other side, where the ball struck him on his upper thigh.

"Take your base!" said the umpire, and Shreck lumbered into first. The runner on third trotted in to score, and the bases were still loaded with two outs, but the Goats' lead had been cut to a single run.

"One!" Shreck said from first base. "That's only one more run we need, ah-ha-ha-ha!"

Skip was still cursing and kicking dirt at the top of the dugout steps, and Sparky believed he hadn't seen anything since LeStrat reached first. He would have at least one more chance before Skip noticed and pulled him, he figured, so he had better make the most of it. Meanwhile, Lou called for time and brought the rest of the infield to the mound.

"This ain't looking so good, kid," Lou said. "These vampires are tricky as all get-out."

"So what do we do?" Sparky asked. "I don't know anything about playing vampire baseball!"

"Fuzzy knows what to do," Fuzzy said, "but don't get mad if it don't work, okay?"

"Whatever, man, I'll try anything at this point."

"Okay." Fuzzy tugged on the bill of his cap, causing his hair to wiggle like a Jell-O mold. "The thing about vampires is, they can't come into anyone's home without being invited, okay? That's a vampire thing."

"Invited?" Sparky said. "You mean like…?"

Fuzzy was already headed back to the infield. "Just give this guy something to hit, right? Fuzzy takes care of the rest." The other infielders began to hustle back to their positions.

"What makes you so sure?" Sparky asked.

"Fuzzy's Aunt Zelda was a gypsy," Fuzzy said. "The gypsies, they know all kinds of stuff about all kinds of stuff, you know? So she knows all kind of stuff about vampires, right?"

"If you say so," Sparky said to himself as he looked in at Vlad Romaine, the Blood Sox player at bat. Romaine pulled his batting helmet on over his widow's peak and stepped into the batter's box. Sparky glanced back at Fuzzy, who just nodded. Sparky's pitch was low but in the zone, and Romaine made contact with it for a short flare out into the gap in right field.

"Ha!" Romaine laughed as he made his way to first. "Somebody stop the bleeding!"

At the moment, Fuzzy reached into his jersey and pulled out a gold cross that he had hanging around his neck. He dangled the cross in the direction of the Blood Sox's third base coach, who hissed and recoiled in horror at the sight of it. The vampire curled up in a ball on the ground, leaving the Blood Sox baserunner on third confused. His eyes were fixed on home plate, but he wouldn't move.

"It's a hit!" the baserunner exclaimed in a thick Hungarian accent. "It's a hit! Tell me to go home!"

LeStrat, running from second base, collided with the baserunner on third. "What are you doing?" he said.

"I can't go home!" the baserunner moaned. "He's not giving me the signal!"

Fuzzy waved frantically at Lance, who had come up with the ball in right field. "Throw it home!" he shouted. Lance lobbed the ball across the infield, and Lou came up with it on two hops. He stepped on the plate, and the umpire signaled the runner on third out. Sparky dropped to his knees on the mound. The game was over, and at long last the Goats had notched their first win of the season.

The good feelings were short lived, however, as the Blood Sox came right back in the next game and handed the Goats their next loss, 14-1. The lone Goats run came, naturally, in the first, when Lance clobbered another solo home run to give the Goats a 1-0 lead that was subsequently erased when Antonio served up a bases-loaded double to LeStrat. And it was all downhill from there.

The scoring outburst from the Blood Sox, combined with the usually late start time to accommodate the Transylvania crowd, meant it was well after midnight when the Goats staggered back into the dreary visitors' clubhouse that night. Skip spent several silent minutes in the manager's office and then came out and wordlessly slapped the next game's lineup on the bulletin board. Only Sparky took the time to look it over – the rest of the team knew exactly what to expect at this point: Bright, Cabarellos, Fernandez, Houston, Hurzberk, Munson, Odinson, VORP, pitcher's spot – sure as the sun would rise in the morning, although Sparky had his doubts about the sun in Transylvania.

Scowling as he read the lineup, Sparky turned to Lou. "How many games have we lost because of this?" he said, tapping the bulletin board.

"At least a couple," Lou said with a sigh.

"Isn't Skip supposed to be a baseball lifer? Doesn't he know anything about filling out a batting order?"

"Kid, believe me, I thought the exact same thing you did when I first saw that lineup. Lord knows these dusty old bones ain't the thing you need to drive in a bunch of runs, but Skip's the man in the office and we're not, so..."

"So we just do whatever he says, even if it's a stupid idea?"

Lou smiled. "Well hey, now you're starting to get it. I knew you'd already played a season in the Big Leagues."

"I'm not putting up with this anymore," Sparky said as he stormed into the equipment room. Yoshi was busy pressing the Goats' gray road uniforms for the next day's game. "Yoshi, I need your help with something."

"Just one thing?" Yoshi asked.

There was a new lineup card posted on the bulletin board the next morning, which caught the Goats by surprise. Now VORP was leading off, followed by Fuzzy, Carlos, Lance, Thor, Bobby, Blerk, Lou and Willie in the pitcher's spot. The handwriting was unmistakably Skip's – no one else could have duplicated his caffeinated jitters or the multiple coffee stains – but a closer look would have revealed the marks where each name had been carefully cut out and glued into their new positions.

"Skip, about this lineup..." Lance said as the manager came striding out of his office minutes before the game.

"If I told you bums once, I told you a thousand times: The lineup is set and that's that!" Skip interrupted. "Every year some jerk comes into my office and thinks he knows more about the game than I do, tries telling me how to set the lineup. Do you think you know more about this game than I do, Bright?"

"I'm just saying..."

"You wanna get cut from this team and wind up somewhere they'll make you work for a living?"

"No, but..."

"Then get your mouth shut and go play some doggone baseball already!"

Sparky and Yoshi shared a secret smile as Lance scowled and trudged his way out of the clubhouse. The first part of the plan had gone off without a hitch – now they hoped the second half worked just as well. The whole thing hinged on the fact that the lineup cards Skip handed to the umpire before each game was filled out with uniform numbers only...

In the top of the first, VORP stepped up to the plate with Lance's uniform number – 1, of course – hastily stenciled onto his back. In the dugout, Skip stood with his arms crossed over the rail and squinted in the direction of home plate.

"Somebody oughta tell Bright he needs to eat more red meat," Skip said. "His legs look like pretzel sticks!"

"Will do, Skip," Sparky said. "You're absolutely right, Skip."

"About time somebody in this clown college agreed with me," Skip said. VORP cracked a slow ground ball to third that he was able to leg out for an infield single. Fuzzy was up next, with Carlos' number 17 stitched to the back of his jersey. Even though Fuzzy grounded out to second, VORP's speed made it possible for the lanky robot to slide safely into second.

After Carlos struck out swinging wildly at a fastball that was outside the zone, Lance swaggered up to the plate. "Don't feel so bad, Carlos," he said as he passed his sullen teammate. "I would have swung at that exact same pitch."

With VORP taking his lead at second base, the Blood Sox pitcher decided he didn't want to enable any of Lance's usual first-inning efforts, so he intentionally walked him on four pitches well outside the strike zone. Lance looked like he was going to cry.

"A WALK?" Lance wailed at the pitcher. "Do you know what that does to my power numbers?"

"It's great for your on-base percentage!" VORP offered cheerily.

"Nobody gives a rat's butt about on-base percentage, you stupid garbage can!" Lance shouted from 90 feet away. "Do you think the ladies swoon over the Bright-man because of his freaking ON-BASE PERCENTAGE?"

It was Thor's turn at the plate next, and after the clearly rattled pitcher staked him to a 3-1 count, there came the sound of distant thunder. The Goats had seen this act before, of course, but with two men on and a hitter's count, there was a real chance for something to happen. Without the softer-hitting Goats surrounding him in the lineup, the pitcher was in a position where he had to give Thor something in the zone, something he could hit. And that's exactly what he gave him.

A bolt of lightning cracked the ebony sky over the ballpark, and a massive thunderclap followed as Thor connected with the belt-high fastball and sent it rocketing into the air. It climbed higher and higher until it finally knocked a heavy iron weathervane off the highest parapet behind the center field scoreboard. The bat-shaped weathervane came crashing down into the bleachers, sending a cluster of vampires, werewolves and mummies diving out of the way. Thor, who was rounding second base, laughed heartily at the sight.

"Deathless denizens of the underworld!" he cried out. "Send thy bill for thine repairs to the God of Thunder!"

The Goats' 3-0 lead held up until the fourth inning, when Willie let a slow roller go between her legs, which allowed a Blood Sox run to score. Another Transylvania run came in the fifth, when Bobby got winded while chasing a lazy pop-up into shallow left field and let it drop as he stopped to catch his breath. The score was 3-2 headed into the ninth, and the Goats needed some insurance runs with VORP, Fuzzy and Carlos due up.

VORP used his speed to turn a ground ball between third and short into a sliding double. Fuzzy hit a deep fly to right field that allowed VORP to tag up and take third with one out. Carlos came up to the plate, waggling his bat and taking some serious practice swings.

"Don't swing for the fences, Carlos!" Sparky shouted from the dugout. "All we need is a base hit!"

"Carlos?" Skip asked. "You need glasses, kid. That's Fernandez up there, I can tell by his number!"

"Uh, sorry, Skip. You're absolutely right, as always."

Carlos looked into the dugout at Sparky and nodded with a smile. From the on-deck circle, however, Lance whistled and shook his head. He pointed at Carlos and mimed a home run swing. Adjusting his batting helmet, Carlos turned to the pitcher and got set.

He took a massive cut at the very first pitch, a high fastball that he caught on the underside and sent spinning off into foul territory. The next pitch was a slow change-up that caught Carlos swinging hard but way too early for strike two. With another nod of encouragement from Lance, Carlos swung so hard at the next offering that he wound up twirling out of the batter's box like a ballerina. The ball, however, made it safely to the catcher's mitt unharmed. Lance gave Carlos a friendly pat on the shoulder as they passed each other.

With first base open, two outs and the Goats' two heaviest hitters up next in Lance and Thor, the Blood Sox manager made the decision to walk both men intentionally to load the bases. This made it possible to get a force-out at any base, something that was more or less assured with Bobby up next. He was still huffing and puffing from chasing down the pop fly from the previous inning.

Bobby was so winded he didn't even swing at the first pitch right down the middle of the plate. Once the count reached 2-2, however, he was able to manage a lazy swing that tapped the ball and sent it bouncing weakly to the mound. The pitcher scooped up the ball as the runners advanced, but with Bobby wheezing and shuffling down the first base line he was the easiest target. The pitcher ran up to tag Bobby out himself, but once he was within a few inches of him he suddenly looked nauseated and dropped to his knees. The ball squirted out of his glove and rolled across the line into foul territory. Bobby collapsed with his forehead landing on first base and VORP made it across home plate easily. Even though Blerk popped out to end the inning, the Goats were sitting in a better position, leading 4-2.

"Nice job, Bobby," Sparky said as he congratulated the still-panting Munson on his RBI hit. "What happened out there on that play?"

"I don't know," Bobby said through a cloud of pungent odor. "But I'm never eating that much garlic bread before an at-bat ever again. I'm exhausted!"

The Goats were all smiles again in the clubhouse that night. As the rest of the team celebrated, Yoshi slipped into Skip's office with a telegram from Go-Town.

"This just came from Mr. Mint," Yoshi said. "He saw the game tonight and wants you to use this same lineup from now on."

Skip snatched the telegram out of Yoshi's hand and read through it, moving his lips as he did. The lineup Sparky and Yoshi had devised was spelled out as the one Mr. Mint preferred.

"He wants this?" Skip asked. "But those bums were finally starting to hit in the old lineup!"

Sparky was loading up his duffle bag when Lou approached him. "Some little birdie told me that whole batting order stunt tonight was your idea," he said.

"What's it to you?" Sparky said without looking up. "Are you and Lance going to ask me to put it back the way it was? I don't want to be wasting my time on any lost causes, here."

"Whoa there, cowboy, I come in peace," Lou chuckled, his hands up in mock defense. "Look, I know what I said probably came across like I was telling you to give up, but that ain't it at all."

"Oh no? Could have fooled me."

"All's I was saying was, I've seen a lot of dudes in your situation, more or less." Sparky looked up into Lou's eyes and immediately knew that Lou knew what he was talking about. There was a look of sympathy but mostly regret. "Most of these guys, they thought they knew what they were doing, too. They thought all they had to do was go out there and give 110 percent and they'd beat that old devil by playing the game. But not a one of them ever pulled it off, and I know why."

"Why's that?"

"Because it turned out they weren't playing the same game as him. But you..." Lou waggled a finger at Sparky. "You're the first guy I've ever seen who gets it, and it looks like you're getting the help those other poor scrubs never got. Now, I ain't saying you're gonna pull it off, necessarily. But I think you've got a shot."

"Thanks, Lou. Thanks for saying that."

"If you need old Lou Houston's help with anything from here on out, you just whistle, you hear?"

"Listen up, you jerks!" Skip bellowed from the door to his office, holding the telegram from Mr. Mint over his head. "Apparently there's going to be some changes in the lineup from now on!"

NEW-LOOK GOATS DEFYING EXPECTATIONS
By Roy Myko, *Go-Town Gazette* Sports Columnist

What do you call it when you're 10 games out of first place at the end of May? If you're the Goats, you call it your most successful month in a long time, of course. Even though they're still looking up – way up – at the Canaries in the standings, the fact that the Goats have managed to break even since their typically disastrous 0-15 start has some players feeling uncharacteristically optimistic as of late.

A lot of that has to do with the performance of phenom starter Sparky Katakura, who has come to life after a shaky Opening Day start to win his last six starts in a row. Just don't tell him that fellow starters Antonio de la Goya and Willy Wilbur have been less than impressive behind him.

"I think we have a good staff here," Katakura said after the Goats' 5-4 win over North Haverbrook last night. "All we need is for a couple of the guys to get some confidence and we should start winning some more ballgames."

"De la Goya has confidence," De la Goya said later. "How can he not have confidence when each pitch that leaves his fingertips is a thing of beauty?" That "beauty" has come with a price, however, as the eccentric hurler sports an ERA that's downright abstract at 7.11.

Katakura's pitching makes up a big part of the Goats' story, but more surprising than the young ace's performance is the revised batting order the team sports these days. Now that the team's power hitters have been relocated to, shall we say, more logical spots in the order, the Goats' run production is up and so is the win column. Manager Skip LaRoche said the change was handed down from the front office in a shocking display of baseball acumen, but this reporter has it on good authority from inside sources that Katakura was at least partially responsible for making the suggestion.

"He was?" right fielder Lance Bright said, seemingly caught off-guard by the implication. "That's not really his job, is it?"

Sparky's dreams that night were troubling. He was back in his old bedroom, back with the familiar old shoebox filled to the top with baseball cards. In his dream, however, the shoebox was impossibly deep. Looking down into it, Sparky couldn't find the bottom, only endless stacks of cards. He could hear Ken's voice from somewhere deep down inside of it, echoing as if the box led to a dungeon.

Sparky began digging through the cards, checking each one to see if he could find the card that bore his brother's picture. But somehow every single card in the stacks was of Lance Bright. Lance Bright playing right field. Lance Bright playing shortstop. Lance Bright, manager. Lance Bright wearing a Go-Town Goats uniform. Lance Bright wearing a Cleveland Optimists uniform. Hollywood Bellhops, Arlen Armadillos, Bogota Sunscrapers – Lance Bright, Lance Bright, Lance Bright.

He kicked the box off the end of his bed, sending an endless shower of cards raining down on him. Sparky couldn't see through the blizzard of cardboard surrounding him. He felt the bed and then the entire room fall away from him until he was sure he was floating, held aloft in an endless blackness. And there was laughter. Mocking, malicious, familiar laughter.

When Sparky finally opened his eyes, he was still floating. He threw off the blankets and jumped out of bed to get back on solid ground, but instead he found himself suddenly submerged in four feet of icy cold water. As he splashed around, he heard the same laughter from his dream. His bed was floating in the middle of the hotel pool, and laughing at him from a balcony above were Fuzzy, Bobby, Carlos...and Lance.

"Hey, good idea, Katakura!" Lance said. "Nothing better late at night than a nice swim to clear your head, right? I mean, you've probably got a lot on your mind right now, trying to run my team and everything!"

"Dude, that's the funniest thing I've ever seen!" Bobby said.

"I don't know how you stayed asleep that whole time we were carrying your bed down there, Sparky!" Fuzzy said. "It's amazing!"

As Sparky was wringing out his t-shirt alongside the pool, Carlos and Fuzzy appeared with a bundle of white hotel towels.

"Come on, Sparky, you gotta admit, that was pretty funny!" Fuzzy said, his laughter making his hair wobble.

"I guess," Sparky said as he dried himself. "Whose idea was that, as if I have to ask?"

"It was Lance," Carlos said. "We were playing video games in Fuzzy's room and he came and asked if we were bored. No hard feelings, right?"

Sparky glanced up at the balcony, which was now empty. "I'm not so sure about that, guys," he said.

7. CLUBHOUSE CHEMISTRY

"Salutations once again from West Side Grounds here in Chicago! Mel Fuller with the Goats legend Randy Sandies here in the top of the sixth inning with the Goats and the Butchers all knotted up at 2 runs apiece. Randy, we've seen some really good pitching here today from Sparky Katakura and the Butchers' Ed Crane, but on a hot day like today you're going to have to dip into that bullpen at some point. There's just no way these two pitchers can keep up this level of performance for nine whole innings."

"You got that right, Mel."

"And that's exactly what the Butchers have done here, as the Goats have runners on the corners with two outs and Lance Bright up to bat. Coming out of the Chicago bullpen is Grandel Whitebeard, who in the course of his career has really given Thor Odinson fits, so can we expect the Butchers to walk Bright to get to Thor, Randy?"

"Uh, yup. Probably, Mel."

"Lance is set, and the first pitch is...well outside, looks like you were right, partner. Whitebeard is going to intentionally walk Bright to face...whoa!"

"Huh?"

"Bright just swung at that pitch! Nowhere near the strike zone, not even in the same area code, and Bright took a swing at it for strike one! Whitebeard and the Chicago catcher are looking at each other like they can't believe it! The count is now 1 and 1 and...he did it again!"

"Did what?"

"Another intentional pitch outside of the strike zone and again Bright swings at it for a strike! He's now in a hole 1-2 and I can't imagine what must be going through his head right now, Randy, can you?"

"I don't think so..."

"The 1-2 pitch...is another pitchout, swung on and missed for strike three! Bright goes down swinging and the inning is over!

Ladies and gentlemen, I have seen this team do some unbelievably stupid things in my day, but I have never seen them turn an intentional walk into a swinging strikeout. Skip LaRoche is absolutely furious in the dugout and we go to the bottom of the sixth, the score still tied 2-2. How about that!"

The score remained 2-2 until the bottom of the ninth, when Sparky's Phantom Slider broke a bit too far outside on Roma, the Chicago second baseman. Roma wound up on first on the base-on-balls, and with Levene's single preceding it, the Butchers had men on first and second with just one out. Sparky felt the hot sun on the back of his neck and imagined it more as a spotlight than anything else. His undershirt was drenched with sweat, and his pitch count had passed 100 a long time ago. Skip emerged from the dugout and joined Sparky, Carlos and Fuzzy on the mound. As he slammed the ball into his glove in frustration, Sparky noticed Lance trotting in, as well.

"All right, kid, you've given them all you got today," Skip said. "I'm going to have one of the Ballpino kids come in and mop up."

"No way, Skip," Sparky protested. "I've still got plenty left in the tank, just give me a shot at getting Blake!"

Skip lifted his cap and ran his fingers through his silvery-white hair, then made a face. "Well, to be honest with you, I ain't crazy about sending any one of those three dopes out here in this situation," he said. "Tell you what, you get Blake here and I'll give you a chance to get out of the inning."

"That's all I ask, Skip."

"Whoa, hey, wait a minute," Lance said. "Spark, old buddy, don't let pride get in the way of your better judgment!"

"What are you talking about, Bright?" Skip asked.

"I think it's clear to everyone here that Katakura is tired, Skip." Lance lifted his sunglasses and made a show out of giving Sparky a quick inspection. "Frankly, I'm impressed that he's been able to gut it out even this long, what with everything he was up to last night..."

"What's he talking about, Katakura?"

"Nothing! I wasn't doing anything last night!"

"Carlos, didn't we see Sparky in the hotel pool around 1 o'clock last night?"

"Yeah, but..."

"All I know is I woke up to the sound of splashing in the pool, and when I came out on the balcony I could see Sparky down there," Lance said. "Now, I know every ballplayer has his own routine before a big game, but I think the kid just didn't realize how strenuous an activity swimming is..."

"Wait a minute, this is complete crap, Skip!"

"No, no, no, I heard enough! You got a lot of spunk, but if Bright says you're pushing yourself too hard, then I don't want to see you all tapped out by August." Skip signaled to the bullpen and Ted Ballpino came jogging out to the mound. Slapping Sparky on the butt, Skip pointed him to the dugout. On the way there, Sparky turned back and glowered at Lance, who smirked and gave him a jaunty little wave goodbye from the mound. Six minutes later, Levene crossed home plate for Chicago's winning run.

Sparky was still dressed in his uniform when the rest of the team filed into the clubhouse. As soon as he saw him, Sparky made a bee-line right to Lance.

"Problem, bro?" Lance said as he tossed his cap into his locker.

"Yeah, you can say that again," Sparky said.

"Problem, bro? Haha, just messing with you, little guy. Why so serious?" Lance found his boombox and hit "play," filling the room with the twangy, warbling sound of his attempt at country music. Sparky immediately punched the "stop" button. Lance flashed Sparky a hateful look, but then took a deep breath and folded his arms. "Okay, I guess you want to talk about something, so go ahead and get it off your chest."

"I want to know what your damage is, Lance. The rest of us are trying to win, but you only seem interested in yourself!"

"Win? Yeah, see, the thing about that is, you're wrong." Lance gestured around the entire clubhouse. "There's nine guys out there on the field, and they have nine different reasons for being out there. The robot is there because he's programmed to. The big Viking dummy thinks he's still fighting trolls or whatever. Munson wants to eat a hot dog in every Big League ballpark, right Munson?"

"Only 84 more to go!" Bobby said.

"See, the rest of these Goats understand something you haven't figured out yet – there's no such thing as winning in Go-Town, not with these players, not with this manager, not with this franchise. This is baseball limbo, Katakura – this is where the game goes to die. All you can do is focus on yourself and maybe you can play your way out of this open grave of a team. Me, I'm only 100 or so home runs away from having a shot at the Hall of Fame, so excuse me for trying to make the most out of this puke sandwich I've been served."

"But you..."

"And even you've got some other reason for being here, don't you? The old cowboy seems to think you're here not because you want to win one for the pathetic losers who stumble into that old dump 81 times a summer, am I right?" Sparky clenched his fists and tried as hard as he could to keep from crying.

"Yeah, you've got your own problems, don't you? And if you listen to the cowboy they're real serious, a bona fide stone-cold bummer. If it's true, that sucks for you. But that's your baggage, amigo, and don't expect me to give a hoot about your situation. Because you sure as heck don't care about mine."

With that, Lance hit "play" again and the clubhouse buzz was drowned out by the syrupy sound of his music.

"As long as we're both here, compadre, you better realize that this is my clubhouse."

With the music swelling to near-deafening levels, Sparky retreated to his locker. He took a look around the clubhouse – with the exception of Lance and VORP, who was humming to himself as he tightened his elbow joints, there wasn't a smile in the room.

"Come on, kid," Lou said, "I know a place not too far from here that makes the best dang quesadillas in the Midwest."

Two okay-but-not-really-anything-special quesadillas later, Lou and Sparky sat across from each other in a mostly empty Mexican restaurant in a sleepy neighborhood of Chicago.

"The problem is, Bright is right," Lou said. "We all do have our own reasons for being here, and asking all of us to rally behind your reason isn't going to get it done, no matter how good a reason it is."

"Have you ever been on a winning team, Lou?"

"Long time ago, rookie season, as a matter of fact." Lou paused to load a chip with a heap of chunky salsa and devour it in one bite. "Believe it or not, my first Big League at-bat was with the New York Emperors."

Sparky's eyes went wide in amazement. "You played for the Emperors? The 35-time World Champion New York Emperors?"

"Now hold on, don't go asking me for Louie Calder's autograph or anything," Lou cautioned. "I wasn't nothing more than a late-season call-up. To call it a 'cup of coffee' is overstating it a little. It was more like a 'walk past a coffee shop and smelling the beans a little.'"

"Oh."

"In fact, that one at-bat was the only one I ever had with New York. They shipped me off to Graviton City the next week. But even when I was in the minors, the one thing the Emperors coaches drilled into you from day one was that the team is the most important thing. Nobody's more important than the team, and the most important thing for the team is to back up your teammates."

"All for one and one for all, right?" Sparky flicked a jalapeno seed from the table into a potted cactus on the other side of the restaurant. "So what happened to that attitude?"

Lou smiled and dunked another chip. "That's a fair question, and I guess when you've played for 26 different teams in the course of an 18-year Big League career, it's kind of hard to feel much of a connection to any of them."

"But that's not the issue with the Goats. It's like they expect to lose."

"And why not? They sure as heck have enough practice with it. What you need to do is show them they can have it another way."

"But we already have a better record than the Goats had last year, isn't that enough?"

Lou shook his head. "You jumbled the lineup around a little bit, yeah, but that's not gonna be enough. It doesn't matter where these guys hit in the order if they go up to the plate expecting to fail every time. We need to give them something to believe in besides you, Sparky. After all, you can't be expected to do everything yourself."

That night, Sparky met Yoshi on the mound for another round of lessons. "What is a strikeout?" Yoshi asked as he picked up a bat and waddled to the plate. Sparky shook his head and shrugged.

"Is this the remedial course or something? When I make the right pitches in the right spots, I strike a guy out. That's what a strikeout is."

"But what IS a strikeout? Show me a strikeout pitch, Sparky."

Sparky cleared his mind and went into his motion, hurling a perfect Phantom Slider that disappeared just as it crossed the plate and reappeared on the other side before plunking off the backstop.

"Okay, good," Yoshi said. "But humor me and throw that same pitch again."

Sparky shrugged and Yoshi stepped into the batter's box, smiling. With a go-ahead nod from his diminutive coach, Sparky concentrated and threw another perfect Phantom Slider, one that Yoshi nonetheless managed to clobber even as it vanished from sight.

"Again," Yoshi commanded, and Sparky obliged with another Phantom Slider. Yoshi swatted it directly back at the mound, knocking Sparky off his feet and actually out of his shoes.

"Good grief!" Sparky exclaimed as he dusted himself off and pushed his feet back into his shoes. Now more than a little annoyed with the grinning old man, Sparky took the mound again.

"Sorry about that," Yoshi laughed. "Let's try that same pitch again, and I promise I won't try to hit you with it!"

Instead, Sparky reared back and unloaded the Blazing Fastball, envisioning the look on the Yoshi's face when it blew right by him. The ball's fiery tail scorched the green grass below it until Yoshi calmly swung and belted it somewhere into the trees beyond the outfield wall.

"Okay, I think I've made my point, so I'll ask again," Yoshi said. "What IS a strikeout? Here, your turn."

Sparky stood in against Yoshi, and he threw Sparky a half-dozen decent pitches. A few of them Sparky was able to make contact with, even if they didn't travel as far as the ones Yoshi hit off of him.

"Now, watch carefully," Yoshi said, and began his motion. Sparky gripped the bat tightly, his eyes fixed on the old man's bare hand as it came out of the glove. He caught sight of Yoshi's grip on the ball and anticipated a four-seam fastball. He watched him raise his arm and noted that it would be a relatively straight pitch. He saw the release point of the ball and readied himself to swing. The pitch was coming, twirling through the air. Sparky was ready to swing. He was still ready to swing. The ball continued to tumble toward home plate. It was still coming.

"Wait," Sparky thought, "shouldn't it have gotten here by now?" On the mound, he could see Yoshi's back foot was still hanging in the air behind him, and his right arm was still swinging slowly downward. The ball continued to spin languidly toward home plate. One one-thousand, two one-thousand, three one-thousand...it's still on its way.

"I need to swing at it," Sparky thought. "I'm definitely going to swing at it. Here goes..." It was strangely quiet all of a sudden, Sparky realized.

As soon as he swung, the sound rushed back to his ears like a flood rushing from a broken dam. The bat cut swiftly through empty air, and when he looked back he saw the ball resting comfortably on the dirt beneath the backstop. Yoshi was laughing next to him.

Sparky wheeled around at the mound, and sure enough Yoshi wasn't there. "What was that?" he asked. "How did you get back there so fast?"

"Sparky, in the time it took you to swing at that pitch, I stretched my legs, got a drink of water from the cooler over there in the dugout and even thought about making myself a sandwich," Yoshi said. "But I wanted to make sure I was back here in time to see the look on your face. It was worth it." Yoshi handed the ball to the perplexed young pitcher.

"I asked you what a strikeout is, and you told me it is what happens when a pitcher makes the right pitches in the right places," Yoshi continued. "But that's only half-right. A pitcher is only successful when the hitter fails. The two are fully dependent on each other, each makes up half of a whole. The batter fails when he expects something different than what you give him, as you have seen with the Cosmic Change-Up just now."

"So what you're saying is a strikeout is something the pitcher and the batter work together to create..." Sparky said, his eyes now wide with understanding.

Yoshi grinned and nodded. "Yep, now you got it. Feel better?"

"Oh yeah, totally, but it's not just me you've been helping out tonight," Sparky said.

The next morning, Sparky ran out onto the field for workouts with the rest of the team. As he threw in the bullpen, he noticed Antonio conducting a strange pitching drill on the other end. Antonio had set up an easel and picture frame directly over the plate, with the frame outlining the strike zone. Around the edges of the frame, pointing inward, he attached paintbrushes, each one dipped in a different color of paint. He would throw the ball so that it would graze each paintbrush as it crossed the plate, and after a dozen or so pitches, the ball was streaked with a criss-crossing rainbow pattern. Antonio noticed Sparky watching him and held up the color-streaked ball for him to admire.

"Magnificent, is it not?" Antonio asked with pride swelling in his voice.

"That's really impressive, Antonio," Sparky replied. "Can you hit the brush you want every time?"

Antonio looked insulted. "What kind of a question is that?" he demanded. "Did Michelangelo always chisel away the right piece of marble? Did da Vinci always sketch the perfect representation of the human form? Did Raphael always use the proper colors for his compositions?"

"Sorry, I was just asking..."

"Did Donatello...? Ah, but I am sorry, my friend. I take such pride in my work, you know."

"No, don't worry about it, I just wanted to know if you always had such great control."

"Certainly," Antonio said with a bow. "It is the hallmark of a great artist to have a full understanding of his instrument. It is almost as if it is a part of you, yes?"

"So why don't you just make the pitches you need to get guys out? It looks like it should be easy for you."

"Sir, others may be concerned with something as pedestrian as an out, but Antonio de la Goya creates art!"

"Well, no offense, man, but your art is getting us killed out there. You're making the wrong pitches most of the time."

"Beauty, my young friend, is in the eye of the beholder." Considering the conversation over and the argument won, Antonio returned to his pitching drills and another basket of rainbow baseballs.

GOATS STARTER IMPROVES HIS PORTFOLIO
By Roy Myko, Go-Town Gazette

For the Go-Town Goats, improvement is often measured in baby steps. Old-timers might remember the hullaballoo that erupted when outfielder Howard Gerber notched a batting average of .245 after a .235 season the previous year. But to say there's been a marked improvement in the performance of starting pitcher Antonio de la Goya over the last few weeks would be an understatement, especially when compared to the type of improvement Goats fans are used to.

Since taking the hill and giving up five home runs against the Jewels in Shanghai earlier in the month, de la Goya has become a formidable weapon in the Goats' arsenal, taking some of pressure off of phenom Sparky Katakura and helping the Goats inch ever closer to the .500 mark. Lest anyone out there shrug at the idea of the Goats breaking even on the season, remember this: The last time they were at the .500 mark was 38 years ago.

When asked, de la Goya says his recent resurgence is due in no small part to the influence of Katakura, who has certainly been making his mark on the team since coming over from the San Carlos Stars under mysterous circumstances.

"Sparky, he told me my approach to pitching was all wrong," de la Goya said as the Goats prepared to head back home for their last homestand before the All-Star Break. "At first, I think he is crazy, because my approach is to treat each pitch as one piece of a work of art. But Sparky, he let me see, there is more to each pitch than what I do. The batter, the way he swings contributes its own texture and color to the at-bat, and it is, how you say, a collaboration between the two of us. A strikeout is the product of two artists, each working in his own medium, and the final result is a thing of beauty to behold."

That change in attitude has gone a long way to improving de la Goya's numbers, dropping his WHIP from a gob-stopping 7.90 before the Shanghai series to a far more formidable 0.82 in the last few weeks. With Katakura and now de la Goya providing power in the rotation and a batting order better suited to driving in runs than helping school kids remember their ABCs, the Goats find themselves in a position completely alien to them – contending.

Yes, the Canaries continue to keep pace in the Central League's Green Division, but one could also say they've been treading water. Fort Clark Manager Cyrus O'Malley has been playing these mid-season games the way he's accustomed to – resting his star players often in an attempt to keep them fresh for the postseason. With the level of competition the Canaries have faced in recent seasons, he can hardly be blamed for that, but out of nowhere here come the Goats. Go-Town's boys are just two games under .500 now and only six games out of first place in the division. Does this team have the stuff to make history, or will it only echo history and wind up burning out down the stretch? The next homestand will provide some clue to the answer, as the Goats face off against division rivals Smallville, Minnesota and, naturally, Fort Clark.

8. BETWEEN THE NUMBERS

Sparky arrived at his locker one day to find a large black binder inside. A note attached to the cover read: "I happened to notice what happened with the lineup, nice work. FYI, Caballeros' OBP is slightly better against lefties, so you might want to consider having him lead off in those situations, but I'm getting ahead of myself. I thought you might be interested in some advanced statistical analysis for the series against Smallville. Hope it helps! Signed, the Go-Goats Girl."

The binder was filled with hundreds of pages of charts, graphs and mostly numbers. Sparky flipped through them rapidly, finding individual sections detailing the tendencies of each Smallville hitter on a pitch-by-pitch basis. Roger Swan, for example, tended to be much more aggressive on a 2-1 count than a 2-2 count. Kara Anderson, on the other hand, would keep the bat on her shoulder if there were 2 balls or more, regardless of how many strikes there were. Every pitcher in the Smallville bullpen had at least a few pages devoted to their pitch selection, top speeds for each pitch, etc.

"Oh my God," Sparky said out loud. "Now I have homework."

As he continued scanning the pages, Sparky noticed a web address at the top of most of them – GoGoatsGirl.com. Making sure Skip was on one of his extended coffee breaks, Sparky snuck into his office and found a computer buried underneath six months' worth of newspapers. Even with Zigleaf Field's ancient Internet connection, Sparky found the site quickly. The blog looked like it was updated almost every day, and the latest entry had been posted only a few hours ago.

"Goats fans, I'll be honest with you," it began. "This is weird. Can you remember the last time this team had a positive win expectancy in any inning? Or when a pitcher wearing the red and orange posted an xFIP as low as Sparky Katakura has over his last few starts? Comparing the team's Pythagorean rating now to where it was at the start of the season..." Sparky scrolled down past all the numbers to where his name showed up again.

"...Katakura's ERA+ has been one of the most consistent factors..." Sparky scrolled down again.

"...normally the truth about a pitcher can be found in his or her BAbip, but Katakura's numbers in that category are exceptional..." Sparky kept scrolling.

"...and remember, any fans who want to get together and talk numbers in person are welcome to come down to The Goat's Pen Baseball Card Shop on Holtzman Street tomorrow, just like every Wednesday. See you there!" Sparky decided she would.

An hour after Thor hit a game-winning double to the gap in right-center that sent a sun-dried Zigleaf Field crowd home crackling with energy, Sparky was standing in front of The Goat's Pen. Even though it was nothing more than a one-story storefront with big glass windows, it was unlike any other building Sparky had seen so far in Go-Town. It was covered from foundation to roof in Goats orange and red. The sight of it was almost too much for Sparky to take in all at once. In a town that hardly seemed willing to admit it even had a baseball team, here was the first evidence Sparky had seen outside of the tiny crowds at Zigleaf that there was such a thing as a Goats fan.

The effect was doubled when Sparky entered the shop. Every inch of wall was covered with memorabilia – pennants, flags, old programs from the ballpark, black-and-white photographs marked with autographs in faded blue ink and, of course, thousands and thousands of baseball cards. The sight of so many cards in one place immediately recalled dusty Sunday afternoons spent bartering with Ken over prized cards, their collections inching closer to perfection with each swap. In the dead center of the wall, Sparky saw a Terrzax the Tormentor rookie card, from his first season with the Alphaville Superiors, the very card that provoked a week-long negotiation after Ken came home from school having swindled a second-grader for it. Next to Terrzax, a Frank Bendis card from the season he hit 75 home runs for the Waffletown Syrups, setting an Intercontinental League record. Next to Bendis, with a price tag of $500, the extremely rare team card of the Area 51 Majestics, which, as the story goes, was pulled off the market by the government because it confirmed the team's existence.

As he scanned the rows of cards lining the walls, Sparky heard himself mumbling to himself: "Need it, need it, got it, need it, got it, got it..." He was so distracted he didn't even notice someone standing next to him.

"Can I help you with something?" she asked. Sparky

straightened up like a solider called to attention. He tried to remember if he had seen her face anywhere in the stands, but even though he admitted to himself that she was kind of cute and even though there hadn't been more than a few hundred people in the stands for most of the Goats' home games, Sparky couldn't remember seeing her before. Her dark hair was pulled into a ponytail that poked out of the back of her faded orange cap. There were freckles on her nose and her face was pleasingly round. She looked very much like the type of girl Ken would have made an idiot of himself around, Sparky realized.

"Uh, yeah, I was just here because of the blog?" Maybe if he phrased it as a question, he could take it back when he thought of something better, Sparky thought. "You must be the Go-Goats Girl."

"It's Katie. Nice to meet you. You're a fan of the blog, huh?" Katie swept some dust off a display case with her fingers. "I didn't think pro ballplayers actually read anything."

"Sure. Well, I mean, I didn't start reading it until last night, but it's, ah, pretty informative."

"Usually when someone says that it means they couldn't make it past the first graph," Katie said, raising one eyebrow and smirking.

"No, no! I just mean that there's a lot of…stuff going on with it," Sparky stammered. "So anyway, do you have like a little group discussion or something for these things?"

"Actually, I don't get that many people coming into the shop," Katie said sadly. "Most of the people reading the blog are from out of town, or if they're from Go-Town they prefer to keep the baseball talk on the Internet. I don't know if you've noticed, but most people in this town like to pretend baseball doesn't exist."

"I have. So, this is your shop? I've gotta say, it's amazing. My brother and I would have loved this place when we were kids. We had to settle for buying up wax packs at the gas station, and then waiting for them to get a new box."

"Thanks, but this place is really my grandfather's," she said as she dusted off a shadow box containing a pristine white ball. It was signed: "To Frank, thanks for everything! Duke Hobbs."

"Whoa, Duke Hobbs!" Sparky leaned in so close to the case his breath fogged up the glass. "Heh, sorry," he said, catching himself. "I was just a huge fan of Duke growing up, so…"

"My grandfather was, too, don't worry about it. Duke sent him that a few years ago, after Duke made it to the Hall of Fame. Grandpa gave him some pointers when Duke was still in the minors, showed him how to throw a curve. Duke likes to say he owes Grandpa his career."

"Holy cow, that's...wow! Your Grandpa played in the Big Leagues?"

Katie pointed to a faded photograph further down the wall. It was of an old-time ballplayer, down on one knee and propping himself up with a bat. He looked to be in the middle of a practice field, with palm trees behind the chain-link outfield fence. A handwritten note at the bottom of the photo said, "Spring Training Camp," dated more than 60 years ago. The smiling young man with the "G" on his cap was looking somewhere off beyond the camera, clearly expecting something wonderful that he was sure was coming soon.

"That's Grandpa at Spring Training."

"He was a Goat?"

"Frank Spalding, one season at third base for the Goats, although it's okay if you've never heard of him," Katie said. "I know nobody really pays much attention to the Goats, not even here."

"Grandpa gave practically his whole life to the Goats," Katie said. "He used to tell me he would have done anything as a kid to play for them. After he had to stop playing, he still went to every game. And he brought me with him, most of the time."

"Why did he end up leaving the game?"

Katie just led Sparky to another framed photo, this one behind the counter. In it, Frank looked even older than in the previous photo, even though he was still in full uniform. A number of Goats players were with him, all laughing at some joke presumably told by a short little man in the center of the picture – a short little man wearing a dark suit.

"Grandpa loved this town, loved the team," Katie said. "All he ever wanted was to be a Go-Town Goat. And when that man showed up, promising him he could make it happen...well, he always used to tell me, 'What else could I say, Katie? What else could I say?'"

Sparky's stomach froze solid in his gut, and his fingers began to tremble. In the center of the photograph, surrounded by Frank Spalding and his Goats teammates, looking no different than he did a year ago, was the rotund, greasy, smiling face of the odious Mr. Stitches.

"No way..."

"Grandpa said he didn't know what he was getting into at the time, but he learned soon enough," Katie continued. "The little man said he could help him make it onto the team, which he did."

Sparky's eyes wandered around the store, and he caught sight of several photographs of Frank as an older man posing with various Goats over the years. The most recent one, it appeared, was of him standing next to a younger Lance Bright. By the look on Lance's face, it was clear he had other things on his mind and other places to be.

"The Goats were at the top of the standings at the end of the season," Katie said, "but what Grandpa wasn't prepared for was the fact that Fort Clark was there, too. They had to play a one-game playoff for the division title and the playoffs. Zigleaf Field was packed solid, standing room only. The game was tied until the bottom of the eighth, when Grandpa hit a solo home run to give the Goats the lead. They were only three outs away from the team's first trip to the playoffs, ever."

Katie's eyes went blank as she gazed straight ahead. Her voice became almost a whisper. If she hadn't been so young, Sparky would have believed she had seen the game with her own eyes, but the effect of her grandfather telling her the story so often made her a virtual eyewitness anyway.

"The first two Canaries batters grounded out weakly – Grandpa said they looked like a team that was already thinking about next year. But the next two batters drew walks, and a wild pitch moved them into scoring position. The bottom of the Canaries' order was due up, and their catcher hit a pop fly that drifted into foul territory on the third base side. Grandpa chased it. He still had a play on it. But one of the fans, he was so excited, just like they all were, he reached out... He said later it was because he wanted to shake Grandpa's hand after he made the last out, but instead he got in between the ball and Grandpa's glove."

"Oh no..."

"The ball bounced off of the fan's hand and fell into the seats," Katie continued. "It was just a foul ball, but it kept the inning alive. The next pitch was hit softly into shallow left field, but Grandpa was so rattled by what had just happened that he..."

"Katie, it's okay," Sparky said. "You don't have to finish..."

"He was so rattled that he lost sight of the ball," Katie said, her voice suddenly strengthening. It was important that she finish the story, as it was every time she told it. "The runners came in to score and the game was basically over. The Goats went down in order in the bottom of the ninth. Grandpa said the city was as silent as a tomb for five whole days afterward."

Sparky and Katie stood in silence as they stared at the photo of Frank with his teammates. Frank looked happier than any person had a right to – he was a man who knew he was going to get everything he ever wanted out of life. The moment when he learned the horrible truth was far away, but not far enough.

"The newspapers were merciless – they called Grandpa every name in the book, and some more they made up just for him," Katie continued. "He said the thought of putting on a uniform again made him sick to his stomach, but the team saved him the trouble of deciding what to do. The owner called him into his office one day that winter and told him he was off the team, said it was in everyone's best interests." She paused as she watched an older man slow down in front of the shop's window. One of the old cards in the window had caught his attention, and for a moment a portion of a smile crept onto his face. But after a second it was gone, and he was on his way again.

"When Opening Day came the next season," Katie finally continued, "no one showed up. It wasn't just a small crowd; there was no crowd. Every seat was empty, and there wasn't a single ticket sold until May. Grandpa said it wasn't unusual for him to play in front of 100 people, if that. Just as quickly as the city was repainted orange and red, it was all scrubbed away and washed down the gutters."

"But you've kept it, even just a little piece of it," Sparky said. "At least someone still believes in us."

"Grandpa kept going to the games, even though it made him miserable," Katie said with a touch of anger in her voice. "He would carry me on his shoulders on the way into the ballpark, but after the ninth inning I would always be the one dragging him away. If the Goats got swept, and they almost always did, he would be in a funk for days. I would pray for the season to end some Septembers, just so I could see him smile again. He just wasn't the same person with the Goats hanging over his head. It was almost like he was paying for the break he got when he was a kid, like karma was coming back to take back what he had been given."

Katie finally broke her thousand-yard stare and looked into Sparky's eyes. "Grandpa loved baseball. He loved it so much he let it control every emotion he had. When he died, he told me I had to keep going to the games. 'Just keep score for me,' he said, 'and I'll be happy.' So I went, and I kept score, and I found out what baseball is."

"What is it?"

"Baseball is math, it's science. The ball goes where it goes not because the hitter has 'grit' or 'hustle' or any of those other things. It goes where it goes because of velocity, air currents … real things that you can see and measure. Grandpa always said, 'Sometimes this game doesn't make any sense, Katie. That's what's so amazing about it.' But he was wrong. The game makes perfect sense if you strip it all the way down to the numbers. All those years, that's what he was making himself sick over. He may as well have been depressed about the stock market, or the weather.

Baseball is a complex system, and once you crack the code it makes sense."

"And that's why you've been feeding me all these scouting reports and stuff," Sparky asked, "because you think you can help me crack the code?"

"No one else on the team would ever listen to me, so I thought it was worth a try," Katie said with a shrug. "To be honest, it would sort of be a relief if it was just over with once and for all."

At that moment, the store's door swung open and a pair of kids no older than 10 jostled their way inside. The slightly older of the two was holding a baseball card out of the younger one's reach and fighting him off with his free hand.

"I wanna hold it!" the littler one protested. "Come on, Danny!"

"You're gonna mess it up!" his older brother stated. "Shut up and let me do it!"

"Afternoon, gentlemen," Katie said as she took her position of authority behind the cash register. "What can I do for you today?"

The older boy held the card high in the air. "How much is this worth?"

Katie carefully plucked the card out of his hand and inspected it closely. "Well, it's in pretty good shape, but that's not surprising because it's only a few years old," she said. "The blue border means it's from the first series that year, which is a little better...I'd say five or six dollars."

The kids' jaws dropped in unison. "Five dollars?" the older one said.

"Or six," Katie corrected.

"But that's a Jim Priest rookie card! He hit .400 last year!" The boy pleaded his case with the intensity of an innocent man facing murder charges.

"Sorry boys, but it's not a Jim Priest rookie card," Katie said sympathetically. "This is from his second season in the Big Leagues. See, he's wearing his Hodgmanville Hobos uniform, but everybody forgets he actually came up with the Lake Wobegon Whippets in his rookie season and got traded a few weeks later."

"Oh..." the older boy moaned.

"We're sorry," said the younger one, suddenly assuming control of the transaction. He began to pull his brother away by his sleeve, but then his eyes grew wide as he finally took notice of Sparky's presence behind the counter. "Hey! Are you Sparky Katakura?"

Both boys immediately began hopping up and down in place in front of the counter, talking over each other in a jumble of high-pitched squeaking. The word "autograph" was the only thing that came out clearly.

"Okay, okay," Sparky said, trying to calm them down. "I'd be happy to sign an autograph, for each of you. What do you want me to sign?"

The boys looked at each other. "We don't have anything," the older one said, suddenly crestfallen. "Our dad won't let us collect anything from the Goats...he says it's a waste of time."

"Oh!" the younger boy went shuffling through a box of cards in neat little plastic sleeves and pulled out two. They were Sparky's most recent card, showing an unflattering picture of him squinting on the mound in the bright Spring Training sunshine, his Goats uniform still missing a uniform number. Sparky quickly signed the cards, returned them to their sleeves and handed them back to the chattering boys.

"You know, those are two bucks each," Katie told them. The boys looked back at her in disbelief. Sparky arched an eyebrow. "What?" she said to Sparky, smiling. "A girl's gotta make a living, right?"

"I'll cover you guys, don't worry about it," Sparky said. The boys bolted for the door and raced down the street, each one boasting that his card would be the more valuable of the two.

"So can I count on you to supply me with more of that interesting number stuff?" Sparky asked.

"If you come back in a week for an autograph session, it's a deal," Katie said, shaking his hand.

9. FLU-LIKE SYMPTOMS

The Goats managed to win two out of three against Smallville, and then split the four-game series with Minnesota. As the team relaxed in the locker room following the fourth game of the series, Sparky had once again sequestered himself at his locker, flipping intensely through the binder containing all of Katie's notes on the Canaries. He was so busy memorizing each batter's hot zones in anticipation of his start the next day, he didn't even notice Carlos standing in front of him until Carlos started snapping his fingers.

"Hey, roomie," Carlos laughed. "You getting ready for the SATs or something?"

"No, sorry, I was just doing a little scouting," Sparky answered, a little annoyed that he was seemingly the only one in the clubhouse who was. "What's up?"

"A bunch of us were going to hit the town, grab something to eat, maybe see a movie," Carlos said, looking around the locker room. Lance noticed him talking to Sparky and waved his arms like a third-base coach trying to stop a runner from heading home. "Do you wanna come with?"

"Thanks, Carlos, but I think I'd better get to bed early tonight," Sparky said, glaring at Lance. "You guys have fun, though."

"But you say that every time," Carlos protested. "Fuzzy says he thinks you're Amish or something. Come on, what's the big deal? You could mow those guys down even if you didn't get any sleep! Heck, I bet you could strike them all out even while you were sleeping!"

"I don't know, Carlos..."

"Dude, Lance says he's paying for everything tonight! Says he's so sure he's going to get his All-Star bonus that he wants to take us all out for steaks!"

"Lance is paying for everything?" Sparky asked as he caught Lance rolling his eyes and shaking his head. "In that case..."

Lou declined the invitation, saying he preferred to spend the night soaking his wobbly knees in the hot tub. Nonetheless, the majority of the Goats roster took Lance up on his offer and climbed into the team bus for a night on the town. Carlos wore a suit jacket and tie, but immediately felt foolish when he got on the bus and found his teammates dressed much more casually.

Lance, wearing a pair of mirrored sunglasses despite the fact it was already past sundown, rolled up the sleeves of his white tuxedo jacket and stood at the front of the bus like a military officer addressing his troops before sending them out into the fray.

"Gentlemen...and Katakura," Lance began, triggering some snickering in the back of the bus. "I know a lot of you are ready for some rest and relaxation with the All-Star break coming up..." Lance paused for effect. "But when you party with the Bright-man, rest and relaxation are the last things you get!" A loud cheer erupted from the team, with the exception of Sparky.

Thor stood up and threw his arms open wide. "A flagon of mead for all!" he shouted. The team let out another cheer.

"Wait," Fuzzy said, "is that a good thing?"

"Yeah, what's mead?" Bobby asked.

"Okay!" Lance shouted, clapping his hands together sharply. "Let's get this show on the road!"

More than an hour later, as the Goats sat contentedly around a massive table in Carl's Steakhouse – often recognized as Go-Town's best – they picked their teeth and marveled over the empty plates had only recently been covered with huge slabs of steak. Bobby was swirling the end of a breadstick around the edges of his plate, careful to swab up as much of the juice as he could. Sparky, for his part, ate nearly half of his ribeye before pushing the plate away. Not only was he skinnier than many of his teammates, but he also wanted to avoid feeling sluggish and weighed down for his start the next day.

As the busboys cleared away the stacks of dirty dishes, Lance called for the check. The manager, a stick-like man who looked like he had never eaten a steak in his life, came to the table waving his hands.

"No, no, I couldn't ask you gentlemen to pay," the manager said in a surprisingly deep voice. "Tonight's meal is on me, please."

The Goats let out a cheer and began pulling away from the table, slapping the manager on the back heartily as they filed out of the restaurant. Lance stood at the head of the table with a confused smirk on his face. "Thanks a lot, compadre," Lance said, "I guess all those years of me coming into this dive and classing it up are finally paying off, huh?" Lance gave the manager a friendly shove and pointed to a photo hanging over a nearby table. Sparky squinted in the dim light and made out that it was a photo of Lance, more than a few years younger, sitting at the very same table, surrounded by other ballplayers. Lance was in his Goats uniform, but the others were dressed in Fort Clark Canary yellow.

"Oh, it's not that, Mr. Bright, although we do appreciate your business," the manager said nervously. "We're just thrilled to see the Goats doing so well, and less than 10 games out of first place, no less! And we're so happy to have Sparky Katakura himself dining here!" The manager came up to Sparky and shook his hand enthusiastically.

"Wow, that's nice to hear," Sparky said, watching Lance grind his teeth out of the corner of his eye. "Lance didn't even want me to come along tonight!"

Lance's grimace flipped immediately to a beaming grin. "Ha-ha! What a kidder! Like I would ever turn a cold shoulder to the kid who's going to be the face of this team...after I retire, of course. Years from now."

"Think nothing of it, Brighty," Sparky said with a wink, "I know it's all part of hazing the new guy, right?" Sparky felt like he might be pushing his luck by needling Lance so much when it was bothering him so obviously. Then again, he thought, this guy's been a huge jerk all season, why not have a little fun with him?

The manager insisted on having Sparky sign a photo to display in the restaurant and engage in a little baseball talk, and when he finally emerged he found the rest of the team still standing in front of the bus, surrounded by fans. All of them were holding out baseball cards, pennants and balls for the Goats to sign. Some of them, caught by surprise by the team's presence, thrust paper napkins and scraps of pizza boxes in hopes of getting a few signatures.

"Hey Sparky!" Bobby called out, smiling. "Can you believe this?"

"I haven't signed so many autographs since the last time I had to get my driver's license renewed!" Fuzzy said. A crowd of kids huddled around VORP, who dispensed laser-printed autographs from a slot on his chest.

Lance stood off to the side, still seething. A little boy approached him with a card and pen in hand. "Mister Bright, could I have your autograph?" the boy asked.

"Sorry little guy, but I'm already doing a book signing at Midtown Books this Thursday night," Lance said coolly. "Why don't you tell your daddy to bring you over, buy a couple copies of my book and I'll be happy to sign them. Signature only, no special inscriptions."

Within minutes, Sparky was in the middle of the fray himself, signing an endless succession of memorabilia. One doughy man even asked Sparky to sign his pitching arm, explaining that he believed the autograph would give him some of Sparky's power and help him win his softball league. He told Sparky he would never wash his arm again, and when he lifted it for him to sign, Sparky believed he could keep that promise.

Meanwhile, a group of college-age girls had gathered around Fuzzy and Bobby, cooing as they touched Fuzzy's hair and giggling at Bobby's repertoire of lame jokes. Both made sure to include their phone numbers with several of the autographs.

With the crowd finally satisfied and the streetlights beginning to take over for the sun, the Goats piled back onto the bus, buzzing with excitement. "Man, I've got a cramp in my writing hand," Carlos said. "Hey Lance, is it always like this for you?"

"Nah, that was nothing," Lance said as he stared out the window. "Remind me to tell you the story of the time me and Oscar Philbert did a collector card show in Albany. Signed so many cards I actually got tired of seeing my own face. That was nothing."

"Jeez, you guys, if people get this excited about us when we're six games out of first place, imagine how they'd treat us if we actually won a pennant!" Bobby gushed.

"'If?'" VORP asked. "Heck, I think we WILL win the pennant this year, guys!"

"That's because your head is full of dead batteries, man!" Fuzzy replied. "Come on, it's nice to win a couple, but we're the same guys who lost 112 games last year! What makes you little guppies think we're just gonna come in outta nowhere and catch Fort Clark? Those guys kick our butts all the time!"

The mood on the bus became more subdued. Even VORP slunk back into his seat. Looking embarrassed, Bobby pulled a purloined breadstick out of his back pocket and began nibbling on it. Sparky watched as Lance chewed on his thumbnail, his eyes darting back and forth between each of his teammates. He wasn't sure, but it looked like Lance smiled ever so slightly as the bus pulled away from the restaurant.

The next morning, Sparky awoke with a slight tingle in his throwing arm. Great, he thought, of all the nights to sleep funny on his arm. But rather than work itself out, the tingle remained even after he got up and dressed, throughout his ride to the ballpark and his morning workout. In fact, the tingling continued to intensify until he was standing on the Zigleaf Field mound, in uniform, in a cold sweat as he tried to ignore the uncomfortable sensation and wondered how he would be able to pitch through it. He looked so rattled that Carlos visited him on the mound just moments before the first pitch.

"You don't look so good, Sparky," Carlos said.

"I'm fine," Sparky said quickly. "Just slept on my arm a little funny last night."

"You're sweating like a pig!"

"I'm okay, Carlos, really. Don't worry about it." Lance jogged past the mound on his way to right field.

"Looks like somebody partied a little too hearty last night, eh?" Lance smirked his signature smirk and tipped his cap to Sparky. "Just giving you a hard time, Sparkers, go knock 'em down."

"Yeah, maybe I will," Sparky said.

"Mel Fuller with Goats legend Randy Sannies at beautiful Zigleaf Field, and Sparky Katakura hasn't been knocking them down with the same efficiency we've become used to seeing from him, wouldn't you say, Randy?"

"Right."

"There's only one out here in the top of the first, and Sparky's pitch count is already in double-digits. He got the lead-off man Rickert to ground out to first, but allowed a walk to Lewis, who advanced to second after Cage grounded out to third. Now the Canaries have their heavy hitters coming to the plate, and up first is the heaviest hitter of them all, Bert Backlin. What would you say Sparky needs to do here in this situation, Randy?"

"Uh, strike him out, I suppose."

"Succinct as always, partner. Backlin is ready, and here's the pitch...and Backlin slaps a base hit between first and second into right field! Bright is slow to get to it, and Lewis comes around from second to score. Canaries lead 1-0, boy oh boy."

From first base, Backlin casually removed his batting gloves and gave Sparky a jaunty salute. "Hello there, friend! Nice to see you again!" Sparky didn't acknowledge the friendly greeting.

"That fastball didn't quite have the snap I'm accustomed to seeing from you. I do hope you're feeling all right!"

Sparky threw a fastball down the middle of the plate that the next hitter missed by a fraction of a second, eliciting a cheer from the Go-Town faithful in the crowd.

"If you're not quite feeling right, I could recommend a tonic that would put you right as rain again, if you'd like!" Backlin continued to chatter away from first base. "In the meantime, I hope you'll understand if I take full advantage of your condition."

Sparky's next pitch was a slider that broke too far across the plate and forced Lou to dive for it.

"It's normally my habit to hit for the cycle at least once each month, and I'm afraid I've fallen a little behind on that particular little chore," Backlin continued.

The next pitch dropped into the dirt, but the hitter was anxious and swung over it.

"As you can see, I've already collected a single, so perhaps the next time I see you I'll try to get the triple out of the way." Enraged by Backlin's insipid frivolity, Sparky forced his noodle-like arm to spit out an average fastball that caught the hitter by surprise for strike three. Sparky felt lucky to get out of the inning giving up just the one run, but with his arm becoming more and more tired with each passing moment, he wondered exactly how long he could continue.

Sparky took the mound in the top of the second with the game tied at 1, thanks to a stolen base from VORP that turned into a run when Carlos singled him home. But it seemed Sparky was destined to be off his game today, as he gave up a single, a walk and then a sacrifice groundout that moved both runners into scoring position. His arm was burning, it was unlike anything he had ever felt before. Each pitch caused his arm to scream in silence with pain, commanding him to stop immediately and get some rest.

The pain became overwhelming, and soon it was so intense Sparky couldn't see the single that put the Canaries up 2-1 through the tears in his eyes, nor the next one that made it 3-1. The next man up walked to load the bases. Lou approached the mound, but Sparky angrily waved him away. No matter what he was feeling at that moment, he thought, it couldn't be worse than what Ken was going through at that moment.

When Sparky finally blinked away the tears and regained his sight, he wished he hadn't – Backlin was striding to the plate, twirling his mustache to a mixture of catcalls and cheers from the half-and-half crowd. Glancing behind, Sparky could see one of the Ballpinos warming up in the bullpen. Backlin was likely to be the last batter Sparky would face today, so he resolved to get him out by any means necessary.

The first pitch was pure agony, a lighting bolt of pain that struck Sparky directly on the shoulder. Backlin watched it strike the mitt just outside the strike zone. Sparky shook his arm to try and get any kind of feeling other than pain into it, but he could barely lift it without wanting to cry. Nevertheless, Sparky clenched his teeth as hard as he could and served up the next pitch, one that sailed through the air with the sound of a gentle breeze instead of the sharp whoosh he was used to hearing. The next sound was the crack of the bat.

Sparky didn't even look up, just watched his shoes as he heard the roar of the crowd and Carlos calling for the ball. Then Fuzzy was calling for it. Then Bobby. When Sparky finally looked up, Backlin was standing on third, smiling serenely at Bobby. In left field, Thor was kicking at the grass and muttering curses to himself in some ancient language. Three runs scored on Backlin's promised triple, and now the Canaries led the Goats 6-1 in the top of the second inning. When Skip came to the mound, Sparky said nothing and handed him the ball. His afternoon was over.

The innings ticked on, with Sparky slumped on the dugout bench. Despite his teammates' insistence, he wouldn't go to the clubhouse to shower and change. Ordinarily all a pitcher can do after a bad outing is to try and wash it off, get a fresh start for the next time. But Sparky couldn't let it go, his numb arm a constant reminder that something might have just gone seriously wrong. The trainer and Skip looked his arm over from a hundred different angles, but physically there didn't seem to be anything wrong with him.

Even worse, the game seemed to have shifted into fast-forward, and time was running out. The Canaries cruised along through the third, fourth and fifth innings, and although Ted Ballpino didn't have his best stuff, the Canaries didn't seem all that interested in padding their lead any more than they already had.

As the bottom of the fifth began, Carlos sat down on the bench and peered down to the other end of the dugout. Sparky was still motionless, holding his right arm and looking for all the world like someone who had lost the most important game of his life. On the opposite end of the bench, Carlos watched Lance root around in a gym bag he had plopped down at his feet at the start of the game. Lance's eyes shifted around the entire dugout as he felt around for something, and finally he produced a small bundle wrapped in a small white towel. He placed it carefully by his side on the bench. Skip was pacing back and forth in front of the bench, muttering to himself.

"Bright!" Skip barked. "I thought I told you those gloves aren't allowed in my dugout!" Lance was wearing a pair of rhinestone-encrusted batting gloves, a gift he made sure to tell everyone he met that came from a big-time rock star and personal friend of his. Skip hated the way they glittered in the sunlight, and their appearance as a part of Lance's uniform was a constant source of strife between the two.

"Oh, sorry, Skip," Lance said flatly. "I'll switch them out for another pair tomorrow."

"You're gonna run back into that clubhouse and get another pair right now!" Skip growled. "I don't want anybody on my team wearing anything prettier than me, you got it?"

"Hey, if that was true, we'd all be wearing paper sacks, Skip!" Fuzzy chuckled from the middle of the bench.

"Shaddap, Fernandez! Bright, go change those glitter gloves right the heck now!" Lance scoffed, but peeled the twinkling gloves off his hands and trudged into the clubhouse, leaving his mysterious bundle behind. As soon as he was sure Lance was gone, Carlos scooted to the end of the bench and unwrapped the towel. His eyes went wide upon his discovery.

Resting in the middle of the white towel, like a baby in a hospital blanket, was a crudely made doll that nonetheless looked very much like Sparky, complete with a tiny glove made from a small scrap of leather. Sparky's glove – which he still hadn't removed – was missing a square patch of leather from the back of the webbing. Most troubling of all, the doll had several large pins sticking out of its shoulder and elbow. Carlos quickly removed these and scattered them underneath the bench. Almost immediately, Sparky began rubbing his arm and curling and extending his fingers as the feeling came back to them. The look of relief on his face was unmistakeable.

"Doesn't make any darn sense..." the sound of Lance's voice approaching from the tunnel spurred Carlos to hastily bundle the doll back up in the towel and dump it back on its spot on the pine. "Tell me something, Carlos..." Lance held up his gloved hands in front of Carlos' face. "What do you see here?"

"Uh, just a pair of batting gloves?" The ferocious look in Lance's eyes made Carlos worry that somehow he had seen Carlos messing with his voodoo doll. Voodoo doll! The words stood out in Carlos' head like they were written in 20-foot-high neon. How could anyone do something like that to a teammate? Especially when the league penalties for using voodoo are so strict! Carlos' mind was racing.

"'Just a pair of batting gloves,' exactly!" Lance huffed. "People come to the ballpark expecting a little razzle-dazzle from Lance Bright, and instead they have to be subjected to this...mediocrity. It's a real shame, you know? Wouldn't surprise me if attendance started dropping."

"Thine complaints are the same every time thine gauntlets are besmirched, noble Lance," Thor offered. "For the sake of thine compatriots, cease thy prattling and earn huzzahs for thine deeds!"

"What?"

"He says shut up about your stupid gloves and play some stupid baseball," Fuzzy translated. Lance scowled and dropped back onto the bench next to Carlos.

"Houston grounds out to lead off the bottom of the fifth for the Goats, and now the count is 2-1 for Ballpino. Hetfield hasn't been overpowering for the Canaries on the mound today, but he's been effective nonetheless. Here comes the pitch, and Ballpino lines one into shallow center for a base hit! That'll bring VORP to the plate, and how do you think Hetfield is going to approach pitching to the speedy android, Randy?"

"I think he's going to try and get him out, Mel."

"Only fifteen years in the Big Leagues will give you that kind of insight, folks. Hetfield works the count to 2 and 2, and there's another base hit! Ballpino takes second, VORP cruises into first and the Goats are in business here as they try to crawl out from under that six-run deficit! Are you feeling optimistic, Randy?"

"Uh, well, um. I mean, well..."

"That's the spirit, partner! And here comes young Carlos Cabarellos to face the increasingly shaky Hetfield. Look at the concentration on the face of the Goats' first baseman, he understands what's at stake here. No one up in the Canaries' bullpen, their manager O'Malley famous for being stingy with his relievers in preparation for the playoff stretch, but let's see if the Goats can give him a reason to change his mind in this one. The windup and the pitch from Hetfield, and it's a wild pitch! It gets away from the catcher, Ballpino and VORP advance and now we have two men in scoring position, still only one out! Excitement starting to build here at Zigleaf Field, right, Randy?"

"Yes sir."

Carlos dug his cleats into the dirt of the batter's box and tightened his grip on the bat. From the dugout, he could hear Lance still complaining about his batting gloves. Energized once again, Sparky leaned over the dugout rail and started clapping with enthusiasm.

"Come on, Carlos! Just put it in play!"

"Swing for the fences, kid!" Lance countered. "What good is one run going to do now, anyway? Go for the gusto!"

The sound of Lance's voice was like sandpaper on Carlos' ears now. He narrowed his eyes and watched as the ball came hurtling out of the pitcher's hand. It looked hittable, a straight fastball without a lot of extra velocity on it. Carlos reached out with his swing and felt the contact sting his hands. The runners took off, and Carlos sped down the first-base line, but before he could touch the plate he saw the ball strike the first baseman's glove with a pop. He turned around to see Ballpino crossing home plate, then jogged sullenly back to the dugout.

"Nice job, kid," Skip said as Carlos passed.

THE BIG LEAGUES

"I could have done better," Carlos responded.

"Don't beat yourself up, hoss," Lou said. "A run's a run, and it's better than nothing at this point. This game ain't over yet."

"So with that groundout, the Canaries' lead is trimmed down to 7-2, and here's Fuzzy Fernandez, who has walked and rapped into a double play already today. Is it me, Randy, or does Fuzzy seem agitated to you?"

"Uh, yeah, a little bit, Mel."

"He appears to be yelling something at the dugout, I don't know if he's talking to Skip LaRoche about the signs or what's going on, but...wait, it looks like right fielder Lance Bright is at the railing, I think they're having some kind of disagreement about something. Randy, can you hear what they're saying to each other?"

"I think I heard Fuzzy say something about gloves, Mel."

"I heard that, too. And the two are still chattering away as Hetfield gets set for the pitch. Here it comes...and it's high for a ball. Boy, Fernandez is really upset, Randy. We've seen Fuzzy argue with umpires, we've seen him get into it with the fans on occasion, but I don't think I've ever seen him this irritated before, and at a teammate, no less. The next pitch is low for ball two."

"Jeez."

"Now Fernandez is really getting into it with Bright, and I'm sure I heard him say, 'Shut up about your stupid gloves, already, you big blonde monkey-boy!'"

"Yikes."

"Indeed, Randy. Now the 2-0 pitch from Hetfield...is lined into left field for a base hit! VORP comes around to score and now it's a 7-3 ballgame!"

Sparky watched helplessly from the dugout as Backlin approached the plate with a man on first in the top of the sixth. His arm had snapped back to working condition, and he felt like he could throw 18 innings. Ted Ballpino, on the other hand, was looking as nervous as a rookie on the last day of Spring Training before the final roster cuts. He couldn't stop scratching his nose as Backlin loitered outside the batter's box, clearly relishing the fear he instilled in the reliever.

Finally, both pitcher and hitter were ready. Ballpino rocked back and sprung forward, his arm whipping forward like a catapult. Backlin heaved a sigh and effortlessly cut through the warm summer air with a swing that caught the ball directly over the plate. The outfielders jumped to attention, but in an instant they dropped their heads. The ball landed in a forest of grasping hands in the bleachers, another in a long line of souvenirs Burt Backlin had given crowds at Zigleaf Field. After the Goats worked so hard to scrape together a couple of runs, the Canaries had taken them back as easily as having the bat boy deliver a new bat. It was a six-run game again, 9-3 Fort Clark.

Carlos was furious. As the bottom of the sixth began, he paced back and forth in the dugout, his batting gloves on and tight.

"You know you're probably not going to get an at-bat this inning, right, sport?" Lance was peeking out from under the brim of his cap as he tried to catch a quick nap.

"Maybe I just want to be ready, Lance," Carlos replied. His preparedness was about to be rewarded.

Thor led off the inning with a walk as Hetfield deliberately avoided the crackling lightning of his bat. Bobby struck out swinging, but Blerk tried to headbutt a pitch and was given first base for his plunking, which O'Malley protested vigorously but fruitlessly. With two on and one out, Lou waited Hetfield out and took a full-count ball four to load the bases.

Ballpino stepped up to the plate and took a few nervous swings. Hetfield looked incredibly annoyed, not because he was afraid of giving up runs but because his gum had lost its flavor and he wanted to get a new stick from the dugout. He pulled the colorless wad out of his mouth and stuck it to the back of his cap.

The first pitch to Ballpino was a tailor-made strike, straight and belt-high. Ballpino watched it whiz by. The next pitch was slow enough for the stocky reliever to take a swing at it, but fast enough to evade his bat. On the third pitch, Hetfield uncorked a breaking ball that only broke halfway, and with a look of absolute surprise Ballpino slapped the mid-speed meatball over the head of the Canaries' second baseman for a solid single. The crowd erupted as Thor crossed the plate, and with Ballpino standing slack-jawed on first the Goats still had the bases loaded. Carlos smiled as he watched VORP clank and clunk his way to the plate. As long as there was no double play, Carlos would get his chance. Lance had managed to doze off on the bench.

"Oh boy," VORP chirped once he reached home plate, "this is swell! Bases loaded, only one out! Even if I make an out, this is drama right here! This is why we play the game! This is why..."

"This is why nobody in the Central League can stand listening to you," snarled the Canaries' catcher. "Just hurry up and bounce into the DP so we can get this stupid game over with? At this rate we're gonna miss our dinner reservations!"

"Well, that's a pretty lousy attitude to have, pal! We should all be happy that we're lucky enough to play Big League baseball! Why, ever since I was booted up, I wanted to play Big League baseball, and every day I want to just keep playing until they shut me down for the night!"

"Jeez, where's the off switch on this guy?" the catcher shouted at the Goats' bullpen.

"Don't listen to that guy, VORP!" Sparky shouted back. "You can do it! We're not out of this yet!"

"Yeah, man, let's go!" Carlos said from the on-deck circle. He turned to give Sparky a thumbs-up.

"Well gosh," VORP sputtered, "if you really think so..." The robot's arms whirred and buzzed as he hefted the lumber off his shoulder and took a powerful swing. The crowd practically jumped out of their seats as the ball came screaming through the air, curling toward the third baseline like a comet plummeting through space. Blerk and Lou came around to score. The players on the Go-Town bench stomped their feet and exchanged high-fives. Skip even gave Blerk a bear hug as he came down the dugout steps.

Carlos was beaming as he stepped up to the plate. He watched the first three pitches whiz by without batting an eye. He knew the pitch he was looking for, and he knew Hetfield was going to give it to him. Now that the count was 2-1, Carlos knew Hetfield was going to try to overpower him, and he didn't look capable of that at the moment. Sweaty and puffing his cheeks out with each breath, Hetfield looked wiped out. O'Malley, leaning over the Canaries' dugout railing, showed no signs of sympathy from behind his sunglasses. There was no way he was going to use a reliever unless absolutely necessary.

Carlos watched Hetfield fling the next pitch off his fingertips. Drops of sweat flew off his forehead as he snapped forward across the mound. The pitch was spinning madly through the air – just as Carlos predicted, it was the fastball, but it wasn't moving nearly as fast as it was two innings ago. The crack of the bat reverberated throughout the stadium, followed by the elated screams of thousands of Goats fans and the irritated groans of slightly more Canaries fans. The ball skidded on the grass to the right fielder's left, careening toward the wall. The right fielder gave chase, giving Ballpino and VORP enough time to scamper across home plate. As he touched first base, Carlos saw the right fielder bobble the ball in his glove. A two-run single was nice, but Carlos knew he could do more good from second base. He turned the corner.

"Hold up, kid!" Carlos could hear Lou calling from the dugout, along with several other of his teammates, but the voice that stood out above the rest was Sparky's.

"Go, Carlos! Go!" Carlos felt his legs burning as he closed the gap between first and second. The shortstop planted his foot on the base and stretched out his glove in the direction of right field. Carlos reached out and left his feet, as if he could grab second base out from under the infielder with his hands. His body landed in the crushed brick infield and he slid for what felt like a mile, just waiting to feel the base with his fingertips. Instead, Carlos felt a strong tap on the top of his helmet, heard the umpire bark "Yer out!" Holding back tears, Carlos slumped back to the dugout.

"I messed up, Sparky," he said with his head down.

"That was my fault, roomie, I thought you had it for sure," Sparky said. "You were flying, he just made a heck of a throw. What are you so worried about, anyway? You just made it a one-run game!"

"An out's an out, Sparky. I just brought us closer to the end of the game by wasting an out. I won't let you lose this game, Sparky. Lance has had me playing for myself and just myself this whole time, when we all should have been playing for each other. I can't be that stupid anymore."

"It's okay, man," Sparky said as he grabbed Carlos by the shoulders. "I know you can do it."

The seventh and eighth innings passed quickly, as neither Ballpino nor the relief pitcher finally brought in to replace Hetfield allowed any runs to score. Each Goats out caused the Go-Town dugout to groan and the Canaries dugout to sigh in relief. The game had finally moved into the bottom of the ninth inning, and O'Malley – with a pained expression on his face – called for the Canaries' closer, Clint Burton. Skip shook his head upon seeing the stone-faced Burton take the mound. Burton had saved all 30 games he had entered up to this point, and saved his last 45 of the previous season, and his tendency to work a quick 1-2-3 inning was well known even outside of the Central League. The sight of Burton on the hill sent a shiver through the Goats' bench, all except for two.

One of those Goats was Carlos, who stood in the on-deck circle and took his practice cuts. Carlos was most definitely aware of Burton's reputation, but he couldn't think about it at the moment. He tried to convince himself that the pitcher was nothing more than a faceless rookie, more afraid of Carlos than he was of him. Maybe if he had been given another hour to warm up, he might have started to believe it.

The other Goat who was unfazed by Burton's appearance was Lance, who was still too sleepy to pay much attention to what was going on.

Carlos' attempt to pretend there was any fear on the pitcher's mound failed the second he stepped into the batter's box and saw Burton's unblinking gaze fixed squarely on him. The pitcher's eyes were as gray and cold as tombstones, his face as blank as a brick wall. Carlos took one look at Burton and thought about asking the umpire if he could forfeit his at-bat just so he could go sit down again.

Nevertheless, Carlos turned to look into the dugout and saw his teammates standing and clapping for him. They were shouting words of encouragement, and even if Carlos couldn't make out what they were saying exactly he understood the meaning perfectly.

Burton nodded at the sign from the catcher and went into his windup. The first pitch zipped in and Carlos decided in a fraction of a second it was a good one to hit. He swung with all the force he could muster, but came up with nothing. The Go-Town crowd groaned as one.

As Carlos waited for the next pitch, he could hear Lance's voice inside his head, chiding him for all the times he had overexerted himself trying to get a hit in a meaningless game.

"What's a meaningless game?" he asked once back in April.

"With this team? All of them," Lance replied with a snort.

How many times had that advice hurt the team, Carlos wondered? How many times had Carlos given away a game for the Goats because he was only concerned with following Lance's formula for a sure-fire successful Big League career? How badly had Carlos hurt his teammates because he wasn't thinking of anyone but himself?

The next pitch came in just as fast and as straight as the first one, but this time Carlos didn't see the ball. Instead of the familiar white with red stitches, he saw the smirking face of Lance Bright, his thinning hair fluttering through the air.

"Come on, kid," Carlos swore he could hear the ball say, "The last thing you want to do is wear out your shoulders trying to win a game for these losers."

There was a jolt that went straight up Carlos' arms as he struck the ball with all his strength. For the first time, Burton's eyes were diverted from the death-stare he had been giving Carlos. Now, his eyes were fixed instead on the ball as it arced high above the outfield in a booming rainbow of a shot that ended in the hands of a skinny kid with glasses and a Goats cap. The game was tied.

Carlos returned to the dugout through a forest of high-fives. When he emerged from the giddy mass of teammates, he was nearly eye-to-eye with Lance. "That sure was something, buddy," Lance said flatly as he plopped his batting helmet onto his head. He curled his lips into a smirk and slapped Carlos on the shoulder. "Next time, though, how about you have some consideration for your teammates who weren't planning on taking another at-bat, huh?"

"Man, don't even start with that," Carlos said as Lance brushed past him.

"Come on, bro, it was just a little joke, okay, hombre?"

"And what you did to Sparky, was that just a little joke, too?"

Lance stopped dead in his tracks and turned slowly to look he rookie right in the eyes. "What the heck are you talking about?"

"Yeah, what are you talking about, Carlos?" Lou had pulled himself away from the railing after hearing the two jawing at each other. "You think Bright did something to the kid? That's a pretty serious accusation."

Carlos stared down Lance, trying to will him into confessing, but of course the cagey veteran only glared back at him. Just then, Skip's broken-glass voice snapped the tension between the two of them.

"Bright! Get your butt out there in the on-deck circle, for crying out loud!" Without another word, Lance turned and stomped out onto the field.

"What were you talking about with Bright?" Lou inquired.

"I'll tell you later. I'll tell everybody later. Right now, we have to win this game."

"You'll get no argument from me, kid. Whatever you and Golden Boy have going on can wait until later."

"Mel Fuller with Randy Sannies welcoming you back to Zigleaf Field, where a game that looked like a sure thing for Fort Clark has just gotten a lot more interesting, right, partner?"

"For sure."

"And just in case you folks at home can't tell through Randy's excitement, the score is 9-9 in the top of the 10th. The Canaries have a man on second and at the plate is that old Goat-slayer, Bert Backlin himself. Ballpino still on the mound in relief for the Goats, unless that's not still Todd and it's his brother Ted instead. Or I suppose it could be Tad – Randy, what's your call?"

"Hm. Ah..."

"Here's the pitch from the Ballpino currently on the mound, and it's in there for strike one."

"Gee, um..."

"The next pitch from Ballpino is swung on, here comes trouble! Curling into the right field corner, Bright chasing after it! Ulrich being waved around third, he'll score from second to break the tie! Backlin motors into second standing up, and the beefy Canaries infielder has hit for the cycle today – a single, triple, home run and now the double to complete the collection. Boy oh boy, what a blow to this Goats team who had made such a startling comeback on the shoulders of young Carlos Caballeros."

"I think that's Ted Ballpino out there, Mel."

"You can only wonder what must be going through the mind of the Goats' rookie first baseman right now."

"We're screwed," Carlos said as he tossed his glove onto the dugout bench.

"Hey now, come on, that ain't no kind of talk when we still have three outs to use," Lou said as he pulled on his batting gloves. "A lot can happen with three outs. Years ago, I was playing in San Diego, and there was this dude, not unlike yourself, who had been struggling at the plate for a heck of a long slump. With the team down three in the last of the ninth, that kid hit a grand slam and got his team the win."

"Let me guess," Fuzzy chimed in, "it was you, right, cowboy?"

"Nope," Lou said. "But I was the guy who called for the fastball on the 3-0 count."

The bottom of the inning did not begin promisingly. Lou was able to work the count to 3-1, but he wasn't able to make good contact on the next pitch, and ended up bouncing it to short for the first out. Ted Ballpino couldn't manage any better than a soft roller down the third baseline, and he was easily thrown out for the second out of the inning. Carlos stepped into the on-deck circle as VORP stood in at the plate, twirling his bat in the air and humming a jaunty tune through his buzzy speakers. At first base, Backlin yawned and lazily slapped his glove against his leg.

VORP cheerfully took the first two pitches outside and away for balls, then fouled off the next two to even the count. Then Burton uncorked a fastball that rode high and tight on VORP, causing him to extend his neck a good six inches to avoid being hit in the face with it. The count was full, but VORP continued to hum to himself without a care in the world. On the next pitch, what looked like a sure-fire strike right down the middle ended up breaking late and low, practically scraping the plate as it crossed. With the crowd exhaling a sigh of almost-relief mixed with irritation, VORP jogged to first. Carlos would get to the plate after all.

From the dugout, Sparky watched as Carlos took a deep breath before stepping into the batter's box. The anxiety that had always been there in the corners of Carlos' eyes were gone, at least from Sparky's point of view. He didn't expect Carlos to look into the dugout for encouragement or advice, the way he had all season. The crowd in the bleachers might have seen the same rookie from Opening Day, but Sparky knew just by watching him that Carlos had done a lot of growing up over the course of this game. Nine opponents on the field, 40,000 in the stands, millions watching from home – all with their eyes riveted to the young man at the plate.

"Caballeros having a tremendous day at the plate, but in danger of being overshadowed by the achievements of Bert Backlin. Still, even if nothing else happens today, you have to be impressed with the progress this kid has made, Randy."

"Oh, sure."

"Caballeros takes the first pitch from Burton for strike one. On any other day, Randy, nine runs from this Goats team ought to be enough to win. The next pitch is high for ball one, and the count is even. But today, the Goats just happened to run right into the immovable brick wall of the Fort Clark Canaries, and you just have to tip your cap to them."

"Mmph."

"And the next pitch is...in there for strike two, and now Caballeros and the Goats are down to their last strike. Time to name our Player of the Game, and today the always impressive Bert Backlin hit for the cycle and drove in nearly all of the Canaries' runs, so we name him our Player of..."

"Hey!"

"There's a drive to left! Goats win! Goats win! Carlos Caballeros hits a deep drive that clears the left field bleachers to score two! He did it again! He did it again! Can you believe it? In a game in which the improbable was not expected, the impossible has just happened!"

Carlos watched as the ball cleared the fence and soared past the massive trunks of the zigleaf trees, but he knew from the moment he hit the ball that it was going out. He felt the ball collide with center mass on the barrel of the bat, the vibration jolting his hands cleanly with no stinging. Most of all, he felt the roar of the crowd as the legions of Goats fans became one voice, drowning out the Canaries fans for the first time all year. The noise swallowed him up, and he couldn't even hear his own footfalls as he rounded the bases. The next thing he heard was the screaming of his teammates as he met them at home plate.

The clubhouse was still in a state of euphoria more than half an hour later as the Goats celebrated. Sparky, Fuzzy, Thor and Bobby were gathered around Carlos' locker.

"Verily, friend Carlos, thy deeds today are worthy of being retold around the table in Valhalla!" Thor declared, lifting his hammer into the air and punching a hole in the ceiling in the process.

"Hey, what did Backlin say to you when you touched first, man?" Fuzzy said as he playfully knocked Carlos' cap off of his head.

"Aw dude, I don't know if I can say it out loud with Bobby standing right here," Carlos said.

"Hey, what the heck is that supposed to mean?" Bobby asked.

"This is what I've been talking about since Spring Training, you guys," Sparky said. "Isn't this a whole lot more fun than getting stepped on every day?"

"Well of course it is," Bobby said. "But up until now we didn't even know we could do this!"

Just then, Carlos' expression went sour, and the rest of the Goats turned to see Lance standing behind them. He was holding out his hand to Carlos, grinning his same old made-for-TV grin.

"Way to go out there, rookie," Lance said with a half-hearted laugh.

"Yeah, well, someone had to step up out there." Carlos didn't return the handshake.

"That's what the Bright-man likes to see in a rookie, someone just says to heck with it and does it himself. Good to see I'm starting to rub off on you."

"Oh yeah? So how long do you think it'll be before I start trying to sabotage my own teammates?"

Lance's face went white, no small feat considering the amount of tanning he had done over the years. "Buddy, hey," he stammered. "What the heck do you mean?"

"Sparky wasn't sick today – Lance put the voodoo on him."

The Goats gathered at Carlos' locker immediately stood up to look Lance right in the eyes. Lance put his hands up and started tip-toeing away from the increasingly hostile scene in front of him.

"Hey, come on you guys...are you really going to believe the kid? He's all amped up from the game, he doesn't know what he's saying! I mean, what kind of proof does he have?"

Just then, VORP came ambling up and handed Lance the doll Carlos had found in his equipment bag during the game. "Hey, Lance! I caught Blerk poking around in your locker and he was playing with your Sparky doll," VORP said. "It looked kind of fragile, so I thought I should give it to you for safe keeping. Boy, what a game today, huh? Makes me wish we were playing again right now!"

VORP sauntered off to his locker again, leaving Lance holding the voodoo doll with a contingent of angry teammates staring him down. "Really, guys? This is an, uh, art project! Yeah, I was going to make one for each of you guys as a gift at the end of the season, but now that robot had to go and ruin the surprise, heh! Well, guess I better get back to working on this one..."

"Not so fast," Sparky said. "Correct me if I'm wrong, guys, but isn't the use of voodoo strictly forbidden outside of the Midnight League?"

"Aye," Thor said. "It would appear that Lance hath broken league rules."

"And against his own teammate, too," Fuzzy said. "Man, what kind of a cockroach do you have to be to do something like that?"

"You'd have to be some kind of mega-uber-super-jerk to do that," Bobby said. "Wow, getting caught with something like that would do all kinds of bad things to someone's image, wouldn't it?"

"Verily. Such a despicable act could make the cur an outcast, banished for all time to the wilderness to atone for his crime!"

"And worse than that, it would ruin his chances for getting into the Hall of Fame, right?" Sparky couldn't help but smile a little as Lance began to sweat. "But this is a team matter, so I say we deal with it as a team. Fair is fair, right Lance?"

"What are you talking about?"

"Kangaroo court," Sparky explained. "We get the team together and we vote on what your punishment should be. No managers, no league officials. You agree to take your punishment or we take this to the Central League office."

Lance furrowed his brow and stuck out his jaw, as if readying himself for a punch to the face. "Okay, fine," he said. "I'm not worried. You guys can't do anything to me, anyway. I'm the All-Star on this team, so I'll still be living it up with my peers – my real peers, that is – while you losers come up with your little punishment."

"Hey, you bums," Skip said as he waddled up to the group. His belt was unbuckled and his gut spilled out from under his jersey. "I just got a message from the Big League Baseball office about the All-Star Game that everybody needs to hear right away!"

"I hope they're sending a new limo service to pick me up from the airport," Lance said. "Can you believe they didn't have satellite TV last year? That's just a lack of respect, am I right guys?"

"The starting lineups for the game just got posted, and one of the starters is going to be Katakura! Nice job, kid."

As the rest of the Goats started applauding, Lance grabbed

Skip by the arm. "Skip, what's going on? How is this going to work? I thought they only allow one player from a team to play in the All-Star Game."

"Yeah, that's right," Skip said as he jerked his arm out of Lance's grip.

"So how am I going to be in the game with Katakura?"

"You're not," Skip said bluntly. "Jeez Louise, you been licking pine tar or something?" Skip returned to his office, leaving Lance standing alone in the center of the locker room, watching Sparky receive congratulations from the rest of the team.

"Well, anyway, I'm not worried about your little kangaroo court," Lance told Sparky after the last Goat had shaken his hand. "I've played with most of these guys for years, they think I'm a god. You're going to have one heck of a time convincing them to side with you over their old buddy the Bright-man."

BRIGHT ANNOUNCES ABRUPT RETIREMENT
By Roy Myko, Go-Town Gazette
After 10 seasons of coasting, it seems inertia finally has brought Lance Bright's career to a halt. The never-camera-shy right fielder for the Go-Town Goats suddenly announced his retirement Wednesday, just days before the Big League All-Star Game in New York City. At a hastily assembled press conference yesterday, Bright said what many have been saying for some time.

"As painful as it is to admit, my baseball career is over," Bright told the assembled reporters, some of whom came from as far away as three blocks over to pay their respects to one of Go-Town's baseball icons.

A controversial figure when anyone bothered to talk about him, Bright became well-known in Go-Town more for his propensity to shill for any product rather than his skill on the diamond. For years, Bright's face was as common a sight in downtown Go-Town as a traffic light, even if more people paid attention to the latter.

Many forget that Bright's career in the Big Leagues actually started promisingly, as he slugged 221 home runs over his first five seasons with the Ivy Town Professors in the Zenith League. Over time, however, Bright seemingly became more interested in promoting himself than helping his team win, and he bounced from city to city over the course of the next decade.

Although he should have been on the brink of retirement, Bright signed a 15-year contract with the Goats after a disappointing season with the El Dorado Gold Caps. Rumors that Goats owner Arthur J. Mint IV signed Bright believing him to be much younger have never been confirmed, nor should they be expected to.

When asked if his retirement had anything to do with the selection of pitcher Sparky Katakura to represent the Goats in the All-Star Game over himself, Bright remained, as always, obtuse. "I wish the little guy all the luck in the world," Bright said through his teeth. "But I just felt the time was right to move on and wait to hear from the Hall of Fame, who shouldn't pay attention to any strange rumors about me that may or may not be floating around."

10. THE ALL-STAR BREAK

Sparky took a deep breath before stepping onto the field. Even though he had been tested against cyclops, robots, vampires and golem, it was hard for him not to feel a little intimidated by Imperial Stadium, even when it was empty. The outfield grass was freshly mowed, and if Sparky had taken the time to get down on his hands and knees he would have found that each blade of grass was exactly the same height. A breeze caused the Emperors' multitude of championship pennants to flap and flutter proudly. There had been so much history on this field, much of it before Sparky was even born. He could rattle a hitter with a well-placed fastball, but there was nothing Sparky could do to face the jitters he experienced now.

There already was a small crowd of players standing in center field, where a heavy-set man in a suit held court. It didn't take long at all for Sparky to recognize the man in the suit as Bob Honcho, one of the Emperors' all-time great third basemen and now a liaison from the Commissioner's Office. Even though his face was puffy and wrinkled, Honcho still wore the same confident grin he brought to the plate in his playing days. The players who gathered around him were rapt, hanging on his every word. Honcho held a sealed gold envelope in his hand, casually waving it around as he joked around with the players. He was in the middle of telling a story when Sparky approached the group.

"...and as I'm sure most of you know, back in those days they hadn't built the dome over Atlantis, so those games were all played outside, as it were," Honcho said.

"So how'd you guys play underwater?" asked the player representing the Vermont Tappers.

"Well, you ever been scuba diving?" Honcho said. "Just like that, you put your tank and your mask on and you just hoped you didn't use up your oxygen supply during warm-ups. So anyway, we're down there for a series against the Mermen, and I hit this ball, but I get on top of it. Now, in any other ballpark in the galaxy, that ball bounces in front of home plate and becomes a hard chopper, maybe an infield hit, right? Not in Atlantis, buster. That ball went right into the sandy ocean bed and just – POP! – sunk in there. And I mean it was deep, boy. By the time they finally found it and dug it out, I was backstroking my way across home plate."

The assembled ballplayers collectively "ooh"ed in amazement.

"So, if you look up the longest home run ever hit in the Big Leagues," Honcho continued, "you'll see my good buddy Captain Awesome and his 1,321-foot homer in the Worlds Series. But, you're not ever going to see the ball old Bob Honcho hit that day – 34 inches." That sparked a round of laughter from the players on the field, and Honcho took the opportunity to excuse himself from the group and make his exit. On the way out, however, he stopped to extend a big meaty hand to Sparky.

"You're Katakura, aren't you?"

"That's right," Sparky said as his hand was engulfed by the big outfielder's handshake.

"I'm real glad you're here, son, because it saves us a little bit of trouble. Why don't you and I take a walk while the other guys get the lay of the land? I don't think there's any doubt you'll actually be playing in the game this year."

"You don't think so? There's 200 ballplayers out there and only 25 roster spots on each team. How do you know I'll get picked?"

"Because I'm one of the captains this year, that's why," Honcho chuckled. As he led Sparky off the field, Sparky could feel someone staring at him. He turned to see a player in the familiar New York Emperors pinstriped uniform watching him from outside of the group of All-Stars. The mysterious Emperor didn't look away even when Sparky spotted him, but that wasn't the strangest thing about him – it was the painted metallic mask that covered his face. He was still watching Sparky, motionless, as Honcho led him off the field.

Honcho brought Sparky to an elevator at the end of a long corridor under the grandstands of Imperial Stadium, which was guarded by a mean-looking security guard who let them pass without a word. When the doors opened, Honcho showed Sparky into an office even bigger than he remembered Mr. Mint's being. Seated at a desk that looked more like the wall of a fortress was a smiling old man in a crisp suit with wavy silver hair. He stood as soon as Sparky entered the room.

"Sparky Katakura," the old man said warmly. "I'm so glad to finally meet you in person. I've become a big fan of yours over the course of this season."

"Uh, thanks a lot," Sparky said.

"My name is Mr. Oni, and I'm the current owner of the New York Emperors. When Mr. Honcho informed me that you would be taking part in the All-Star festivities here this weekend, I was thrilled."

"I have to say, I'm pretty excited to be here myself. I was a San Carlos fan growing up, but seeing the Emperors on Game of the Week was always exciting for me." Sparky felt a twinge of pain as he remembered watching those games with Ken after Little League on Saturday afternoons.

"That's excellent, excellent. I'm happy to hear that the team has meant a lot to you over the years. In fact, that makes what I wanted to talk to you about all the more special."

Mr. Oni was interrupted by the sound of a toilet flushing from inside the wall of his office. A hidden door opened and Mr. Mint emerged, drying his hands on a snow-white towel monogrammed with a golden "O."

"My, my, my," Mr. Mint exclaimed. "Solid gold fixtures! You really do know how to live big here in New York City, Mr. Oni! Oh, Sparky! I didn't see you there! Whatever are you doing here in New York?"

"I'm here for the All-Star Game, Mr. Mint."

"Well, that's splendid! You see here, Oni? My players are so dedicated to the game of baseball that they will travel to watch an exhibition even during their vacations!"

"No, Mr. Mint, I'm here to play in the All-Star Game."

Mr. Mint blinked his eyes several times. "Oh, I see. Was Lance not able to attend for some reason? If he's injured, our entire season goes down the drain, you know!"

"Lance retired a few days ago, Mr. Mint."

"He did?"

"...And this leads directly into why I asked you gentlemen to join me here in my office this morning," Mr. Oni broke in. "My general manager noticed your need of a right fielder, and I believe we can be of service to each other." Mr. Oni motioned to the back of the room, and Sparky jumped when he saw the same masked Emperor from before standing silently behind him.

"Oh, he's quiet!" Mr. Mint said.

"He also has the best slugging percentage in the Metropolitan League," Mr. Oni added. "Not to mention one of the best on-base percentages and a league leader in all the pertinent fielding metrics. Number 7 is, quite honestly, one of the best players in the game right now, and I am offering him to you and your Goats, Arthur."

"Well, that's mighty generous of you, Oni! He sounds like a

real corker of a ballplayer!" Mr. Mint leaned over and whispered to Sparky: "Say, have you ever heard of this 'slugging percentage?'"

"Just a moment, Arthur," Mr. Oni said. "I know you're a shrewd businessman, and as such you wouldn't expect me to simply give Number 7 away without asking for something in return, would you?"

"Ah, well, no, I suppose not," Mr. Mint said, disappointed.

"What's up with the mask?" Sparky asked.

"When I purchased the Emperors some years ago, I understood that I wasn't simply buying a baseball team," Mr. Oni said, turning his back to gaze out the enormous window of his office with its view of the New York City skyline. "I was buying a legacy, an institution, a way of life. The Emperors are more important to this city than the Empire State Building, the Brooklyn Bridge and the Metropolitan Museum of Art put together, and that means that no one player should ever become more important than the team. That's why, when a player puts on the Emperors uniform, he must keep his identity concealed. I believe players play for the name on the front of the jersey, not the one on the back. If we allowed names on the backs of the jerseys, that is."

"I don't remember ever seeing this before," Sparky said.

"Well, you probably wouldn't have, unless you were one of our Emperor Vision subscribers. I won't allow games to be broadcast to just anyone – I only want true Emperors fans to have the privilege of watching their team, and what better way to determine a fan's loyalty than charging admission?"

"You have some very interesting ideas, Oni," Mr. Mint said. "I should like to discuss these with you further once we settle the little matter of your trade here. Now tell me, what were you seeking in return for that silent specimen over there?"

"I think you'll find it a fair offer," Mr. Oni said. "All I ask for in return ... is Sparky."

"Hmm..." Mr. Mint mused. "You drive a hard bargain, Oni, but I'm inclined to say...it's a deal."

Sparky quickly pulled Mr. Mint aside. "Mr. Mint, you can't do this," he said. "I have to finish the season in Go-Town, it's extremely important."

"Son, you're too young to know this yet, but in the art of negotiating, you have to be willing to let your most cherished possession go at the drop of a hat."

"But you didn't negotiate with him at all! You just caved in immediately!"

"You say I caved, and I say I made a split-second decision with clarity and determination," Mr. Mint said, nudging Sparky away from him. "This team needs to fill the void left by Lance

Bright, and Mr. Oni is making a fair offer to do so. As a businessman, I don't see how I can pass up this deal."

Mr. Mint strode back to Mr. Oni's desk and raised a hand high into the air. "Mr. Oni," he proclaimed, "I believe we have some paperwork to sign, but it seems young Mr. Katakura isn't too keen on the proposal."

"Really?" Mr. Oni said with an arched eyebrow. "Is there anything that troubles you about the prospect of playing for the winningest baseball team of all time, Sparky?"

"Ordinarily, no, sir. But I've sort of made a promise to someone that I would try to win a championship this season, with the Goats. If I don't, well, I don't really think I'd be willing to play baseball for any team after that."

"Oh dear, that does seem to be an issue," Mr. Oni said. "On the one hand, your employer and I have already made a gentleman's agreement to complete the trade, but on the other hand I don't want to have a starting pitcher whose heart isn't in the game."

Sparky took a deep breath before speaking up. "Okay," he said. "Here's the deal. If Number 7 over there can get a hit off me in the All-Star Game tomorrow, I'll go to New York without a fight. But, if I can strike him out, then the trade's off. What do you say to that, Mr. Oni?"

Mr. Oni raised an eyebrow, but then smiled. "A very interesting proposal, Sparky. Very interesting, indeed. I see no problem with your terms. That is, of course, if Arthur doesn't object?"

"Why, that sounds absolutely ripping to me! These games usually bore me to tears, anyway, so it would be smashing to have something to pay attention to for once! I'm all for it!"

"Yes," Mr. Oni said, "Regardless of the outcome, I think this will make for the most interesting All-Star Game in some time."

That afternoon, Sparky stood assembled with the other 199 Big League Baseball All-Stars in center field of Imperial Stadium. The All-Star Team selection ceremony had always been a big event, and this year was no exception as more than 50,000 fans crowded under the blazing July sun to watch the honorary captains select players who would actually take the field for the game – the very best of the best.

From his podium representing the All-Star Red team at first base, Bob Honcho hitched his pants over his gut and waved to the crowd. On the third base side representing the All-Star Blue team, the legendary shortstop for the Buenos Aires Silver Spikes Emilio Faustino smiled and tipped his cap to the throngs. As Sparky strained to see over the rows of taller players in front of him, he

126

caught sight of the masked Number 7, who looked to be taking the selection ceremony as seriously as he did everything else.

Honcho won the coin flip, and stepped proudly in front of the microphone. "As honorary captain of the Red team, I, Bob Honcho..." He paused for a thunderous round of applause from the New Yorkers in attendance. "...I select my starting pitcher with my first pick. From the Go-Town Goats, Sparky Katakura!"

Sparky was stunned. Even though Honcho had told him earlier in the day that he would be selected for the team, being the first overall pick was not something he could have ever been prepared for. In his head, he saw a flipbook of baseball cards bearing the flag "All-Star Game First Pick," and it was a virtual Hall of Fame of some of the game's all-time greats. To have his name counted among them was something Sparky had always wanted, but within moments he was overcome with guilt. How could he think of what it would say on his baseball card when his brother was depending on him?

He was brought back down to Earth with Faustino's first pick. "As the honorary captain of the Blue team, I choose the right fielder for the hometown New York Emperors, Number 7!" The crowd's reaction was loud and sustained as 7 made his way deliberately up to the podium. He shook Faustino's hand and took his place along the third baseline, arms folded, never moving. His eyes were locked onto Sparky, and while Sparky wanted to stare him down, something about 7 made him extremely uncomfortable. He was beginning to regret his bold wager in Mr. Oni's office – at this point he wasn't even sure he could get the ball over the plate against this stone-cold specter of a man.

An hour later, the rosters were set. Those who had been chosen for either the Red or Blue teams stood on the baselines and shook hands, exchanged high-fives, and generally behaved as though they would never have to go back to being competitors when the regular season started again. First-time All-Stars jumped around the field and snapped pictures of themselves in their red and blue caps with their phones. Veterans stood to the side and snickered at the youngsters, doing their best to hide how excited they themselves were. The 150 who remained on the outfield put on brave faces, maybe wiped something out of their eyes when no one was looking. They waved to the crowd as they came to grips with the fact that they wouldn't do much more than sign autographs or participate in skills competitions for the rest of the weekend. After all, there was always next year, wasn't there?

The Red and Blue teams lined up on the infield for the customary handshake. As the respective first picks, Sparky found himself immediately lined up with 7. The tips of Sparky's fingers went cold, and there was a quiver in his stomach. He tried to see beyond the mask and look 7 directly in the eyes, but there was only darkness past the slits cut into the polished steel. Nevertheless, 7 offered his hand and Sparky shook it, an act that seemingly drew all the heat out of his body. Sparky moved down the line like a robot in a factory.

"That fellow from the Emperors sure is a strange duck, eh?" Sparky turned around to see the imposing figure of Bert Backlin standing behind him in line, his oblivious smile creeping out from under the weight of his mustache. With everything else going on in his head, Sparky had neglected to pay attention to the rest of the selection ceremony, and now he was wearing the same cap as one of the most irritating players he had ever met.

"I bet you'd never go for that whole thing they have going on in New York, huh Backlin? Wouldn't your mustache get caught in the mask?"

Backlin laughed loudly and slapped Sparky on the back, hard. "Oh, I've forgotten that there was anything I liked about you, Katakura! Your sense of humor is just tops! No, I shouldn't like to have to shave my face of one of my crowning achievements, but to play for the New York Emperors is an opportunity you would have to be crazy to turn down. Wouldn't you agree?"

"Maybe I would," Sparky said, "if things were different."

The sun broke over the New York City skyline the next morning to reveal a perfect, cloudless midsummer day. Fans packed themselves into their seats long before first pitch and continued buzzing for hours. The players took the field for warmups and stretching, but 7 remained conspicuously in the dugout, quietly listening as he shared the bench with a smiling and talkative Mr. Oni.

Pregame ceremonies concluded with a storm of fireworks that drowned out the crowd noise for a few brief moments. Punching the inside of his glove, Sparky took the field with the rest of the Red team. As he stood on the mound, Sparky wondered for a moment if Ken could see him, the starting pitcher in the All-Star Game. If he could, he hoped his brother could take enough pride in that to hold on for the rest of the season.

Sparky used the killer combination of the Blazing Fastball and Phantom Slider to strike out the first two Blue hitters, bringing up Urgh, the great third baseman of the Savage Land Sabretooths. As Urgh dragged his knuckles to the plate, Sparky saw Number 7 step into the on-deck circle. As always, the masked man's eyes were staring right through Sparky. With two outs already in the inning, it didn't look like they would have their fated meeting until later. Still, 7's gaze bothered Sparky, jarred something loose in the pit of his stomach that was now sloshing around free and splashing his insides with ice water. To put it plainly, Sparky was terrified of Number 7.

Sparky's first pitch to Urgh was a wobbly breaking ball that flopped into the catcher's mitt well outside the strike zone. Sparky's distraction carried over to the next pitch, a fastball that whizzed high and outside, catching the catcher by surprise and forcing him to miss it. The ball careened off the backstop and into the stands, to the horror of the crowd. Number 7 continued to glare at Sparky from the on-deck circle.

On the next pitch, Sparky rediscovered the strike zone, but this time Urgh was ready, as well. With a swing of his hairy arms, Urgh hit a chopper that bounced several feet in front of the mound. Sparky instinctively ran up to make the play, but by the time he had the ball in his hands, he glanced over to see Number 7 still on deck. Enough waiting, Sparky thought.

"Come on now, let's have the ball!" Backlin called from first base, where he kept one eye on the lumbering form of Urgh making his way down the baseline. Sparky turned in Backlin's direction and cocked his arm, but double-clutched and Urgh beat the throw by half a step. The crowd's voice was a mixture of disappointment and confusion. Sparky just stepped back onto the mound and saw Number 7 already standing at the plate. No matter how scared he was, Sparky knew that he held his and his brother's destinies in his hands, and he was going to make it count. He could see Backlin shaking his head in frustration and disgust at first base, but Sparky figured he wouldn't ever be on the big guy's Christmas list, anyway.

Number 7 stepped to the plate with calm determination. If he was feeling as much anxiety over this at-bat as Sparky was, it didn't show. Was he even aware of what was at stake? Was he that confident he could get a hit off of Sparky, or did he just not care? Did Oni even allow his ballplayers to show emotion, or were their feelings as tightly controlled as a team's haircut policy? Sparky got the feeling he never wanted to find out for himself.

For the first time since he arrived in New York, Sparky missed having Lou behind the plate. He had come to depend on his teammate's steely glare as a source of reassurance. Instead, he found himself looking into the eyes of Earl Tribeca, the rocket-armed catcher for the Paris Professionals. Completely unaware of what was riding on it, Earl called for a first-pitch fastball high. Sparky nodded slowly, checked the runner Urgh at first base, and got set for the windup.

Sparky's Blazing Fastball tore through the air and popped

right into Earl's mitt, curls of smoke swirling around the point of impact. Strike one. Number 7 took a step out of the batter's box and casually adjusted his batting gloves, then tugged on the brim of his helmet so that it came down a little further over his mask. The masked man stepped back into the box, took his stance and twirled the end of his bat over his head in little circles as he awaited the next pitch.

Earl decided to catch the hitter off-guard with a breaking pitch, and Sparky agreed with the strategy. He took a deep, cleansing breath before pulling back and unleashing the Phantom Slider. True to form, the ball curved slightly outside before vanishing altogether for the critical moment when it crossed the plate. Number 7 flinched, but never took the bat off his shoulder. Earl did his best to keep his mitt inside the strike zone, but the pitch had moved too much and the count was now even.

Again, the Emperors' All-Star representative stepped out of the box and performed his little hitter's rituals. He stepped back in again, tugged his helmet back down over his brow, twirled his bat again and was ready. Sparky got the call for a curve this time, and he obliged with a beautiful 12-6 curveball that started out almost high enough to knock off the umpire's mask, but gracefully dove right through the zone. Number 7 timed it wrong and swung right over the top of the ball, and now Sparky was in control of the at-bat.

Earl wanted to close out the at-bat and the inning in dramatic fashion, and called for the fastball. As Sparky glanced over to check the runner at first, he caught Urgh digging in his ear with his crooked index finger. Obviously, there was no threat of a hit-and-run situation. Number 7 stepped back in and twirled his bat again. This time, however, Sparky thought he could see the mighty right fielder trembling a bit. He could see Number 7's fingers shaking as he flexed them around the bat handle. Sparky grinned to himself – he had gotten inside his head. For all his stony intimidation, it was now the grim mystery man who was standing in fear of Sparky.

Feeling the heat pooling in his elbow and shoulder as he went through his wind-up, Sparky was like a coiled spring that finally exploded in a burst of motion. The ball streaked toward home plate, actually picking up speed and trailing tongues of flame behind it. Number 7 continued to tremble as his unseen eyes tracked the pitch from Sparky's hand. The ball was now practically a stream of fire connecting the pitcher's mound to the plate. Sparky allowed himself to relax as the pitch crossed the plate. But then Number 7 swung.

The Emperor's swing was more like a flash, a hummingbird-fast blast of speed that redirected the flaming ball and sent it screaming in the opposite direction just as fast as it had arrived. Sparky wheeled around just in time to see a streak of scorched turf pointing in the direction of the left-field corner, where Olen Fjordson from the Reykjavik Springs was trying to corral the careening ball. Urgh was charging at full speed around second base and would score easily. Number 7 himself trotted into second, but this time he would not make eye contact with Sparky at all. The score was 1-0, Blue team. Sparky would pitch the next three innings, but the game was already over.

11. ON THE TRADING BLOCK

Once the game was actually over, Sparky had been sitting at his locker for at least an hour and a half. He had gone straight to the showers after being taken out of the game. His eyes were red and sore. The players began filing into the locker room, and Sparky quickly composed himself. No one paid him any attention at first, until he felt the unwelcome presence of Bert Backlin casting his big, dumb shadow over him.

"Say there, friend," Backlin said, "you look as though you've been overcome with emotion!"

"And?" Sparky said as he wiped his nose with the back of his hand. "So what? You got something to say to me about being a warrior or some other garbage? Maybe I don't give a crap about your manly manliness thing or whatever it is you won't shut up about, did you ever think about that, Backlin?"

"Well, no," Backlin said. "I can honestly say I never have thought about that. But I was only asking because I was concerned for you."

"Oh sure, I'll bet. And why's that?"

"We're all part of the same brotherhood, young Sparky. Regardless of the uniforms we wear, we all share a bond, wouldn't you say?"

"Yeah, well, I'm having a hard time seeing it that way right now, okay?"

"I understand. I've heard stories told of what brought you to Go-Town, and if they're true I can only offer my condolences. I wish you success, so long as it doesn't come against the Canaries, of course."

"Yeah, right. I hear you. But you probably won't be seeing much of me any more, Backlin."

"Well, then I wish you nothing but success, Sparky. You've been a fine competitor, and I tip my cap to you." And he did.

"Thanks. You're a real jerk, Backlin. But thanks."

Meanwhile, deep within the tunnels and corridors that criss-crossed the foundation of Zigleaf Field, Yoshi was awakened from a brief nap by the sound of the clubhouse telephone.

"Hello? Hello! Hello hello hello hello! I'm awake, I've been awake the entire time!"

"Mr. Kawaii, it's Arthur Mint calling from New York City. Listen, I need you to get to work right away on some uniforms for a press conference tomorrow morning."

"Uh, all right," Yoshi said, scrambling around the office for a pad of paper and a pencil. The pencil he found resting behind his ear, but in lieu of paper he decided to scribble on the wall. "Go ahead, sir."

"Now, we're going to need a uniform for our new right fielder. Eh, who wears number 7 for us right now?"

"That would be Thor, sir. Thor Odinson."

"Mm, I see. Well, that will have to change. So make up a new jersey with number 7 in...uh...well, let's play the percentages and say medium size."

"And the name on the back?"

"That's a good question, Mr. Kawaii, a very good question indeed. Leave it blank for the moment."

"You're the boss, sir. Anything else?"

"Hm? Oh, yes! Box up anything belonging to Sparky Katakura and have it prepared to ship to Imperial Stadium in New York. We have a big trade to announce tomorrow, Mr. Kawaii, a very big trade indeed!" With that, Mr. Mint hung up, leaving Yoshi scrambling now for his address book. He flipped through it and found the first number he needed to call. There were now a lot of people he needed to talk to tonight, but this one was the most important.

"Hello, Katie? It's Yoshi."

By the time Katie hung up the phone, there was a cold feeling in the pit of her stomach. This was the exact opposite of what she had been wanting for the last three years. She was almost in the position to finally let go of all her wasted time, the promise she had made to her grandfather that she had been robotically carrying out since then. Why, after so many seasons of trying to distance herself from this cruel game and this crueler team, was she being pulled back into its orbit? Why her, and not someone else?

"Who was that on the phone, Katie?" her mother asked as she carried an unbalanced stack of legal briefs into the kitchen. She dumped them onto the kitchen table, where they more or less held their shape as a teetering column of pages.

"It was Yoshi, you know, from the Goats."

"Oh, another insider scoop for the blog, huh? Your grandfather would be so excited to hear about it, I'm sure." Katie's mom slipped on her delicate reading glasses and began to sort the pile of pages into neat little stacks according to a system only she understood.

"Not this scoop, probably," Katie replied. "It's kind of bad news for the team."

"Bad news for the Goats?" her mom said with mock surprise as she flipped pages. "Heavens to Betsy, is there any other kind of news?"

"Yeah, well, Yoshi thought I should know, thought maybe I could do something about it with the blog."

"And are you?"

"I don't know. I'm sort of done with baseball right now."

"No court would convict you of that, that's for sure." Katie's mom chuckled. "Not in this town and especially not with that team involved."

"Grandpa would be disappointed in me, wouldn't he?"

Katie's mom looked up at her over her glasses. Her constant page-shuffling ceased for the moment. "I guess he would be, a little bit. But he knew you were going to grow up sooner or later. He knew you were going to make your own decisions and leave your mark on the world your own way. I remember when I was a little girl and he would be watching the Goats, he would always something like, 'I wish there was something I could do for them, they need help!' There are some things you really can't do anything about, like baseball."

"They always have needed help," Katie said. "Thanks, Mom."

"Mm-hm. Are you going to the store at all today?"

"No, I don't think so," Katie said. She went upstairs and locked the door to her bedroom. Within minutes, she had her blog opened up to a fresh entry. She titled the new post "The Go-Goats Girl Needs Your Help, Go-Town!"

The next day, Sparky was sitting in Mr. Mint's office, but this time he paid no attention to the sunny summer baseball diamond on the other side of the big glass picture window. Instead, he focused on the mitt that was sitting in his lap. He had carried it all the way up from his locker without even thinking about it, and now he was picking at the seams holding the contoured leather panels together in the rough shape of a hand. On the other side of the desk sat Mr. Mint, who was babbling excitedly on the phone, seemingly paying no attention to the fact that Sparky was in his office or that it was he who had told Sparky to be there.

"Yes, it will be sensational, absolutely sensational!" Mr. Mint gushed. "Biggest trade in Goats history, I tell you!" There was a pause, and Mr. Mint's expression soured. "Well, I suppose that would be... Yes, that one was... Listen, Fred, let's be clear – this will be the biggest trade in Goats history that will actually benefit the Goats, all right?"

Mr. Mint hung up the phone with a scowl on his face, but brightened once he caught Sparky's eye. "Ah, the press are always trying to put a spin on things, aren't they?" he chuckled weakly. "Well, no matter. What do you say, son? Shall we get down there and make history?" The question was, of course, rhetorical.

Sparky followed Mr. Mint down the elevator and through the endless tunnels that honeycombed Zigleaf Field on their way to the press conference Mr. Mint had scheduled to announce his trade to New York. Mr. Oni and Number 7 would be waiting down there to sign the paperwork and make everything official. On their way down, they were intercepted by Yoshi.

"Sorry, Mr. Mint, but there's a bit of a problem with the conference room," Yoshi said as he waved them down another hallway. "Pipe burst, the whole place is flooded. We moved the press conference into the clubhouse."

"Oh dear, that is troubling," Mr. Mint stammered. "Lead on, then, Mr. Kawaii, lead on."

Yoshi shuffled ahead of them and showed them through the big double doors of the clubhouse. A podium and lectern had been hastily assembled in the back of the room, and in front of it sat row after row of reporters clutching notebooks, holding tape recorders and nervously clicking pens. A few of them were wearing orange Goats caps, and Sparky noticed that Roy Miko wasn't in his usual spot in the front row. In fact, he couldn't see Miko's beat-up brown hat anywhere in the assembled crowd of press.

"I see our friends from New York aren't quite here yet, but that doesn't mean we can't get started," Mr. Mint said as he pulled a stack of index cards from his coat pocket. "First of all, I want to thank all of you – and there are a lot of you here today, I see – for coming here today to witness a very important day in Go-Town Goats history, as we say goodbye to one player but welcome in another who will certainly become one of the all-time greats someday..."

"Question, Mr. Mint," interrupted one of the reporters in the front row.

"Please, hold all your questions until the end of the presentation..."

"Is it true that Sparky Katakura is going to be traded to the New York Emperors for their right fielder?"

"Ah, well, you haven't really given me a chance to make my announcement yet, so if you'll just..."

"Mr. Mint," called out another, "isn't it true that Number 7 has one of the most expensive contracts in Big League Baseball, and would likely bankrupt the Goats if he was traded here for even one full season?"

"That's, that's purely speculative, young man, and I won't subject myself to any baseless..."

"Isn't it true," said a third reporter, "that Number 7's home run totals are inflated significantly due to the nature of the wind at Imperial Stadium? He hits far fewer home runs anywhere else, and would likely see a huge drop in production if he played half his games at Zigleaf Field?"

"Uh, I'm not sure where you're getting that information, but I..." Mr. Mint was beginning to sweat noticeably.

"Mr. Mint, isn't it true that...um, uh..." the reporter began flipping through his notebook. "Wait a second, I had it here a second ago..." He turned to a reporter seated behind him and shrugged his shoulders. The other reporter stood up quickly and pushed her glasses up the bridge of her nose. Even with the wig, glasses and a fake British accent, there was no mistaking who it was, for Sparky.

"What my colleague is probably trying to ask," Katie blurted out, "is why you would agree to this deal when the team already has power but is so shaky with starting pitching?"

"Now see here," Mr. Mint spat, "I'm of the opinion that a team can never have too many home-run hitters, so if you're trying to suggest that this is a bad deal, I'll kindly ask you to leave!"

"But Sparky Katakura has a Wins Above Replacement rating almost twice as high as Number 7!"

"Numbers don't take grit and determination into account, young lady."

"He has the second lowest WHIP in the Central League!"

"The best defense is a good offense, as they say."

"But Katakura has one of the best strikeout/walk ratios in the Big Leagues!"

"Young lady," Mr. Mint chuckled, "am I running a baseball team, or an algebra class?"

Katie looked dejected. She glanced around the room at the rest of her assembled "reporters," but none of them could think of anything else to say. Sparky tried to look her in the eyes and offer her a smile as a way to at least say "nice try," but Katie wouldn't look back at him.

Then, suddenly, the look on her face shifted. The defeat and despair dissolved in an instant, and there was a confident gleam in her eyes again. Sparky recognized it as the same look she had when arguing all-time great pinch-hitters with the customers at her shop.

"So then, Mr. Mint," she said, remembering her English accent after the first few words, "I trust you're not worried about...the curse?"

Mr. Mint, who only moments ago wore the look of a school teacher doling out extra homework on a Friday afternoon, now began to shrink away from the lectern. "Curse? I-I'm not sure what you're talking about."

"The Curse of Number 7, of course," Katie continued. A few of the fake reporters looked extremely confused, but they came to understand as she continued. "It's extremely well-known that Emperors who wear number 7 inevitably experience severe injuries after signing with a new team."

"You don't say...like who?"

"Jess Allen, 32 seasons ago – he slipped on a wet spot on the warning track in Lumberton only a week after being traded by New York, ruined his career. There was Harris Monroe, who was traded to Gateway City and was hit by a bullpen cart while running laps before a game. And let's not forget Brett Manger, who accidentally cut his thumb off with a bandsaw while building a canoe in his garage over the winter. All wore number 7 with the Emperors, none of them played baseball again."

"I see," Mr. Mint said as he motioned for Sparky to follow him and backed toward the doors. "Well, thank you all for coming once again. Come along now, Sparky, quickly!"

Yoshi led them down the corridor before they were intercepted by a very perturbed-looking Mr. Oni and the stoic-as-always Number 7.

"Arthur, where have you and Katakura been?" Mr. Oni asked. His calm expression was marred by a rapidly twitching right eyelid. "We were waiting to start the press conference."

"I've been thinking about that, Mr. Oni, and as a gentleman I must inform you that I no longer wish to complete this deal. It's off, I'm quite sorry."

Mr. Oni closed his eyes and forced a smile. "What do you mean, Arthur? I thought we had come to an understanding that would be beneficial to both our ball clubs."

"I'll tell you what I mean, I mean I know about the curse, is what I mean!" Mr. Oni's eyes went wide, and now they were filled with a white-hot rage that seemed to make them glow on their own.

"How...?" But Mr. Oni stopped himself, ran his hand over his silvery hair and composed his face back into a cool, knowing smile. "I guess it's not important," he said. "You have the right to change your mind, of course. It's a shame, really." He turned to look directly into Sparky's eyes. "I have a feeling you'll come to regret this decision more than anyone, Sparky. But that's business for you." Mr. Oni snapped his fingers and started down the hallway. Number 7 followed dutifully behind, hanging his head.

Moments later, Sparky returned to the clubhouse to find Katie's army of ersatz reporters long gone. Yoshi was busy folding up the chairs in the middle of the room.

"Now that was a close one, kid," Yoshi said without looking up from his task. "You're lucky the boss hates signing players without a big press conference."

"I owe you one, Yoshi."

"One?" Yoshi let out a booming laugh. "Kid, you owe me a lot more than that. But not for today. This whole thing was her idea." Yoshi nodded in Sparky's direction, and Sparky turned to see Katie standing in the doorway, still wearing her wig and reporter glasses.

"Tell me, how did you...?"

"It wasn't that hard, really," she said. "I just put out a call on the blog for a fake press conference, and Yoshi got us set up."

"No, I mean all that stuff about the curse of Number 7. Was that something your grandfather told you about?"

"Hardly. It's complete crap. I just named three former Emperors who wore number 7 and suffered career-ending injuries off the top of my head."

"But they did all have bad things happen to them, right?"

"Duh, but do you know how many guys have worn number 7 for the Emperors over the last 750 years? Most of them turned out fine, but everyone remembers the weird cases. Psychologists call it confirmation bias, but ballplayers call it superstition."

"You're awesome," Sparky said. "I mean, that's awesome."

"I do what I can," Katie said.

"Hey wait," Sparky said. "I thought baseball was just a game, not worth any more of your time and all that."

"Nothing's just a game, Katakura. Now don't make this whole thing a waste of a good fake British accent."

"It wasn't that great."

"Just shut up and pitch."

Just then, Mr. Mint appeared in the clubhouse, followed by Skip and Lou, both of them wearing street clothes – Lou in jeans and a crisp button-down shirt, Skip in a turtleneck sweater and a very obvious toupee.

"Look, I don't do a lot of complainin' about how you run your own baseball team, Mint, but yer screwing around with lineup is going too far this time!"

"LaRoche, I know I promised to replace Bright in right field, but if you knew half the things I've learned about Number 7, you and I wouldn't be having this conversation!"

"Hey, what's she doing in here?" Skip said, suddenly noticing Katie. The dark curls of his wig bounced in front of his forehead like Slinkys. "No press in the locker room, huh?"

"She's not press," Sparky said. "She's a blogger."

"And a season ticket holder," Katie added.

"What's going on, Lou?"

"What's going on, Spark, is that we start the regular season up again tomorrow and we got nobody in right field."

"Why don't we call someone up from the minors?" Skip offered.

"Naw, I've been looking over our farm team reports, and the best outfielder we got down there is hitting .178," Lou said.

"Hey, cowboy, why don't you go chase a tumbleweed or something and let me manage my team?" Skip said as he waved a threatening finger in Lou's face.

"Aw, come on, Skip, you know it ain't like that."

"I would appreciate any suggestion, seeing as how we're running dangerously short on time," Mr. Mint said.

"How about Katie?" Sparky suggested to the surprise of everyone in the room. No one was more surprised than Katie, however.

"Her?" Skip asked, his shiny artificial hair still bobbing and swaying of its own accord. "But she's just a...what did you call it? Something about jogging?"

"She was a top outfielder in high school and college, even had a couple of tryouts with Big League teams," Sparky continued as Katie's face was frozen in wide-eyed panic.

"So why isn't she playing now?" Skip prodded.

"Her grandfather needed her and she had to stay close to home, but now she's available and she's ready to play, right, Katie?" Katie remained frozen, forcing Sparky to give her an elbow to the side.

"Oh, yeah," she said finally. "I'm totally ready to play. For the Goats. Tomorrow."

"Hmm, I don't know," Mr. Mint said.

"I have a lifetime .296 average," Katie said.

"She's never played in the Big Leagues before..."

"I'm fast and I have a great arm."

"It just seems like such a risk..."

"You don't have to pay me."

"Get her a uniform."

12. MID-SEASON ACQUISITION

The next day, Katie followed the rest of the Goats out onto the field at Milwaukee's Schotz Field for the first of a three-game series against the Vagabonds. She took her spot in right field in the bottom of the first and lobbed a few warm-up tosses in Carlos' direction before the first at-bat. The rest of the infield had gathered around Sparky on the mound.

"This has the potential to be fascinating," Blerk said. "The opportunity to study the psychological impact of baseball on a human female as both spectator and participant is one I look forward to."

"You think she's nervous?" Bobby asked. "I know my heart was pounding in my first game in the Big Leagues."

"That's because you probably ate three cheeseburgers on the way to the park," Fuzzy said. "She's nervous, but she's probably worried about impressing Fuzzy." He waved to her. "It's okay, Katie! Fuzzy likes you no matter what!" Katie didn't appear to notice the attention.

"Based on data previously collected about this subject, I would assume that the female known as Katie Spalding is preoccupied with exposing flaws in the opposing lineup," Blerk said.

"Maybe she's trying to imagine what her baseball card will look like," Sparky guessed.

In the relative solitude of right field, Katie had only one thought: "Please don't let me screw up, Grandpa."

The score was 2-2 in the top of the fifth inning, and the Goats were in the middle of a rally. At first base stood Blerk, the beneficiary of a five-pitch walk. At second base was Bobby, who had managed to pop a bloop single over the infield into shallow center field. Thor had struck out to start the inning, and now the infield was at double-play depth for Katie, who had only grounded weakly to third her first two times at bat. Tweedy, the Milwaukee pitcher, looked in at Katie with an expression that suggested he may as well be pitching to a coat rack. Her mind was racing, trying to recall as much information about Tweedy as possible. He had gone low and away from her for much of the previous at-bats, and he usually tried to mix it up more on the third time through the order. His fastball had some zip, but he made his living on fooling hitters with breaking pitches. It calmed Katie down to imagine seeing Tweedy's percentages superimposed over his beefy frame, just like on TV.

Just as predicted, the first two pitches stayed down and near the outside half of the plate, with one catching the corner of the plate for a strike. Katie tried to imagine the stat splits for Tweedy in this situation, and likely he was to throw something hittable with a 1-1 count with one out and two on. Was it 35 percent, or 53 percent? She couldn't remember, and now her brain was being cluttered with numbers. If Skip attempted a double-steal here, it had a 15 percent chance of success. The wind was now blowing softly in the direction of left center field, meaning she was approximately 4 percent more likely to hit a good pitch in that direction. But her spray chart from college indicated she was more likely to pull the ball. Tweedy checked the runner at first – did that have any bearing on the next pitch? What had started out to be a calming influence on Katie was now causing her to tense up. Then, she remembered something her grandfather had said to her all the way through Little League:

"If it looks good, swing at it."

Katie cleared her mind's eye of charts, graphs and other overlays. She focused all her attention on Tweedy's right hand. She watched it disappear behind his back, watched it swing up over his head and watched it propel the ball forward in one smooth motion. The ball was definitely coming faster than before, but that was okay, because it was also coming in straighter and higher than before. In other words, it looked good. Katie coiled her body like a spring and released all the energy in a tight swing that caught the pitch right over the plate and sent it screaming, belt-high, through the gap between first and second base.

Bobby was already red-faced and sweaty by the time he reached third base, but the third base coach was waving him home as the ball was plucked off the grass by Milwaukee's right fielder.

"Oh, come on!" Bobby wheezed, but he made the turn nonetheless and began pumping his legs like a man possessed. Blerk and Katie were cruising into third and second as the relay throw reached the catcher's mitt. Bobby pushed off the ground and hung in the air for one brief, glorious moment, like a cow that has somehow learned ballet. Reaching out with his left hand, Bobby slapped home plate before the rest of him came crashing down onto the dirt. The Goats took a one-run lead. Katie looked down to make sure her foot was indeed still touching second base. Once she was sure that it was, she allowed herself to exhale.

"Okay, Grandpa," she said. "I think I can take it from here."

In the dugout, Lou gave Sparky a slap on the back hard enough to make him spit out his gum.

"You're starting to look like a real smart son of a gun, you know that?" Lou said.

"I told everyone she could play."

"I got a real interesting feeling about this team all of a sudden, Sparky."

"Interesting in what way, Lou?"

The old cowboy curled up his mouth in a smile and grabbed his bat out of the rack. "Interesting in the sense that it don't feel like the worst thing in the world to be a Goat anymore."

GOATS STAND ON BRINK OF HISTORY
By Roy Miko, Go-Town Gazette

In their 250-plus-year history, the Go-Town Goats have been to many places. They've toured the United States as a barnstorming team in their earliest incarnation, played throughout the world as one of the first Central League teams following the organization of Big League Baseball, and just this year their schedule has taken them to Transylvania, the Himalayas and even Milwaukee. But in all that time, there's one place the Goats have never visited – first place.

And yet, here they are, ready to begin a three-game series against – who else? – the Fort Clark Canaries that will decide the Central League championship. For Fort Clark, the division pennant would be the 46th in team history. For the Goats, it would be No. 1. Despite the history at stake, however, the Goats seemed upbeat and optimistic in the clubhouse after last night's 7-6 win over the Brockway Conductors. Combined with a 5-3 Ogdenville victory over Fort Clark, last night's victory put the Goats 2.5 games out of first place. They would need to sweep the series against Fort Clark to win the division, something that hasn't happened since an outbreak of stomach flu weakened most of the Canaries' constitutions several seasons ago. The Goats won't be able to count on assistance from viruses this time, but that doesn't bother Goats manager Skip LaRoche.

"When you get right down to it, there ain't nothing about those guys that makes them any different from us," LaRoche said. "In fact, if you take away all those pennants they got, that fancy ballpark, the fact that they got five guys on the current roster who could be in the Hall of Fame, and they fact that they're better than us, they ain't no different at all."

"I have been positively giddy with anticipation for this series," said starting pitcher Antonio de la Goya. "The way the smoothness of Bert Backlin's swing counters the sharp movement of my sinker ball is something that honestly takes my breath away every time I see it. And when the entire piece is capped off with the violent sound of ball striking mitt…I don't believe there is anything else that qualifies as a work of art so much as that."

"I can't say this situation is all too familiar to me, but just the same I'm itching to get out there and show everybody in the Central League just how far the Goats have come," catcher Lou Houston said. "For a lot of these young guys, these are gonna be the most important games they've ever played."

"These are the most important games I've ever played," starting pitcher Sparky Katakura said, declining to elaborate.

No matter the outcome of these final three games, this season has been one of startling metamorphosis for the Go-Town Goats. By the time the dust settles, all of baseball will know whether or not the team has become the one thing no one has ever thought they could be – champions.

The noise in the stands at Canaries Stadium in Fort Clark was something like a fleet of fighter planes throttling up their jet engines, but deep within the visitor's clubhouse there was little evidence of it. As Sparky laced up his cleats, he could hear the distinct sounds of the hot tub bubbling and gurgling as Fuzzy sighed.

"This is the life, man," Fuzzy said with a wet washcloth draped over his eyes. "How come we don't have anything this nice at our place, huh?"

"Because," Lou said as he walked by and yanked the hot tub's power cord out of the wall, "the Canaries want you to be so relaxed you go out onto the field and play like garbage. Get the heck out of that thing, Fernandez."

"Ah, come on," Fuzzy said as he lifted himself out of the now-still water. "Every time Fuzzy wants to have himself a nice time, the old cowboy here has to ruin it." He balled up the washcloth and lobbed it in Lou's direction.

"That's because every time Fuzzy wants to have a nice time, it's when the rest of his team is counting on him to stay focused," Lou said, effortlessly deflecting the washcloth with a wave of his hand. "I don't care how many hot tubs they have here, and I don't care how nice the lunch buffet is, we're here to beat these guys and take their dang pennant from them."

"But you have to admit," Bobby said from behind the buffet table, "the lunch spread is pretty good here, right?" He carefully balanced one final buffalo wing on top of his teetering plate.

"Aye, tis a feast truly worthy of the mead halls of Valhalla," Thor boomed through a mouthful of roast beef sandwich. "Have I ever told the tales of the great boar hunts in Asgard?"

"Yeah, yeah, you threw some sticks at a pig, big deal," Fuzzy said. Thor and Fuzzy immediately began arguing over the proper method of hunting and skinning a boar, with the rest of the team tossing in the opinions as they felt necessary. While the fracas dominated the center of the clubhouse floor, Katie found Sparky sitting at his locker, deep in concentration.

"Oh! I didn't mean to interrupt," she said.

"No, it's no big deal, just trying to keep my heart rate consistent. I get a few more MPH on my fastball when I'm centered."

"And all that noise over there doesn't bother you?"

"This is pretty quiet for them, believe it or not," Sparky said. "I think everyone's trying to keep their mind off of the game."

"I'm worried about their starting pitcher," Katie said as she took a seat across from Sparky. Behind them, Fuzzy could be heard making an argument in rapid-fire Spanish while Thor attempted to drown him out by loudly repeating "Nay, nay, nay…"

"Why?"

13. PENNANT CHASE

Later, in the dugout, Sparky got the answer to his question. Warming up on the mound for the Canaries was a brick wall of a man whose uniform was augmented with a golden chestplate and a headdress of brilliantly-colored feathers attached to the top of his cap.

"That's Marty Zuma, the Aztec Ace," Katie said. "Just came off the disabled list this week."

"Why was he on the DL?"

"Broken hand."

"Fielding drills?"

"Human sacrifice."

Zuma took his spot on the rubber and clutched the ball in his left hand. He wore no glove on his right. Zuma looked up into the sky and screamed at the top of his lungs.

"WAAAAAAAAAARRRRRRRGGGGGGHHHHH!" With that, he tossed the ball softly in the air with his left hand and then punched it with his right. The result was a blistering fastball that the stadium radar gun clocked at 126 miles per hour. The knuckles on Zuma's right hand were smoking.

"Do me a favor," Sparky said without taking his eyes off the human volcano pitching for Fort Clark, "don't let the rest of the guys watch him warm up."

Despite Sparky and Katie's best efforts, however, the Goats saw all they needed to see of Zuma in the top of the first.

"Boy oh boy, what a day for a ballgame!" VORP chirped in the batter's box. "And how exciting is it to have the division pennant riding on this series? Makes me wish we could play all three games at once, know what I mean?"

Zuma glowered at the robot from the mound and sneered, "Quiet yourself, metal man, or else I will make you quiet myself!"

"Hey, didn't mean to break your concentration there, buddy!" VORP continued. "I know this game means a lot to you guys, too. Sometimes my enthusiasm subroutine overwhelms my main programming and I just can't help myself, so you'll have to forgive me if I seem a little…"

With a terrifying growl, Zuma punched the ball directly at VORP, and the impact sent the robot's limbs and head flying in all directions like some kind of disturbing party favor. The sound was something like a hand grenade being tossed into a metal garbage can. The field was showered with nuts and bolts.

"Is that the way you tell your guys to play ball, O'Malley?" Skip shouted across the field at the Canaries' dugout. "I always knew you were a dirty son of a gun, and now I have the proof!"

O'Malley took the top step of his dugout and called back to Skip with a slight grin on his puffy red face. "He lost control of the ball, LaRoche! He just got back from the DL, he needed to knock some of the rust off! He just decided to knock it off of your guy, that's all!" This sent a chuckle through the Canaries' bench.

"Take your base!" the umpire shouted while pointing at first base.

"Oh, absolutely," VORP's head said from its resting place a few feet away from home plate. "There's nothing I would like more than to move on to first base, but as you can see, I'm in kind of a difficult position here."

The umpire pointed into the Goats dugout at Skip. "Either get this guy to first base or put in a pinch runner, and do it quick or you forfeit the game!" This resulted in more general guffawing from the Canaries' bench.

"Pinch runner?" Skip said, scratching his head. "We don't have no pinch runners on this team, this ain't no track and field meet!" Skip grabbed one of the bat boys and put an equipment bag on his back. "Get out there and gather up as much of that bum as you can," Skip told the terrified young boy. "And then go stand on first base!"

And so, as Carlos stood in, it was with a visibly nervous bat boy standing on first, his knees wobbling under the weight of an equipment bag stuffed with most of the Goats' center fielder. VORP's head and one arm were hanging out of the zipper, still chattering away as if nothing had happened.

"Come on, Carlos! We all know you can do it!" VORP said as he waved his one functional arm in the air. The bat boy struggled to stand up straight.

"Is there anything you can tell us about how to hit Zuma?" Lou asked Katie.

"I wish there was," she replied, "but with the time he spent on the DL I just don't have enough recent data about him. And his fastball's not behaving like it was before he got injured. We're going to be flying blind with him."

"Strike three!" the umpire called out after Carlos whiffed badly on the third straight fastball from Zuma. The massive pitcher spread his arms and screamed into the sky in triumph, his roar overwhelming the sound of the crowd.

Zuma's voice was still reverberating throughout the gleaming steel of Canaries Stadium when Fuzzy took his spot in the batter's box. "You like to yell a lot, huh?" he said as he looked directly into Zuma's wide, burning eyes. "Well, I can yell a lot, too, man. Let's see who's louder, okay?"

With that, Fuzzy started screaming at the top of his lungs as he got into his batting stance. Zuma punched another blazing fastball toward the plate and Fuzzy, still screaming, swung quickly enough to get wood on the ball. He continued screaming as he took off down the first base line, frantically waving his arms in the air in a mockery of Zuma's antics.

Meanwhile, the bat boy carrying VORP was having a difficult time running between first and second. "Way to show some hustle, kid!" VORP encouraged him from just over his shoulder. The ball shot through the gap between third and short and rolled to a stop in shallow left field. The left fielder, seeing the bat boy huffing and puffing and still not yet at second base, scooped the ball off the grass and lobbed it over to the second baseman for the easy out. Fuzzy finally stopped screaming when he noticed the bat boy crawling past him on his way back to the dugout, a look close to relief on his face.

"Hey, that's okay," Fuzzy said loudly, clapping his hands. "Mr. Featherhead over there is probably going to tire himself out with all that screaming pretty soon, so we'll start hitting him!"

Zuma scowled and turned his attention to Thor, who was striding to the plate with a defiant gleam in his eye. The thunder god tapped his bat on home plate and the skies answered with a faint rumble in the distance on an otherwise cloudless afternoon.

"Uh oh, I don't like the sound of that," Fuzzy said in Zuma's direction. "That sounds to me like the big guy is getting ready to pop one out of here. So it's a two-run homer instead of a three-run homer, big deal! That's just for starters, too. You think you're gonna last the whole nine innings today, Mr. Headdress? Mr. Feathered Serpent? Mr. Pour Molten Gold Down Some Guy's Throat?"

Fuzzy took a step off the bag and pointed out to the deepest part of center field, 428 feet away from home plate. "You see that guy in the stands eating the two jumbo chili dogs?" Seventeen rows up in the bleachers did indeed sit a gaunt young man who was nevertheless alternating bites between two jumbo chili dogs, and not getting a drop of anything on his immaculately white T-shirt. "I bet I can tell you what's going to happen. Thor is

147

going to clobber one deep into the center field bleachers, and the ball is going to come straight at that guy with the chili dogs. And when it does, he's going to drop both of them on that lady with the big hat sitting below him when he tries to catch it."

"Yer out!" the first base umpire shouted. The crowd surged and cheered, causing Fuzzy to look around frantically. Finally, Fuzzy saw Backlin's glove resting on his shoulder, the ball nestled snugly in its webbing. While Fuzzy had been concocting his elaborate scenario for Thor's at-bat, Zuma had tossed Backlin the ball, and Fuzzy had never put his feet back on the bag. The game was off to a very ominous start.

Sparky did his part in the bottom of the first, striking out the first two hitters. It wasn't until the Canaries' #3 hitter, Mustaine, stepped to the plate that Sparky began to feel dread pulling down on his confidence.

Mustaine fouled off the first two pitches, then took a slider down low for a ball. Sparky knew he would be aggressive with a 1-2 count, and decided it would be best to avoid giving him something hittable. The look in Lou's eyes conveyed the same feeling, and he gave Sparky the signal for an upstairs change-up. Sparky delivered, but Mustaine was able to slow his swing down enough to catch the ball's underside. The result was a high pop-up that drifted lazily out to center field.

"Oh wait," Sparky said to himself. "Center field?"

VORP had his glove in the air, drawing a bead on the pop-up as it arced in front of the sun and began falling back down to earth. But the ballboy, who was still carrying VORP's jumbled components on his back, was frantically scanning the sky, looking for anything that in any way resembled a baseball.

"It's right in front of you!" VORP called out. "Six steps toward home! No, wait, now five! Take another step to your left! No, left!" The ballboy staggered around in center field like a zombie, in danger of tripping over his own cleats. Thor and Katie watched nervously from both sides.

"Hast thou the ball?" Thor said. "Be you in need of assistance?"

"We got it, we got it!" VORP insisted. But the ball dropped a good two feet from the ballboy's feet. Katie rushed in to make the play, firing the ball into second base and holding Mustaine to a single. The crowd roared in hysterics. Lou kicked at the dirt in front of home plate. He and Sparky exchanged a look that seemed to say, "What in the heck do we do about this?" Into the batter's box stepped Bert Backlin.

"My my," said the massive slugger, "That's quite a way to get into a jam, isn't it? I hope you understand that it's nothing personal, but I would anticipate that my teammates and I will be doing our best to exploit your specific deficiency in center field."

"Right, right," Sparky spat back. "Just get in there and swing the bat, Backlin."

"I intend to do no less!" Sparky watched as Lou flashed the sign. Briefly looking over his shoulder to check Mustaine at first, Sparky went into his motion. His first pitch was a slider that broke inside a bit too far, causing Backlin to take a half-step backward.

"I say, are you trying to get my attention, young man?" Backlin said, smiling.

"You'd know if I was," Sparky mumbled quietly. His next pitch was a fastball, high and tight. Backlin offered a half-swing and shrugged his shoulders when the umpire called a strike.

"My mind must have been elsewhere," Backlin sighed.

Lou gave Sparky the sign for another fastball, which Sparky delivered so forcefully that he almost fell off the mound. This time, Backlin caught up with the pitch, and the contact was strong enough to cause the bat to splinter into a thousand pieces. The sound of the explosion rocked the stadium, followed by the awestruck exhalation of the fans. The bat fragments showered the grass in front of home plate, and in the meantime the ball was curling through the air toward the left field corner. Thor gave chase, his glove pulling him across the outfield.

With his beard trailing behind him like the tail of a fiery red comet, Thor streaked his way toward the foul line. The ball seemed to be running away from him, almost like it was a game of tag the ball was determined to win. His teeth gritted together, Thor pushed off the ground with his tree-trunk legs and stretched out. He flew through the air, his glove like the head of some magnificent winged serpent. When Thor finally landed, he left an impact crater carved into the outfield grass. When the ball finally landed, it was foul by 50 feet.

The Fort Clark crowd showered Thor with mock applause, cheering him for the ultimately useless and misguided defensive effort. Thor slowly climbed back onto his feet, shaking clumps of grass and dirt out of his beard. On the mound, Sparky began to panic. Every pitch now was an opportunity for something to go wrong, and there was no margin for error today.

With Backlin ready for the 1-2 pitch, Lou gave the sign for a curveball. Sparky shook him off. Lou then flashed the sign for a slider, and again Sparky refused the pitch. A fastball, a straight change and a splitter all got the same reaction from Sparky. Lou let out deep, mustache-rustling breath and gave the sign for the Phantom Slider, and this time Sparky finally nodded.

"All right, kid," Lou said to himself. "Let's not step on the gas too early here."

Sparky twisted into his delivery and sprung, the ball rocketing off his fingers and curling toward home plate. The ball vanished from sight, and Backlin took a whack at the space where it had been just a moment earlier, but it reappeared safely inside the catcher's mitt. Backlin slumped his massive shoulders and dragged his bat back to the dugout as the Goats whooped and hollered their way off the field. Sparky felt a twinge of soreness in his elbow, but ignored it.

In the top of the second, Thor came to the plate to a round of laughter and more insincere applause from the Fort Clark fans. Many of them pantomimed his clumsy fall, their eyes agog as they reached out for an invisible ball that they would never catch. Thor rubbed some of the infield dirt on his gloves and gripped his bat.

"Hear the words of thy son, mighty Odin," Thor said to the sky as he stepped into the batter's box. "The God of Thunder humbly beseeches you to bestow upon him some of your infinite power. I know my decision to play baseball on Earth displeases you, father, but now in this mortal arena I fight for the glory of all Asgard!" A low rumble rolled through the sky as clouds began gathering. "Grant me the power to bring honor back to Asgard, grant me the strength to redeem myself in thine eyes, and most importantly, grant me a home run so that I may SHUT YON FORT CLARK JERKS UP!"

Thor's request was punctuated by a peal of thunder, and as he got into his stance his eyes began to crackle and glow with electricity. Unintimidated, Zuma screamed his war cry and hammered a fastball toward the plate. With the laughter of the crowd still ringing in his ears, Thor swung his bat. The sound of bat meeting ball was impossibly loud, and accompanied by a bright flash of light. Trailing a tail of sizzling lightning behind it, the ball soared over the left field wall and struck the giant neon canary that hung over the bleachers. It exploded into a firework of glass and sparks. The once boisterous Fort Clark crowd was suddenly silenced.

"The God of Thunder thanks you, mighty Odin," Thor said as he circled the bases. "Thor doth promise to visit more often, and he shall call Mother before the next setting of the sun."

The score remained 1-0 in favor of the Goats for the next several innings, thanks to Sparky dominating the Canaries' lineup with a steady diet of special pitches. He struck out Mustaine on the Phantom Slider, took out Halford with the Blazing Fastball and got several more swinging on the Cosmic Change-Up. By the bottom of the sixth, however, Lou called time and rambled out to the mound.

"You all right, kid? You look like you're pressing a bit up

here."

"I'm fine, Lou," Sparky said as he hastily wiped the sweat off his forehead and jammed his cap back on his head.

"You've been throwing every piece of junk in your arsenal at these guys, and I'm worried you're going to tire yourself out before too long."

"Really, Lou, it's fine, okay?" Sparky slammed the ball into his glove. "Are we trying to win this game or not?"

"You're gol-durn right," Lou replied forcefully. "We're trying to win this game, not just you. You try and win this whole thing by yourself again, like you did on Opening Day, and you're gonna put yourself out of commission when we need you the most."

Sparky looked over his shoulder and saw the rest of the Goats watching him. "Don't think you have to blow the ball past these jerks every time up," Lou continued. "Give your teammates a little bit of credit, huh?" Lou handed the ball back to Sparky and hustled back behind the plate.

Sparky turned his head and took a long look at his teammates. Carlos was hopping up and down at first base, trying to calm down. Blerk was busy rubbing some of the infield dirt between his fingers, watching it carefully as it sprinkled back down to the ground. Fuzzy was having an animated argument with a Canaries fan in the front row, with lots of pointing and yelling. Bobby was trying hard to catch his breath after bending over to pick up his glove, which he had dropped while trying to eat a hot dog he had just purchased from a vendor.

In the outfield, Katie was staring intently at a notepad and scribbling notes with a tiny pencil she pulled from behind her ear. VORP chattered away in the ballboy's ear from inside his bag. And Thor was bent over, adjusting the laces of his shoes. Seeing Sparky looking at him, Thor gave Sparky an enormous smile accompanied by a thumbs-up. Sparky sighed and realized that, no matter how much he wanted to, he couldn't lose faith in his team now. And it was a good thing, too, because his arm was starting to feel like a dead elephant dangling from his shoulder.

There were two out, and Mustaine was back up at the plate again. Mustaine spit out a mouthful of sunflower seeds in front of the batter's box, leaving a trail of spittle trickling down his chin. He narrowed his eyes and sneered at Sparky, but the sight of his spit-stained face inspired little more in Sparky than nausea.

Being careful not to put too much strain on his tender arm, Sparky lobbed a sinking fastball over the plate. Mustaine rapped a ground ball that skipped past the mound and took a funny bounce. As Blerk ran in to make the play, the ball hopped up in the air. Blerk's shiny black eyes grew wide, and he began backpedaling.

The ball continued twirling in the air, climbing higher and higher in the air and threatening to sail completely over Blerk's head. He put his glove up in the air.

Sparky held his breath as he watched the ball arch through the air. Blerk continued stumbling backwards as he tried to keep his eye on the ball. Suddenly, Blerk's feet went out from under him and he toppled backwards, his arms flapping at his sides like the wings of an inexperienced bird. Mustaine charged down the first base line as Carlos covered the base, cringing.

Blerk crashed to the ground, but he managed to keep his glove over his head, where the ball dropped right into the center. With a single motion, Blerk hopped to his feet and flipped the ball to Carlos. With Mustaine bearing down on him like a freight train trailing streams of spittle behind it, Carlos shut his eyes and waited for the ball. Sparky's eyes were shut, too.

"Out!" shouted the first base umpire.

The Goats managed to hold onto their 1-0 lead into the ninth inning. However, the Canaries' lineup had come back around to the top of the order, and Sparky would be facing their 1-2-3 hitters. Backlin was at the end of that unappetizing menu in the #4 spot, of course. Before Sparky left the dugout, Skip pulled him aside. "You think you got one more inning left in you, kiddo?"

"You bet your butt I do," Sparky replied.

"Good, because I don't trust a single one of those dopes in the bullpen to rub out a pencil mark with a dime store eraser! Now get the heck out there and get this thing over with!"

Lou caught up with Sparky before he reached the mound. "I hope you weren't just blowing sunshine up old Skip's skirt there, Sparky," he said. "But, just in case you were, Katie and I have been talking about ways we can help you out."

"Like what?"

"Aw, heck," Lou said with a glimmer in his eye, "You gotta leave this cowboy some surprises, okay?"

The Canaries' lead-off man started the inning off uncomfortably by clipping a fastball and sending it careening into short left field for a single. Sparky watched him out of the corner of his eye as he took a step off of first base, then another. Sparky whipped a pick-off throw to Carlos, but the runner dove headfirst and missed the tag. He slapped the dirt off his uniform and took another two steps toward second. Again, Sparky tried to pick him off first base but was a split-second late. He did manage to keep the runner from taking as big of a lead the next time, however, and Sparky felt comfortable enough to finally give the hitter his attention. His first pitch was on the outside corner for a strike. The runner stepped back onto first.

When the runner took only a one-step lead toward second again, Sparky let loose with a slider that tailed inside too close to the hitter's knees, evening the count at 1-1. Now the runner had taken another one-step lead, but Sparky could see his feet creeping closer to second by a fraction of an inch at a time. The next pitch was fouled straight up and behind the hitter, landing safely several rows into the premium seats. The runner ambled back to first.

As Sparky got set for the 1-2 pitch, he saw the runner crab-walking slowly toward second. There was no doubt the hit-and-run was on, so even with his shoulder crying out in anguish, Sparky reached back and hurled a Blazing Fastball with as much force as he could muster. The hitter's bat could only tickle the tail end of the flames as the pitch scorched the plate and struck the inside of Lou's mitt for strike three. But Lou had no time to shake off the sting in his left palm – the runner had jumped on the pitch and already was nearly at second.

Hopping up to his feet with a grimace, Lou fired the ball toward second, where Blerk was waiting with one foot on the bag. The other was planted right in the basepath in the hopes that it would create an obstacle for the runner. The ball found Blerk's mitt and the bulb-headed spaceman swiped at the cloud of dust that was quickly rolling across his feet. By the time Blerk completed the motion, the dust had blown away and the runner was standing upright with a toe on the corner of the base. Just like that, there was a runner in scoring position with only one out.

"Ah, dang it," Sparky said under his breath. Behind the plate, Lou dropped his head and held up a hand, accepting full responsibility for the stolen base. Sparky forgave him with a quick shake of his head. He turned to Blerk and they shared a similar exchange of brief yet meaningful head nods.

The next hitter stepped to the plate and again the runner took a couple of steps off the bag. Blerk stood behind the base, ready for the pickoff throw, but it didn't come. Sparky's first pitch was met with a swift crack of the bat, and a deep drive soared out to right field. The runner planted his left foot on second base, prepared to run no matter what. The entire stadium's eyes tracked Katie as she locked onto the ball and chased it toward the right field wall. The Canaries fans stood in their seats, already cheering as if the game were over. And for a moment, it looked like it might be.

Katie felt her footing change from the soft grass of the outfield to the compact dirt of the warning track. At best she had one more stride before she came face-to-face with the wall, which was covered by a yellow padding but nonetheless looked like the last thing she wanted to introduce her face to. The ball continued its trajectory, not giving up any of its velocity or altitude despite the distance it had traveled already. Unless somebody stopped it, it was going to end up in the bleachers. Katie decided it was time to be somebody.

Her next step didn't hit the ground – instead, she planted her cleats into the soft padding on the wall and used her momentum to carry her one step up the wall. Then, both feet were on the wall and Katie could already feel gravity trying to assert its influence over her. She grabbed onto to the top of the wall with her ungloved hand and reached up. If she had timed it right, the arc of the ball would intersect with her glove right...about...now.

As she felt the ball smack the inside of her glove, Katie looked into the crowd and saw a sea of faces, all wearing the same disbelieving, anguished expression. Two of them, however, stood out especially – the two Fort Clark fans she had been seated above on Opening Day. Seated in the front row of the bleachers, the two Canaries fans' faces quickly changed from amazement to anger when the out was recorded on the scoreboard.

"Hey guys," Katie caught herself saying, "The seats are better at Zigleaf, aren't they?" And just like that, Katie was dropping back to Earth like a stone.

Meanwhile, the runner saw the long fly ball turn into an out, tagged up and started hustling toward third. Bobby crouched into a sumo wrestling stance and punched his glove in anticipation of the throw. Katie's throw came in like a bullet to Fuzzy on the edge of the outfield, and Fuzzy relayed it with a bullet of his own. The impact nearly forced Bobby to take a step backward, but he held his ground. Unfortunately, the runner again slid in just under the tag and was now safe at third. The Canaries' dugout was loud with players clapping and shouting encouragement for the runner. Mustaine walked purposefully off the on-deck circle and strode to the plate.

Sparky watched as Mustaine stared him down, but he wasn't paying attention to the yellow-toothed sneer the hitter was showing him. He was silently and subtly testing his arm, checking for pain and looking for any sign that he potentially had at least one special pitch left. He found his shoulder feeling almost numb – that meant there was little chance the Phantom Slider would break properly, and even less chance it could fully disappear from sight. His elbow felt soft and sluggish, so his Blazing Fastball wouldn't produce much more than a puff of smoke as it slowly rambled across the plate. The Cosmic Change-Up also was out of the question, if the nagging pain in his bicep was any indication. Lou had been right, Sparky realized. By trying to carry the whole game on his shoulders, there was almost nothing left when his team needed him the most.

Nevertheless, he couldn't give up on anything now. He slapped his glove against his leg and looked in for the sign from Lou. The runner on third took his lead. Sparky's first wobbly pitch was called a ball as Lou had to lunge to the outside to catch it. Mustaine smirked and spat another stringy wad of saliva and seeds into the dirt. Sparky's arm was really starting to burn now, and he reasoned that if he couldn't get Mustaine, there was no way he'd be able to get Backlin. The Canaries' first baseman stood in the on-deck circle, rubbing dirt on the barrel of his bat and humming a jaunty tune to himself.

The next pitch felt like Sparky was trying to swim through sand, and again Lou had to come out of his stance to reach way outside of the strike zone for it. Now Mustaine was smiling openly, so much so that Sparky could see the flecks of sunflower seeds stuck to his teeth. He tossed another pitch that took far too long to reach the plate, and this time it came close enough to the corner of the plate to cause a half-second hesitation from the umpire before he called it ball three.

"Time!" Lou called as he hopped up and jogged out to the mound. The crowd was restless.

"My arm is a mess," Sparky said with his glove over his mouth.

"Oh good," Lou said, deadpan. "Here I was thinking you were screwing up on purpose for dramatic effect. What do you say you just concentrate on getting the ball over the plate, okay? This guy's not all that good, anyway."

"Lou, this guy's hitting .342 this season."

"That means he ain't hitting point-seven hundred and sixty, uh, no, wait...point-seven hundred and fifty... Heck, I'm not good with numbers like the blogger, but the point is even the best guys get out more often than they don't, so play the percentages and let's at least make him work for it."

"And what if that doesn't work?"

"Well, then I guess we'll have to think of something."

Lou slapped Sparky on the back and returned to the plate. Sparky fixed his eyes dead-center on the middle of Lou's mitt, which was itself centered directly in line with the point of home plate. Mustaine twisted his cleats into the dirt and stood ready. Sparky rotated his aching shoulder and checked the runner at third. The 3-0 pitch was on its way.

It was a fastball, but only in name. Sparky watched the ball hurtle toward the plate with all the urgency of a sleepy elephant and saw Mustaine's eyes gleam with malicious delight. He didn't just intend to hit this ball – the look in his eyes signaled nothing short of homicide. The bat came off his shoulder and within a second there was the cringe-inducing sound of contact. Katie immediately began backpedaling, but she was only trying to catch up to it. The ball caromed off the wall, and the stadium erupted in joy. A shower of popcorn and soda rained down on the expensive seats from the upper deck.

As soon as the ball struck the wall, the runner started jogging toward the plate. Lou took off his mitt and mask, dropping them to the ground in disgust. He shook his head sadly. Seeing Lou give up, the runner slowed into a triumphant trot, taking time to wave at the multitudes along the third baseline. Someone tossed him a cap bearing the words "Central League Champions," for which he proudly swapped his yellow Canaries cap.

Suddenly, however, the sound of cheering dropped off, replaced by a more frantic, pleading roar. The crowd was now waving its arms, pointing at home plate with intensity and screaming through cupped hands at the runner. He continued to home plate, giving the crowd a puzzled look. Then he felt something bump his chest. He looked down to see find the ball, in Lou's bare hand. The umpire screamed, "Out!" It was the only sound in the entire stadium.

"Kid's got a heck of an arm in right, doesn't she?" Lou asked the speechless runner. "Next time, keep your eye on the play and don't let yourself get fooled by an old fool."

The stadium had been drained of all life as the Goats celebrated their way off the field. There was hardly a sound in the entire building, save for the laughing and high-fiving that followed the Go-Town nine into the dugout. Within moments, all that was left on the Canaries Stadium field was a very irritated and angry Fort Clark Canaries team, who to a man kept their eyes locked onto the visitors' dugout.

In the Goats' clubhouse, the jubilant mood quickly subsided as the team took stock of their condition. Sparky laid back against his locker, several bags of ice strapped to his arm and shoulder. Thor rubbed his knees, still stinging from the dive he took. VORP had been dumped out in a pile on the floor, with the trainer sifting through his parts for anything salvageable.

"How's he looking?" Skip asked the trainer.

"Still mostly functional," the trainer replied. "But he's going to need some replacement parts."

"Kid, run down to the nearest hardware store and get the doc whatever he needs," Skip told the batboy. Exhausted from carrying a robot on his back for nine innings, the batboy slowly got to his feet, but the trainer stopped him.

"You don't understand, Skip," the trainer said. "VORP is

practically an antique, a collector's item."

"Hey, I might be worth money!" VORP said cheerily.

"I'm going to have to go online and see if I can find parts, and that'll take at least a few days."

"Well, kid," Skip said, slapping the batboy on the back, "Looks like we're gonna need that strong back of yours for a little bit longer."

The next day, the second game in the series started with a greater feeling of tension in Fort Clark. The Goats were now just one and a half games behind the Canaries, and the local newspapers were dominated by screaming headlines such as, "GOATS OUTSMART CANARIES," "CANARIES FALL FOR CHILDISH RUSE," and "O'MALLEY PROMISES 'COMPENSATION.'"

"Welcome back, Goats fans! Mel Fuller and the legend Randy Sannies here to start the bottom of the fourth in a game that, if the first three innings are any indication, should be another fine pitching duel between these two rivals. We've seen some fine work by Antonio de la Goya as well as the Canaries' starter, Cad Lawless. Wouldn't you agree, Randy?"

"Yep, you bet."

"The Goats' artistic lefty is facing the heart of the Fort Clark order now, with Mustaine, Backlin and Butler due up. Antonio's first pitch to Mustaine is right on the money for strike one! Randy, you played a lot of games here in this stadium against the Canaries in your career."

"That's right."

"How would you describe being a part of that rivalry, and a rather one-sided one, at that?"

"I didn't like it."

"Not at all?"

"Nope. Those guys were jerks."

"The 0-1 to Mustaine is in there for strike two! But surely, Randy, after you retired...there had to be some guys from those Canaries teams of your playing days that you've become friends with? Old-time players often talk about the community of baseball transcending old rivalries and..."

"Nope. Jerks."

"Well, there you have it, folks. And there's a line drive over Fernandez's head on the 0-2 pitch that'll skid to a halt in short left field for a base hit. Mustaine is safe at first with nobody out, and here's Bert Backlin. Well, regardless of how you feel about some of the Canaries you played against, Randy, you have to admit that it is a unique pleasure to get to visit this beautiful ballpark in one of the best baseball cities in the world."

"Nope. Hate it."

"De la Goya's first pitch to Backlin is high for ball one. Now Randy, I can understand some of the frustration you experienced losing to some of those great Canary teams of the past...coloring your experience somewhat, but most objective observers would agree that Canaries Stadium is a great, modern place to watch a game."

"Always smells like paint, gives me a headache."

"Just a reminder, folks, that the views and opinions expressed by Goats legend Randy Sannies do not necessarily reflect the views and opinions of this station. The 1-0 pitch to Backlin is high again, 2 and 0 the count."

"Just don't like Fort Clark."

"All right, Randy, we'll try to change the subject for you, then. Goats center fielder VORP continues to be carried around in an equipment bag by one of the team's batboys. Have you ever seen any arrangement so unusual in all your days as a player, Randy?"

"Mm...no."

"And we're back on track, ladies and gentlemen. The next offering to Backlin...is hit high in the air, deep to right field. Spalding chases it down, but this ball is going to land in the corner for a sure extra-base hit! Mustaine, with that great speed of his, rounds third and comes home easily as Backlin rumbles into second. The throw is late, Backlin is safe and the Canaries break through the scoreless barrier and lead the Goats now, 1-0."

"Hmph."

In the bottom of the seventh, Backlin connected on a solo home run that extended the Canaries' lead to 2-0. Even though Antonio was pitching a brilliant game, there was nothing the Goats could do to get to Lawless. In the top of the eighth, Lou dropped down on the bench next to Sparky and began strapping on his shin guards.

"It can't end like this, Lou," Sparky said as he stared out of the dark of the dugout into the endless sunshine on the field. The dugout was feeling smaller and smaller with each out, and Sparky imagined that by the end of the game it would completely surround him and shut out the light.

"Nobody said it was going to end like this, Sparky," Lou said to his shoes. "We still have four outs left, and as far as I know that's the only clock there is in this game."

"Yeah," Sparky said, watching Antonio knock a lazy pop-up into the sky directly above the Canaries' shortstop, who put it away for the final out of the inning. "But still."

The game moved quickly into the top of the ninth, with Lou, Antonio and VORP due up. Lawless remained on the mound, already doffing his cap to the fawning crowd in preparation for the complete game and pennant-clinching win. Relaxed and confident, Lawless ran the count to 3-2 against Lou. With a full count, Lawless went to his signature knockout pitch, a slider that broke far inside.

Seeing the pitch coming toward him, Lou leaned back slightly. The pitch had the spin of a breaking ball, but he needed a fraction of a second more to determine how it would break. Keeping his eyes riveted to the ball, he detected the faintest wobble, little more than a twitch as the ball closed the distance between the mound and the plate. It wasn't much. In fact, to the untrained observer the ball didn't deviate at all from its path. But to Lou's cultivated gaze, the ball's intentions were clear, but what he couldn't determine was whether or not the umpire would rule it a strike. He had less than a fraction of a second to decide whether or not to swing. In that fraction of a fraction of a second, Lou decided to choose "none of the above."

Leaning forward ever so slightly at the last possible moment, Lou put his forearm directly between the ball and the catcher's mitt. The pain jolted his mind back into regular speed again. Ignoring all impulse to rub the sore spot on his arm, Lou calmly dropped his bat and jogged to first base. The Goats dugout came to life, clapping and shouting their encouragements at the wily veteran, who only exhaled sharply as he touched the base. From the dugout, Sparky thought he saw a tear run quickly from Lou's eye, but the catcher immediately rubbed away all evidence that being hit was anything other than a pleasant experience.

Antonio came to the plate and watched Lawless' first pitch spiral across the plate for a strike. "Ah, such wonderful fluidity!" Antonio gushed. The next pitch blazed down the middle for strike two.

"Amazing!" Antonio enthused. "Pure, raw ferocity to counterbalance the grace of the previous pitch. You, sir, are a truly exceptional artist!"

Lawless only scowled and tugged the bill of his cap. Antonio looked into the dugout and saw Skip giving him a sign. Nodding his head, Antonio readied himself for the 0-2 pitch.

"Yes, you are quite the artist," Antonio continued. "Your precision and control are certainly laudable, make no mistake. However, if it's balance you're trying to create, perhaps I need to complement your order with a little...chaos!" At that, Antonio squared up to bunt, and the pitch bounced off the barrel of his bat with a weak "pop."

His eyes wide with shock, Lawless scrambled off the mound

in pursuit of the bouncing ball, which had taken a strange hop toward the third base side. Lou was able to slide into second safely, and Antonio's long legs were carrying him swiftly toward first. Lawless barehanded the ball and sailed it to Backlin, who made a game attempt to catch the high throw and keep his foot on first. However, Backlin had to hop ever so slightly to reach the toss from Lawless, and in the moment his toe came off the bag, Antonio was able to plant his foot firmly on the side of the base.

Inside the Goats' dugout, there was an explosion of excitement as the umpire called Antonio safe, but Skip tore his cap off his head and tossed it onto the ground. "What the jumping blue heck is he doing out there?" Skip sputtered. "I told him to swing away, not bunt the dang ball!"

"Aye, but he doth given our side greater numbers on the field of battle!" Thor offered. "Antonio did show the valiant courage of a warrior born this day! The god of thunder stands with you, friend Antonio!"

"Ah, it's the principle of the thing that bothers me, is all," Skip muttered. Looking around the dugout, something in Skip's expression changed. At least, that's the way it looked to Sparky. The sternness in his eyes dissolved, and his typical frown had vanished. Sparky had expected him to continue seething, or maybe take out his frustration on the bat rack, but instead he old man stood at the top of the dugout steps and started clapping his hands.

"That a way, Antonio!" Skip shouted toward first base. "Let's keep these bums guessing! They ain't gonna know what him 'em!"

On the bench, Bobby, Thor and Fuzzy shared a confused look. Carlos pulled his bat out of the rack and stopped in front of them. "What's the matter, guys?"

"It's Skip, man," Fuzzy said. "What's he doing?"

"It looks like he's cheering," Carlos said.

"Yeah, I know," Bobby said. "Isn't that weird?"

It was time for VORP and the batboy to take their at-bat, and the batboy had to duck out of the way every time VORP took a practice swing. "All right, yup yup yup, ready to knock 'em in, buddy!" VORP said. "Get ready to hustle up that base line, pal!"

"I'm so tired," the batboy said. "Can't you just work the count and try to draw a walk?"

The batboy got his wish, as VORP patiently took a few pitches and fouled off a few borderline ones to get to a full count. However, the next pitch was a hanging curveball that stayed in the zone just a tiny bit too long, and VORP was able to lay into it for a deep line drive into the left field gap.

"Oh man!" the batboy exclaimed as he began trudging toward first. Lou took third and headed home at the third base coach's insistence. Lou scored the Goats' first run of the game, and by the time the ball was tracked down and thrown back to the infield, Antonio was standing on third and the batboy had collapsed onto second base with VORP patting him on the shoulder repeatedly.

Carlos stepped gingerly into the batter's box, like an old lady testing the temperature of a bath before stepping into the tub. He was barely into his stance before Lawless started jawing at him. "Hey, rookie! Bet you never came up in a situation this big in the diaper leagues, huh? Why don't you just go stand over there in the corner so you don't embarrass yourself swinging at these sweet pitches I'm about to blaze your way?"

"Just stay calm," Carlos said to himself as he heard the catcher snickering behind him.

"I say, rookie, the gravity of your current situation must be weighing on your shoulders," Backlin called out from first base. "I should hate to add to your burdens, but surely you must be aware that your team's entire season now hinges on this at-bat! It might behoove you to spend some more time in the Big Leagues before attempting an at-bat of this magnitude. There's no shame in admitting this, you know!"

"Just stay calm, just stay calm," Carlos repeated as he rubbed his sweaty palms against the tape around the bat handle. The Goats' bench was standing and voicing their support, but between the hostile Fort Clark crowd and the Canaries' sustained verbal assault, they were difficult to hear. Carlos realized he was even having trouble hearing his own words.

"You're not going to make this happen, rookie," Lawless said as he stared down the middle of the plate for the sign. "Who knows? Maybe you'll have another chance like this in a few years when your peach fuzz comes in. And, you know, once you get shipped off to another team that isn't such a collection of losers!"

The first pitch came sailing in high and tight, looking like a giant snowball rolling straight down a high mountain peak straight at Carlos' ski lodge. Reflexively, Carlos swung at the pitch the way someone would swing at a bee at a picnic, spinning out of the way and falling into the dirt, triggering a wave of laughter throughout the stadium.

As Carlos pulled himself to his feet, he could see the Canaries' infielders struggling to contain their giggling. Every instinct in his body told him to just go. He could drop his bat, kick off his spikes and take the next plane right back to his village. He could become a fisherman, like his father and his brothers, and there would be absolutely no chance he'd ever run into anyone from Fort Clark ever again. It would be so easy, it had to be the right thing to do.

At least back in the village, the sun was welcome. It would coat the entire world in warm, syrupy light, comfortable as a blanket. Carlos could float out on the water in his little boat and feel safe. But here, the sun's rays felt like a spotlight, focusing all of its heat and blinding light right on top of Carlos' head. It would be so easy to just leave. Maybe the Fort Clark fans would even like him if he just quit. He looked down at his shoes – one of them was already untied. How hard would it be to slip it off?

Then, Carlos looked up into the Goats' dugout. Every single Goat on the bench was on their feet, leaning over the railing and waving towels over their heads. Sparky, standing next to Skip on the top step, looked right into Carlos' eyes and saw the look. He saw the look of all the players who found themselves in an impossible situation, the same look he was sure he had had at one point himself. He caught Carlos' eye, and nodded his head in such a way as to say, "I know."

Carlos knocked the dirt off his cleats with the bat and got back in the batter's box. Lawless shook his head and smiled, then shrugged. "Your funeral, kid," he said. The next pitch crossed the plate like a dart and now the count was 0-2. Carlos started looking around the ballpark, just to see if maybe there was an exit he hadn't seen before that was close. There wasn't, and Carlos began to imagine himself sitting in his tiny boat in the clear blue ocean with his father, their fishing lines dangling in the water.

He remembered one time in particular, when he was no more than 10 years old. Carlos had just spent 20 minutes trying to haul in a big fish, only to watch in dismay as the line snapped and the fish swam triumphantly away.

"We can get him tomorrow, right Dad?" he asked through tears.

"I don't think so, Carlos." His father looked out into the endless blue from under eyebrows like evergreen branches.

"Why not? He'll be here again tomorrow, most likely. All we need to do is be in the same spot, with the same bait, and..."

"And that is exactly why we won't catch him," Carlos' father said in his strong but soft voice. "He won't fall for the same trick twice. Sometimes, son, an opportunity only presents itself once, and you can either take it or wait for something else that's close, but not the same."

Taking a deep breath, Carlos dug his feet into the dirt next to home plate. Lawless smirked and tumbled the ball around and around in his hand. "Okay, rookie," Lawless shouted at Carlos over the thunderous noise of the crowd, "I'm going to put this one right over the middle of the plate, okay? I know you're not even capable of catching up with this pitch, which is the only reason I'm telling you this. Get ready!"

With that, Lawless went into his windup. The batboy took two painful steps off of second. Backlin turned and gave the fans a thumbs-up. Sparky thumped his fists against the dugout railing. Carlos reminded himself not to take his eyes off the ball.

The ball came spinning off the tips of Lawless's fingers, traveling in a bullet-straight line across the infield toward home plate. There was nothing out of the ordinary about its spin, to Carlos's eyes. He had seen many balls just like it in batting practice and on the playgrounds of his village. There was absolutely nothing special about it, it was as familiar to Carlos as the feather-stuffed cushions on his mother's old blue couch. And yet, Carlos knew this pitch was another big fish, one he might never have the chance to see again.

Carlos's eyes followed the ball all the way to the plate, where he watched it collide with the barrel of his bat. He watched it climb through the sky and fly toward the gap in right field. Antonio charged home, with VORP and the batboy chugging toward third to take their place. The ball continued its flight, with the center fielder and right fielder both trying to claim it. Neither caught up to it, and it bounced off the outfield grass and off the wall.

Antonio made it home easily for the tying run, and now the third base coach was waving his arms, urging VORP and the batboy to try for home. As he crossed first base, Carlos watched the right fielder scoop the ball off the warning track and hurl it like a shotput. The batboy scrambled and lurched down he third base line with his heavy load yelling the entire way.

The ball made it to the cutoff man, who wheeled around on his heel and aimed for home plate like a sniper. The batboy continued huffing and puffing, until finally his toe caught a tiny bump in the dirt and, for a moment, he was completely airborne.

The ballboy hung in the air for a brief moment, then came crashing to the ground with a disastrous clatter. The equipment bag's flap fluttered open, and all the assorted pieces of VORP came spilling out. The ball smacked the inside of the catcher's mitt, but the umpire didn't say a word yet.

Instead, the umpire looked down at the plate and saw VORP's finger already touching the corner of the plate. His finger was still connected to his hand, which was still connected to his arm, which was still connected to his body, which was touching his broken leg, which was touching his other broken leg, which was dangling out of the equipment bag, which was still on the back of the batboy.

"Safe!"

The stadium erupted. The Goats came pouring out of the dugout to celebrate at home plate as the Canaries stood at their positions in complete shock. As Sparky followed his teammates onto the field, he caught sight of Bert Backlin standing at first base, shaking his head. Tossing his glove to the ground, Backlin began striding purposefully in Sparky's direction. Sparky stopped and braced himself, but Backlin merely extended his hand.

"Ripping good show, Katakura," Backlin said as Sparky cautiously shook his enormous hand. "I dare say this has been the most memorable regular season I've ever experienced in the Central League, and it looks like I have you to thank for it."

"Uh, it's no problem at all, man," Sparky said. "Maybe we can do this again next year."

Backlin threw back his head and laughed uproariously. "Not bloody likely," he said, his expression becoming suddenly stern. Backlin released Sparky's hand and trudged off the field.

The Goats looked like they were in the middle of a group hug around home plate, but suddenly Sparky saw them hoist a laughing Carlos over their heads, to the crowd's delight. Katie looked like she was in a daze.

"Did this just happen?" she asked Sparky. "Did the Goats just win the pennant?"

"We just won the pennant," Sparky said. "And I'm just as shocked as you are."

"Don't be," Lou said, a smile creasing his face.

Even after an hour of celebration, the Goats fans were still hanging around the stadium when the team finally entered the clubhouse. Amidst all the hugging and high-fiving, Skip called the team to order.

"All right, all of you settle down," Skip said. "Now I want to say a few words."

"Good, because that's all you know," Fuzzy shouted from across the room.

"Under the circumstances I'm going to pretend I didn't hear that, Fernandez!" Skip replied. "Anyways, I just want to say that I'm proud of you bums. You stood up and delivered when your team needed you to, every last one of you. Now, I don't want to say this whole thing was because of one guy, but I think we all know that this wouldn't have been possible without the contributions of one specific individual..."

Lou slapped Sparky on the back and Bobby gave him a thumbs-up.

"...so I just wanted to say...you're welcome."

The team groaned in unison as Yoshi entered the room

pushing a huge laundry cart.

"Yoshi, I just wanted to say thanks again for everything you've done for me so far," Sparky told him. "And I'm sure my brother would thank you, too, if he was here."

The little old man squinted up at him through his thick glasses. "Gee, lay off the mushy stuff, will you? Besides, all you've done so far is make the playoffs."

"But I couldn't have done it without you."

"Wonderful, I'm touched. Now put this on." Yoshi tossed Sparky a new orange Goats cap, this one padded with thick wool and sporting ear flaps.

"What's this?" Sparky asked.

"Your official cold-weather gear," Yoshi said as he began distributing new caps and uniforms to the rest of the team. "The playoff match-ups for the first round were just set. You guys are going to Amundsen City to play the Polar League champs."

"Amundsen City?" Bobby said. "Isn't that...?"

"At the South Pole, uh-huh," Yoshi said flatly. "I'd pack some warm undies if I was you."

14. PLAYOFF PUSH

The city sparkled like a jewel against the icy Antarctic landscape, its crystalline towers rising out of the snow like they were part of the continent themselves. As the plane descended, Sparky could see hovercars shooting along the gleaming highways surrounding the spires and domes that made up much of the city.

"I'm shivering just looking at all that ice," Carlos said.

"It's probably not really that cold once you're inside the city," Sparky said. "Come on, you really think all those people down there would be happy living like penguins?"

By the time the Goats checked into their hotel, however, Sparky was rubbing his hands under his armpits just to keep the feeling in his fingers. A chubby man with rosy cheeks at the front desk cheerfully handed Sparky his room key.

"Not used to the cold, eh?"

"The rooms have heat, right?" Sparky said, shivering.

"Ho-ho, not here! The entire hotel's made of ice, you want the place to melt down? But don't worry, we'll make sure to send some extra blankets up to you!" Sparky's teeth chattered all night, making it exceedingly difficult to get any sleep that night.

Polar Park was an impressive sight from the outside. Thousands of interlocking ice blocks were stacked like Lego pieces, and many of them glowed with colored lights that changed to create shimmering displays. A series of glowing blocks formed the words "Go Explorers," then a fluttering pennant in the team's ice blue and gold, and then "Beat the Goats!"

"Sakes alive, they still use artificial turf down here?" Lou said as the Goats trudged across the rock-hard field.

"Nay, tis permafrost," Thor said. "This field reminds me of the realm of the frost giants in Niffleheim, a frozen place where the warmth of life can nary be found."

"Hey Bobby, I'll give you a hundred dollars if you lick the wall in the clubhouse," Fuzzy said.

On the mound, Sparky had to work hard to keep his footing, even with the extra-long cleats he put on before the game. He walked the first batter he faced and was in a 3-0 hole with the #2 hitter. Lou flashed the sign for the Blazing Fastball, and Sparky nodded enthusiastically.

He delivered the pitch, which caught fire just as it had hundreds of other times before. However, before the ball even made it halfway to the plate, the flame sputtered and flickered before finally being snuffed out. Trailing a tiny wisp of gray smoke, the ball fluttered over the plate, where the Explorers hitter made solid contact and sent it hurtling over Fuzzy's head and into left center field. Sparky slammed his fist into his mitt and looked up into the pale blue sky that was now indistinguishable from the sheets of permanent ice all around. A double-play ball from the next hitter advanced a runner to third, who scored on another failed Blazing Fastball. After the next Explorer to bat popped up softly, the score was 1-0 Amundsen City.

The Goats looked to answer right back in the top of the second, and there was hope in the dugout after Thor drew a leadoff walk. Bobby managed to slap a ground ball into left field, and Thor hustled into second base. Seeing the left fielder plant his feet to make a throw to second, Thor dropped down to slide into the bag. He slid...and slid...and kept right on sliding on the icy infield dirt until he slid completely over the base and halfway to third. Before the burly thunder god could get back to his feet, the second baseman had the ball in his mitt. He calmly trotted over to the still-scrambling Thor and tagged him out. The inning ended without further incident.

Thor slammed his batting helmet onto the dugout bench. "Fie on these wretched conditions!" he grunted. "How can these mere mortals play baseball on a surface that only Ymir, lord of the Frost Giants, would call suitable?"

"It's just going to take a little getting used to," Katie offered. "Didn't you guys read the park factor report I printed out for you yesterday?"

"Is that what that was?" Bobby asked. "Looked like a tax form to me."

"Yeah, you gotta remember to make those things look like a menu, or else Bobby's never gonna read it," Fuzzy said.

"Hey, lay off, puffball! Skip, tell Fuzzy to knock it off!"

"S-s-stop mouthing off, you jerks!" Skip said, his teeth chattering.

Katie stopped Sparky on his way onto the field. "Sparky, I know the weather's a little too cold for your Blazing Fastball, so I'd advise you to stick to your breaking stuff for most of the Explorers' lineup."

"Most?" Sparky crinkled his nose at the suggestion. "Why not all of them?"

"Ugh, you guys never read anything I give you!" Katie grumbled. "The Explorers have a bunch of guys who can't hit a breaking pitch to save their lives, but they also have that guy." She pointed to the on-deck circle and Sparky saw him – or it, he wasn't sure.

Rising nine feet over the on-deck circle was a beast covered in white fur that burst out of the sleeves of its jersey. Its feet were so big that each individual toe was shod in its own normal-sized cleat. Its red eyes glowed like lava rocks melting their way through a snowy field. The monstrous hitter carried the largest bat Sparky had ever seen.

"That is Gogrogog," Katie said. "He's a Yeti, in case you couldn't tell by looking at him. He's far and away the best hitter the Explorers have, especially when it comes to offspeed and breaking pitches."

"And that's all I have left in this cold," Sparky said flatly as the reality of the situation began to sink in. "Okay, so maybe I should have read your scouting report, you win. What's your advice?"

"Well, stay away from the strike zone, for one thing. He's not the most patient hitter, but he's got a good eye."

"Good enough to pick out a baseball during a snowstorm?"

"He spends his offseasons hunting polar bears, so I'd say so. Go get him, buddy."

"Yeah, thanks."

Sparky's first offering to the snowy monster flirted with the edge of the plate, but was called a ball. With the next pitch, he tried to make the Yeti chase a pitch up and inside, but the creature only watched it sail by for ball two. Two pitches later, Gogrogog was lumbering to first base with a walk. The next hitter whiffed on three straight pitches, but the one after that drove a ball deep into the gap that advanced the shaggy Yeti to third. Sparky found himself beginning to sweat despite the cold, and soon there were little ice crystals forming at the tips of his hair, pulling it down into his eyes.

The next hitter worked the count full, and by this point Sparky could feel his heart beginning to pound with anxiety. His pitch tumbled toward the plate, and when the hitter made contact it was like someone had punched him in the gut. The ball rocketed to Sparky's left, just inches from the webbing of his glove as he dove after it. Picking himself off the frozen ground, Sparky watched as Blerk shoveled the ball to Fuzzy for the force at second, then saw Fuzzy whip it to a waiting Carlos to complete the double play. Gogrogog trudged off the field with his head down.

Sparky exchanged high-fives with his infielders, but he was far from settled down. There was no way he'd be able to avoid pitching to the Yeti a second time, and he was starting to get tired.

"And we're back in Amundsen City, where the score remains 1-0 in favor of the Explorers, and the Goats are having some trouble adapting to the cold, wouldn't you say, Randy?"

"It's pretty cold, yeah."

"Well, here's hoping the Goats can start to warm things up here in the top of the eighth, with Houston, Katakura and VORP due up. A sellout crowd of 56,402 here today to witness this historic first-ever meeting between these two teams. The last time the Goats matched up against the Polar League was more than 75 years ago, and at that time Amundsen City was little more than a research outpost housing less than 100 people."

"Is that right?"

"Indeed it is, partner. Houston ready for the first offering from Perry, Lou is one-for-two so far today with a single in the third. Perry rocks and fires...Houston hits it on the ground, left side, not hit very hard. The shortstop charges in, scoops it up, throws over to first and it's in time to retire Lou Houston. The Goats are running out of time, and it would certainly be a shame to see such an amazing season end in such an ignominious fashion, wouldn't you say, Randy?"

"No."

"Is that because you have confidence that the Goats can pull it out here?"

"No, because I don't know what 'ignominious' means."

"Fair enough. Katakura up next, and he takes the first pitch for a strike on the outside corner, 0 and 1. Here comes the next offering from Perry...Katakura swings over the top of it and chops the ball off the ground directly in front of home plate! The ball shoots straight up into the air, Perry is camped under it but this is a high bounce, very high! Finally, the ball lands in Perry's glove, but Katakura is already safe at first on that high Baltimore chop off the rock-solid frozen tundra here in Amundsen City! Randy, have you ever seen a ball bounce that high off the infield before?"

"Uh, nope."

The Goats dugout came alive after Sparky's infield single, and they carried that energy through the rest of their half-inning. VORP let the pitcher's frustration with the infield hit hurt his control and patiently waited out a walk to put two runners on. Carlos followed that up with a line drive that just nicked the top of the second baseman's glove as it soared over him and into center field, loading the bases with just one out.

With two balls and two strikes on Fuzzy, he stepped out of the box and shook his head vigorously. "Hey man, this weather is brutal on my hair," he said to no one in particular. "It's all like, crunchy and everything. Can't get comfortable, dang!"

Fuzzy stepped back into the batter's box, took his stance and awaited the next pitch while twisting his neck around in an attempt to find a comfortable angle to hold his head. As he did, his batting helmet teetered precariously on top of his dry, brittle dome of hair. Just as Perry released the pitch, Fuzzy's helmet slid off the top of his head and down into his face, covering his eyes and causing him to swing blindly. The ball passed by untouched for strike three.

"Dang it!" Fuzzy spat as he tore his helmet off his head and slammed it to the ground, where it bounced up and smacked him directly in the mouth. "Gang id!"

It came down to Thor, with the bases loaded and two out. Thor stepped to the plate and took a moment to knock the ice off his cleats with a few taps from Mjolnir. On the mound, the pitcher, Perry, spat at the ground, the spittle freezing into an icy stalagmite before it even touched the ground. He started his windup, and all around him the winds began to swirl, collecting the snow that hung in the air and creating a frosty vortex that surrounded him completely.

"Oh gosh," Katie said in the dugout, almost too quietly for Sparky or anyone else to hear. "It's the Avalanche Cutter."

Perry was now practically invisible on the mound, wrapped up in a funnel cloud of swirling snow. Suddenly, the snow curtain dropped and Perry released the pitch. The ball was concealed inside a massive cloud of snow and ice that rumbled toward the plate at a frightening speed. It looked like a ton of snow was sliding down a mountain at Thor, and the red-bearded Asgardian was taken completely by surprise.

Shutting his eyes tight against the onslaught of frozen annihilation coming straight for him, Thor took a blind hack at the center of the snowy mass. There was a sharp crack, and Thor opened his eyes. He scanned the skies for any sign of the ball, but saw only the right fielder chasing after it toward the stands. The outfielder pulled up before running into the wall, and the ball dropped harmlessly into the seats several rows deep. Thor breathed a deep sigh of relief and tightened his grip on his enchanted bat.

"Hey, so tell me why that pitch wasn't on those fancy spreadsheets you keep yelling at us to read, huh, Miss Spalding?"

Skip had marched over to Katie and waved a copy of her scouting report in her face like a teacher confronting his student with another failed quiz.

"Perry hasn't used that pitch in two years," Katie stammered. "He had the Rowengartner procedure on his elbow, so he shouldn't be able to throw like that!"

"Well, I guess that son of a gun out there didn't get the memo," Skip snapped back. "You wanna head out there and show him the pie chart that tells him he shouldn't be able to throw that pitch, or should I?" With that, he stomped away to lean against the dugout railing and grumble to himself.

Thor clenched his fingers around the handle of his bat and stared out at Perry. The fans were still buzzing at the long-delayed appearance of the Avalanche Cutter, and for the first time that day their voices overwhelmed the whistling of the cold wind overhead.

Perry checked the runners and went into his windup again. The winds enveloped him once more, and the rush of snow came rumbling across the infield. Again, Thor closed his eyes against the pelting ice crystals and swung without looking. This time, he clipped the underside of the ball and sent it hurtling straight up in the air. The catcher jumped up and began chasing the ball toward the backstop. Thor looked up helplessly as the catcher tried to keep his mitt directly underneath the ball, but the wind eventually caught it and caused it to flutter erratically in the air before dropping softly into the netting over the first few rows of seats.

Thor took a step out of the batter's box and adjusted the straps of his batting gloves. "Wouldst thou try to use the winds themselves against the son of Odin?" Thor said to Perry. "Against the god of thunder himself?"

Stepping back into the box, Thor tapped his bat on the center of the plate. Perry checked the runners again, and found all the Goats on base were shivering and hugging themselves to stay warm, clearly not in any mood to start running. The pitcher began his windup.

"Know this, mortal," Thor continued, "to toy with the elements is to invite the wrath of Thor!"

Perry emerged from the center of the tiny ice storm around the mound and delivered the next pitch, which again was swallowed up in the swirling, rushing cloud of cold. Thor stood defiant this time, not even closing his eyes. Instead, he held his bat on his shoulder and continued bellowing at the mound.

"The winds obey only THOR!" As he shouted his name, the wind suddenly changed direction, and the wall of snow and ice rushed back toward Perry. The pitcher threw his glove in front of his face for protection. The ball continued coming toward the plate, deadened by the force of Thor's voice. What was once a mighty fastball concealed in a whistling torrent of icy chaos was now a batting practice cream puff, seen as plain as day. Thor lifted the bat off his shoulder and swung with the power of a warrior on the field of battle. All four Goats on the field at that moment would touch home plate.

The score was 4-3 in favor of Go-Town headed into the ninth inning, and Sparky was on his way to a complete game. However, by the bottom of the ninth the atmosphere had become much colder and more bitter. It had nothing to do with the weather. The Explorers had loaded the bases with two outs, and the man coming up to bat wasn't a man at all. With his lumbering gait, Gogrogog strode to the plate, snorting and chomping and all the while burning through Sparky with his glowing red eyes. Sparky blew into his cupped right hand, trying in vein to warm it up, but the truth was he hadn't had any feeling in his hands for the last three innings. Lou called time and ran out to the mound as fast as his knees could carry him.

"Well kid, I'd sure like to know how you plan to get yourself out of this one," Lou said, spitting at the ground.

"You and me both, Lou."

"Normally, I'd say give the big lug a free pass to first base and take our chances with the rest of the lineup, but there ain't no way we can afford to give up a run here." Lou spat again.

"I know, man, I know." Sparky pounded his mitt and looked up into the pale blue sky. "He's going to crush anything I give him in the strike zone."

"Maybe we just have to let him put it into play and count on the defense to pull us out," Lou said, with another spit. Sparky looked around the diamond and saw his teammates shuddering in the cold. He looked back down at his shoes, and caught sight of Lou's shoe. Lou's spit had already frozen solid into a spiky little icicle.

"Okay, I've got it," Sparky said. "I'm gonna give him something nice and easy, slow and straight right down the middle."

"Sparky, this danged Yeti is going to make contact with a pitch like that for sure," Lou said.

"That's okay," Sparky said as he spit into the center of his glove. "I need him to. You just stay on your toes, okay?"

Lou nodded slowly and smiled. "You got it, kid." Sparky spit into his glove again and set himself for the pitch.

True to his word, Sparky delivered the slowest, straightest "fast" ball he could muster. And, just like Lou said, Gogrogog turned on it and smacked it squarely with a reverberating crack. The Yeti flipped his bat in front of the plate and took off toward first. The runner on third started running home. The outfielders snapped to attention and began scanning the skies, but none of them could find the ball. They all turned to look at each other in disbelief, and Katie looked back into the bleachers for a sign that the ball had left the yard. But no fan in the stands held the ball.

By the time the runner made it near home plate, he took notice of the confusion that had gripped the players on the field. Everyone had heard the ball strike the bat, but moments later no one in the entire stadium had found it – or so it seemed.

The runner trotted up to home plate, half-watching the Goats looking around helplessly for the ball. He was met just before the plate by Lou, who was holding the bat Gogrogog had tossed away just a few seconds before. He tapped the runner on the top of the helmet with the bat, and for a moment there was nothing but confused silence. Then, Lou turned the bat around and showed the umpire the ball, frozen to the spot where it made contact by an icicle made of spit.

"Out!" shouted the umpire.

The Goats converged on the mound in a chaotic group hug of sorts, with Sparky crushed in the middle. As he was tossed back and forth like a sock in an otherwise empty dryer, Sparky suddenly felt something cold and wet pelting his face. He looked up and saw a barrage of snowballs raining down on the jubilant Goats from the angry Explorers fans in the stands.

"That was a heck of an idea, Sparky!" Lou said as he clapped his pitcher on the shoulder. "I hope you got a few more of them up your sleeve before the playoffs are over!"

"Well, here's one," Sparky said, wincing as more ice and snow struck him on the back of the neck. "Why don't we get into the clubhouse?"

Fuzzy broke for the dugout first, his hair almost completely frosted with particles of ice like an evergreen tree in a blizzard. "Come on, holy cats!" he said. "They're running out of snow and starting to throw ice!"

Once they were all back in the relative safety of the clubhouse, the Goats immediately began clustering around the few heaters in the room, warming their hands and faces. Bobby cracked open his locker and pulled out a large box. He started tossing little paper-wrapped packages to his teammates.

"What the heck is this, Bobby?" Katie said as she picked at the paper.

"Celebratory ice cream sandwiches!" Bobby said holding one in each hand over his head triumphantly. "Are we going to do this right or aren't we?"

"You better watch how many of those you put away, unless

you want to play third base from a wheelbarrow," Lou said.

"What do you mean?" Bobby said with his mouth full. "That's it, right? We won!"

"We only won the first round of the playoffs, amigo," Antonio said. "There are still several rounds left to go before we reach the Worlds Series."

Bobby's mouth hung open long enough for a dribble of ice cream to fall from his lips. "What?"

"Man, I knew beating Amundsen City was too good to be true," Bobby said a few days later as he fastened his seat belt. "This isn't what I signed up for, no way!"

"Still thy mewling, friend Bobby," Thor said sternly. "Tis no true warrior who girds himself for battle in such a childish, cowardly manner!"

"Wh-what?" Bobby gripped the armrests on his seat so tightly his fingernails punctured the upholstery.

"He says you're being a big baby, dude," Carlos said, then turning to Lou, who had his arms crossed in front of him and his seat tilted back as far as it could go. "That is what he said, right?" Lou nodded without opening his eyes or saying a word. Carlos smiled broadly.

"Man oh man, I wish we could just get this over with as quickly as possible so we can just go home," Bobby whined as sweat began to appear on his forehead.

"I don't understand," Blerk said from his seat behind Bobby. "Unless I am misunderstanding, the object of this contest is to progress as far as you can. The length of time you require to do so is irrelevant."

"No, man, not the playoffs," Bobby said, his voice quivering. "I mean this weirdo road trip!"

"Please fasten your seat belts," a calm female voice said over the speakers. "The captain has turned on the 'no gravity' sign. We will begin our trip momentarily. Thank you for traveling with Relativistic Spaceways, and we hope you enjoy your journey."

"Oh no oh no oh no oh no oh no," Bobby repeated quietly to himself.

"Ten, nine, eight, seven, six, five, four..."

"Oh no oh no oh no oh no oh no..."

"...three, two, one. Blast-off."

There was an intense rumbling, and then the Goats were suddenly pressed flat against their seats by the force of gravity. Bobby continued to dig his nails into his arm rest while Lou snored away next to him.

Sparky watched the stars streak by through the window

until he saw a shining globe appear out of the darkness of space, growing slowly larger as they approached. "Check it out, Lou," he said. "It looks like the moon."

Lou opened his eyes and sat up for a moment. He took a quick look out the window and then sunk back into his seat. "That's no moon," he said. "That's the ballpark."

As the ship grew nearer, Sparky could see how massive Orbit Stadium was. Half of the massive globe was a transparent dome that covered the field and the grandstands. Outside the dome, floating in the space just beyond the outfield walls were a set of floating platforms that contained the bleachers. It was unlike anything he had ever seen in his life, even watching on TV.

The view inside the stadium was just as impressive. From the mound, Sparky could see an asteroid belt floating directly over his head, and a massive ringed planet loomed in the distance behind the left field stands. He was so transfixed by the wonders of infinite space during his warmup tosses that he almost didn't notice Lou had left home plate and was standing directly in front of him.

"Didn't mean to startle you, kid, but I thought you should know we might be in some trouble here," Lou said, nodding in the direction of the umpires. In the center of their cluster was an imposing figure, easily a foot taller than any other umpire. His black chest protector was covered with lights that slowly pulsed red. His face was completely obscured by a black, featureless mask that reflected a dark, twisted version of the world across his visage. The sight of him caused a shiver up Sparky's spine.

"That's our home plate ump," Lou said. "They said his name is Drax Crater, and word is he's a real hard case."

"Really?" Sparky said with his mouth agape. "What tipped you off?"

Sparky took the mound in the bottom of the first, learning through the PA system what his name sounded like in an alien language. It sounded like someone trying to sing "Funky Town" with their head submerged in pudding. Blerk stifled a giggle.

"What?" Sparky asked him. "What did they say about me?"

"I'm afraid the joke doesn't really work unless you can hear in subsonic frequencies," Blerk said, wiping a tear away from one of his enormous eyes. "But on some planets it's actually preferred to have hair like a Pandulvian Glistshiffer, so I wouldn't worry too much about it."

The first batter for the Rigel 7 Conquerors settled in behind the plate. It was an oozing glob of green goo that gripped the bat with one tentacle. Its hat was half-submerged in the gelatinous mass that was where its head would have been. Drax Crater took his position behind the plate and raised his hand above his head.

"Play ball!" Crater called out in a booming register that sounded like it came through a megaphone.

Sparky sized up the hitter and went into his windup. The first pitch whizzed over the plate and struck the inside of Lou's mitt more or less in dead center of the plate. Might as well try to intimidate the hitter with a little bit of heat right out of the gate, Sparky thought. Crater snapped his wrist and pointed to the side. "Strike one!" he said with authority.

The next pitch was another fastball, slightly lower than the previous one, and the jiggling batter waved his bat at it unsuccessfully. "Strike two!" Crater called.

Sparky checked the sign from Lou – the old catcher wanted a curveball right over the middle to catch the batter swinging. Sparky nodded and delivered a perfect 12-6 curve that dropped from a dizzying height right into the center of the strike zone. The hitter was clearly baffled, as it didn't even swing at the pitch. Sparky looked up at Crater, but the umpire hadn't yet signaled a strike. Instead, the helmeted Crater just straightened up, turned to the side and said, simply, "Ball."

Lou tossed the ball back to the mound and turned slightly to look over his shoulder at the umpire. "That one missed?" Lou asked casually.

"The pitch was too high as it crossed the plate," Crater said. "The count is 1 and 2." Lou shook his head but focused his attention back on Sparky. He gave the sign for the next pitch and Sparky delivered another fastball that crossed the inside corner of the plate. Again, the quivering mass of jelly at the plate was too petrified to swing. And again, Crater nonchalantly adjusted his jacket before announcing, "Ball two."

"Having a hard time seeing where that missed, I'll tell ya," Lou said.

"I have an innate knowledge of the strike zone, as do all umpires," Crater said. "I find your lack of faith disturbing."

"Yeah, all right, all right, just saying, is all."

Sparky gave Lou a puzzled look, and Lou just shook his head. The next sign came in, and Sparky reared back to hurl another blistering fastball that tickled the outer half of the plate, a surefire strike if Sparky had ever seen one. The batter winced but didn't move the bat. Lou glanced behind him and saw Crater tugging on his black leather gloves. "Ball three," he said.

Sparky looked up into the dome and beyond into the infinite darkness of space that surrounded the ballpark. What was it going to take to find this guy's strike zone? Exasperated, he got the next sign from Lou and threw a Phantom Slider that the batter finally took an ugly hack at and missed. Crater called "Strike three!"

and the blob wiggled its way back to the dugout.

Sparky continued to struggle with the strike zone for the next two batters, running both of them to full counts before inducing a pop fly for one and getting the next one to slap a sharp grounder to Bobby that he just barely threw to first in time to get the runner. As he left he mound, Sparky glared in Crater's direction, but the umpire only stood there behind home plate, arms crossed, his shiny black helmet reflecting Sparky's scowl right back at him.

By the bottom of the second, Sparky felt like he had pitched both ends of a day-night doubleheader. It seemed like Crater wouldn't call anything a strike unless it was belt-high and down the middle or swung on and missed. Sparky had racked up five walks trying desperately to nudge the boundaries of the strike zone out an inch or two, but Crater was unyielding. There was only one out, but there was a liquid metal robot on second and a two-headed runner on first, both beneficiaries of 3-2 pitches that were deemed unworthy by the implacable Crater.

Sparky stepped off the rubber to wipe the sweat off his forehead with his sleeve. Lou shifted his weight from one foot to the other as he crouched behind the plate. Neither one of them looked like they could take much more of this.

The next hitter was a towering blue humanoid with four arms, and he used all four to wave the bat over the plate. Sparky's first pitch was popped back over Lou's head and into the stands for the first strike. Taking a deep breath, Sparky checked the runners and delivered the next pitch, a breaking ball that the hitter swung through for strike two.

Lou called for the Blazing Fastball for the third pitch, hoping that Sparky could close the door on the hitter swinging through another pitch. Sparky nodded, checked, and pitched. The Blazing Fastball burned through the air, startling the hitter so badly he actually let go of the bat with two of his hands to throw them in front of his face defensively. However, the ball was resting just two inches off-center to the inside of the plate, so Crater crossed his arms and announced "Ball one."

Sparky slammed the ball into his mitt and kicked at the mound. For his next offering, Sparky served the Cosmic Changeup, and again the batter twitched but didn't offer at the pitch. The hitter stepped out of the batter's box and tilted his helmet back to reveal a pair of glimmering insect-like eyes just above his normal ones.

"Cosmic awareness, human," the hitter smirked. "You can't sneak one of those past me!"

Sparky just shook his head and rolled the ball around in his hand. If he couldn't trick the hitter into swinging at a ball outside of the zone, and if the zone was only about the size of a baseball to begin with, there was really only one thing he could do, he figured. He kicked his leg high and fired the next pitch straight down the middle of the plate. It was slow and level – any hitter would have had to be blind not to get a good look at it. The batter tensed all four of his arms and belted the ball into deep right field.

Katie chased after the ball, which was rapidly leading her onto the warning track. She had less than two steps before she would collide with the wall. Ignoring every self-preservation instinct that was screaming in her brain to stop, Katie lifted her glove into the air and braced for impact. She collided with the padded wall with a cringe-inducing "thump" as all her momentum was stopped suddenly dead. The ball, however, was cradled safely in the center of her glove, and it stayed there even as Katie crumpled to the dirt.

Within moments, the Goats all were huddled around Katie as she lay on the warning track. The trainer sat down on the grass next to her. "Katie?" he said. "Can you hear me? Say something if you can hear me, come on."

Sparky dropped to his knees and leaned over the right fielder. "Nice play out there, Spalding," he said.

"Nice pitch, Katakura," Katie said without opening her eyes. "I've seen practice tees that could fool a hitter better."

With Katie icing her knee in the dugout, the Goats went to bat in the bottom of the inning. And while Sparky had been struggling to fit his pitches inside Crater's tiny strike zone, the Conquerors' starter was having no trouble at all. Of course, as a robot, FERG-1E had little trouble doing anything without accuracy, thanks to his computerized brain and a targeting system capable of hitting any target within one micron.

The robot had been fooling the Goats' hitters all day, changing speeds and the arc of each pitch but still managing to fit it into the strike zone when they didn't swing. When it was Sparky's turn at bat, he tried to talk himself into a different approach. "Come on, man," he told himself, "you know the pitch is going to be right down the middle of the plate. No matter what the pitch looks like, there's no way he's going to put it anywhere but right there in the center of the zone. Just swing in the same spot it's going to be and you'll hit it!"

FERG-1E's first pitch came catapulted out of his hand high. It looked like it would miss the strike zone by more than a few inches, but Sparky knew it would drop eventually. "Just swing," he told himself. "Swing right through the center of the plate. It'll be there."

A fraction of a second later, and the ball was still coming in high to Sparky's eyes. "Just swing belt-high," he reminded himself.

"Don't try to swing any higher, you'll just swing over the top of it when it comes down. And it's coming down...now! No! Wait! It's still too high! Don't swing! No, I have to swing! But I can't swing at a pitch that high, Coach will make me run laps! You're not in high school anymore, genius! Just SWING!"

And he did. But it was several seconds after the ball had landed safely in the catcher's mitt. Crater watched Sparky take his belated hack and called out, "Still only one strike."

"Yeah, thanks," Sparky said without looking up from his shoes. "Wouldn't have to swing like an idiot if you opened that strike zone up a little bit," he muttered under his breath, or so he thought. Crater tilted his head slightly to one side and then crossed his arms slowly.

FERG-1E got set for the 0-1 pitch. As the robot released the ball, however, the dirt of the pitching mound shifted ever so slightly under the robot's weight and crumbled out from under his left foot, causing him to land awkwardly on his right. Instead of hitting the target square, the pitch came in about an inch and a half above Crater's zone. Sparky took a step back, expecting a 1-1 count.

"Strike two!" Crater bellowed, pumping his fist straight out. Sparky nearly dropped his bat. Knowing that arguing balls and strikes would mean a quick trip to the showers, Sparky instead sighed deeply and stared up into the dome.

"That one, uh, that one missed?" Sparky said, as meekly as he could.

"The count is 0-2," Crater droned.

"Right, right, it's just that there were, um, a few pitches in the last inning that were right around there, and they were called balls... so..."

"I am altering the strike zone. Pray I don't alter it any further."

Sparky grumbled to himself and waited for the next pitch. FERG-1E settled in and delivered a fastball that came screaming in at Sparky's hands. Reflexively, he hopped out of the way, the catcher's mitt stabbing across his chest to get between Sparky and the ball. Sparky turned to watch Crater, who twisted his hand into a tightly clenched fist.

"Strike three!"

The altered zone carried over to VORP's at-bat, as the Conquerors' robot quickly dispatched the Goats' with three called strikes that looked to be well outside even another umpire's strike zone. Sparky retrieved his glove from the dugout bench and started out onto the field, only to be stopped by Lou.

"I'd advise against trying to ring up any more K's today,"

Lou said in an even graver tone of voice than he normally used.

"What are you talking about? He finally loosened up the strike zone!"

"You think he's going to give you the same looks he gave that robot fella? Ump's got it out for you, kiddo. He won't call another strike for you the rest of the day."

"So what do I do?"

"Well, you have seven other guys out there literally watching your back," Lou said. "I'd say keep your wits about you, trust your teammates to do their jobs, and for God's sake, keep the ball down."

Sparky kept Lou's words in the back of his mind as he pitched the next inning. He concentrated on throwing sinking balls that resulted in ground balls. Meanwhile, Sparky started kicking at the dirt in the mound, loosening a little bit more of the mound before each pitch.

By the top of the ninth inning, the situation couldn't have been more nerve-wracking unless the Worlds Series was on the line. Sparky stood next to Katie in the dugout and watched FERG-1E erase Carlos on yet another strikeout.

"This is hopeless," Katie said flatly. "That robot isn't showing any signs of slowing down."

"Isn't there some kind of pattern to his pitch selection we could try to exploit or something?" Sparky asked.

"No, he must be using his computer to randomly generate pitches. It's possible that even the robot doesn't know what he's going to throw until he starts throwing it." Sparky kept his eyes fixed on the front of the mound.

"Maybe we just need to be patient," Sparky said.

"That makes sense from a statistical standpoint," Katie said, "I mean, if you stretch out our at-bats to infinity, the odds that we get a hit against the robot become even, but we probably won't get infinity at-bats, Sparky."

"That's not what I meant," Sparky said, pointing to the spot on the mound where FERG-1E's foot came down during each delivery. "Look!"

As the robot went into his delivery for the next pitch to Fuzzy, his foot landed in the same spot that Sparky had been kicking at for most of the game. The dirt crumbled underneath his foot just enough to cause FERG-1E's entire body to shift ever so slightly to his left, causing the pitch to wobble off its intended flight path and right into Fuzzy's hot zone.

Fuzzy gave the ball a jolt and sent it high into the artificial air. As Fuzzy dropped his bat and took off for first, the ball continued traveling higher and higher, until it finally struck the clear dome with a "plunk" that echoed throughout the stadium. The ball's spin caused it to skid across the underside of the dome, hugging its curvature all the way around, over the heads of the fans in the outfield stands and straight down to the ground on the far end of the dome for a home run. Fuzzy pumped his fist as he circled the bases, and the rest of his teammates celebrated in the dugout. Sparky had been staked to a one-run lead with only three outs to get, but Crater loomed imperiously over the plate.

Sparky continued to keep the ball down and rely on his defense to bail him out, but with so much pressure placed on them for so long, some cracks were bound to show. Twice, a ground ball squirted past Bobby along the third base line, putting two runners on the basepaths with two outs and the Conquerors' cleanup hitter stepping to the plate.

Standing straight and flaring his nostrils as he examined his bat for flaws, Tork was one of the few Big Leaguers to come from the mysterious and storied Krangling Galaxy. Word around baseball was that the Kranglings' warrior mentality made the very thought of playing baseball for merely recreational purposes blasphemous. Many Big League scouts had left for the Krangling Galaxy on recruiting trips, never to return. What few Kranglings had come to Earth to play in the Big Leagues refused to discuss their home world or the circumstances of their emigration. All Sparky could see was a bulky man with blood-red skin, horns that poked through his batting helmet and a frightening power swing.

Sparky concentrated, tried to envision the strike zone sitting dead center in Lou's mitt. Maybe there was a chance he could sneak one or two past the hitter, put him in a hole so he could catch the big guy swinging at something funny-looking. Sparky's fingers curled around the surface of the ball, the stitches falling in line with where he wanted them. He checked the runners, coiled and released.

There was no fooling a Krangling, however. The bulky batter flared his expansive nostrils, reared back and hacked. He cracked a screaming line drive no more than seven feet high that looked like it was a sure thing to hit the right field wall and rattle around in the corner for an extra-base hit. Sparky watched with his heart nearly in his throat, but the ball eventually veered over the foul line and ricocheted off the head of a fish-faced fan wearing a large breathing dome. Sparky was ahead in the count, but there was no way he'd feel comfortable taking another chance like that again.

Lou gave Sparky the sign for the Cosmic Changeup, and after a moment's hesitation Sparky okayed it. Even if the Krangling could somehow figure out the timing on that pitch, its lack of speed would result in a ball with a much better chance of staying inside the confines of the ballpark.

With the strain on his arm beginning to make its presence known to him, Sparky fired the Cosmic Changeup. He could see the Krangling's eyes zero in on the ball, watched him track it on its way to the plate. He watched the pupils of the hitter's eyes grow huge as the pitch's movement took effect and time seemingly stopped for him. Too late, the batter lifted the bat off his shoulder, and by then the ball was resting comfortably in Lou's mitt.

Infuriated, the Krangling hitter stomped his feet outside the batter's box and cursed Sparky's name in a language very few outside of the Krangling Galaxy ever heard. The fearsome hitter adjusted his helmet, looked in at Sparky and nodded his head solemnly. He didn't say a word, but Sparky took the meaning well enough: "Now that I've seen that pitch once, I will absolutely destroy it the next time you attempt it." Sparky swore he could see actual steam blasting out from the hitter's impressively large nostrils.

With Crater crossing his arms and staring Sparky down, he knew he wouldn't be able to sneak one past Tork. There was one thing he hadn't tried yet, however. Catching Lou's eye, Sparky tapped the side of his head with one finger. "I have an idea," the gesture said. Lou nodded and put up his mitt.

Sparky held the ball up in one hand. "I have the ball," he announced. Tork snorted and looked confused. "Can you see that I have the ball?"

"Yes!" Tork shrieked. "Now throw it so that I can destroy it!"

Sparky started his motion, kicking his leg high in the air, bringing both hands up close to his face, then whipping his pitching arm forward while holding his glove hard close to his body. No sooner had Sparky brought his arm all the way around did the Krangling batter unload instinctively with a massive swing. And just as Tork finished the backswing on his massive swing, Sparky plucked the ball out of his glove and underhanded it to Lou.

"Strike three," Crater stated. "Most impressive."

Exhausted, Sparky collapsed into the folding chair in front of his locker. His pitching arm felt like a sack of wet sand grafted onto his shoulder. A large group of Goats had gathered around the clubhouse TV to watch the end of the other crucial Game 7 taking place that day, between the Athens Olympians and the San Diego Whales. The only thing Sparky cared about was getting some ice on his arm.

"You're looking kind of run-down there," Lou said as he passed by.

"Doesn't matter," Sparky replied wearily. "At most there's fourteen games left to go, and then I'm done."

"With the season? With your quest? Or done...for good?"

Sparky closed his eyes and leaned back in his chair for a long moment. "I don't know," he said finally. He had been so focused on his goals that Sparky had never thought much about what he would do if he failed. If Ken really did belong to the Baseball Devil for all eternity, how could he even pick up another ball as long as he lived? Where could he go where he wouldn't be reminded of the game constantly, except Go-Town, the would-be home of his greatest failure? If he couldn't lead the Goats to victory in the Worlds Series, Sparky might as well be trapped in Mr. Stitches' accursed card album himself.

Sparky's introspection was interrupted by a raucous cheer from the other end of the clubhouse. The players who weren't watching before were now crowding around the television, and Sparky was the last to join them.

"What happened?" Sparky asked as he tried to rub the feeling back into his arm.

"Athens just got a walk-off grand slam," Bobby said excitedly. "They're moving on to the next round."

"We have to play Athens next?" Carlos said. "That's a killer lineup they've got, man."

"No, Athens was a lower seed than San Diego," Katie corrected. "They're get to play New York."

"Whoo, lots of luck to you guys," Fuzzy said, pointing to the screen and the jubilant Athens players celebrating on the field. "The Emperors are gonna tear through you like you're wet toilet paper."

"That's disgusting, dude," Bobby said.

"So where does that leave us?" Antonio asked.

"Now that Athens is moving on, we're going to be playing the higher seeded team left," Katie said. "We're going to Graviton City."

"I don't even know where that is," Bobby marveled.

"No kidding, the only thing you can find on a map is the nearest Taco Taco Taco," Fuzzy snorted.

Bobby slapped Fuzzy on the back of the head, and the two began playfully shoving each other away from the TV. The others soon pulled themselves away from the screen to get their showers and finally change out of their uniforms. Katie and Sparky were the only ones left as the professional voices of the post-game show hosts took over.

"A walk-off grand slam," Katie said. "Just goes to show you how anything can happen in this game."

"Guys hit home runs all the time, Spalding," Sparky said.

"Even guys with no career home runs and .075 lifetime averages versus left-handers? There's a first time for everything, I guess."

"I know," Sparky said. "I'm counting on that."

"This is seriously making me real nervous, you guys," Bobby said as he stepped onto the glowing circle in the center of the room.

"Don't worry about it," said the technician as she tapped on the touchscreen in front of her. "Teleportation is the safest form of travel, and it's the only way to reach Graviton City." The tone in her voice made it clear she had delivered that information thousands of times.

"Quit being a baby and just get microwaved already," Fuzzy shouted from the back of the line. "You worried that thing is going to make you uglier somehow?"

"Valiant Fuzzy speaks the truth, Bobby!" Thor said. "Where is thy sense of adventure?"

"Probably the same place I ralphed up my breakfast a little while ago," Bobby said. He shut his eyes tightly as the teleporter began to hum ominously. A brilliant white light appeared in the center of Bobby's body and soon enveloped him and his luggage completely. When the light finally died down, Bobby and his bags had disappeared.

"Did he make it?" Fuzzy asked, hopping up and down to try and see over the heads of his teammates.

"Yep, he made it," the technician answered.

"Whew," Fuzzy said. "I'm glad he went first instead of me!"

"Aye, verily. Yon device doth creepeth me out."

The Goats were soon assembled in the main teleporter station of Graviton City, a massive metropolis that hung suspended in the clouds. Sparky saw a colorful banner hung over the teleporters that read, "Welcome to Graviton City, home of Earth's greatest heroes!" The station was ringed with golden statues of heroic-looking men and women in tight outfits. Names like "Captain Champion" and "Luminous Lass" were chiseled into the bases. Sparky rolled his eyes.

"That wasn't so bad," Bobby said. "Kind of felt like my stomach when I eat too many hot wings, only all over."

"Speaking of food, how soon get we get to the hotel?" Katie asked.

"I think I see a hoverbus coming to pick us up," Carlos said as he squinted into the bright, sunlit sky.

"That's just a flock of birds," Sparky said, gazing up into the sun and shielding his eyes.

"You sure that's not a plane or something?" Lou said.

"Nah, it's some of them super-jerks," Fuzzy said without even looking up from his mirror, where he was trying to arrange his hair back under his cap.

Sure enough, swooping out of the sky and landing directly in front of the Goats were a legion of nine figures of dynamic proportions. They were clad in uniforms made of materials Sparky had never seen before, materials that looked like they gave off their own light instead of simply reflecting it. Some of them wore gleaming capes that fluttered in the breeze like the flags of great conquering nations. The Graviton City Lasers had arrived.

"Face front!" called out the Laser in the center of the formation. "Our global monitoring system has alerted us to the fact that you are to be our opponents in the next round of the playoffs! As captain of the Graviton City Lasers, I, Sergeant Southpaw, welcome you!"

"Uh, thank y-"

"But let me also bring you a dire warning!" Sgt. Southpaw shouted. "Graviton City's honor on the baseball diamond is ours to defend, and it is a task we shall never waver in! Challenge us at your own risk, Go-Town Goats!" The Goats just stood there, too stunned to say anything in response. After an awkward moment of silence, Sparky cleared his throat.

"I'm sorry, are you waiting for us to-"

"Graviton City Lasers, away!" Sgt. Southpaw and the rest shot straight up into the air, their fists pointing into the sky.

"Ah, they're scared," Skip said as soon as they were out of sight.

"Hey," Bobby said as he rummaged through his luggage. "Where'd my gerbil go?"

Sparky ended up rooming with Bobby, which meant a steady stream of room service carts were in and out of the hotel room that night. At one point, Sparky rolled over in bed to grab a scouting report off the night table and his elbow ended up landing right in the middle of a Fiesta Nacho Platter.

"Ugh, dude, seriously," Sparky said as he mopped the steaming cheese sauce off his arm with a formerly snow white bath towel. "Can we kill it with the room service already?"

At the other end of the room, Bobby looked up from his ribs with a pained expression. His cheeks were stuffed full of pork and glistening with barbecue sauce. "Ooh, sorry, Sparky," he said, his words muffled by meat. "But Graviton City is supposed to have the best ribs in the world. The sauce is made with mongoose blood, can you believe that? It's supposed to be how Captain Zip got to be so fast. Mongoose blood, isn't that something?"

"Yeah, but there's no way you're going to be any faster tomorrow after eating all this heavy crap," Sparky said. "Don't you think you'd perform better on the field if you didn't eat like this all the time?"

Bobby sighed and dropped the bare rib bone to his plate. "Of course I do, dude," he said. "But I just can't help it, you know? When I was playing softball in the park district league, we'd always go out after a win for an extra-large pizza and endless wings at Extra-Large Pizza and Endless Wings, you know, on Fourth Street?"

"Yeah, right, Extra-Large Pizza and Endless Wings. I like the quesadillas there."

"Uh-huh, with the hot salsa and everything? But anyway, I guess I end up eating so much because I actually get really nervous playing Big League Baseball, and, well, I kind of like feeling like we won something no matter what." Bobby looked up at Sparky with panic in his eyes. "Does that make me weird? You're not going to tell the rest of the guys all that stuff I said, are you?"

"Nah, don't worry about it," Sparky laughed. "And I know exactly what you mean. I know for a fact that some people will do anything to feel like a winner."

The next morning, Sparky woke up to find Bobby sleeping in the center of a nest made of what looked like the shredded remnants of his bedsheets. Bobby was curled up in a ball, his nose twitching as he snored.

"Bobby, hey man, wake up," Sparky said as he shook Bobby's shoulder. "What the what happened to your bed, dude?"

Bobby smacked his lips as he woke up, yawned and looked around him. "Whoa, that's weird," he said. "Heh, I've never done anything like that before. Hey, are they still serving breakfast downstairs? I'm uber-hungry for some cinnamon rolls."

During warm-ups that afternoon, Sparky pulled Fuzzy and Blerk aside. "Guys, I need you to keep an eye on Bobby today and let me know if he does anything weird."

"Regular weird, or weird for Bobby?" Fuzzy asked.

"Making-a-nest-out-of-his-bed-and-sleeping-in-it-like-a-hamster weird," Sparky said.

"Okay, that's weird."

"The one called Bobby, his behavior seems no less out of the ordinary than usual to my observations," Blerk said. "However, if my fellow Goats so desire, I could subject him to a full diagnostic scan after the game."

"Would that take long?"

"Not at all, once I remove the top of his skull."

Sparky looked over at Bobby, who was playing catch with Thor in-between bites of a giant soft pretzel. "Let's put that idea in the 'maybe' pile, okay, Blerk?" he said.

Once the game got started, both Sparky and Sgt. Southpaw established themselves early, each notching four strikeouts in the first three innings. Sparky was having good luck with the Phantom Slider, as the Lasers couldn't find the pitch even with their x-ray vision. Even though he could feel the first twinges of pain creep into his arm, Sparky was determined to stick with what worked. Meanwhile, the Goats found themselves hacking away at Sgt. Southpaw's Krackling Knuckleball, a pitch that seemed to be everywhere at once as it sizzled through the air surrounded by a fizzing purple light.

In the fourth inning, however, things started to come a little unglued for Sparky on the mound. He was having difficulty hitting the strike zone, and the Lasers had one of their most dangerous hitters at the plate, the third baseman Hot Corner.

"You may have defeated my teammates," Hot Corner said as he tightened his grip on his glowing blue bat, "but you can't keep this up forever! Sooner or later, justice will prevail!"

Sparky ignored the batter's bombastic blathering and concentrated on hitting his spot in the strike zone. He released a spinning breaking ball that would have just nicked the outer edge of the strike zone, if Hot Corner hadn't connected with it and sent it humming down the right field line.

Sparky wheeled around to watch the ball shoot over Carlos' head, hugging the baseline as if it were on a track. Katie made a bee-line to the corner, her path and the ball's forming a perfect right angle, but she wasn't going to catch it on the run. With the ball's trajectory dropping to within mere inches of the turf, Katie sprang straight out, perpendicular to the ground for a brief moment. At the last possible second, her glove came between the ball and the ground, saving it from ricocheting off the turf and sending it who knows where. On the mound, Sparky finally exhaled.

The game still was scoreless going into the bottom of the seventh, and the Lasers had the top of their order coming up to face Sparky and his increasingly tired arm. He had been able to power his way through the Graviton City lineup with his power pitches up to that point, but by now he was losing velocity on his Blazing Fastball and the Phantom Slider would only flicker into transparency instead of vanishing altogether. It wouldn't be enough to get through the Lasers again without incident, and Sgt. Southpaw continued making things difficult on the Goats offensively.

"Batting next for your Graviton City Lasers, the center fielder, Leadoff Man!" Despite the fact that he had struck out twice before, the smiling Leadoff Man was the picture of confidence as he approached the plate. He adjusted the bright gold visor that covered his eyes and pulled his finned batting gloves tighter over his hands.

"You look pretty cocky for a dude halfway to a golden sombrero," Lou said as he watched Leadoff Man flex and stretch outside the batter's box.

"That's because I know there's more than one way to take first base, old-timer! Stand aside and watch the fastest man on two legs take the first step toward victory!"

Sparky narrowed his eyes and caught the signal from Lou. Without the power pitches to rely on, Sparky would just have to work with good old-fashioned changing speed and eye level. He reared back and delivered. Leadoff Man squared the bat to bunt, and the ball bounced off the barrel, landing dead on the ground in front of home plate.

Lou jumped to his feet and reached out to pluck the ball off the ground, but by the time he fired the ball to Carlos, Leadoff Man was already standing on first base, stuffing his batting gloves into a pouch on his utility belt. Carlos caught the throw and was startled by the sight of Leadoff Man standing next to him.

"Ah-ha!" Leadoff Man boasted. "As you can see, my unique physical structure makes it possible for me to run at speeds beyond human comprehension! The lab accident that replaced my blood with concentrated liquid time made me fast enough to be faster than a pickoff throw, speedier than..."

"Okay, okay, we get it," Carlos said. "You're really fast."

"I have a feeling you're about to find out just how fast I can really be," Leadoff Man said with a wink.

With the next hitter at the plate, Sparky glanced over his shoulder to first base. Leadoff Man wasn't taking a lead off the bag, wasn't even leaning toward second, but Sparky knew what was coming. Lou nodded at him and Sparky nodded back. With as much arm, strength as he could muster, Sparky hurled the pitch well outside the strike zone, and Lou jumped to his left to receive the pitchout. Out of the corner of his eye, Lou could see that Leadoff Man wasn't at first base, and he whipped the ball to Blerk at second as hard as he could. It was a bullet, maybe the fastest throw Lou had ever made to second base, but Leadoff Man appeared on the base as soon as the ball left his fingertips.

"Don't you get it?" Leadoff Man laughed. "There's no man in the universe who can run 90 feet faster than me! You're just going to have to accept the fact that I'll claim third with the next pitch, and then home after that!"

"Time!" Lou called, and he motioned for the infield to join him on the mound with Sparky.

"All right, so that speedy son of a gun is going to take third, is he?" Lou said, taking the ball from Sparky and tossing it casually in the air a few times. "I say, let's give it to him."

"That's a great plan, cowboy," Fuzzy said. "Let's buy him dinner, too, while we're at it."

"I never thought Fuzzball would ever say anything I agreed with, but this is it," Bobby said, his nose twitching. He began frantically scratching behind his ear.

"You okay, Bobby?" Carlos asked.

"Worry about it later, I want to hear the rest of Lou's plan," Sparky said. "There is a rest of the plan, isn't there?"

"Aw, you know me, kid," Lou said. He stuck his glove hand in the center of the circle. The others looked at each other and then put their own glove hands in, as well. "'Goats' on three. One, two, three!"

"Goats!" the team shouted in unison.

Lou then clapped Sparky and Bobby on the shoulder at the same time. "Let's beat that cocky little so-and-so to the punch, fellas." Sparky and Bobby looked down into their gloves, smiled, and everyone returned to their respective positions.

At the plate, the Lasers hitter wiggled his fingers as they coiled around the handle of the bat. There wasn't a single indication of worry on his chiseled face – he may as well have been waiting in line for a cup of coffee. At second base, Leadoff Man kept both feet firmly planted on the bag, just as before. He allowed a confident smile to cross his face as Sparky glanced back at him. At third base, Bobby continued twitching his nose and scratching behind his ear, but he kept his eyes fixed on the mound.

Sparky accepted the sign from Lou, took his position and began the stretch. There was a rush of wind behind him, but all Sparky did was smile and continue his throwing motion. The hitter tensed up, but he didn't move the bat. Lou clapped his mitt closed, a sound that was followed immediately by the sound of "Out!" echoing throughout the ballpark. The crowd murmured, heads snapped back and forth as they tried to find the epicenter of the action.

The action, as it turned out, was centered on third base, where Leadoff Man stood just inches away from the bag. Preventing him from reaching the base was Bobby's outstretched arm. At the end of his arm was his glove, and inside his glove, to the crowd's astonishment, was the ball. Lou opened his mitt to reveal...nothing at all. The Goats had passed the ball into Bobby's glove during their conference on the mound, and Sparky had simply gone through the motion of pitching.

"That's just simply unsportsmanlike!" Sgt. Southpaw cried from the Lasers dugout. "What unmitigated villainy!"

"Hey, not all of us can fly around with laser beams coming out of our noses," Fuzzy said as the Goats trotted off the field. "How do you think we feel watching you guys zipping around like bacon grease in a skillet?"

"Dude, what does that even mean?" Bobby asked.

In the top of the ninth inning, Bobby found himself on second base after a walk and a fielder's choice ground ball. Blerk stepped to the plate and promptly delivered a hot ground ball to second base. The second baseman saw Bobby break for third and, after seeing him take a few lumbering steps in that direction, decided to make the throw to third to get what he thought would be an easy tagout.

Halfway between second and third, however, a startling metamorphosis occurred. Bobby began to pick up speed, his naturally stubby legs began rapidly skittering across the infield dirt. By the time the ball reached Hot Corner's glove, Bobby was scampering on all fours like some kind of giant rodent, and it was because of this that Hot Corner's tag wound up sweeping over Bobby's head and missing him entirely. The crowd, which was already getting restless following Bobby's trickery in the previous inning, was now whipped into a righteous frenzy, hurling as many nasty words as they could think of in Bobby's direction. For his part, Bobby simply stood up and dusted himself off. The angry taunts of a hostile crowd was nothing new to him, although it was unusual to hear them coming from the opposing team's fans, he thought.

There were runners on the corners and only one out, and with the game still scoreless late in the game the Lasers manager stepped onto the field and asked Sgt. Southpaw for the ball. Grimacing, the muscular super-pitcher reluctantly gave up the ball and hovered slowly off the mound. Inside the Graviton City dugout, a red telephone sat under a protective plexiglass dome. The pitching coach gravely lifted the dome and issued a terse, whispered command to whomever answered him on the other end.

Within moments, there appeared in the sky above the ballpark a brilliant light, a light that projected the outline of a baseball onto the clouds. Although moments before they had been frothing and foaming over what they thought to be Bobby's unethical play, now the Graviton City faithful were oohing and ahhing, many with broad smiles replacing their gritted teeth. In the Goats' dugout, the team strained to see past the roof. The Lasers' manager stood alone on the mound, looking up into the sky as if expecting someone or something to come down from the clouds to join him.

The answer came mere seconds later, as a shadowy figure appeared on the roof of the stadium, high above the grandstands and home plate. Swinging from a rope, the mysterious presence swooped off the roof, executing a double backflip before landing in a dramatic crouch on the pitcher's mound. The ballpark's PA system buzzed to life.

"Now pitching for the Graviton City Lasers...The CLOSER!" Shrouded in a black cloak, only the Closer's eyes pierced the shadows that surrounded him. An ebony-gloved hand emerged from inside the swirling cape and took the ball from the Lasers' manager, who quickly retreated to the dugout. Backstop, the Lasers' catcher, motioned for some warm-up tosses, but the Closer waved off the suggestion with a curt gesture. The meaning was clear – the Closer was ready to strike.

As soon as the crowd had settled down following the pitcher's ominous entrance, Lou stepped into the batter's box. Eyeing the black-clad stranger with a skeptical eye, Lou spat into the dirt and held the bat over his shoulder. "All right, so you can do a somersault," Lou said. "Let's see how you hurl the horsehide, jasper."

In response, the Closer reached back and flung the ball off the tips of his fingers. His delivery was unlike any Lou had ever seen before – instead of throwing with an overhand or sidearm motion, the Closer threw his arm straight out in front of him, the same way Sparky remembered ninjas tossing their deadly shuriken in a hundred movies. Concealed inside his cape until the moment of release, there was no way to see how the Closer gripped the ball. His first pitch to Lou took the old catcher by surprise and was counted a belt-high strike.

Two more inscrutable pitches like the first one and Lou was on his way back to the bench with nothing to show for his trip to the plate but an ache in his lower back. That brought up Sparky with a chance to at least tie the game.

Sparky tried to see into the eyes of the Closer, but all he could see were two white slits that were fixed in a look of pure determination. The Closer's first pitch was delivered with the same forceful flick of the forearm as the others, but this time the ball climbed for an instant high out of the strike zone before sinking back into it. By the time Sparky noticed what was happening, he had no time left to swing the bat. The count was 0-1.

With the next pitch, the Closer again whipped the ball toward the plate with an identical motion, but now the ball moved laterally across the width of the plate, curling from the far inside area of the strike zone to the far outside portion. Sparky misjudged where the pitch would be and ended up catching it with the very end of the bat, tapping it into a right-angle trajectory for a foul ball. The count suddenly became 0-2.

"He's getting all kinds of movement on those pitches without even changing his motion!" Sparky thought to himself. "There's no way to tell what I'm going to be getting!"

Sparky tried to clear his mind and anticipate the next pitch. If he couldn't figure out what the Closer would be throwing him next, he would have to guess. His mind raced through the possibilities. The first pitch looked like a 12-6 curve, and the second was another breaking ball, a slider. So would he try to get him swinging on a high fastball? Or maybe he would try another slider, one that broke in the opposite direction? What kind of fastball does he even have? Forkball? Splitter? Four-seam? Wasn't there a page in one of Katie's scouting reports that covered this guy? He couldn't remember seeing anything about the Closer in anything he had read about the Lasers, and now the cold feeling in the pit of his stomach was beginning to spread throughout his body. He tried to tamp it down as the Closer stood as still as a statue on the mound.

Before he knew it, the pitch was on its way to Sparky. His mind still swirled with possibilities, but he was somehow able to drag the bat off his shoulder and across the plate. All he felt was the bat slice through the air, untouched by anything. The fans erupted in a great cheer, and Sparky trudged back to the dugout without looking up. He didn't want to see the look on Bobby's face.

The bottom of the ninth arrived, and with neither team able to put a run across the plate to that point, the Lasers were thinking about the walk-off win. Sparky's arm felt slow and sluggish, but he managed to induce a weak ground ball for the first out. Out of the corner of his eye, he could see one of the Ballpino brothers warming up in the bullpen. The next hitter cracked a line drive on an 0-1 count that ricocheted off the infield grass and bounced right over Blerk's head. A full-count walk and another seeing-eye single later, and the bases were loaded with only one out.

Skip scampered out of the dugout, huffing and puffing as much from frustration as he was from the running. He stopped at the base of the mound and bent over, trying to catch his breath.

"What are ya…what do ya…what's the deal with you, kiddo?" Skip wheezed.

"I'm slowing down a little, I know, but I'm still good to go," Sparky said with as much confidence as he could muster. The Laser hitter in the on deck circle was hovering, cross-legged, arms folded in front of him as the bat hung suspended in the air in front of him. With a look of serene concentration on his face, he took telekinetic practice swings without moving a muscle. The bat moved so fast it could barely be seen. The Ballpino brother in the bullpen was watching with such slack-jawed intensity that he was hit in the face with a toss from the bullpen catcher.

"Really, Skip, I'm okay," Sparky protested. "I just need to mix up my spots a bit more."

"Well, I don't believe you," Skip said, "but I don't want to put any of those Ballpino chumps in the game. If you can get me another out, you can have your shot at finishing it. Because I'm only making one more trip out here, and that ain't just because it's in the rulebook. Dang air's way too thin up here."

Skip shuffled back to the dugout and left Sparky there to ponder his fate. The hitter floated up to the plate and the umpire called for play to resume. Sparky's first pitch was high for ball one. With the next one, he tried to keep it down, and it was fouled to the first base side. With his 1-1 pitch, Sparky wanted to get a ground ball to the left side of the infield, maybe force a double play. Instead, the hitter swiped the bat across the plate and hit an uppercut fly ball that rose high above left field. Sparky slapped his glove against his thigh as he watched the ball climb into the air, with Thor circling under it.

The runner on third had his eyes locked on the ball, too, and as soon as Thor closed his glove around it he started breaking for home. Thor narrowed his eyes, planted his back foot and threw the ball toward home plate. The ball was hurled with such force and such speed that Fuzzy, who had set up to cut off the throw, leapt out of the way just before the streaking missile caught him square in the center of his helmet.

Lou set his feet in front of home plate, holding his mitt out in front of him to receive the mighty left fielder's throw. The throw hit the mitt dead center, staggering Lou backward half a step. The runner from third lowered his shoulder, and caught Lou right in the chest. Both men tumbled to the ground in a heap, a tangle of limbs suspended in a cloud of dust. When it settled, the runner reached down and slapped home plate. The umpire ran circles around the scene, trying to spot the ball anywhere in the mess. Fifty thousand people held their breath. Sparky had been holding it since the batter first made contact.

The runner rolled off the top of Lou, leaving the catcher flattened against the ground. But when Lou opened his mitt again, the ball was still cradled inside, like a bird's egg in a nest. Now there were two outs, and Sparky would have his chance to close it out.

The Lasers' last chance in the inning would be Hot Corner, who flipped down his cybernetic visor as he crouched into his batting stance. Thor's throw had denied the previous man the sacrifice fly, but as Lou blocked the plate the other two runners had seized the opportunity to take an extra base, and now there were men on second and third with two out.

Sparky didn't even think about his arm, which was now as sore as he'd ever felt it before. He didn't think about Bobby, whose weird behavior would probably be something the team would spend the next 24 hours before Game 2 worrying about. He didn't even think about his brother, the pennant or the Baseball Devil. All he thought about was what Hot Corner's expression would be as he marched back to the dugout empty-handed.

Sparky delivered the first pitch with a loud grunt, but nothing he could have done would have added any speed to it. It came in low and slow, giving Hot Corner and his cyborg implants plenty of time to calculate its velocity and trajectory. The Graviton City third baseman swung the bat with the graceful sweep of a robot arm on an assembly line. It caught the ball in the perfect spot, pushing it to the third base side.

Fortunately, it seemed as if Bobby was in the perfect spot to field the ball and make an easy throw to first for the forceout. Unfortunately, as soon as Bobby made the move to his left to field it, he let it skip right past his glove. Just before the ball reached him, Bobby began spinning around in a tight circle on the infield dirt. The ball rolled into left field, the runner from third touched home plate, and the Goats had started the series with Graviton City in an 0-1 hole.

The mood in the clubhouse was understandably a little grim, but for the moment the team wasn't focused so much on losing the first game in the series as it huddled around a much sweatier-than-usual Bobby. Perched on a tiny stool like an egg balanced on a golf tee, Bobby winced each time the doctor prodded or poked at him.

"What's the diagnosis, Doc?" Skip asked without a hint of worry or compassion. "Is he going to be okay to go tomorrow?" He could have been asking a mechanic about his car.

The doctor leaned away from Bobby, pulled his tiny glasses off his face and started rubbing the bridge of his nose. "It's a little early to say for certain," the doctor began, "but you said you lost your gerbil just after arriving in Graviton City?"

"Yeah, I had him in his little traveling habitat, but when I checked on him at the teleport station, he was gone," Bobby said, his voice quivering and squeaky.

"Mm-hm, well, I think I know what happened, then." The doctor leaned forward and placed his hand on Bobby's shoulder. "Son, your gerbil…is in you."

"Doc, I know I've eaten some crazy stuff in my day, but Chester was practically family to me!"

"No, what I mean is the teleporter operator must not have known about, eh, Chester, and as a result the teleportation sort of fused your DNA with his. You are now part man, part gerbil."

The team reacted with nearly unanimous shock. Blerk rubbed his chin and stared intently at Bobby. Fuzzy just started laughing. The doctor cleared his throat.

"Now, this is something that isn't all that uncommon here in Graviton City," the doctor said. "In fact, people are always having their DNA changed by a radioactive animal of some sort – spiders, lizards, cats, bats…I have a colleague in town who once treated a man who had been bitten by a radioactive skunk! Those were not pleasant house calls, let me tell you."

"So, what's going to happen to me?" Bobby stammered, his nose twitching like crazy.

"Well, these things tend to clear up on their own after a few days, but if you get plenty of bed rest it can be shorter. Sometimes it's permanent, and then you may feel compelled to join a super-team, depending on your powers and abilities. For the time being, however, I'd say you can expect to have all the special powers and abilities of a gerbil."

There was a moment of silence.

"Like what?" Bobby asked.

"Oh, enhanced speed, super scampering ability, greater metabolism…"

"Does that mean he'll be able to eat more?" Fuzzy asked.

"Yes."

"You better pencil him out of the lineup tomorrow, Skip, he's going to be stuck at the hot dog cart all day!"

But the truth was that Bobby was in the lineup again the very next day. Skip explained his decision to the media that morning by saying, "I don't give a dang if his DNA is spliced with a block of gouda cheese, Bobby Munson is our starting third baseman, and that's that! I once played with a guy who went out late one night before a game, got into an argument with a gypsy and got a curse put on him. Poor son of a gun had his head turned completely backwards when he showed up to play the next morning, and I'll be danged if he didn't go 2 for 4 with a home run that day!"

Bobby's rodent-enhanced DNA helped him scamper his way to a stolen base, but the overall story of Game 2 was more or less the same as Game 1. Neither team could generate much offense with the starting pitchers Antonio for the Goats and The Knuckler for the Lasers being locked into the strike zone. A late sacrifice fly with a runner on third drove in a run for the Lasers, but in the bottom of that same inning the Goats had VORP flexing his knees on second base after hitting a long fly ball that smacked the wall and bounced out of the reach of the center fielder.

However, Carlos was caught looking at a backdoor slider for his third strike and Fuzzy chopped a ground ball to the shortstop. Suddenly, there were two outs, but the Goats were a little less than worried because their own god of thunder was waiting to take his turn at the plate.

The Knuckler tugged at the corner of his mask and wiped away the rivulets of sweat that were trapped underneath. Thor tapped his enchanted bat on the ground in front of the on-deck circle, and a peal of thunder could be heard miles in the distance. Lightning crackled around the barrel of the bat for a brief second and then dissipated. Even with the flawless engineering of his cyborg arm, The Knuckler looked worried.

Just then, there was a flash of light in the sky, stamping the shape of a baseball on the clouds above. The call for The Closer had gone out once more, and in the dugout Sparky shook his head.

"Where does that guy come from?" he asked his teammates. "Katie doesn't even have him listed in her scouting reports."

"It's the weirdest thing," Katie said. "I can't find any proof he even exists except on the Lasers' roster, but when it just said 'The Closer' I thought that meant they forgot to fill it in!"

"If we could just figure out who that guy is and where he comes from, maybe we could figure out how to beat him," Sparky said.

With those words, The Closer appeared, this time emerging from a door behind the scoreboard and gliding his way down to the mound with his cape stretched between his arms like wings. Four pitches later, Thor's bat was as quiet as a spring rain shower, and the thunder god was dragging it back with him to the dugout.

Not long after, the Lasers were celebrating a 2-0 series lead in the center of the field. The Closer, however, was nowhere to be seen.

"We've got to find out who that Closer guy is," Sparky said

as he watched the celebration through narrowed eyes in the dugout.

The series returned to Go-Town, and the locals were restless. The Goats were greeted at the airport by a large group of fans, but instead of cheering and waving banners, they were mostly quiet. They held up handmade signs bearing sayings like "Please Don't Embarrass Us!" and "Maybe It's For The Best..." and "You Tried Pretty Hard, At Least!"

"Dude," Sparky said as he and Katie got off the plane. "This town turned on us pretty fast."

"This is actually the biggest turnout I've ever seen for a Goats team coming back from a road trip," Katie replied nonchalantly. "Also the most enthusiastic one. Usually the signs are a lot less...appropriate for general audiences."

"Huh?"

"Never mind."

As the Goats prepared for Game 3, Yoshi came around collecting towels from everyone. The giant cart, overloaded with damp terrycloth, wheeled in front of Sparky's locker. "How you holding up, kid?"

"We're getting killed by this Closer guy, Yoshi," Sparky said. "I don't suppose you know anything about him through your super-secret connections?"

"My connections are all older than I am, and they've never even heard of you," Yoshi snorted. "Heck, they don't even remember who I am half the time. Anyway, don't worry about the mysterious superhero reliever, Sparky. I'm working on it. In the meantime..."

Yoshi paused to toss a fresh towel out of the cart, which ended up covering Sparky's head completely.

"...try to score more runs," Yoshi grumbled as he wheeled the cart away.

The stands at Zigleaf Field were packed for Game 3, but it was eerily silent when the Goats took the field. As the Goats tossed the ball around the field, Sparky could hear individual coughs echo throughout the ballpark. At one point, he could hear a splash coming from the right field bleachers, followed by a plaintive, "Aw man, I spilled my soda!" During the national anthem, the crowd murmured their way through the words, never rising above a low groan. Fuzzy did his part to try and wake up the crowd by insulting individual fans, but no one bit. Sparky and Lou just looked at each other in the dugout and shook their heads.

The Goats didn't give the fans much of anything to cheer about through the first three innings, either. Only VORP and Bobby, with the proportional speed of a small rodent, were able to reach base, and the other hitters could do nothing to bring them home. Against the Lasers' starting pitcher, Colonel Comet, there was very little anyone could have done.

Meanwhile, the Lasers had given Willie Wilbur as much as she could handle in the first third of the game, putting her in a bases-loaded jam twice and leaving runners on the corners once. All three times, Wilbur had been able to get some key strikeouts, all on pitches that looked suspiciously greasy. In short, the situation was not promising.

At the end of the third inning, Willie slammed her batting helmet down on the dugout bench next to Lou. The sound, by far the loudest thing that had happened in the stadium up to that point, didn't even faze the veteran catcher as he strapped on his gear.

"What the crap, man?" Willie spat. "These superhero dudes, man, they don't even give you a fighting chance!"

"Maybe they don't, but maybe they do," Lou said.

"Aw come on, don't give me that magic cowboy stuff! What the crap are you talking about?"

"These superhero dudes are a lot like cowboys," Lou continued. "And part of that 'magic cowboy crap,' as you so eloquently put it, includes a code."

"What, like a secret code or some garbage?"

"Not quite so secret, no. What's been our problem against this Comet guy?"

Willie scratched her nose and frowned. "We can't tell what he's going to be throwing us."

"And that means he ain't tipping his pitches. That's okay, a good pitcher won't tip his pitches. But we just haven't tried asking him yet."

Lou hustled out onto the field, leaving Willie alone in the dugout, looking confused. After a moment, and at the umpire's heated insistence, Willie finally ran out to the mound. The Lasers ended up clogging the bases yet again, and this time Willie's luck didn't hold up as well. A single drilled by Hot Corner between first and second drove in a runner from third, and the Goats took a 1-0 deficit into the bottom of the fourth.

Lou called a conference of the Goats before the bottom of the inning started, and Fuzzy approached the plate with much more confidence than any of them had until then. Colonel Comet toed the rubber and looked in for the sign. Before he got set into his motion, Fuzzy nodded in his direction.

"Hey man, what are you looking to throw me here?"

Both the catcher and the umpire turned to look at Fuzzy, then they looked out at Colonel Comet. The pitcher kicked his armor-plated boot at the dirt and stood perfectly still for a moment. Finally, he smiled nervously and tipped his cap to Fuzzy, saying, "Why, a fastball, of course."

"Fastball?" Fuzzy confirmed. "Okay, sounds good. Where at?"

"By the rings of Saturn, Colonel!" Baron Backstop shouted. "Don't give this hirsute miscreant such vital information!"

"I know, my faithful compatriot! But I won't deliberately tell a lie, it violates everything that's good and decent about the game!"

Armed with the word straight from the pitcher's mouth, Fuzzy squared up on the next pitch and slapped it down the third baseline, hustling into second with a sliding double. The noise from the stands began to climb from a dull murmur to a modest buzz. The buzz continued as Thor knocked the dirt from his cleats and hacked a few practice swings.

"Tell me, yon pitcher, how dost thou plan to pitch to Thor, son of Odin?"

Again, Colonel Comet looked down at his feet, dried some sweat from his forehead and took a deep breath. Then, with a look of steely confidence in his eyes, the pitcher called back to the Goats' massive red-headed outfielder.

"I plan to start with an off-speed pitch low and inside, then counter that with a slider moving outside, then finish with the fastball up," Comet stated with confidence.

"Aye, that sounds like quite the plan, indeed, friend Colonel!" Thor shouted back. "The Odinson hopes thou does not mind if he adds his own ideas!"

Thor watched as the first two pitches came in exactly as Colonel Comet described them, an off-speed pitch low and inside for a ball followed by a slider off the plate that caught enough of the plate for a strike. After each pitch, the thunder god simply nodded his head. Before the third pitch, however, Thor had his bat clutched tightly over his shoulder and his eyes were sparking with blue lightning.

Comet heaved a mighty sigh and checked back over his shoulder at Fuzzy. The pitcher's face was stony and fixed like a statue whose sculptor had been given only one word: "Determination." He kicked his leg high in the air and sprang forward to deliver the pitch – the fastball, high and tight, just like he promised.

Thor rocked back and swung, timing the path of his bat perfectly with the trajectory of the ball. They connected as if they were both on the same schedule – a fantastically choreographed dance that featured the crack of the bat as the crescendo. The ball pulled all of the electricity off the bat as it pulled away from the plate as fast as it had arrived. There was a collective gasp from the fans, and they all held their breath while the ball cut its crackling arc across the sky. They released it as soon as the ball cleared the fence and landed in the tangled forest of arms reaching up for it as if it were a single drop of rain in a parched desert. The Goats had finally cracked through the scoreboard, and they weren't done yet.

With each Goats hitter asking for and receiving Colonel Comet's plan of attack, the Go-Town nine racked up another six hits and three runs in the inning, giving them a five-run lead going into the top of the fifth. As she took the mound, Willie looked like a woman who had just avoided being hit by a car after slipping on a winning lottery ticket. The lead gave her the added confidence she needed to be more aggressive against the Lasers lineup. She notched another four strikeouts through the next three innings, her pitching leaving some odd stains in Lou's mitt but fewer Graviton City runners on the basepaths.

By the time the top of the ninth rolled around, the Goats were out to a very comfortable 11-4 lead, and now there was no doubt that Zigleaf Field had been packed to the rafters. A constant roar of cheers and whistles accompanied Willie's final pitch, and it became even louder when that ball was tapped weakly to Fuzzy for an easy out at first base.

GOATS SHOW SIGNS OF LIFE
By Roy Myko, Go-Town Gazette
After a showing in the first two games that made them look deader than the Monroeville Zombies, the Goats managed to stay alive yesterday, beating Graviton City 11-4. The series is still weighted in favor of the Lasers, however, and the strategy that brought Skip LaRoche's team the win probably won't be so successful the next time the teams meet tomorrow at Zigleaf Field.

"Yes, it's true that the Goats were able to exploit one of our only weaknesses, but you can rest assured that their nefarious schemes won't bear fruit a second time," said losing pitcher Colonel Comet. "The Lasers are hereby remaining silent for the remainder of the series. We don't have to worry about telling a lie if we don't speak at all."

"Let them keep their yaps shut," LaRoche said immediately following Comet's announcement. "Our guys just happened to get hot at the right time, it had nothing to do with anything they said. I couldn't hear nothing from the dugout, anyway."

However the Goats were able to solve the Lasers' pitching,

it kept them from facing their chief nemesis from the first two games, Graviton City's The Closer. The mysterious masked man shut down potential rallies in the first two games, and if the Goats can't find a way to break through tomorrow against the Lasers' ace Sgt. Southpaw, they may well find themselves baffled at the plate late in the game again. Worse, they may find themselves and the entire city of Go-Town wondering how they could get so close and come up so short.

The off day between games 3 and 4 provided the Goats with a little extra time to rest their sore joints and tired legs, but it also gave them a lot of time to think. Sparky sat in the clubhouse to watch the third game of the New York-Athens series, in which the Emperors had already seized a commanding 2-0 lead. Athens had only scored two runs in the entire series to date, both of those runs coming off a home run in the first inning of the first game from slugger Apollo Ambrosia. From then on, it was all New York.

Lou joined Sparky on the clubhouse couch just in time to see a bases-clearing double give the Emperors a 3-0 lead in game 3. New York's Number 7, the player Sparky was nearly traded for just a few months earlier, was at the plate. The announcers' voices droned on without emotion, giving the entire game the feeling of something inevitable, something that was going to happen no matter what anyone else thought.

"Why are you doing this to yourself, Sparky?" Lou asked after a few pitches.

"What? I'm just watching the game, man."

"What you're watching is a train wreck, and I know for a fact that you're thinking about what it would feel like to be the engineer."

"I want to know who wins this series, that's all." Number 7 had patiently let a few pitches outside the zone whiz by, giving him a full count and a very nervous pitcher dealing to him.

"Kid, we both know New York is going to win this series," Lou said. "You think that old devil's going to make things easy on you?"

"You think he's helping the Emperors?"

"I know he wouldn't offer you a chance unless he knew that chance would be as small as it could possibly be," Lou answered as Number 7 fouled off a tough pitch. "But hey, at least the number's not zero, buddy." Lou stood up with his knees popping and creaking, then slapped Sparky on the back.

"Right, right," Sparky said.

Game 4 of the series began early in the afternoon, with the

sun high in the sky but a gentle breeze keeping the assembled fans cool in the stands. The previous day's win did a lot to bolster the spirit of the Go-Town fans, and they gave an enthusiastic cheer at the end of the national anthem.

The sound of their excitement traveled throughout the corridors of Zigleaf Field, all the way down to the Goats' clubhouse, where Yoshi slept at his tiny desk in the corner of the laundry room. He awoke suddenly, yanking his head off the desk and pulling off a sheet of paper that had stuck to his face with a spot of drool. Yoshi peeled the sheet off his face and took a quick look at it. He had spent the entire night before scribbling down the names of relief pitchers who had left the Big Leagues within the last three seasons. All of them were known for their devastating control and ability to deceive hitters with the placement of their pitches, but according to Yoshi's research, they were all happily retired and accounted for. He was no closer to discovering the secret identity of the Closer than he was when Sparky first asked him.

Jolted awake by the start of the game and feeling frustrated, Yoshi hopped off his stool and shuffled out onto the park's cavernous concrete concourse. There were clusters of fans standing in line at the concessions stands, walking away with cardboard trays overflowing with hot dogs wrapped in foil and popcorn that spilled out of its striped boxes with each little jostle. Cups of soda were cradled in the crooks of their arms, sometimes sloshing over and dribbling down onto the brick floor. Kids chased each other back to their seats, holding out ice cream cones like cavalrymen charging with their swords.

Yoshi was so used to having the park all to himself at this time of year. The sounds of baseball clashed with the cooler temperatures and the changing colors of the leaves, to say nothing of the crowds of people swarming in and outside the ballpark. The difference was striking, almost irritating for someone who had spent more than 60 years tending to a building that was more graveyard than ballyard.

Emerging from one of the tunnels, Yoshi strolled through the aisles as the fans buzzed around him. The game was in the middle of the third, no score. Even if the Goats won this game, the series would be going back to Graviton City for the deciding Game 5. After that, it was either off to New York or back to thinking about next year. Either way, this could be the last game of the season at Zigleaf Field, Yoshi reasoned. It might be a good idea to spend a little bit of time enjoying the atmosphere before closing everything down for the winter.

Yoshi leaned up against a steel beam and focused his weary

eyes on the field as Sparky warmed up for the top of the fourth. Yoshi's gaze kept drifting down to the condition of the mound – he thought it maybe looked a little soft, maybe he should call the grounds crew over to take care of it at the next opportunity. But no, he thought, it was probably time for him to watch an actual inning of baseball under God's own sunshine for once. There was a sound of rushing wind as Sparky retired the hitter with his Blazing Fastball.

There was another sound, too, one that was able to assert itself over even the sounds of the game and the crowd. It was the sound of the vendors, roving through the stands with their bags and trays slopping over with snacks and cold drinks. A good vendor, Yoshi noted, was able to make himself or herself heard no matter where they were in the ballpark. Looking around, he could pinpoint a cry of "Ice cream cones!" coming from the left field bleachers, while "Hot buttered popcorn!" rang out from the seats in right.

"Peanuts!" sounded one vendor with a booming delivery, "Get'cher peanuts right here!" Yoshi craned his neck to find the source, and quickly found the athletic-looking peanut vendor hawking his goods a few aisles away from where Yoshi was standing. The young man's dark blue vendor cap was pulled down over his eyes, but he was tossing red bags of roasted nuts with unerring accuracy, hitting his targets from as far as nine rows away without missing a single customer. He caught the coins that the customer tossed back to him with his other hand just as easily. Yoshi wondered why he had never noticed this vendor before, but then again it wasn't uncommon for vendors to cycle in and out of Zigleaf Field during the season. It was a tough job, after all.

But there was something very unusual about this vendor, Yoshi thought. He had seen plenty of them who could lob a bag of nuts or a hot dog right into a fan's hands, but most of them would underhand the snacks to give the fans a better chance to catch them. This guy was throwing pretty hard, and with a sidearm delivery that looked awfully familiar. Yoshi pulled his cap off his head and scratched his scalp while he puzzled over the problem.

Meanwhile, the Goats had something brewing on the field. With the proportionate speed and scampering of a gerbil, Bobby was able to stretch an infield grounder into a single. Even though he had to stop halfway between first and second to sneak a handful of nuts from his back pocket, Bobby was able to move over 90 feet on a sacrifice fly to deep left by Katie. That put the go-ahead run in scoring position, and Blerk only needed to get a base hit to put the Goats in front.

Blerk's big, shiny eyes watched one pitch whiz past him for

a strike, then another. A long, sustained moan rolled through the crowd as Blerk twirled his bat over his shoulder. Bobby took a little hop off of second base, causing the pitcher to glance over his shoulder. The second baseman edged in behind Bobby, and in one swift motion the pitcher spun around 180 degrees and whipped the ball to second. The second baseman swiped his mitt, but it didn't find Bobby, who had skittered back onto the base safely, flattening his stomach with a deep inhale.

With the pitcher ready to deliver once again, Bobby took another couple of tiny hops off the base. The second baseman crept in behind him again, and again the pitcher made a quick toss to second. And again, Bobby was back safely. The scene repeated itself two more times before the pitcher took a step off the rubber to spit at the dirt in frustration. Sweat was beginning to bead on his forehead.

Another big lead by Bobby, and by now the Graviton City pitcher was beginning to grumble as he needed to continuously keep his eyes both behind and in front of him. For his part, Blerk continued to calmly wait for another pitch to come his way. Finally, the pitcher glanced back and saw Bobby only a step and a half away from second base. Seeing this as his opportunity, the pitcher at last set himself into the stretch and began his delivery to the plate for the 0-2 pitch. His teeth gritted in aggravation and drops of sweat leaping off his brow, the pitcher uncorked a high-speed pitch that trailed a beam of green light behind it as it darted through the air. It was a ferocious pitch.

The pitch was so ferocious, in fact, that its velocity caught Backstop completely off-guard. Behind the protective visor of his mask, the Lasers' catcher flinched, squinting his eyes reflexively and jabbing his mitt out in front of him without any real idea of where the pitch would end up. Where it went turned out to be directly into the brick wall behind home plate, with such terrifying force that the ball wound up lodged inside a small crater. Backstop jumped to his feet and began trying to pry the ball loose from the wall as Bobby hustled to third base. The third base coach kept his eyes locked on the scene behind home plate, but as Bobby reached the bag all he could do was throw his hands up in the air as if to say "I have no idea what you should do here!"

Backstop continued trying to pop the ball, which was still giving off a faint green glow, out of the wall. But the ball proved to be too hot from its high-speed journey to remove from its spot with Backstop's bare fingers.

"Great galaxies, man, hurry!" the pitcher pleaded with Backstop. "We haven't a second to waste!"

"If I could just..." Backstop had one foot up against the wall as he tried in vain to wrest it from the wall's unrelenting grip, but still it refused to yield. Bobby decided to take the chance and made a big turn around third. With a resounding "pop," Backstop finally dislodged the ball from the still-smoking crater it left behind in the wall, but his momentum carried him tumbling backward. The catcher landed flat on his back just as Bobby crossed the plate with the go-ahead run.

In the broadcast booth, Mel Fuller could hardly contain his excitement. "Munson scores! The Goats lead 1-0 on a remarkable play that I don't believe I've ever seen the likes of before! How do you think they'll score that, Randy? Is that a wild pitch, a passed ball or a fielding error?"

"I don't know," Randy said. "What happened?"

There were high-fives all around in the Goats' dugout for Bobby, who mumbled his appreciation for the support.

"Are you okay, man?" Fuzzy asked him.

"Hm?" Bobby answered without opening his mouth.

"Thy speech is garbled," Thor explained.

"Iffs nuffs," Bobby said, pointing to his cheeks, which were puffy and swollen.

"It's what?" Fuzzy said.

Bobby held his hands out in front of him and opened his mouth wide, spilling a huge pile of peanuts, still in their shells and dripping wet. "It's just nuts, guys," Bobby said. "I was holding onto them for later."

"Truly unappetizing, friend Bobby," Thor groaned.

"Hey, nuts have a lot of protein and are a great source of energy for humans!" VORP offered. "It makes perfect sense! Maybe all of you guys should be like Bobby!"

"Uh, that's okay," Sparky said as he put on his batting helmet and prepared to walk out onto the on-deck circle. Just then, Yoshi came hustling down the tunnel and grabbed Sparky by the arm.

"I got him!" Yoshi said breathlessly. "I know who he is!"

"The Closer?" Sparky asked with his eyes widening. "So who is he? Some unheard-of prospect? A veteran come out of retirement? A position player pulling double duty?"

"He's a peanut vendor!" Yoshi pointed across the diamond into the stands, where the unusual vendor was slinging peanut bags with the same deadly accuracy as before. Sparky watched his unique sidearm delivery for two tosses before slapping Yoshi on the back.

"Holy moly, you're absolutely right, Yoshi!"

"Well, I mean, of course I was," Yoshi grumbled. "It's not like I've been right about everything else so far this season or anything..."

Sparky took a quick look at the scoreboard – it was the bottom of the seventh already. "If the game stays this close they're sure to bring him into the game to shut us down," Sparky said. "We have to find a way to keep that from happening."

"You score a whole buttload of runs," Yoshi said with a shrug. "Or else you let them score a buttload of runs, but I don't think that's really what you want to do."

"No, the way this game's been going so far, we're going to need to find a way to keep him from coming into the game no matter what," Sparky said. He grabbed his bat and ran up the dugout stairs. "Let me know if you think of anything!" he called back to Yoshi.

"You'll be the first to know," Yoshi said, shaking his head.

At the dish, Lou hit a humpbacked liner that sailed over the infielders' heads and dropped in a perfect position in shallow left center field. Blerk hustled into second base and with one out the Goats were threatening to extend their lead.

Sitting on a 2-0 count, Sparky jumped on a straight fastball right now the center of the plate, which became a sharp liner than skipped over the lip of the infield. Bouncing high and rising quickly, the ball looked like it would reach the outfield for sure. However, Hot Corner broke for the ball with a burst of speed so explosive that Sparky could swear he saw jets of flame erupt from the soles of his shoes. The Lasers' third baseman improbably caught up to the ball while it rose through the air. He left his feet and, with only a half-second before the ball was out of his range entirely, made a backhanded clutch at it.

From the bleachers, the fans watched in amazement as Hot Corner pinched the ball between the edges of his glove like chopsticks snatching a fly out of midair. Then, as he still hung in the air, he twisted himself over so that his back was parallel to the infield dirt and swiped the ball out of his glove with his bare hand, firing it to second base with a flick of his wrist. Even taking into account the effort Hot Corner needed to put in to get to the ball, his throw still was in time to nail Lou at second base.

Lou trotted back to the dugout, shaking his head sadly at Sparky as he passed first base. "Goldurn knees of mine," he groaned. "I'm sorry I let you down, kid."

"It's all right, Lou," Sparky countered, hoping to hide the disappointment in his voice. "The guy made a heck of a play. You can't always...what the heck is going on there?"

Sparky pointed to the bullpen, where Ted Ballpino was hustling across foul territory with his glove on his hand. Lou looked back at Sparky with a confused glint in his eye.

"Lemme go see what's up," Lou said. "Just concentrate on running the bases, you hear me?"

"Where are you headed, pilgrim?" Lou said as he caught up with Ted on the dugout steps.

"I don't know," Ted answered with a shrug. "All of a sudden I get a call in the bullpen to get in the game, but Skip says I'm going to play third!"

"Third?!?"

"Yeah, he's playing third!" Skip said gruffly. "Believe me, the list of things I'd rather do than put one of those Ballpino kids in the game playing the infield is long and detailed, but I've got no choice with Munson out of the game!"

"Bobby's out of the game?" Lou said. "The guy's gone 2-for-3 with three stolen bases so far, Skip! They can't catch up to him if they were all riding jackrabbits!"

"You don't have to tell me that," Skip shot back. "But Yoshi says he's got a bad blister on his foot or something and now he can't finish the game, so you can sort of see how that puts a bit of a wet blanket on things."

Lou looked to the end of the bench and saw Bobby standing against the rail, his right foot wrapped in enough gauze to keep the Giza Pharaohs from falling apart for half a season. When Bobby saw Lou staring at him, he quickly shook his head and gave them the thumbs-up.

"That crafty little so-and-so," Lou said, smiling.

With runners on the corners and VORP coming up to the plate, the Lasers' manager hovered out to the mound and motioned to the bullpen. He spent a few moments conferring with his pitcher before placing a hand on his shoulder and nodding solemnly. The signal appeared high in the sky – The Closer was being summoned once again.

Graviton City's manager waited on the mound for a moment. Then another moment. Then the home plate umpire joined him out there to ask him politely just what the heck he thought he was doing, and gently reminded him that there was a baseball game to be played and no one there had all day to wait around. The manager looked perplexed, and began waving out in the direction of the bullpen, but the bullpen coach could only offer him a confused shrug.

Meanwhile, in the stands, a familiar-looking peanut vendor was being gradually relieved of all his stock.

"Give me another bag, would ya?" Bobby stood on his tiptoes to address the vendor from over the roof of the Goats dugout. The vendor complied, tossing him a fourth bag of peanuts and collecting the money from him. By the time the vendor had made change, Bobby had emptied the bag into his ever-expanding cheeks.

"Mmpf, these'r relly good," Bobby said through a mouthful of salted shells. "Hey, I'll take anuffer bab."

"Of course, sir," the vendor said, then turned and began talking to himself under his breath. "Great golden gloves! This ravenous rogue is keeping me from answering the signal! And yet, I can't break away without revealing my secret identity!"

"Wha wuzzat?" Bobby asked.

"Nothing, citizen!" the vendor replied nervously. "Just getting you your peanuts!"

After a few more moments of the umpire gently reminding the Graviton City manager that there was no way he was going to allow him to stand out there on the mound like an idiot, the manager finally surrendered and made another motion to the bullpen. A few seconds later, another reliever took the hill for the Lasers.

VORP practically sprung from the on-deck circle into the batter's box, his motivators and actuators making happy little chirping noises. He took a few practice swings and waved to the Lasers' manager as he floated back to the dugout like an overloaded blimp.

"Did you guys get everything straightened out there?" VORP asked after the opposing manager. He scowled back at VORP with glowing yellow eyes.

"Boy, I sure hope that Closer guy is okay," VORP continued. "That's the strangest thing I've seen in a really long time!"

A few pitches later, VORP turned on a low fastball and sent it screaming over the infield, past a diving shortstop and into left field, where it skipped across the grass and took a hard hop off the base of the outfield wall. Blerk jogged across homeplate, and as Sparky touched second base he saw the left fielder was still chasing down the ball. His legs already burning with exhaustion, Sparky leaned forward and sprinted toward third base. The third base coach's eyes darted back and forth between Sparky and the play in the outfield, but he hadn't given Sparky any kind of signal yet.

To heck with it, Sparky thought. If it's that close...

He could feel the pull of gravity dragging on him as he came charging down the third baseline. Sparky almost was outrunning himself, and he felt as if the only thing keeping him from falling flat on his face was the frantic movement of his legs. The sound of the crowd grew to a furious roar. It was the only way Sparky could tell he still had a chance to score. He watched Backstop plant his feet in front of the plate, trying to create a wall with his body. He dropped his mitt down in front of him, gut level, ready to receive the throw from the outfield.

Sparky's feet were having trouble keeping up with the rest of him. He was only a few feet from the plate, and if he took another step he would end up tumbling to the ground too early. So, with the last of the strength left in his aching legs, Sparky tried to give himself one last little push through the air. He was suspended in midair, feeling the roar of the crowd rumbling underneath him like a riptide carrying him out to sea. His fingertips were stretched out before him, eager to make contact with the hard rubber of the plate. Backstop caught the throw and clutched the ball firmly in his mitt. Sparky reached out...but the familiar smell of leather filled his nostrils before he felt the hard ground collide with his body. He didn't need to hear the umpire say anything to know that he hadn't made it. The Goats' rally would be limited to one precious insurance run.

And so the Goats took the field for the top of the ninth, the air inside Zigleaf Field heavy with the held breath of an entire city. The ballpark's organ played a bouncy, upbeat tune that nevertheless sounded like mocking laughter compared to the intense anxiety that crackled through the stands and kept the fans paralyzed with tension. Sparky could feel it as he took the mound. Every eye in the stadium was on him.

The first two batters of the Lasers' half of the inning were retired on long fly balls that stayed in the park despite jumping off their bats with vigor. Each time the bats made contact with the balls, the crowd started as if they had witnessed a car accident, settling down only when the ball came to rest inside an outfielder's glove. Some of the fans chuckled to themselves, realizing how silly they must have looked, but most still bore a mesmerized look.

Unfortunately, the next hitter cracked a bouncer up the third baseline, where Ted Ballpino was watching it with terror-stricken eyes. Ted's eyes were so fixated on the ball that he seemed to mirror its movement. The ball took a big hop off the dirt, and so did Ted, jumping in the air in perfect synchronicity. This brought him directly in front of the path of the ball, but instead of putting his glove in front of it, Ted put out his chest like a sumo wrestler preparing to take a hit from an opponent severely above his weight class. The ball struck him right in the "A" in the word "GOATS" on his jersey, then skittered away from him into foul territory. The umpire behind third base signaled a fair ball, and by the time Ted finally was able to corral it, the hitter was taking a big turn around first. Sparky slapped his glove against his leg, but then turned to Ted and nodded at him to let him know it was okay.

But the Lasers could see the Goats' infield now had a

glaring weakness. The next batter slapped a few foul balls just outside the third baseline before tapping a slow roller in Ted's direction. As Ted scrambled after it, the ball quickly deadened to a trickle on the thick infield grass, causing Ted to overshoot it. He tried to double back, but his momentum meant all he could do was fall backwards while swinging his glove in the direction of the ball. Both runners were safe.

Stepping to the plate was the Lasers' slugging left fielder, The Blue Bomber. Sparky looked back at Ted and gave him a reassuring nod, but in truth he wasn't sure how he was going to escape this situation. The Bomber's eyes were blank circles of white under his shimmering blue cowl, but Sparky could tell he was hungry nonetheless. His previous plate appearances had ended in an intentional walk and a sharp single off the right field wall, and with runners on base there was no way he was thinking anything but extra bases.

The runners took their leads and Sparky delivered the first pitch to the Blue Bomber, a fastball down and in. If the Bomber was determined to make contact, Sparky at least would try and keep the ball down. But the Bomber didn't flinch at the pitch, and it was called ball one. Exhaling deeply, Sparky looked in for the next sign from Lou, and seeing what he wanted straightened up, ready to deliver. This time he went fastball up and away, hoping he could maybe fool Bomber into chasing it. But there were keen, finely-tuned eyes hiding underneath the Bomber's reflective lenses, and he didn't so much as twitch. Sparky had quickly fallen behind 2-0. His next pitch was a slider that brushed through the strike zone for a moment but ended up falling over the outside edge of the plate. Again, Bomber just watched the ball whizz by and took it all the way.

Lou called for time and half-ran out to the mound. "I think we need to give the gentleman first base," he said. The way his mustache rustled, Sparky could tell it wasn't what Lou actually preferred.

"Load the bases for Hot Corner?" Sparky thumped his glove with his fist. "No way, Lou! I can get the Bomber, just let me throw him some of the special stuff."

"Kid, you throw any more of the special stuff and there ain't gonna be much stuff left in that arm, special or not," Lou argued.

"Just give me the chance to get him," Sparky pleaded. "My arm feels okay, really."

"If you were anybody else, I'd slap you on the back of the head and tell you you're an idiot," Lou said. "But at this point I'd say you've earned the benefit of the doubt. Go get 'em, kid."

Lou trotted back behind the plate and Sparky relaxed his

shoulder as much as he could. He looked in, past Boomer and his massive arms and zeroed in on Lou's mitt. Sparky drew a deep breath and went into the stretch. He could feel the burning flare up in his shoulder almost immediately, much sooner than it did normally, but he ignored it. The sensation traveled quickly down his arm, bursting at his elbow as he cocked his arm. Both joints were on fire as Sparky stepped forward and pushed off with his back foot.

The burning consumed his right arm, now surging through his wrist and swallowing up his fingers. There was pain, more intense than he was used to. As the ball spun off his fingertips, Sparky felt the pain and burning explode through the palm of his hand. The Blazing Fastball tore through the air toward the plate. Boomer's mouth opened slightly with surprise, but he clenched his teeth and took a full swing from the back of his heels. If he made contact with the ball at all, it was at least two bases, for sure.

But there was no contact. With the explosive speed of the Blazing Fastball, Boomer's bat could not catch up. The sweet spot of the bat instead passed harmlessly through the fiery tail of the pitch and completed its arc on Boomer's opposite shoulder, bearing scorch marks and a halo of smoke hanging over it.

Sparky pumped his fist and Lou nodded as he threw him a new ball. He stood motionless on the mound, resting the ball in the recesses of his glove as he again targeted the mitt. His eyes darted around to check the runners – the runner at first had taken a single step off the bag and Fuzzy was playing at his normal position. There was no threat on the basepaths.

Sparky lifted his arms above his head and started his motion. There was a sensation traveling up his arm now, from the tips of his fingers creeping slowly toward his shoulder. Sparky could sense the feeling in his fingers disappear, as if they had been separated from his body. Although his eyes could tell him everything still was where it should be, if he didn't know better Sparky could have sworn that his hand and forearm had simply vanished. Without the feeling in his arm, Sparky needed to trust his mechanics, switch over completely to instinct. Controlling the Phantom Slider was all about discipline.

When the ball left his fingertips, it felt as if Sparky's entire arm was following it to the plate. As the feeling quickly returned to his throwing arm, he watched the ball twist toward the plate. Boomer's eyes had trouble picking up the pitch at first, but within a fraction of a second he focused in on it, and he tensed up again for another big hack.

Boomer's bat slashed across the plate, making a bee-line directly for the ball. But just before the two intersected, the ball flickered out of sight, leaving Boomer swinging through nothing but empty air. With the bat now safely out of the danger zone, the ball rematerialized on the opposite side of the plate in time to reach the safety of Lou's mitt. The umpire threw his hand in the air to signal strike two.

On the mound, Sparky exhaled with relief and no small amount of amazement. He knew the Phantom Slider could vanish from sight, but the break on that last pitch was greater than anything he had ever seen himself pitch before. Had the ball actually traveled outside of regular time and space? Sparky made a note to ask Yoshi about it later.

By now, Boomer was grumbling to himself at the plate. What had been a sure hitter's count before was now full, and he had been fooled badly on the last two pitches. The look on his face said he only expected one outcome on the next pitch – complete and utter ownage. Whether it would be Boomer or Sparky on the receiving end of the ownage remained to be seen.

Sparky was ready to deliver the 3-2 pitch. He didn't even check the runners – he knew they would be on the move. As he brought his arms down from over his head, time began to slow down. His arms felt like they were buried in oatmeal, and the ball became as heavy as a shot put. Sparky strained to push his arms forward – the air itself felt as thick as wet cement and what was once a sphere of twine and horsehide now felt like a cannonball in his hands. With sweat streaming down his face, Sparky released the ball. It felt as if it should have plummeted straight now into the dirt, but instead the Cosmic Change-Up floated through the air on a straight line that would be impossible under the normal rules of physics.

The action around the ballpark slowed down, as well. Sparky broke his gaze from the path of the pitch for a moment to watch the fans. Many of them were standing, fists clenched, eyes wide with anticipation. Sparky had seen the crazed look in the eyes of Goats fans before. There were only a few of them on Opening Day, but today he could see the look in almost everyone wearing the red and orange.

When he turned back to the pitch, he noticed that Boomer didn't seem the same as the rest of the crowd. He wasn't standing stock still, as everyone else in the ballpark seemed to be. In fact, Boomer broke from his stance to adjust his batting gloves and spit a sunflower seed into the dirt. The burly hitter assumed his stance once again and kept his eyes fixed on the ball. He looked up momentarily, with the ball still slowly rotating its way to the plate, and winked maliciously at Sparky. Sparky felt his stomach drop past his knees.

The slugger's swing was timed perfectly to match the glacial speed of the pitch. He caught the ball directly in the center of the bat's barrel, and with the crack of the wood time caught up. The ball climbed through the air as the runners took off. Thor gave chase, but couldn't catch up with it in the air. Sparky watched with horror as the ball landed squarely on the left field grass in front of Thor's feet.

The runner from second base touched third as Thor scooped the ball off the grass, and the third base coach waved him around. Thor reared back and hurled the ball in, with Fuzzy ready to cut it off and possibly try to make a play at home. With the ball speeding toward the infield and the Graviton City runner hustling to home plate, Fuzzy reached up to receive the throw, but he didn't make it.

That's because Ted had jumped in front of Fuzzy and cut off the throw himself. As Fuzzy started shouting something at the diminutive reliever pitcher-turned-infielder, Ted spun around and fired a fastball strike right at home plate. Lou slid in front of the plate, took the throw dead-center in his mitt, then went sprawling as the runner barreled straight into him.

Lou came off his feet and went flying through the air, and the runner crumbled in a heap in front of the plate. Lou landed flat on his back, kicking up a cloud of dust like a building collapsing. There was a moment of silence as the crowd strained to see what had happened. And then Lou pulled the ball out of his mitt and held it over his head, and the crowd went wild.

15. DOWN THE STRETCH

"Good morning, Go-Town, and what a good morning it is to be in this city and to be a Go-Town Goats fan! This is Mel Fuller alongside the Goats legend Randy Sannies welcoming you to a very special edition of 'The Bleat.' It's special not only because we're on the air in October, but also because we're here to talk about something we've never discussed before. Can you guess what we're talking about today, Randy?"

"Uh, besides the Goats in the Worlds Series?"

"You've hit the nail right on the head, partner, albeit in your own inimitable roundabout fashion. Yes, Go-Town, the Goats captured a trip to the Worlds Series with their series victory yesterday afternoon against the Graviton City Lasers in a dramatic climax that I'm sure will go down in the annals not only of Goats history, but in the history of all Big League Baseball."

"That was something, all right."

"Indeed it was, Randy. The Goats will be moving on to face the New York Emperors for the title of World's Champion of baseball, a position that is completely alien to the Goats but all-too-familiar for the Emperors. Before we get to breaking down the respective merits of each ballclub, Randy, why don't we talk about home field advantage?"

"Okay, sure."

"As you know, the Goats entered the playoffs after winning the Central League crown. However, based on the Goats' overall record at the end of the regular season, they were awarded the #10 seed in the Doubleday Memorial Bracket. New York, on the other hand, easily captured the Metropolitan League pennant and entered its playoff bracket with the #1 seed overall. Are you with me so far, Randy?"

"Wait, so, uh..."

"The Goats went on to beat the Polar League champs, Amundsen City, and then moved on to the next round to play the Galactic League champs in the form of the Rigel 7 Conquerors. That brought them to the series they just won against Graviton City and now the Worlds Series."

"Okay, but..."

"The Emperors reached the Worlds Series by defeating Athens in the previous round of the playoffs, and as a #1 seed logic would dictate that they would receive home-field advantage."

"That's true..."

"But hold on, Randy. As everyone knows, the outcome of the All-Star Game has bearing on home-field advantage. But that can be negated based on the outcome of the Home Run Derby, and that's what has happened this year, of course. So the Emperors were in good shape to retain home-field advantage at the end of the regular season."

"Oh, is that so?"

"But, the Goats held some key tiebreakers heading into the playoffs, most notably for complete games, overall team batting average and stadium cleanliness. That meant the Emperors needed Athens to make the playoffs but not LV-426, because the Xenomorphs had the better record in spring training."

"Uh-huh."

"Of course, LV-426 was eliminated from playoff contention by losing the second-to-last game of their season to Magrathia, and now the Goats had to watch and wait for the outcome of the Graviton City-San Diego series to see if they could overcome that situation."

"Mm."

"And as we all know, Graviton City came out on top of that series, and under the new playoff-opponent rating system that was introduced three years ago, now the scales were tipped in Go-Town's favor. That is unless, of course, the Emperors had lost their series against Athens, in which case the team with the higher attendance figures would be subject to having its regular-season opponents put through the Beatability Matrix established by the Expansion and Realignment Agreement of 58 years ago. If the Beatability Matrix score of the team with higher attendance was under 78.4, then the team with the higher average temperature in October would receive home-field advantage."

"..."

"But of course all that was rendered moot with the Emperors' victory over Athens, and determining home-field advantage was left to the old-fashioned method of calculating the relative strength of each team's regular-season opponents, factoring in the performance of other playoff teams and weighing those figures against where each team stands in terms of the standard statistical categories. And all that, of course, leads us to where we are today and with who else having home-field advantage for the Worlds Series, Randy?"

"Buh?"

"Your very own Go-Town Goats will host the first two games of the series before traveling to New York City for games 3, 4 and 5, and then if necessary the series will return to Go-Town for games 6 and 7."

"Right."

"Of course, this marks the first time the Goats have advanced to the Worlds Series in the team's entire history, and as a founding member of the Central League, you know that history goes back a long way. We'll be back in a moment to break down the match-ups that will define this monumental Worlds Series, but first, Randy and I just want to remind you that if you happen to see a Goat today, make sure you say, 'Thanks!'"

Sparky, frankly, had been thanked enough by the time he left his apartment building that morning. From the moment he left the ballpark the night before, Sparky and his teammates had been mobbed by Go-Towners wanting to shake their hands or get an autograph. There had been a traffic jam of hovercars stretching back a full mile when someone spotted Thor and Katie crossing the street to get to the parking lot.

Pulling his old high school team cap over his eyes and flipping up the collar of his varsity jacket, Sparky took a deep breath before opening the front door to his building. Carlos had texted him half an hour earlier to suggest they try to meet for lunch at the Mexican place. There was no way Sparky thought he could avoid being swarmed by a city full of suddenly-rabid baseball fans, but there also was no way he could go all day without eating something, and there was nothing in his fridge but protein shakes and sports drinks.

Sparky poked his head out of his front door and saw...nothing. There was no mob of fans waiting outside his building, just the normally busy rush of people that made up a typical morning in Go-Town. Maybe no one knew this was where he lived, or maybe Go-Town just needed to get back to work. Whatever the reason, Sparky decided to take advantage of the situation and walked briskly down the street.

Even with his sunglasses on, Sparky could see that red and orange had completely taken over the downtown. There were banners and flags hanging from almost every window, and streamers of red and orange dangling from every lamppost. What startled Sparky wasn't just amount of team spirit he saw – he had witnessed bandwagons in the past, certainly – it was that so many of these flags and banners and bunting looked so old. There was visible fraying on the edges of many of the flags, and the colors were dusty and faded. How long had these things been sitting in these people's closets?

Sparky passed one window in which someone had taped a homemade sign on orange posterboard. In the middle was an old photograph of an even older man, his face not so much wrinkled as it was crumpled, seemingly by rough hands with no regard for what effect they were having. The old man was sitting in what looked like a bleacher seat at Zigleaf Field. He was wearing a battered Goats cap that looked as if it had been through the same process as his face. But he was smiling. He held a cup of some frosty beverage in the air and wore a broad grin that propped up all the wrinkles on his face. Sparky almost walked by without seeing the little boy sitting next to the old man, a little boy wearing his own Goats cap, fresh off the shelf with the brim still flat as a board. The little boy was looking up at the old man and smiling, too. There was a message scrawled in bright red magic marker over the photo: "You'll never believe it, Gramps!"

When Sparky arrived at the restaurant, it was surprisingly empty for the lunch hour. In fact, he noticed only two groups of people: a small cluster of men in fine suits in the far corner of the dining room, and Bobby, Fuzzy, Carlos and Katie at the Goats' usual table in the middle.

"Man," Sparky said as he pulled up a chair and slipped his cap off his head, "I've never seen this place so dead before!"

"They must have found out Bobby was coming and figured there wouldn't be anything left!" Fuzzy exclaimed.

"That's real funny, you human pom-pom," Bobby said. "I'll have you know that I actually haven't been hungry since yesterday. I guess the hamster DNA is finally wearing off. Poor little guy."

"That's too bad, Bobby, because your slugging percentage went up 150 points over your average while you were, uh, mutated," Katie said as she tried to get a chip overloaded with salsa to her mouth without dripping.

"Maybe it's for the best," Bobby said. "I was starting to worry about when my tail was going to grow in."

Sparky laughed, but he couldn't help feel as if he was being stared at. He glanced over his shoulder and saw the three men in suits in the corner looking straight at him. The one in the middle gestured for Sparky to join them.

"Excuse me, guys," Sparky said as he stood up and crossed the room. The corner was dark, darker than he was used to the restaurant being at that time of day. It was almost like the lights had been dimmed on purpose for these men.

"It's good to see you again, Mr. Katakura," came a familiar voice from the center of the group. Sparky squinted, his eyes finally adjusting to the darkness to make out the face of Mr. Oni. "I have to admit, I was hoping we'd run into each other again."

"Hey, if you have something to say about that busted trade, you can take it up with Mr. Mint," Sparky said. "All I care about right now is winning the Worlds Series against your Emperors."

"That silly matter of the trade?" Mr. Oni said with surprise. "Oh no, I can assure you that it's all water under the bridge now, Mr. Katakura. What's done is done."

Mr. Oni took a long drink of water and looked down at the half a burrito on his plate. "Ah," he exhaled. "This place is supposed to have the spiciest food in Go-Town, and I'm happy to say I'm not that disappointed. Do you come here very often?"

"We do," Sparky said, his eyes fixed on Mr. Oni's face. The other two men in the booth sat in total silence. It didn't look like they had eaten anything at all.

"Would you recommend the enchiladas? I was torn between the vegetarian enchiladas and the chicken burrito."

"They're pretty good," Sparky said.

"Oh, that's excellent. I'll have to remember that for next time." Mr. Oni dabbed the corners of his mouth with his napkin, folded it neatly in half and set it down to the side of his plate. He then put his elbows on the table and closed his fingertips together in front of his face.

"I didn't want to talk to you about the trade, Mr. Katakura," Oni said at last. "Rather, I wanted to talk to you about what you gave up by turning us down."

"New York's great and everything, Mr. Oni, but right now I'm just focused on winning here in Go-Town," Sparky said.

"And that's wonderful, just wonderful." Oni arched an eyebrow and smiled at Sparky. "It's really spectacular for Big League Baseball to see a small-market team like the Goats do something improbable every so often. It's good for business if every fan thinks their team has a shot, you know?"

"Thanks," Sparky said sarcastically. "So I guess I didn't need to come to New York to make it this far."

"No," Oni sighed. "But there were some other variables to the deal that I guess you didn't consider." Oni reached into his jacket and pulled out a stack of baseball cards. "These are from the new set, fresh from the factory."

Oni handed the top card to Sparky – it was of Number 7, the same player Oni almost had convinced Mr. Mint into taking in exchange for Sparky. The masked outfielder was wearing the familiar pinstriped Emperor uniform, standing at the plate under the bright lights of Imperial Stadium. His batting stance was the same as Sparky remembered seeing in the All-Star Game, still as strangely familiar as it was a couple months earlier.

"This is really nice," Sparky said as he tilted the card, allowing what little light there was to bounce off its glossy surface. "Sure looks like your guy Number 7 is still happy to be an Emperor. At least, I think he is, I can't tell with that weird mask..."

"Take a closer look," Oni said, waving his fingers subtly at the card. Suddenly, the image on the card began to move, and Number 7 began twirling the head of his bat over his head as he waited for a pitch. "Doesn't that stance look familiar to you?"

Sparky frowned. Whatever point Oni was trying to make, he didn't like how long he was taking to make it. "Yeah, sorta. Come on, what's the deal with this? Are we talking about baseball or telling riddles?"

"Talking about baseball, most definitely," Oni said. "I'm surprised it's taking you this long, frankly." He slipped another card out of the stack and passed it across the table to Sparky. It was a card of Ken, from his first season with the Stars. The scenes on the two cards were virtually identical – both photos were taken from the same angle, both photos were taken at night, the batting stances were...actually identical.

Sparky dropped the card on the table and stepped back quickly. "What is this?"

"You fought so hard against that trade, didn't you, Mr. Katakura?" Mr. Oni slipped the cards back into his pocket and smiled. "All you had to do was accept it, and your brother would have been released from his contract. The rest of his teammates, of course, would have belonged to me for all eternity, but you were never really that concerned about them, were you?"

"So you're...him, then? You're the Baseball Devil."

Mr. Oni held up his hands. "Oh, I don't think there's any need to be so formal," he said. "Please, you can continue to call me 'Mr. Oni.'"

"I can think of a few other things I could call you right now."

"Of course, of course," Oni said. "You ballplayers are always so colorful with your language. You know, I was afraid at first that you and your Goats would have been eliminated from playoff contention even before the All-Star Break." Oni leaned back into the shadows, but his eyes continued to glow like two coals in the back of a dying fireplace.

"Yeah, well I guess we ruined your plan," Sparky said, his voice trembling a little.

"Not at all! It's always disappointing to have a wager settled so quickly, and without drama. But this! This is spectacular, with everything coming down to the very last games of the season. Makes me remember why I got into this game in the first place."

Sparky just stood there, frozen by a combination of rage and fear. He wanted nothing more than to jump across the table and grab Oni's wrinkled old neck in his hands. Would that change anything? Would he even make it halfway there before he was turned to ash, or changed into a gargoyle, or just plain stomped on by those big jerks on either side of the old man?

"I can see you're not as thrilled by the prospect as I am," Oni said. "That's all right, I wouldn't feel too good about my chances in this series, were I in your place. I have the most successful team in Big League Baseball history, I have the reigning Worlds Series champions on my roster, and I have myself. You have one remarkable arm, a collection of players who barely qualify as professional ballplayers, and a significant streak of luck..." Oni's eyes narrowed in the shadows. "...that will run out soon enough."

Suddenly, Sparky felt dizzy. The restaurant seemed to swirl around him, and he was unable to fix his eyes on anything for more than a half-second. He could hear Oni laughing softly to himself in the dark. Sparky had to close his eyes to keep from getting sick. When he opened them again, he was sitting across from Bobby again.

"Sparky! Hey!" Bobby said as he stared straight into Sparky's eyes. "What's the hold-up?"

"Huh?" Sparky looked around the table and saw his teammates staring at him. There also was a waiter staring at him, pad and pencil at the ready.

"Come on, man, what are you having? You've just been staring out into space for like five minutes!"

"I was?"

"Yeah, you said you were going to be right back, but then you just sat there and didn't move," Fuzzy said. "It was pretty weird."

Sparky felt a chill run down his back, but then it was gone. He looked up at the waiter. "Uh, I guess I'll have the quesadillas."

It wasn't the quesadillas. Every time he had rolled over, the story the alarm clock told got worse and worse. Deciding he'd rather do anything than lay there and try to force himself to sleep, Sparky got out of bed and put on his cleats.

Sparky was surprised to find some of the lights on when he arrived at Zigleaf Field, but it somehow made sense when he was met at the gate by Yoshi.

"What are you still doing awake?" Sparky asked.

"I would ask you the same question, but I think we both know the answer, anyway," Yoshi said wearily. "Besides, you're not the only guy who's having trouble sleeping tonight."

Yoshi unlocked the gate and let Sparky onto the field. The stadium lights were on, making the field as bright as day. With the stands empty and the lights off throughout the rest of the stadium, the field was suspended in darkness, like a butterfly pinned to a black background. The batting cage had been set up over home plate, and Sparky could see a pitching machine rhythmically launching pitch after pitch from on top of the mound. As he got closer, Sparky could see it was Carlos in the cage, turning each pitch into a line drive with a crack from his bat.

"Hey," Carlos said as he saw Sparky approaching the cage.

"Hey. Been here long?"

"What time is it now?"

"Almost 2."

"Then yeah."

"You mind if I take over for the machine? I feel like I could use a little exercise."

"Go right ahead, man."

"Thanks."

Sparky rolled the pitching machine off the mound and took the hill. He spent a little while throwing to Carlos, never overexerting himself but trying to make the first baseman work a little. For every pitch that danced out of the way of Carlos' bat, there was another he drilled across the infield or into one of the infield gaps.

After a while, Sparky and Carlos heard the stadium gate squeak open again. They stopped their impromptu session and saw Thor crossing the outfield, his glove on his hand.

"Ho, fellow Goats of Go-Town!" Thor called out to them. "The son of Odin did find his slumber this eve to be most fitful and troubled, thus did I make my way to yon stadium to hone mine skills on the field in anticipation of our final battle. May the god of thunder join thee?"

"Sure thing, Thor," Sparky said. "You want to shag some flies out there while Carlos hits?"

"Friends, the god of thunder would like nothing better."

Thor spent some time in the outfield, tracking down fly balls hit by Carlos, but soon there came again the familiar sound of the stadium gate swinging open. This time, it was Katie who stepped onto the field, squinting under the glare of the lights.

"Hey guys," she said. "Looks like I'm not the only one who had this idea, huh?"

"No, but I'm sure you've got a formula that says this is really the best time to work out and we're all dopes for not knowing that or something, right?" Carlos chuckled.

"Well, statistically, uh, the body reacts to certain..." Katie smiled nervously and then laughed. "Okay, I couldn't sleep, either."

The sun rose over Go-Town like a pennant climbing a flagpole. On an ordinary October morning, the city's streets and skyways began pulsing with activity slowly but steadily until it reached a peak, like a jogger's heartbeat on their morning run. On this morning, however, there was a ragged randomness to the routine, with buses running late, traffic backing up at stop lights and hovercars floating just inches above each other. It was obvious that the Goats weren't the only citizens of Go-Town who had been too wound up to sleep that night.

Sparky had woken up in the dugout, his head resting on a duffel bag filled with towels. Carlos had fallen asleep in a giant laundry hamper in the clubhouse, while Thor had taken his rest in the topmost row of the outfield bleachers. His snoring rumbled like a storm brewing miles away. As he lead the still-sleepy Katie down onto the field, Yoshi reported that he had found her bundled up in a bunch of dugout jackets sleeping in a seat in the upper deck, not quite in the middle of a row. Still half-asleep, she had mumbled something about her grandfather and staggered downstairs, he said.

One by one, the rest of the team arrived at the ballpark, most bleary-eyed and sluggish. On the other hand, Skip arrived in a loose, relaxed mood, whistling to himself as he fixed a cup of coffee in the clubhouse. The whistling stopped as soon as he got one look around at the other faces of the team.

"What the heck is all this?" Skip asked loudly. "Why the heck ain't any of you guys look like you got any sleep?"

"Why do you think, old man?" Fuzzy groaned. "It's the Worlds Freaking Series, dude!"

"The Worlds Series?" Skip sputtered, spraying the room with coffee. "Are you sure?"

"Pretty darn sure, Skip," Tod Ballpino said, dejectedly whipping a towel into his locker.

"Why the heck didn't any of you bums tell me?"

"We just made it through three rounds of the playoffs, what else did you think was going to be next?" Bobby asked.

"Hey, don't you goldbrickers turn this around on me," Skip said. "When I was playing the playoffs were 12 rounds, and they lasted from September to December! It's not my fault they go easy on you big babies these days!"

Skip stood quietly for a moment, rubbing his chin as he

closed one eye and stared off into the distance. Then, he clapped his hands together loudly and rubbed them together. "Okay, okay, everybody gather up and take a knee," he said. The Goats looked at each other in confusion but soon all circled around Skip and kneeled down.

"Ah, it's been a while since I had to deliver a speech like this," Skip began. "Okay, I want to say that I'm proud of you guys…"

The team let out a collective "Aww…" followed by a lot of laughter.

"I want to say I'm proud of you guys, but the truth is most of you wouldn't be where you are right now if I hadn't come along," Skip continued. A few Goats rolled their eyes, and some shook their heads. "It's been a long time since I had to give one of these speeches because I've been managing this collection of bums and jerks for more than 10 years! When I first took this job, a bunch of my old buddies pulled me aside and they said to me, they said, 'Skip, don't you take that job. Everybody and their brother knows that the Go-Town franchise is run by a penny-pinching old fop who don't know any more about the game of baseball than he does how to breathe underwater.' And to a man, I grabbed those old buddies of mine by the shoulders and said, 'Come back and talk to me in a year.' Of course, that was before I knew just how bad things were over here. I mean, we had a water heater playing center field back then!"

"That was me, Skip!" VORP said from the back of the room, waving his arm cheerfully. "And I'm still here, too!"

Skip continued, undaunted. "But anybody who knows Skip LaRoche knows that I ain't never heard the word 'quit' before in my life, and at the end of that first year I had those guys playing better baseball than anyone had ever seen out of them!"

"At the close of that season, thine Goats had lost ten score games!" Thor said.

"What's that in regular numbers?" Fuzzy asked.

"One hundred and twenty," Antonio answered.

"Whoo, forget I asked."

"So my estimate was off by about a decade or so," Skip continued, "but here I am, the man who turned around the worst team in the Big Leagues into a pennant winner and the man who's about to lead them into the Worlds Series for the first time in its history. Now, I'm not saying I want a statue built in my honor. Anybody who knows me knows I don't go for that kind of thing. All I'm saying is that when you look back and consider what's been accomplished, and when you see how far this team has come…there's little doubt in my mind that baseball will remember that, and it'll remember who made it happen. And that's all I got to say about that." Skip turned and headed back into his office.

"Hey Skip, what was that?" Willie asked.

"That was my inspirational speech to you guys," Skip said. "Nice job."

"Get out on the field, all of you."

Later, the national anthem was blaring, the whole of Zigleaf Field like a giant mouth shouting the melody straight into the sky for someone on a distant planet to salute. But Sparky wasn't listening. He was standing along the foul line, hand and cap held over his heart, eyes locked on the Emperors standing on the opposite side of the diamond. Their ghoulish masks shone in the midday sun without their caps to shadow them. Sparky narrowed his gaze to Number 7, the one Oni told him was his brother Ken. He could almost believe it, too, if it didn't pain him so much to do so.

Ken could have been free already, Sparky told himself. If only he had just gone along with the trade, if only he hadn't been so headstrong, if only he hadn't been arrogant enough to believe he could turn the Goats into world champions. Defeating the New York Emperors of old was one thing, but when they're owned and operated by the single most evil force in all of baseball? He could have saved his brother's soul already. He would have been on the Goats, sure, but they weren't so bad, given the alternative. Sparky imagined what it would be like to be standing there on the other side of the field behind one of those masks. Did Ken even recognize him? Did he know where he was, who he was, what was going on? They both had just wanted to win so badly…was that wrong?

Antonio had been given the start for Game 1, and for the first few innings he was dazzling, felling four Emperors by swinging strikeouts and allowing only two well-hit balls that dropped for singles. In the bottom of the fourth inning, the Goats had runners on second and third with just one out. Thor stepped confidently to the plate and watched as the anonymous pitcher's first two attempts missed the strike zone. Watching the pitcher's hand like an eagle scanning the surface of a river for the outline of a salmon, Thor readied himself for the 2-0 pitch, and it came off the pitcher's fingertips looking like a beach ball pushed by a gentle breeze. The thunder god actually felt his mouth water as he squared up on the ball, and the contact put a jolt in his palms. The ball began climbing into the sky, but before it could reach the realm of the right fielder it suddenly deviated from its course and broke over the foul line and into the stands. Midway to first base,

Thor scoffed and grumbled as he lumbered back to the batter's box.

The next pitch looked even more enticing than the one previous, hanging in midair like the full moon and growing ever larger as it lazily approached the plate. Thor chuckled to himself and wondered why the pitcher would ever consider throwing something as hittable as this pitch appeared to be. Again he put the full force of his massive form into his swing, and the sound of the impact was not unlike a battering ram making contact with a particularly not well-constructed castle gate. This time, the ball was crushed into straightaway center, and even though the center fielder already was playing deep he turned his back to the plate and gave chase. Thor took off running for first base.

But again, although the ball had been hit on a line off Thor's bat, it suddenly bent out of the way of fair territory and somehow sailed foul, this time landing in the seats along the left field line. Thor actually stopped in mid-stride to watch it happen, and he could swear that the line drive had made a sharp left turn, its flight nearly a perfect right angle. Again he walked back, shaking his head.

The next pitch after that was another would-be hitter's pitch, and now Thor was so flustered that when he made contact it he did so too late and slightly underneath the pitch. There was no way this one was going to need help going foul, Thor thought, and sure enough the ball was popped high in the air and drifting out over the Emperors' dugout. Their third baseman jogged after it, but it was clearly out of play. Thor looked down to make sure his cleats weren't dirty, but when he looked up he saw the ball bending back in the opposite direction and right into the third baseman's glove for a very unlikely out. The next batter struck out looking to end the threat and the inning.

The next time through the order, the Goats were in a very similar situation, with runners on the corners and only one out. This time, it was Bobby at the plate. He swiped the back of his hand across his forehead and his batting glove came back damp with sweat. The count was 2-2, and with a pitch to waste the expressionless hurler flirted with the outside edge of the plate. Bobby decided to take a chance on the borderline pitch and hacked at it, and with a short, sharp shock it hopped off the infield grass and looked as if it would surely split the shortstop and third baseman for a base hit. The fact that none of the infielders even tried making a move for it gave Bobby extra confidence, and the crowd cheered for the players circling the bases.

Just as the ball seemed as if it would skip past the infield entirely, it instead made a sharp right turn and hopped straight into the motionless shortstop's glove. Without a second's hesitation, the shortstop turned and tossed the ball to the waiting second baseman for the force out at second. Another quick throw, and the 6-4-3 inning-ending double play had been completed, and another potential Goat rally was squashed.

"This is insane!" Bobby said as he flipped his bat in the direction of the bat rack. "How the heck are were supposed to make anything happen if they can make an out without even moving?"

"You ain't ever heard of 'hitting 'em where they ain't?'" Skip said through clenched teeth. "Of course they're making outs, because you losers are hitting 'em where they are! You there, Internet Girl!" He pointed menacingly at Katie.

"Me?"

"Yeah, you! When you get up there next inning, I want you to start hitting 'em where they ain't!" Katie and Skip just stared at each other for a long moment, long enough for Skip to flare his nostrils six times. Katie finally raised one eyebrow.

"You got it, Skip," she said, and then trotted out into the field.

"Listen, Bobby," Lou said. "The mojo isn't in the ball, it's in the arm, you ought to know that by now. Just keep wearing that dude down and he'll burn through his hustle soon enough, okay?"

"Yeah, yeah, you're right, Lou," Bobby said slowly. "I'm sorry, man, I just got kind of nervous there for a second, right?"

"It's all right, kid, happens to everyone in the Big Leagues once in a while. Now get out there and play some defense, you hear?"

"You got it!"

"You know that for sure?" Katie asked Lou as Bobby skipped to third base.

"Heck no," Lou said. "I've never seen anything like this before in my life. There's a lot more than hustle in that dude's arm, I know that for sure."

Both sides continued to struggle to put runners on base. Even though they followed Lou's advice and continued hacking away at pitches, New York's starter showed no signs of fatigue, even though the level of hustle he would have needed to expend was well beyond anything any player had ever been seen giving.

For the Emperors, it was the nearly flawless pitching of Antonio De La Goya that kept them from advancing beyond third base. True to the pitcher's form, each delivery over the plate was like a single note that collectively formed a symphony. Every pitch was the perfect follow-up to the one before it, a mystifying melody made up of differing speeds and locations. It was the work of a virtuoso, a siren song that lured the Emperors' hitters to their doom time and time again. But the game was wearing on, the maestro was reaching his limit, and the tempo of the music was slowing down.

In the top of the eighth inning, the Emperors took advantage of a couple of pitches that Antonio couldn't quite keep out of their reach, tagging both for screaming line drives that resulted in runners on second and third with only one out. The public address announcement that followed chilled Sparky's blood more than the crisp October air ever could:

"Now batting for the New York Emperors, Number 7."

Sparky watched as his brother approached the plate with the same confidence he remembered from their childhood. Ken had always been a little cocky, sauntering up to the plate with an attitude that told the opposing pitcher he didn't expect to have any trouble putting the ball in play, but with his terrifying mask and the fearsome faces of his cursed teammates watching from the dugout, his movement was more menacing. Ken looked not so much like a player confident in his own abilities than one who had nothing but contempt for his opponents' abilities.

Sparky watched Ken twirl his bat over his shoulder and felt his face get hot as he was suddenly filled with hate. He hated Oni for turning his brother into this faceless monstrosity, hated him for corrupting Ken's love of the game into a remorseless mechanical arrogance. And, if he was being completely honest, Sparky hated himself most of all for letting it happen.

Antonio was able to fool Ken on the first pitch, tricking him into swinging at a high fastball. But he wasn't as lucky on the second pitch, which Ken made solid contact with and cracked into left field. Thor scooped the ball off the grass almost immediately, but although the fury of his throw made the runner on second think twice about advancing to third, it wasn't in time to stop the runner on third from trotting across home plate. After seven innings of close calls and near-misses, it was the New York Emperors who drew first blood in the Worlds Series, and they took a 1-0 lead. Antonio dropped his head and stood motionless on the mound until Skip made his way slowly up the hill to take the ball from him.

The Goats clapped their hands and spouted encouragements as Antonio slumped into the dugout, but it was clear that the team's mood had been crushed. The bottom of the eighth came and went without incident. Tad Ballpino walked a batter but otherwise made it through the top of the ninth unscathed. Suddenly it was the bottom of the ninth, and the Goats were on the verge of squandering the home field advantage they miraculously had been gifted, and the team knew it.

As Sparky watched helplessly from the dugout railing, the remaining three Goats whiffed, rolled and popped their way out of the batter's box and back to the dugout. There was almost complete silence throughout the ballpark, and the Emperors silently lined up and retreated into the clubhouse. The only thing that marked the official end of the ballgame was the fact that the field remained empty after they had left. The fans quickly and quietly filed out of Zigleaf Field, choosing to hold their tongues until they had returned to the relative privacy of their homes and watering holes.

Later that evening, Skip delivered another one of his patented finger-pointing sessions, finding fault with just about everything the Goats had done on the field that day. In recognition of Antonio's dominant performance, Skip offered only a flip of his hand in the pitcher's direction, followed by a gruff "This guy did okay." Sparky wasn't paying attention to most of it.

Nor was Sparky paying much attention when he found himself taking a walk through downtown Go-Town later that night. He had laced up his running shoes in the hopes that an evening run through the cool autumn air would help clear his head, but instead the city's silence just made him feel guilty, so he just wandered the streets with his head down and his hood up.

"There's something about this weather, isn't there?" Sparky stopped dead in his tracks when he heard the familiar voice oozing out of a nearby doorway. He looked up and saw himself standing in front of the Go-Town Palace Hotel, with its huge golden doors and doormen in their rectangular red coats. One of those doormen held open one of those huge golden doors for Mr. Oni, who was stepping out into the night wearing a bulky black coat over his suit.

"After a long season of playing under the hot sun, baseball in weather like this is very refreshing," Oni continued. "I'd say that you come to appreciate it more each year, but in your case I would advise enjoying it now, while you still can."

"Leave me alone," Sparky snapped as he turned and walked the other way. "I don't want anything to do with you."

"Hm, sportsmanship truly is on the decline these days," Oni said as he followed Sparky. "I weep for the future of the game. Speaking of which, I hope there are no hard feelings once the Worlds Series is over. I could really see you making a big splash in the New York pinstripes. Of course, no one would be able to get your autograph, but I don't want you to think I treat my players shabbily just because I own them completely."

"Not interested."

"Oh, of course, I understand. You have to play the

hometown hero in the press, say all the right things about how you want to retire as a...whatever it says on those ugly jerseys you're wearing right now. But I know how these things work, and eventually you'll decide that if you can't beat them, you'll have to join them. They all come to that conclusion, eventually."

"Not me, old man. And you're going to have an empty roster to fill once this series is over."

"I love the confidence, that's splendid," Oni laughed. "But do you really have that much confidence in that team of yours? The old man? The computer geek? The fat guy? The loudmouth? Oh, or the rusty old robot? He's my favorite."

Sparky had heard enough. "So what? So what if the rest of the team is a bunch of losers? I don't need them!" The words caught Sparky by surprise, but at the moment they felt right. "I've got enough hustle to beat your jerks all by myself!"

"Really?" Oni chuckled. He patted Sparky lightly on the shoulder and turned back toward the hotel. "Now that, I'd like to see. Best of luck to you tomorrow, Mr. Katakura. See you at the game." Sparky watched as the old man strolled out of sight, his blood still boiling.

Sparky arrived at the clubhouse the next day to find it deserted. He circled the locker room three times looking for any sign of his teammates, but there was none, not even an open locker anywhere. Frantically, he scrolled through his phone for any texts or voicemails, but no one had tried to contact him since he turned it off the night before. Finally, after standing at his locker for a long while wondering what he could do, Sparky heard the sound of someone walking down the hallway, accompanied by an odd squeaking noise.

Sticking his head out into the hallway, Sparky saw the incredibly strange sight of Yoshi dragging a red wagon behind him. Slumped inside the wagon like a 100-pound bag of wet gravel was Skip, his jersey half-buttoned, his cap barely clinging to his head and his entire body dripping with sweat.

"Yoshi, what the heck is going on? We've got a Worlds Series game today, don't we?"

"We've got kind of a problem, is what we have," Yoshi sighed. "Everybody..."

"Everybody's sick as a got-dang dog!" Skip croaked. "Must've been that eggplant they served us for lunch yesterday!"

"But I ate the eggplant and I feel fine, Skip," Sparky said.

"What are you, calling me an idiot or something?" Skip said, scowling. "It's gotta be the eggplant, the egg part probably went rotten! You know how touchy eggs can get." Skip moaned and rolled over onto his side.

"So the whole team is sick?" Sparky asked Yoshi.

"They couldn't even get out of bed, they told me," Yoshi said. "Skip made me drag him all the way to the park in this thing."

"Yeah, that's right, because I ain't no creampuff!" Skip said before retching loudly. "Oh God, why did I mention food? Urgh."

At that moment, one of the umpires came marching down the hallway, holding a blank lineup card high over his head. "Hey! I don't see anyone out there taking batting practice, are you guys playing this game today or what?"

"We have kind of a situation here, Blue," Yoshi said as he gestured at Skip's bloated, sweaty form. "Ah, flu-like symptoms."

"Well, I don't care if half your guys are in a coma," the umpire bellowed. "The Big League office says Game 2 gets played today no matter what, so either you get your team out on the field or I'm calling it a forfeit!"

"There won't be any forfeit," Sparky said. "I'll be out there."

"You might be out there, kid, but you still need eight other guys out there with you or you're not a full team," the umpire said, shaking his head.

"Hey, hang on there," Yoshi said cautiously. "If I remember the Big League rulebook correctly, Sparky doesn't need anyone else playing with him."

"He doesn't?" Skip asked.

"I don't?"

"No, look it up – Rule XII, Section IX, Paragraph 3: 'A Big League team must field a team of no more than nine but no less than one individuals to participate in a regulation game.' The rule was changed 31 years ago to accommodate the Blob from Planet X, who could play all the infield positions at once."

"Oh right, the Blob from Planet X," Sparky said to himself.

The umpire stood there for a moment, staring at Yoshi as he searched for something to say. His lips writhed around on his face like a pair of wrestling worms, his eyebrows twitched like barefoot caterpillars on a hot sidewalk. Finally, he pointed one finger at Yoshi. "I'm going to go check on that," he said, and then he stomped away.

"All right, Sparky, come with me," Yoshi said.

Sparky took his place on the mound in the otherwise-empty stadium and waited for Yoshi to return. The little old man returned with a weird-looking contraption that he planted behind the plate. It looked like a bicycle stood on its back wheel, with a catcher's mitt attached to the center of it.

"Okay," Yoshi shouted across the field, "Give it the heat!"

Sparky reared back and uncorked a fastball that struck the

mitt dead-center. The mitt was pushed back by the force of the pitch, setting off a chain reaction of springs, chains and gears that ended with the mitt, launching forward and returning the ball back to the mound.

"Not bad, huh?" Yoshi said. He rubbed the mitt down with a greasy old rag and smiled. "I built it for pitching drills, but I think this will work just fine as a backstop for you today."

"That's great, but the mitt doesn't move," Sparky said. "I'm going to have to keep throwing it right down the center of the plate the whole time!"

"Listen, if we're seriously going to try and pull this off, you're going to have a whole lot more to worry about than painting the corners," Yoshi said.

Soon, the gates were opened and the breathless, nervous faithful of Go-Town streamed into the stands. Many of them decided to save themselves some time and scooted forward to the edge of their seats. With the nervous energy in Zigleaf Field already at a fever pitch, the public address system crackled to life.

"Ladies and gentlemen, your attention please," the announcer crooned in his smooth baritone voice. "Have your scorecards ready, as there have been some minor changes to today's lineup. Starting today for the Go-Town Goats...pitcher Sparky Katakura. Left field, Katakura. Right field, Katakura. Center field, Katakura. Third base, Katakura. Second base, Katakura. First base, Katakura. Shortstop, Katakura. Catching...the Kawaii Catch-O-Matic 5000?"

The sound the crowd made after the lineup was read could have been best described as a confused murmur, and when Sparky took the field all by himself in the top of the first they did no more than clap politely, the way people would applaud for a circus clown that wasn't very funny at all but was clearly trying his best anyway. Sparky tipped his cap to the fans but then focused all of his attention on the center of the Catch-O-Matic's mitt.

Sparky dealt the Emperors' leadoff hitter a Blazing Fastball down and in, followed by another Blazing Fastball just above the belt and then a Phantom Slider that broke across to the far side of the plate. The New York hitter swung right through the slider with a whoosh that could be heard in the outfield bleachers. He tossed his bat up and snatched it violently out of the air with one hand. With the mask covering every inch of his face, his body language was the clearest sign that Sparky had already frustrated one-ninth of the New York lineup. So far, so good, he thought as he rubbed away some of the stinging sensation in his shoulder. One down, only 26 more to go, Sparky told himself, and maybe his arm would live to see tomorrow if he could just keep his pitch count down.

The next two hitters walked away from the plate with as much to show for their efforts as the leadoff man. Sparky set them down on just three pitches each, and he took a deep breath as he pulled his bat out of the bat rack. If he couldn't get a hit in his first at-bat, he thought, he would get at least two more in the same inning.

Sparky's first at-bat ended in a groundout to third base, and the second resulted in a popup on the infield that the first baseman pulled down for the second out. The stinging in his shoulder was still there, reminding him that he would still have to run back out to the mound and pitch another inning, no matter what happened in his next at-bat.

Watching the pitcher shake off signs from the catcher, Sparky tried to slow his breathing and push the odd feeling in his shoulder to the back of his consciousness. He felt his hustle bubbling deep within him, like a mug of warm cocoa drank on a bitterly cold morning. Sparky tried to tap into it, thinking it was better to use it while he still had it, even if he didn't know what it was going to do for him at the plate. The tingling in his shoulder faded away. The pitch came screaming toward him, extremely fast but still straight as an arrow and right through the strike zone. Sparky swung the bat.

The ball rocketed off Sparky's bat, tearing between the first baseman and second baseman before digging into the grass in right field and leaving a divot about the length of the fielder's forearm. Sparky's foot touched first base, and there he stood until the ball had been returned to the pitcher. He ran back to the plate and picked up the bat again.

The pitcher looked over to the first baseman and motioned for him to step on the bag. Instantly, Sparky realized what was going to happen and broke for first base with every bit of speed he had. Even though he was taking another at-bat, technically he was still on first base, and the Emperors were trying to pick him off. He dove headfirst into the base and just avoided the tag. Jogging back to the plate, Sparky saw the pitcher attempt another pickoff, and again he had to dive back into first to avoid being caught. The first baseman patted Sparky on the back, and there didn't need to be a single word spoken for Sparky to know sarcasm when he saw it.

Already out of breath, Sparky tried to rush back to the batter's box to take his cuts, but another pickoff throw forced him back onto the base. The crowd began to groan at the futility of the whole thing. They, along with Sparky, were beginning to see that there was no way out for him the way things were. Finally, Sparky threw up his hands and stepped off of first, allowing the first baseman to gently touch him with the ball and retire the side. On his way back to the mound, Sparky could only shake his head. Clearly, if he was going to get a base hit at all in this game, he was going to have to keep running until he reached home plate.

The next few innings went as routine as they could under the circumstances, with Sparky continuing to frustrate New York's hitters with his repertoire of special pitches, and Sparky unable to hit the ball away from the Emperors in the field. In the fourth inning, however, he ran into trouble. The count was 1-1 on the New York hitter, and Sparky wanted to try and fool him with a Cosmic Changeup. He picked the rosin bag off the mound and tossed it up and down with his bare hand, enveloping it in a cloud of dust that soaked up the sweat that was pooling in his palms. He looked in and started his delivery, but as he pushed his arm forward a drop of sweat rolled off the tip of his hair and landed right between his index finger and the ball.

Sparky could feel the ball slip off his finger just a tiny bit too quickly, and what should have been a time-bending offspeed pitch instead became nothing more than an average batting-practice meatball. He ground his teeth together as he watched the ball lazily roll its way to the plate and saw the Emperor hitter twist his hands greedily around the handle of the bat.

The swing was lightning-quick, a snap of action that looked like a mouse trap sprung by a passing butterfly. The ball instantly vanished from sight, and a fraction of a second later the crack of the bat reached Sparky's ears. He turned and began running before he even knew which direction it was headed.

A few panicked steps off the mound and Sparky finally spotted the ball against the deep green leaves overhead. Fortunately, his instincts had served him well, and he was at least headed in the same general direction as the ball – toward deep right field. Each step he made brought him a little bit closer to catching up with the soaring fly ball, but he was running out of room. He had at best only a few strides before he hit the warning track, so he tried to force his legs to do what he knew his arm could do.

Suddenly, Sparky found himself directly underneath the ball, close enough that he could just pick it out of the air like a low-hanging apple from a tree. The ball was just hanging there in the air, rotating slowly over his head. Sparky reached up and snapped his glove around the ball. The next thing he knew, he felt himself drop to the ground on both feet, and the sound of the crowd cheering madly came rushing back into the ballpark like a tidal wave crashing over a levee.

Splashing water on his face in the dugout, Sparky looked

down at the other end of the bench, where Skip was still splayed out in his wagon, sweating and wheezing.

"You're not spotting your pitches too good," Skip whispered.

"Well, considering that my catcher doesn't move at all, I think I'm doing pretty okay," Sparky said. "Are you feeling any better, Skip?"

"What are you talking about? I'm fine! I'm perfectly fine, and I don't care you many flying purple catcher's mitts you stick on your face!"

"How are you holding up?" Yoshi asked Sparky. "It's actually not going as badly as I thought it would."

"Did you see the way I caught up to that ball, Yoshi? I've never been that fast before!"

"Yeah, I noticed," Yoshi said flatly as he started reorganizing batting helmets.

"Well, that's pretty awesome, right? I mean, this is going to be a lot easier if I can hustle on fielding and hitting too!"

"I hope so, kid. I hope so."

"What? What was that? Come on, why do you always have to say something weird whenever I say something?"

"And why do you always say something like you haven't learned a blessed thing since you got here?" Yoshi said. "I've told you how many times that hustle is something you have to respect? That it's something you use to give your natural talents a boost, not as a replacement for them? That if you overuse it, you run the risk of losing your connection to it forever?"

"What choice do I have, Yoshi? We need to win this series!"

Yoshi reached up and put his hand on Sparky's shoulder. Sparky sighed – he might not have been paying too much attention to what Yoshi had been saying about hustle, but he knew enough by now to know when the old man was about to tell him something he didn't want to hear.

"Sparky, I know you don't want to hear this," Yoshi began, "but you might want to start thinking about yourself. A phenom comes along only once every few seasons, but there's always another one. You have your whole career ahead of you, you could get out of this place and get yourself a chance at a ring or two. You've got the talent and the hustle to make that happen, Sparky."

Sparky snatched his batting helmet off the bench and brushed Yoshi's hand off his shoulder. Glaring at Yoshi but not saying a word, Sparky trudged up the dugout steps and to the plate.

"Your brother knew what he was doing when he signed those papers," Yoshi called after him. "He knew it could ruin his career...don't let him ruin yours, too."

Yoshi's words ran circles around Sparky's brain as he stood waiting at the plate. He was so preoccupied that he ended up swinging late on a pitch and popped it straight up in the air for an easy first out. In his second at-bat of the inning, Sparky caught himself thinking about it so much that he didn't know what the count was, but he was brought up to speed quickly when the umpire called strike three on a borderline pitch he didn't swing at.

When he stepped out of the batter's box, Sparky tapped his helmet with his bat. "Come on, dummy, focus," he muttered to himself. Taking a deep breath, he crossed the white chalk line once again and started concentrating. He could feel the energy start flowing through him, just like it did when he was on the mound, only this time it was in both arms. He swung at the first pitch.

The ball bounced off the barrel of the bat with a loud "bwong," a sound that Sparky thought was extremely unusual, but it looked like a screaming line drive all the same. He took off running, keeping one eye on the flight of the ball. The center fielder came charging in, and it looked like he might be able to make a running catch. Sparky sighed and unconsciously started to slow down.

But instead of a running catch, the center fielder made contact with the ball and was knocked completely off his feet and backwards, like he had been struck by a wrecking ball. The ball went shooting off on a right angle in the direction of left field, losing none of its velocity. As Sparky touched second, the left fielder held up his glove to make a play, but again the ball struck him like a bullet and went off in another random direction.

Charging around the bases, Sparky watched as the ball careened around the field like a pinball, striking almost every Emperor on the field and knocking them all on their backs. Halfway between third and home, Sparky saw the ball "bwong" off the first baseman and take another hard turn, this time toward the waiting mitt of the catcher. The catcher planted his feet and leaned forward. Sparky pushed himself as hard as he could. The ball came screaming through the air. All three converged at the plate at the same time.

Sparky heard the "bwong" of the ball's impact before he felt the catcher's padded chest guard collide with his face. The two players went sprawling in opposite directions. Sparky couldn't see where the ball ended up, but he did manage to reach out with one hand and swipe it across the plate before landing flat on his back. For a second, nothing happened. Then the ball dropped out of the air and landed right in the middle of Sparky's chest with a "thump." The umpire shouted, "SAFE!" and Sparky Katakura had opened up a 1-0 lead on the New York Emperors all by himself.

Another three innings passed and by that point Sparky wondered how he would ever be able to make it to first base again, let alone all the way back to home plate. His legs were weak and rubbery, his arms felt like wet towels hanging off his shoulders. The inside of his cap was soaking wet, and he could feel blisters starting to form on his feet. There were two innings left to go, but Sparky couldn't even conceive of how we was going to get through the next hitter.

Tapping into what little energy had felt he had left, Sparky delivered a Blazing Fastball that barely coughed out a few tiny flames and some smoke before popping the Catch-O-Matic's mitt for a called first strike. Sparky glanced up at the radar gun reading on the scoreboard – the last pitch was clocked at 109. When the game started, the same pitch was breaking 130 and was virtually unhittable. Now Sparky was breaking a sweat to throw a pitch any elite Big League hitter would be ready to turn on.

Sparky tried to make up what he lost in velocity with deception, and he tried to place the next Blazing Fastball on the opposite corner of the plate from the last one. The hitter's swing was a fraction of a second late, but he still made good contact on the ball, and Sparky watched the lazy fly ball arc slowly over the mound. He gave chase, but had to settle for snatching it on a bounce. The runner stopped at first as Sparky stared him down halfway between first and second.

Taking the mound once more, Sparky saw the radar gun reading for the previous pitch – 102. The pain in his arm had returned, he noticed, and his legs hardly felt capable of supporting him standing up. He tried to fool the next hitter with a Cosmic Changeup, but the pitch wouldn't slow down enough, and the hitter tagged it for a sharp grounder between second and third. Sparky caught up to it in shallow left field, with the runner originally on first already rounding third, and the hitter reaching second standing up. Exhausted, Sparky slammed the ball into the center of his glove and watched the scoreboard flip over from 1-0 to 1-1. Soon, it would be 2-1 in the Emperors' favor.

Sparky made it out of the inning, but not before New York score six runs on a flurry of hits. Barely strong enough to drag his bat to the plate, Sparky couldn't make anything happen in the bottom of the inning. Nor could he in the bottom of the next inning, after the Emperors rocked his tired arm for another 12 runs. By the time Sparky weakly swung through the last pitch of his last at-bat of the bottom of the ninth, the score was New York 45, Go-Town 1.

As the game ended, the Emperors walked briskly but

silently off the field. There were no celebrations or displays of emotion. Sparky tossed his bat aside and ran after the player he knew was his brother – the enigmatic Number 7. Catching up to Ken, Sparky grabbed his shoulder and found it cold to the touch.

"Ken!" Sparky said once his shock subsided. "Ken, it's me!"

Ken turned around slowly, his eyes still hidden deep within the darkness behind his mask. He stared for a long, breathless second at his brother, and suddenly Sparky felt hope swelling up inside of him.

"Ken, I've been trying to help you! That little guy, Stitches, he told me I had to win to get you out, get you all out! I've been trying so hard, Ken…" Ken didn't move, just kept staring at Sparky with those eyes that may or may not have actually been there. For all Sparky knew, there was nothing but a void behind that mask, and watching his brother just stand there made him believe that might just be true.

"I'm…I'm sorry, Ken," Sparky said quietly, his voice catching in his throat. Tears were welling up behind his eyes. "I'm sorry, Ken. I've been trying, but…I'm just sorry. I'm sorry."

Then, Ken slowly reached up and placed his hand on Sparky's. Ken's hand was just as cold as his shoulder, but just the feel of it made Sparky feel better. He remembered countless high-fives on the schoolyard baseball diamond as Sparky rounded the bases for a home run, the way Ken used to mockingly tap the top of his helmet when he would slide into home head-first and Ken had him out by a dozen strides. Most of all, Sparky could clearly remember each and every time Ken had offered him his hand to pull him up off the ground.

Then Ken mechanically brushed Sparky's hand off his shoulder and walked away.

It was a chill that Sparky carried with him all the way to New York, and the imposing atmosphere of Imperial Stadium did nothing to warm him up. The Goats all made a full recovery from their mystery ailment, but the way Game 3 went it wouldn't have mattered whether they fielded nine players or just one again. Wilbur served up a dizzying array of pitches that would have bewildered any other squad of players, but it was as if a switch had been thrown in the New York dugout compared to the previous two games. They drilled line drives with deadly precision, placing them perfectly in the outfield gaps, under infielders' gloves and just out of the reach of practically everyone. Wilbur was pulled in the fifth inning after giving up 8 runs, and Tad Ballpino fared no better in relief.

At the plate, the Goats looked lost, completely out of

rhythm. Pitch after pitch resulted either in a weak ground ball, a soft pop fly or a swinging strikeout. Skip kept up his normal rate of chatter, but other than that not a word was exchanged in the dugout.

It wasn't until well after the final pitch was thrown in Game 3 that Sparky said another word to one of his teammates. He just sat at his locker, still in full uniform, staring at his brother's old baseball card.

"You look beat, kid," Lou said as he sat down in the creaky old chair next to Sparky.

"Don't we all?" Sparky replied. "I mean, how else are we supposed to look?"

"Hey, this thing ain't over, and we still have another nine innings to get something done."

"Yeah, in New York," Sparky scoffed. "And even then, let's say we win that game, Lou, then what? Then we have to go out and beat those guys again. And then let's say that somehow we get that miracle to happen and we win Game 5, then what? Well, then we have to go right back out there again and win another game we can't win! And then, even if we somehow manage to beat this bunch of faceless, demon-powered, super-magical all-stars three times IN A ROW..."

Sparky stopped and realized the rest of the locker room had been looking at him. They all had the same weary look on their faces, as if they had been expecting bad news for a long time and were finally getting it. Sparky's eyes met Katie's, and she bit her lower lip and dropped her shoulders.

"Well, I mean..." Sparky said in a much softer voice. "Katie, you know numbers...what kind of chance do we have?"

"It's definitely not impossible," Katie said with a touch of brightness. "A team coming all the way back from being down 0-3 in the Worlds Series – that's happened before, and more than once!"

"How many times?" Blerk asked.

"Uh, let me think ... it's happened five times," Katie said, a smile starting to appear on her face as she ran through the database in her head. "Yep, that's right, five times in the history of Big League Baseball, so it's definitely not impossible!"

There was a smattering of murmurs around the locker room as the Goats started nodding and even smiling a little bit. Fuzzy, who had been stuffing his duffel bag with almost everything from his locker, stopped and started hanging his jerseys back up.

"Okay, fine, but who did it?" Sparky said flatly, knowing the answer. "Which teams have come back from being down 0-3 in the Worlds Series five times, Katie?"

"Um, well, the first time it happened, it was the Emperors," she said. "And then the second time it happened, the Emperors did it again. Same with the third time…and the fourth."

"And the fifth time?" Bobby asked hopefully, to which Katie just sighed and held up her hands. The Goats dropped their heads again.

"Look, guys," Sparky said. "I know this is a real mess we're in right now, and I just wanted to say that, for what it's worth…I'm sorry I got you into this. You guys were doing fine without me here. Uh, except for all the losing and everything, I guess, but you know what I mean. I'm sorry I pushed you guys so hard." Sparky sat back down and covered his head with a towel. The fact that there was still a Game 4 to play the next day barely registered with him. He just wanted to vanish for a long time and not have to think about baseball. Maybe he would wait until the start of spring training, he thought. Or maybe he would just let spring training and the whole following season just go on without him.

"Wait," Fuzzy said from the back of the room. "That's it? Little Baby Fastball don't want to play no more, so we all just give up?" Fuzzy marched to the center of the locker room and pointed directly at Sparky. "You came here nine months ago because you wanted to win. You could have gone anyplace and been the biggest mamma-jamma in the league, but instead you joined up with this pack of jerks because here it was going to mean something, for real. You turned this whole thing around and now we remember what winning felt like."

Fuzzy looked around the room and started pointing at his teammates. "Do you like winning? You? What about you, robot, you like winning better than losing?"

"You know me, I have a great time playing no matter what!" VORP said. "But yeah, winning is just the best!"

"Shut up, but yeah," Fuzzy said. "Blog Girl, you like winning, right?"

"Don't call me 'Blog Girl,' but I do," Katie replied.

"See? Everybody likes winning way more than what we were doing before, and that's all because of you, chico," Fuzzy told Sparky. "That Lance guy was a real cementhead, but he was right about one thing – we all got our own reasons for being here. All you did was come into this clubhouse and make sure everybody had the same reason for being here, and ain't that what a team is supposed to be?"

"Yeah," Sparky said quietly. "You're right about that."

"Oh you better believe I'm right about that, man," Fuzzy shot back. "You've spent this entire season working on us, making us work harder, making things easier for us, giving us a taste of the big time, because you needed us. Well, it works both ways, buddy, and right now we need you."

Sparky looked up, and the rest of the team was looking straight at him. "Is that how everybody else feels?"

"Aye," said Thor.

"Basically," Carlos said.

"Yep," Bobby said. The others nodded their heads in agreement.

"Then I guess we have some work to do," Sparky said, and the locker room erupted in applause and cheers.

"Sounds like you made your choice," Yoshi said later as he stopped Sparky in the empty corridor. "What made up your mind?"

Sparky thought about it for a second, then smiled. "Realizing it's never been just about me," he said.

Yoshi chuckled to himself. "For the great ones, it never is," he said. "Now you're getting it."

"It might be too late, though," Sparky replied solemnly.

"As long as you have at least one more at-bat, you have a chance," Yoshi said.

"That's not the problem," Sparky said as he looked into Yoshi's eyes. "I threw a bullpen session earlier today. I couldn't get any of my pitches to work. My hustle's gone, Yoshi."

"Welcome to Game 4 of the Worlds Series between the New York Emperors and your Go-Town Goats from Imperial Stadium in the Big Apple! I'm Mel Fuller, with me as always is former Goats legend Randy Sannies…"

"Right, Mel."

"And we have a special treat for you fans out there, as we are joined in the booth for today's game by one of the best and certainly most popular Goats of recent vintage, the great Lance Bright. Lance, how are you?"

"Boy, I'm just pleased as punch to be in the broadcast booth with you two amazing broadcasters, it's a real honor."

"What have you been up to since your retirement earlier this season, Lance?"

"Well, you know the Bright-man is never one to let the grass grow under his feet, so I've been doing a lot of thinking about the next step in my career. For a renaissance man like myself, it shouldn't be that difficult to just slide into a new career. Really, leaving the game could be the best thing that's ever happened to Lance Bright."

"Have you ever thought about getting into broadcasting, Lance? Certainly you have a voice for radio and a wealth of baseball experience that I'm sure fans would find extremely illuminating."

"Oh absolutely, Mel. In fact, I'm considering today's game as something of a tryout. I'd love to be able to catch on with a broadcast team just like, well, just like Randy has!"

"Huh?"

"That sounds exciting, Lance, and we hope you'll keep us posted on any future developments in that regard. Turning the focus now onto today's game, after a season that was so unexpected in so many ways, the Goats now find themselves on the brink. Lance, you were in the clubhouse with these guys only a few months ago, what can you tell us about their mentality right now? Do these Goats have the mental fortitude to come back?"

"That's a great question, Mel. Although it breaks my heart to say so, I don't believe the Goats have that killer instinct that it takes to claw their way out of a situation like this. There were so many times that those guys turned to me in dark times and I was able to help lead them out of the woods, help them get their heads screwed on right."

"Uh, Mel, I think the problem in the clubhouse right now is…"

"Now, you look in that dugout – excuse me for a second there, Randy – and you don't see a leadership presence. I mean, you've got Lou Houston, who's bounced between so many different teams that I don't think he's ever unpacked his suitcases. There's Katie Spalding, who was writing a blog before joining the team, and the less said about that the better. And then there's the supposed young ace of this team, Sparky Katakura. Don't get me wrong, Sparky's a great kid and I taught him a lot, but I just think he's too wrapped up in his own agendas and his own concerns to bring this team together."

"All right, thank you for sharing those insights, Lance, and we'll be checking back in with you throughout the game. Game 4 between the Goats and Emperors, coming right up after this!"

The crowd cheered heartily as the Emperors took the field to start the game, although the cavernous dimensions of the stadium made it sound less like a throng of rabid baseball fans than a clock radio tuned to static and fallen behind a nightstand. The plush front rows were half-filled with bored-looking people in dark sunglasses, almost all of them tapping away on their phones while stealing a quick glance at the field every so often. The Emperors' multitude of championship banners flapped and fluttered in the afternoon breeze. An empty flagpole alongside them waited patiently for a new addition.

As the Emperors' starter for the day fired his warmup

pitches, Sparky watched from the dugout and tried to discern which of his old teammates he was looking at. The delivery looked like Milt Smithworth, the Stars' number-3 man in the rotation, but Sparky didn't remember his fastball having that much zip. He puzzled over the mystery for a few minutes, and was glad to have anything to take his mind off the fact that his arm still felt, for all intents and purposes, disappointingly average. The Goats still had a chance to win Game 4, but with Sparky slated to pitch Game 5, their chances might not extend much further.

Leading off the first for the Goats, VORP swung at a first-pitch fastball but missed. "Wow, that was a good one!" he shouted to the expressionless pitcher. The next pitch buzzed him inside and high for a ball. "Trying to back me off the plate, eh?" VORP said. "Can't say I blame you, good idea!" The 1-1 pitch was a slow breaking pitch that came in high. "Oh, where's this one going? Looks kind of high…" As VORP watched, the curveball dropped about four feet and crossed the plate for strike two. "Wow!" VORP said. "That was sure something! I don't think I've seen a better curveball in my life!"

"Something tells me VORP isn't going to get under these guys' skin the way he normally does," Lou said to Sparky.

"VORP can do more than just irritate a starter out of his rhythm," Sparky said. "Give him a chance, Lou."

With VORP happily humming to himself, the pitcher who may have been Smithworth rocked back on one foot and fired the 1-2 pitch. It was a slider that curled outside just enough to spend some time off the plate, but VORP could see the rotation of the ball begin to change ever so slightly. With the reflexes of a jack-in-the-box, VORP swung the bat. The resounding crack of the bat was followed by a streak of white horsehide that cut through the cool air and fell quickly to the grass in left field.

"Atta way, VORP!" Bobby shouted from the dugout, with the rest of the Goats adding their own noise to the scene. On first base, VORP turned and saluted his teammates.

Carlos flew out to center field, but Fuzzy cracked a grounder that kicked off the corner of first base and jumped at a crazy angle out of the reach of the second baseman. The confusion gave VORP enough time to round second and hit the brakes at third base. Fuzzy pulled his batting gloves off and tossed them directly to Sparky in the dugout.

"Did that look like a man thinking about next year, Sparky?" Fuzzy said with both index fingers aimed right at him.

"That looked like a man wanting to win himself a Worlds Series, that's what that looked like!" Sparky returned.

"That's right, baby, you know it," Fuzzy said as he tucked

more hair underneath his batting helmet. He then turned his attention to Thor, who was just stepping out of the on-deck circle. "Hey, RBI chance right now, Big Red! You better not screw it up!"

Thor threw back his head and laughed deeply. "Ha! Think you the god of thunder be a mere stripling?"

"Whatever, man. Stop talking and start swinging, you bearded goon!"

Thor watched the pitcher intently, lightning crackling around his eyes and climbing up his arms to envelop his bat in a sheath of sizzling sparks. The first pitch was low and inside, and although Thor flinched, he did not swing the bat. The next pitch came hurtling in high, but the mighty left fielder from Go-Town got a good enough look at it to take a cut at it.

The impact of bat on ball was punctuated with a thunderclap that shook the cheap seats in the outfield, but the ball's flight path was too low to be a home run. With the center fielder giving chase, the ball smacked the top of the outfield wall and caromed back into the fielder's waiting glove. VORP easily hustled down the third base line and scored, and Fuzzy made it to second on Thor's long single.

The Goats dugout was bursting with excitement, with players stomping on the bench, thunking helmets with bats and whooping as loud as they could. In a stadium filled with 50,000 people, the most noise in the top of the first came from just a dozen.

Go-Town's 1-0 lead lasted until the bottom of the second. With runners on first and second, Antonio made the mistake of focusing too much on the hitter. The Emperors executed a double-steal, both runners moving in perfect synchronization as they zipped around the basepaths. As soon as the ball struck his mitt, Lou bolted upright. But the sudden movement was too much for his knees, and they buckled just as Lou tried to gun the ball to Bobby at third. The throw went wild, sailing over Bobby's head and down the baseline into left field. Without even stopping to look, both the tying run and the go-ahead run crossed the plate before Thor was able to get the ball back to the infield.

"Nertz!" Skip cried out as he tossed his cap to the ground, stomping on it a few times for good measure. "What the heck are you doing out there, you sod-chewing cowpuncher? Do I have to come out there and show you how to throw a ball without spitting up all over yourself?" Lou just stood there behind home plate, watching the two men who had just crossed the plate trot back into their dugout. Bobby smacked himself in the thigh with his glove and kicked third base. Thor snorted and huffed as he paced around left field, his eyes red and fiery.

"That's okay, Lou! That's okay, guys! Plenty of game left! Plenty of game!" Sparky stood up on the top step to make sure the rest of the team could see and hear him. Lou caught sight of him, nodded his head and shook his mitt in Sparky's direction. Lou then caught Bobby's eye and gave him the "settle down" gesture. Bobby caught his breath and nodded, then he turned to Thor and gave him the same gesture. Thor slammed his fist into his glove, but he stopped pacing and nodded back to Bobby.

Later in the game, with the Emperors still leading 2-1, Katie hit a long fly ball that found the gap in left-center field for a base hit, driving in Blerk and tying the game. But the Emperors responded right away in the bottom half of the inning with a solo home run off Ken's bat that landed just inches on the wrong side of the outfield wall, where even VORP couldn't reach it.

The score remained 3-2 Emperors into the top of the seventh inning, and with Blerk standing on second base after a ground-rule double over the right field fence, Lou was at the plate. There was one out, but with Antonio and his .205 batting average in the on-deck circle, everyone on the Go-Town bench understood that Lou was their best chance to even the score.

The wily old catcher watched the first pitch break away from the plate for a ball. Then the second pitch dropped out of the strike zone for ball two. Both times, Lou just chuckled and shook his head.

"You wouldn't be trying to pitch around me, would you, son?" Lou said loud enough for everyone on the field to hear it. Even though the pitcher's mask made it impossible to determine his emotion, the fact that the third pitch was a screaming fastball on the inside corner of the plate made it clear what his intentions were. "Now we're getting somewhere," Lou said, to himself this time. "Lord, if this old bag of bones has another dinger in it anywhere, now would be a good time to make it happen."

The pitch was delivered, and Lou steeled himself for the swing. The bat sliced through the air like a samurai sword through a Jell-O mold, and with a sharp "pop" the ball was on its way toward the stands. Lou hobbled down the first base line, the pain in his knees making it hard for him to do anything else. He watched the ball fly further and further into the distance, the center fielder staying underneath it with his arm outstretched.

"Come on, get out. Get out, get out, get out," Lou muttered to himself with increasing urgency while the soreness in his knees intensified. "Just get out of the dang ballpark so I can go sit down again, please."

Lou's mustache curled upward into a broad grin as the ball finally crossed the top of the center field fence and out of the center fielder's reach. The Goats bench exploded with cheers as the scoreboard was once again in their favor, with the score now 4-3.

But the seesaw was not done tilting, and Antonio was in a jam just an inning later, with the bases loaded and only one out recorded. The Ballpino brothers began working furiously in the bullpen to get loosened up. Sparky could only watch helplessly from the dugout, with nothing but Skip's constant grumbling to distract him from the hopeful cries of the New York faithful. The Emperor hitter lifted a fly ball to deep right field, and the runner on third began to lean ever so slightly in the direction of home plate. Lou crouched over the dish and pounded his mitt in anticipation of a relay throw. Katie planted her feet and positioned her glove underneath the ball's shadow.

The ball landed square in the pocket of Katie's glove. She plucked it out immediately and hurled it to Blerk. The runner tagged and took off for home. Blerk received the throw, spun around and gunned the ball toward Lou. Lou watched the runner get closer and closer out of the corner of his eye, with his other eye tracking the flight of the ball on its way to him. It looked like a photo finish, but by the time Lou had the ball in hand and swung around to drop the tag, the runner had already slid to the ground and hooked his left leg across the plate. The umpire signaled "safe," and just like that the game was back to square one.

The battle continued this way into the ninth inning. Each time the Goats scraped a run across the plate, the Emperors answered right back with one of their own. Soon the score was 7-7 moving into the bottom of the ninth. Antonio goaded a groundout from the first hitter before striking out the second, but now Ken was standing in at home plate. Twirling his bat menacingly, Ken swung at the first two pitches and fouled both of them off to the right side of the outfield. The second foul ball was closer to the foul pole by more than a few feet, and the crowd could sense that the faceless slugger was zeroing in on his target.

For his part, Antonio was the picture of composure on the mound. Perhaps, Sparky thought, his belief in each pitch being part of a great artwork made him immune to big-game pressure like this. How many great painters ever thought about an individual brushstroke so much that they ended up missing the canvas? The pitcher's long arms and legs were bent but he was carrying the weight of the moment as easily as one would carry a single bag of groceries. With no more deliberation or flourish as the one before it, Antonio delivered the next pitch. Ken swatted the ball hard, and again another long fly ball was speeding into right field, but this time it did not look like a foul.

Katie, who was playing somewhat deep to begin with,

started backpedaling. The crowd seized the moment and began cheering wildly, with some in the bleachers tossing their boxes of popcorn in the air. The kernels rained down all around Katie, their irregular shapes flittering across her vision as she tried to keep her eyes focused on the perfectly spherical silhouette of the ball. She could see it begin to descend as the popcorn began dropping onto her head like a hard rain. In her head, she made an educated prediction about where the ball would be based on its trajectory, flight arc, velocity and spin, put her glove at the end of the equation, and closed her eyes. The sensation of the ball falling into her glove was, by all objective measures, very satisfactory.

The air went out of the crowd as the scoreboard operator flipped the inning counter from "9" to "10." Antonio received a round of high-fives when he returned to the dugout.

"We're coming up on extras," Skip said. "You still got anything left in there, or do I send one of those other bozos out there?"

"This game has a certain...rough-hewn quality," Antonio said wistfully. "I like the texture it has, the deep basso profundo sound...but it is not complete yet. It lacks a certain...how shall I say it? It needs balance." Skip stared at him for a moment.

"Grab some bench and get ready to grab a bat when we need you," Skip said at last. "It's easier to just leave you in than listen to you explain stuff to me."

VORP led off the top of the 10th for the Goats, and drove a single into shallow left field. Carlos followed that up with one of his own to the opposite field, moving VORP up to second. Fuzzy stepped off the on-deck circle and got a good look at a few pitches, but his best swing resulted in a lazy pop-up to center field for the first out. It was time for Thor to take his cuts, and the entire stadium suddenly became filled with a nervous silence, everyone too agitated to stand still but too anxious to make a sound. It was as if all the air had been sucked out of the stadium, and only a soundless vacuum remained.

As the massive outfielder stomped his way into the batter's box, the catcher slid over and stood up, his mitt as far away from the plate as possible. Thor noticed and dropped the head of his bat to the ground. "Have you no honor?" he cried. "Would thou rather surrender first base than face a warrior born in his element?" The pitcher, of course, offered no defense. The first pitch was a soft lob that didn't come within three feet of the plate for ball one, and Thor sighed.

"Dost thou fair people of New York not see with thine own eyes what cowards thou cheer for?" Thor turned and shouted to the assembled masses throughout the ballpark, and he was greeted with thunderous jeering. The next pitch also gave the plate a wide berth, and the count went to 2-0.

"Such a display is unbefitting a band of supposedly great warriors," Thor continued, paying more attention to the booing crowd than the pitcher. "Even the trolls of the mountains doth show more courage when they cower among the rocks during a summer rain!"

Again, the pitcher tossed a meatball that bent as far away from the plate as possible. The count was now 3-0, and the crowd continued to boo as Thor protested his case. "Good people, the god of thunder implores you to choose dignity on the baseball field, and not this craven display!" Wadded-up hotdog wrappers and peanut bags were hurled from the stands, and within moments Thor's ankles were buried in trash. "I give you one last chance, on my word as a prince of Asgard! Cease this childish nonsense, or else suffer the wrath of the god of thunder!"

"Go stuff it up your horn, beard-for-brains!" one of the outraged fans shouted.

"Take your base and shaddup!" screamed another.

"We didn't buy a ticket for the Shakespeare routine, ya jerk!"

"Very well," Thor said confidently. He turned his attention back to the mound. The catcher again slid a full step to outside and held his mitt out at arm's length. The pitcher nodded and went into his windup. VORP and Carlos took short leads off their respective bases. Thor wrung the handle of the bat in his gnarled hands.

The 3-0 pitch came in just as slow and as wide as the previous ones, but this time it did not reach the catcher's mitt. Thor, with both feet still planted firmly in the batter's box, stretched himself across home plate, and with both arms fully extended, swung the very end of the bat through the ball's flight path. Any other batter trying anything like this likely would have tapped the ball softly out in front of the plate, but the power of Thor's swing was such that the force of the blow knocked the catcher back on his heels and nearly toppled him over. There was a flash of light followed by a roar of thunder, and the ball soared high over the outfield and into the stands for a three-run homer. When the ball landed, the impact it created was enough to scatter dozens of fans, leaving their seats empty for the moment.

Garbage continued to pile up on the field as Thor circled the bases, his chin jutting out and his chest puffed up to full capacity. The Goats' dugout went crazy with cheers and whistles, and even Skip deemed the conquering hero worthy of a handshake upon his return.

"That was one heck of a wallop, big guy!" Skip

congratulated Thor. "I tell ya, that was one rip-snorting, slobberknocker of a sockdolager, by cracky!"

"The son of Odin demands no great tribute for performing his appointed duties," Thor said. "He only asks that his teammates perform to the best of their...wait, what did you say?"

Bobby knocked a hard ground ball that was scooped up by the shortstop on the lip of the outfield grass and whipped to first to get him by half a step. Antonio prepared to take the mound and potentially seal up a 10-7 Goats' win and extend the season by at least one more day.

He greeted the first batter of the New York 10th inning with a lazy curveball that dropped in for strike one. That was followed by a fastball down around the knees that the batter swung at in a panic for strike two. He closed the performance with another fastball that came close to shining the batter's shoes, but was swung on anyway for a quick strikeout. The other Goats were practically hanging from the dugout rail as they anticipated charging the mound and celebrating, but there were still two outs to get.

The second batter of the inning saw another curveball from Antonio, but this one did not have the same shape to it, and it missed the strike zone high for ball one. The next pitch was a fastball, but instead of hanging down at the knees like previously, it dipped suddenly, and it took Lou's quick reflexes with the mitt to prevent it from bouncing behind him. The 2-0 pitch was outside, and with the count heavily in the batter's favor, Antonio missed again with the fastball to give the runner a free pass to first base.

"Ah jeez, look at this!" Skip said. "Now I gotta go out there and yank him outta the game!"

"Hang on a second, Skip," Sparky said. "He said his game didn't have enough balance, so maybe the walk is there to balance out the strikeout he got on the last guy?"

"This ain't girls' softball," Skip whined. "You don't give another guy a freebie after you knock his block off!"

"Just give him another at-bat," Sparky pleaded. "I think I know where he's going with this."

Antonio's face remained the epitome of calm as he sized up the next hitter. He started him off with a cut fastball, and the hitter fouled it straight back behind him. Next, an offspeed pitch caught the hitter looking and the count was 0-2. But then, Antonio followed that with a curveball that was obviously never going to touch the strike zone, and the hitter let it go by for ball one. Then, a fastball whizzed in low and away, causing Lou to drop to his knees again to block it from escaping. The count was even. Antonio's fifth offering came within inches of making contact with the hitter's hands, and after that the count was full.

The expression on Antonio's face never changed. A casual observer could have mistaken him for a pitcher facing the top of the order in the first inning rather than staring down the heart of the order in the 10th inning of a slugfest. He checked the runner at first and then coolly delivered the pay-off pitch, right down the center of the plate. The hitter turned on it and slapped it hard, and the runner on first went barreling toward second base. Fuzzy made a move to his right, just as the ball hit the infield dirt and bounced upward. Fuzzy got his glove around the ball and threw it to Blerk for the force-out at second. With the batter running hard down the baseline, Blerk made a perfect throw to Carlos to complete a game-ending double play.

The New York crowd had seen enough, and with the Goats streaming to the mound in celebration, the fans began grumbling their way out of the stadium.

"Antonio, you crazy son of a gun!" Lou said. "You were counting on the double play, weren't you?"

"I only put the ball where it needed to be," Antonio said. "The batter, he did the rest."

"See, I told you you couldn't just give up on this losers," Fuzzy told Sparky.

"You were right, okay?" Sparky said, smiling. "What else do you want me to say, man?"

"So we were down three games to none and now we've climbed all the way back to being down three games to one," Tod Ballpino said.

"So what?" his brother Ted asked.

"So now what do we do?"

"What the heck do you expect, dummy? We keep winning."

"Oh." Tod paused. "Can we do that?" Ted just shrugged.

Game 5 started in the mid-afternoon, with the sun just beginning to sink out of the sky. The days were getting shorter, and Sparky couldn't help but think it was fitting that the Goats' chances were just about at their shortest, too. He went through his warmup routine feeling exposed, like one of those dreams where you forget to wear pants to school. His arm still felt normal, but it was the worst kind of normal. It was the kind of normal he hadn't felt since he was a kid playing catch in the backyard with his dad and brother. His fastballs made it to the mitt intact and cool to the touch. His slider remained in plain sight all the way across the infield. Time passed at a normal rate when he threw the changeup. Sparky wished he could pitch the entire game in the dark.

Before the game started, Lou came out to the mound.

"Everything okay?" he said. "You're not using the power pitches."

Sparky thought for a second about telling Lou the truth, but after the team fought so hard to come back in the last game, what would the truth do to them? He saw Carlos and Blerk playing catch on the infield, laughing and joking as if they had just shown up on the first day of spring training. Katie and Thor were signing autographs for young fans straining to reach over the left field wall. The Ballpino brothers were shoving each other around in the bullpen. Was it really fair to burden them with the knowledge that he didn't have his hustle anymore?

"I'm fine," Sparky told Lou. "I just want to keep my arm fresh for the game, you know?"

"I guess there's a first time for everything, isn't there?" Lou said with a twinkle in his eye. "Hey, as long as you still remember how to throw that heater, you do whatever you need to."

After the first three innings of Game 5, Sparky's nerves had settled somewhat, but the anxiety had been replaced by something else, something he couldn't as easily ignore. For the first time in a long time, Sparky felt fear on the mound. Each pitch came with a shudder, as he fully expected it to be mashed straight at him or, worse, over the fence. So far, that hadn't happened, and he had only given up a few hits and a single run, but he knew the second time through the order wouldn't be as kind to him.

Meanwhile, the Goats had mounted a few scoring opportunities of their own, and Thor came through in the clutch once again in the fourth with a double that drove in a pair of runs. With a 2-1 lead, all Sparky had to do was hold the Emperors down, something that felt less and less possible with each hitter he faced.

In the sixth, Sparky gave up back-to-back singles to the first two men who came to the plate. The fans murmured with concern as Number 7 was announced as the next hitter, and suddenly the fear that had been swelling up in Sparky was threatening to burst him wide open. He tried to steady himself as Lou gave him a sign for a first-pitch curveball. He took a deep breath and stood up straight.

The curveball hung in the air above the plate for what felt like forever. Sparky held his breath as he watched Ken closely for the slightest muscle twitch, but his brother just watched it fall in about belt-high for a strike. Sparky exhaled. Lou flashed him the sign for a slider, away. Sparky nodded, set and delivered. Ken watched this one go by, too, but this time it was outside for a ball.

Sparky pulled his cap off his head and wiped the sweat off his forehead with his sleeve, despite the cool temperatures. Lou gave him the sign for a fastball. Sparky put everything he had into the throw, hoping maybe some small connection to his hustle had been reestablished, but there were no flames, no smoke, not even a little shimmer of heat coming off the ball before it was cracked high in the air but twisted foul off to the left.

Lou crouched back down and gave Sparky the sign for the Cosmic Changeup. Sparky shook him off. Lou asked for the Phantom Slider, and again Sparky refused. Finally, Lou signaled for the Blazing Fastball, but Sparky would only shake his head. Lou called for time.

"All right, now you can't tell me you're just saving your arm," Lou said.

"It's all used up," Sparky said. "The hustle, I mean. It's just gone. I'm useless up here, Lou."

"I knew a guy once, a guy a lot like you," Lou said. "He had hustle, boy, he had it in spades. Could throw a knuckleball that would run to the concession stand for cotton candy before crossing the plate for a dead-perfect strike. But then one day, he just lost it. It conked out on him. He just came to me that morning and said, 'I don't feel it anymore.' He never pitched again."

"He was so bad he got dropped from the team?"

"No, he just never pitched again, walked away from the game that day. Sparky, some guys fail because they can't hack it in the Big Leagues. Some guys fail because they never even try to give it a shot. Which kind of failure do you want to be?" Lou slapped Sparky's glove with his own and tottered back to the plate.

Once he was hunched back down behind home plate, Lou gave Sparky the sign for a regular fastball. For the first time in the game, Sparky didn't think about his arm, and how normal it felt. He didn't focus on the feeling in his shoulder, and whether or not he could find any sign of the once-familiar tingle he had felt. All of his attention was concentrated on the center of the catcher's mitt and on the feel of the seams as he tumbled the ball around in his hand. The fear was gone.

Sparky glanced back at the runners, then stretched and hurled a fastball across the plate. It looked perfect, spinning through the air at an impressive speed, the seams blurring into a haze that surrounded the ball. It didn't stop time, it didn't catch fire. It was the pitch Sparky had perfected in the backyard with Ken, it was the pitch that had made him the ace of their high school team's rotation, it was the pitch Sparky realized, in that moment, that he should have been relying on all this time.

It was also a pitch that Ken clobbered into right field for a base hit. Sparky watched the runner from second cross the plate to tie the game. He could only put his hands on his head and wait for the ball to be returned to him. Ken stood on first base, and Sparky half-expected to hear him start taunting him the way he did when they were kids, but of course that didn't happen.

The score was 6-6 in the bottom of the ninth, and the Goats were down to their last out. Bobby stood at third base, after a base hit and two sacrifice flys. Skip was on the top step of the dugout, giving signals to the third base coach. There was a fly buzzing around his head, however, and each time he started to give the signals to third, they were interrupted by his swatting at the bug.

"Whoa," the third base coach said as he watched Skip's gyrations across the diamond. "I can't believe it, but he's the boss. Go get 'em, Bobby."

"Wait, what?" Bobby asked, but before he could get clarification, the pitcher began his delivery. Based on Skip's jumbled signals, Bobby started running, and now the slowest member of the Go-Town Goats' roster was attempting to steal home.

"What in the name of all that's holy...? No!" Skip shouted the second he saw Bobby breaking for home. The fans had essentially the same reaction as they watched Bobby's soft belly ripple and heave with each step. The pitch already had reached the plate, and now the catcher stood facing the lumbering baserunner, ready to tag him out.

Bobby looked back over his shoulder and saw the third base coach throwing his hands up in the air. There was no way he would be able to make it back to third in time. He was caught in no man's land, and the only direction he could go was full speed ahead. The catcher stood his ground. The only way to the plate was through him, and Bobby decided then and there that if his size ever was going to be a positive for him, it was going to be at that moment. He clenched his fists and powered down the baseline, and he was picking up steam. He crossed his arms in front of him like a battering ram and dropped his head. The catcher braced himself, pulling the ball in as close to his body as possible. Bobby aimed all of his mass directly at the catcher's mitt. Then he tripped.

Bobby went sprawling to the ground, his arms and legs stuck out as wide as a skydiver's. Within half a second Bobby found himself face-to-face with the catcher's shoes. But between them, mere inches from his face, was home plate. Before the startled catcher could react, Bobby slapped the plate with one hand, and the game was over. In the dugout, Sparky sighed with relief and looked across the field at the Emperors' dugout. This time, Ken was looking right at him.

"We welcome you back to Zigleaf Field in Go-Town, where the Goats have turned a Worlds Series that was merely historic into one that is potentially legendary, but with New York leading by a run here in the bottom of the 11th, they are in danger of coming up short. Thor Odinson, who has been so impressive all season since taking over the cleanup spot in the lineup, is at the plate with a runner on and two outs."

"Boy, Mel, the Bright-man has certainly been impressed with the way these Goats have made this series interesting, but I have to believe that they're at the end of their rope right now."

"What makes you say that, Lance?"

"Odinson, as good of a hitter as he is, has never shown that he can respond well in this types of high-pressure situations. That Viking temper of his can make him lose his cool at the drop of a hat, and we saw that in Game 4 with that intentional walk."

"Lance, if I'm remembering correctly, Odinson hit a walk-off home run in that at-bat to give the Goats the game, did he not?"

"Sure, but everything we know about the game says that you take the walk in that situation. As I've detailed many times in my best-selling series of instructional books for young ballplayers, any time you can get on base without doing anything, you take it. There's no sense in risking a pulled muscle or something like that, and I think Thor took a big risk by letting his anger get the best of him. I hate to say it, but that's what prevents him from being a true clutch clean-up hitter."

"The first pitch is right down the middle for strike one."

"Uh, Mel, the interesting thing about Odinson's numbers this year, I think, is that..."

"You simply cannot have a guy out there – pardon me, Randy – but you cannot have a guy out there who lets his emotions get in the way of the program. I played with Thor for a number of years, and there was one instance in particular I can recall. This is actually in my memoirs, which will be in bookstores on November 16..."

"The next pitch is swung on and driven deep to center field! It's going back, back, back and...gone! A two-run home run from Thor Odinson, and the Goats win Game 6! We will be here again tomorrow, Go-Town!"

"If I could just finish talking about my memoirs..."

Zigleaf Field had never been as crowded as early as it was on the morning of Game 7. Sparky arrived at the ballpark to find it surrounded by people camped out in sleeping bags and makeshift tents. Yoshi greeted him at the gate and waved his hand at the teeming masses outside.

"Been here all night waiting for standing-room-only tickets," Yoshi explained. "Probably 95 percent of them won't get in. That was quite the gutsy performance you put in the other day, kid."

"Yeah well, I didn't have much of a choice," Sparky said with a smile.

"Think you can do it again today?"

"If I can't, there'll be eight other guys out there ready to pick up the slack," Sparky responded. "So I'm not worried."

Before taking the field, Sparky reached into his locker and pulled out his brother's baseball card. Taking one last look at it, he slipped it into his back pocket and took the field.

"This is it!" VORP shouted as he warmed up in center field. "Doesn't get much bigger than this! No matter what happens, I'm just thrilled to be a part of it!"

"Aye, there is valor in fighting to the bitter end," Thor told him. "But the sweetest spoils of all are those that can be found only in victory, my metal friend! And the god of thunder intends to taste those spoils this day."

"If we can hold a lead into the bottom of the sixth, we stand a lot better chance of winning than if it's tied or we're losing," Katie said. "I think it's something like a 45 percent better chance."

"Man, I'm not going to be happy until we got a 100 percent chance of winning!" Fuzzy said as he fielded a few practice grounders.

On the mound, Sparky took his warmup throws. He noticed Lou trying but failing to hide a smile as big as all outdoors. The ultimate journeyman was in the biggest game of his life, even it had taken almost his entire career to get there.

The first hitter for the Emperors stepped in and the game was underway. On a 2-1 count, Sparky served up a fastball that the hitter got all of, turning it into a streak of light that looked like it would have taken someone's head off if they had been in the way. Fuzzy made sure his head wasn't in the ball's way, but his glove was. The streaking ball burnt a hole right through the webbing of Fuzzy's glove, but charging in from left field was Thor, who dove to cradle the falling streak into his smoking glove. Sparky caught his breath and retired the next two hitters with a swinging strikeout and a weak ground ball.

Katie hit a looping liner in the bottom of the third that arced over the head of the third baseman and dropped in for a base hit, giving Blerk the chance to make it home and score the game's first run. The Emperors answered with two that were scored when a pop-up fell with enough force to cause a small earthquake that knocked VORP off his feet.

Sparky regained control in the middle innings, but without his special arm he was flying by the seat of his pants. The Goats didn't get another scoring chance until the bottom of the eighth, when VORP led off with a walk and advanced to second on a stolen base. Carlos followed that with a base hit that rolled to the left field corner, and VORP was waved around third. His mechanical legs throwing off sparks, VORP slid hard underneath the tag and scored the tying run. He returned to the dugout slowly and without the bounce in his step he normally had.

"VORP, you okay?" Katie asked.

"Oh, I'm just fine, thanks a lot," VORP said, his voice garbled by static. "I just think I might be a little tired, is all."

Katie popped open the control panel on VORP's back and turned to Sparky. "He's down to emergency power," she said. "He might not last the rest of the game."

"I don't know what's wrong," VORP said. "Usually I have plenty of power to make it through the entire season."

"Yeah, but you've never been all the way to the Worlds Series before," Sparky said. "We've got to find a way to keep him in the game."

"VORP, can you go into sleep mode?" Katie asked him.

"Aw, but then I'll miss the rest of the game," VORP protested with a weak voice. "I couldn't do that, I don't want to let the team down!"

"You won't, trust me," Katie said. VORP's eyes dimmed to about half their usual brightness and began pulsing slowly as he stood motionless. Katie motioned to Carlos at first base.

"Carlos! You're playing center in the next inning!"

"What?"

Fuzzy was up to bat next, but he tapped the ball weakly to shortstop to cause a double play. With Thor up next, the Emperors decided to walk him intentionally, but this time they made certain to keep the ball out of his reach. As the catcher stood and watched, the pitcher threw four pitches six feet over his head and into the seats. Thor shook his head, but took first base anyway. Bobby came up next, and when he stepped on an untied shoelace in the middle of his swing, he fell forward into the path of the ball and it struck him in the shoulder. The umpire called for Bobby to take his base, and Thor moved up to second.

Blerk stepped to the plate. "I think I understand what is meant when my teammates talk about 'hustle,'" Blerk said to the catcher. "It is very similar to a concept from my home planet called 'bleemsperk,' a mental discipline that gives one limited control over the environment. This appears to be an ideal time to put this into practice."

The pitcher delivered a hard fastball, and Blerk's hands began to glow. Blerk swung and hit a line drive that the center fielder tracked down and stood ready to catch. The ball traveled through the air on a direct line to the fielder's glove before it just stopped in mid-air. The glowing ball hung in the air, spinning, as the center fielder started running toward it. He was almost within reach of the ball when it suddenly resumed its flight, sailing over his head. By the time he caught up with it, Thor had slid across the plate, kicking up a veritable storm cloud of dust and a thunderous roar from the crowd.

The lead remained a single run as Sparky took the mound for the top of the ninth. Fans were pounding their feet, waving their arms and shouting at the top of their lungs. Sparky mopped the sweat off his forehead and thought about how he was going to approach the next three hitters. If everything went well, he wouldn't have to face Ken again.

The first hitter showed some amazing patience, however, and Sparky threw nine pitches before he finally retired him on a fly ball. The next two hitters seized on Sparky's tired arm and took advantage, one driving a base hit that dropped right at Katie's feet and the next drawing a walk on a 3-2 pitch that missed inside. Lou came out to the mound as the Ballpino brothers started warming up.

"Those last two guys were lucky," Lou said. "Forget about them and focus on the next guy. He's a ground ball hitter, so we've got a good chance to turn two here."

Sparky worked the inside half of the plate against the next hitter, hoping to coax a grounder out of him. But he didn't bite, and the count became a hitter-friendly 2-0. Beyond the hitter in the on-deck circle, Sparky could see Ken selecting a bat from the rack. The fear was beginning to return. With his mind racing, Sparky's grip on the next pitch was too tight, and he missed his spot badly for a 3-0 count. Angry at himself, Sparky overthrew the next pitch and now the bases were loaded. Skip came out to the mound.

"Are you going to mess this up?" Skip asked as he looked Sparky right in the eye.

"No, Skip, I just got in my own head a little bit. I'm over it now, I promise."

"Well, good, because if I have to put one of those bullpen idiots into this game the newspapers will never let me hear the end of it!" With his pep talk completed, Skip retreated to the dugout.

The next hitter watched a few pitches before swatting a high fly ball into shallow center field, where a surprised Carlos nearly stumbled over his own feet trying to get a jump on it. Despite the stumble, Carlos was closing in on the ball as it plummeted to the ground. Finally, he dropped to the ground and slid on his knees, getting the lip of his glove between the ball and the grass. As he brought his arm up, the ball flipped off the edge of his glove and was flung straight up into the air. For a terrible moment, Carlos lost sight of the ball, but he found it just in time to swing his arm back down and capture it in the palm of his glove. Immediately, he whipped the ball to Fuzzy, and the runners had to hold their places.

Sparky didn't have time to be relieved as he watched his brother step to the plate. In his head, he could hear Ken's voice describing the scenario just as he did a million times while they were growing up: "Ninth inning, two outs and the bases loaded! A hush falls over the crowd as Katakura stands at the plate! Will Katakura ever be able to strike out his brother? Or will the older, stronger and much better-looking Katakura brother take him deep like he's done so many times before in the past?"

"Shut up and get ready to hit the showers," Sparky would shout back at his brother back then, and he felt like saying it again. Lou called for time and brought the rest of the team, around the mound.

"Okay, Sparky, forget everything else," Lou said. "All those other at-bats against this guy, they're in the past. What you've got is one at-bat, and even the best hitter in the world is going to fail six out of 10 times when he's only got one at-bat."

"And this guy ain't the best hitter in the world, either," Fuzzy added.

"He doesn't have to be," Sparky said. "I've never gotten my brother out, ever."

"That guy's your brother?" Fuzzy exclaimed. "Yeah, I can see the resemblance."

"Never?" Lou asked.

"Not in our backyard, not in Little League, not in Spring Training...never."

"Whoa, so that guy out there is the dude who got snatched up by the Baseball Devil?" Fuzzy continued.

"That's statistically impossible to never record an out on one player over that many plate appearances," Katie said.

"But that's what happens," Sparky said. "He just knows how to hit me."

"So the Baseball Devil runs the New York Emperors?" Fuzzy asked. "What other kind of secrets have you guys been hiding from me? Hey, is Spalding really my sister or something? Cause that would be totally weird, but I sort of suspected it..."

"Shut up, Fuzzy!" Bobby said. "Jeez."

"All right, we've got no place to put him and there's no way any of the Ballpino brothers are going to get him, so we need to figure out how Sparky can get him."

"Okay, the numbers say you have a better chance if you..."

Katie started.

"Forget the numbers, you gotta go after him hard," Bobby offered.

"Whatever you do, don't count on getting the out at first," Carlos said, pointing at where VORP had been propped up, one foot on first base and his glove arm extended.

"I can't tell you what to do, Sparky," Lou said. "I know you can figure it out on your own."

"All right," Sparky said as he tugged on the brim of his cap. "I've got this."

The Goats returned to their positions just as the umpire arrived to chase them away. Sparky stepped back onto the rubber and looked in at his brother. Ken twirled his bat the way he always did, and it irritated Sparky the way it always did. Sparky got set and delivered his first pitch.

The ball whistled through the air, an arrow-straight fastball that Ken swung right through for strike one. The fans burst into a deafening cheer that shook the leaves above their heads. Lou returned the ball to Sparky with a reassuring nod. Sparky exhaled and nodded back.

With the crowd still roaring, Sparky checked the runners and started his stretch. He shot forward and released the next pitch, a breaking ball that came off his fingers and curved toward the plate. Ken tensed up, but did not swing, and the ball ended up just shy of the outside corner of the plate for a ball. The noise in the ballpark softened by a few degrees.

Sparky's next pitch was a fastball that climbed a hair too high and out of the strike zone, and he grimaced as he watched the umpire step back without calling a strike. Ken took some slow practice swings outside of the batter's box, rubbed some dirt into his glove and stared directly into Sparky's eyes as he stepped back in.

Lou called for the curve. Sparky let it roll out of his hand, starting out high and dropping quickly into the strike zone. Ken watched it slowly approach the plate, but then as it dropped he took a tight, quick swing at the last second. The result was a high pop foul behind the plate. Lou yanked the mask off his face and scrambled around in foul territory, trying to get a bead on it. He chased it all the way to the netting in front of the seats, where the ball plopped harmlessly. The noise from the fans became louder, more urgent. The Goats in the dugout were standing against the railing, pounding it with bats and making as much noise as they could.

Sparky tried to ignore the noise. He tried to ignore the look of breathless anticipation he saw in the face of just about every person in the stands. But he couldn't ignore the sight of a single little girl sitting in the front row with her parents, waving a tiny Goats pennant and shouting at the top of her tiny little lungs. She had the same look on her face as the kid Sparky had spotted in the crowd one year earlier in San Carlos. "Please," her face said. Just "please."

Sparky reared back and threw what he hoped would be his last pitch. It was a slider that slid from the inside of the plate to the outside, but Ken would not swing. The pitch ended up outside the zone to even the count at 2-2. In his mind, Sparky could see a younger Ken already standing on first base, razzing him. With a grunt, Sparky fired his next pitch, a high fastball that felt like it pulled his arm out along with it as it sped toward the plate. It was low, ball three.

The crowd continued to shout their full-throated support for Sparky. The Goats were stomping their feet in the dugout. Sparky looked around the field to see his teammates smiling at him, giving him thumbs-up, or pointing at him. He turned back and saw Ken still twirling his bat, waiting for the payoff pitch. He imagined Ken somehow smiling underneath the mask. Sparky stopped trying to ignore the sound of the fans. He let their cheering fill his head, pushing out anything else he might have been thinking about.

"Sorry, Ken," he said to himself. "I'm not doing this for you anymore. I'm doing this for them." He closed his eyes, went into his windup, and released the ball.

16. Postseason

Somewhere in the desert, the sun was shining bright. A band was playing somewhere, and if you followed the sound of that music it would have led you straight to a practice field on Goats Island. A stage had been built in the middle of the field, with a brass band filling most of it. At the front of the stage was a podium where Arthur Mint IV stood adjusting his green bowtie and shuffling a stack of papers. Standing next to Mr. Mint and wearing a suit, boots and a cowboy hat, was Lou Houston. The rest of the field was filled with reporters, cameras and microphones. Mr. Mint signaled for the band to cut the music and he addressed the crowd.

"Thank you all for being here today as we open Spring Training for the Go-Town Goats!" Lou leaned over and nudged him. "Oh, yes, sorry...the WORLD CHAMPION Go-Town Goats!" The crowd of reporters broke into spontaneous applause.

"Yes, thank you," Mr. Mint continued. I want to begin by thanking our manager, Skip LaRoche, for his many years of fine service to the franchise, and I'm sure we're all looking forward to hearing him in the radio booth with Mel and Randy this season." The applause for this announcement was significantly more reserved.

"But I'm also pleased to introduce the next manager of the Go-Town Goats, Lou Houston!" Lou tipped his hat to the crowd and smiled.

"And we'd like to extend a warm 'welcome back' to the young man who many people say was the catalyst for last year's amazing season, Sparky Katakura, who has just signed a five-year extension with the team!" Sparky came up on stage to more raucous applause. "Would you like to say a few words, Sparky?"

"Ah, I'd rather let my pitching speak for itself, Mr. Mint," Sparky said.

"Fine, fine," Mr. Mint continued. "We're also pleased to announce that another long-time fixture of the Goats family, VORP, has been appointed our new Executive Vice President of Fan Relations. Taking his spot on the field will be our newest free agent acquisition, All-Star Ken Katakura!"

Ken stepped out on stage to more applause and immediately put Sparky in a playful headlock. Once they were separated, Mr. Mint began describing the new facilities on Goats Island. As he stood there, listening to Mr. Mint prattle on, he spotted a familiar and unwelcome face in the crowd. Mr. Stitches glowered at Sparky and Ken for a moment, his greasy eyebrows arched at enraged angles. Then, the stumpy little man in the dark suit slipped his hat onto his head and slinked through the crowd until the brothers lost sight of him. Sparky smiled.

Soon, the press conference was over, and the new Goats lineup entered the clubhouse to get ready for the upcoming season, at last. While Sparky unpacked his bag, Katie entered with another large black binder stuffed with notes.

"Am I going to have to read all of that?" Sparky asked as she set the massive tome on the bench next to him.

Katie smiled. "No, but I think you'll want to." She opened the book and pushed it toward Sparky. He read the first page: "Dear Sparky, I just wanted to say thanks for everything. My sister and I have been Goats fans for a long time, although it wasn't always easy to admit it in public. She moved to Los Angeles a while ago, and yesterday she told me she wore her Goats cap outside for the first time in more than five years. Thank you for making our dream come true. Signed, Terry."

Sparky flipped through the book and found that each page was a letter to him, all different but all saying essentially the same thing. He looked up at Katie.

"People have been flooding the blog with these all winter," Katie explained. "Don't worry, everybody on the team is getting them, it's not all about you."

"So you're putting the calculator away forever?" Sparky asked with a grin.

"Are you kidding? I'm still trying to figure out an optimized lineup now that Ken's here. It hasn't been easy because his splits last season were so heavily skewed, you know. Plus there's park factors to account for, trying to adjust for Thor's improved ultimate zone rating in left field, and I don't know if Fuzzy's on-base percentage will hold up this season or if he'll regress back to his career numbers…" Katie stopped herself when she noticed Sparky's eyes glaze over. "But I wanted to make sure you didn't think all I did over the winter was crunch numbers."

"Of course not."

"Hey, what's goin' on here?" Lou demanded as he

marched up and down the rows. "Isn't anybody here to play baseball? All I'm seeing are a bunch of kids lollygagging around at summer camp! Let's pick 'em up and put 'em down, people! If any one of you are still standing here in the next 30 seconds, you're going to have to wash my car! And people, that car is mighty dusty from driving here through the desert."

The Goats grabbed their caps, gloves, bats and cleats and hustled out of the clubhouse. Bobby grabbed for a box of donuts, but Fuzzy stopped him. Thor roared with laughter as he practically skipped out onto the field like a kindergartener. Sparky felt a sharp "thwack" against the back of his head and when he turned around, it was Ken standing there, grinning like a maniac and holding his glove.

"Nice to have you back," Sparky said to Ken.

"Thanks, but you know I let you strike me out back in Game 7," Ken said coolly.

"You're insane. I thought you couldn't even think for yourself when you were possessed or whatever."

"Nah, I knew what I was doing, figured it was time to throw you a bone."

"Throw me a bone? You're just embarrassed that I got you to whiff in Game 7 of the Worlds Series!"

"You couldn't do that on your own and you know it, Worlds Series or not!"

Sparky and Ken glared at each other for a moment.

"Practice Field B, five minutes!" Ken said. "I'll take any pitch you can throw at me downtown, guaranteed!"

"You're on!" Sparky said, and the brothers bolted onto the field. Next year was here.

THE END

THE BIG LEAGUES

ABOUT THE AUTHOR

Chris Petersen has been a writer and a baseball fan for about the same length of time. In addition to being an editor on a series of business-to-business publications, he also moonlights as a serious fan of a certain underachieving baseball squad. He lives in the Chicago suburbs with his wife. *The Big Leagues* is his first novel.

www.ingramcontent.com/pod-product-compliance
Lightning Source LLC
Chambersburg PA
CBHW022032240626
47154CB00007B/2370